THE RUTHLESS YEOMEN

THE RUTHLESS YEOMEN

Bridges Over Time
Book II

Valerie Anand

St. Martin's Press
New York

This book is for Jean
whose companionship and hospitality
while I studied the landscape of East Anglia
added so much to the pleasure of the research

Library of Congress Cataloging-in-Publication Data

Anand, Valerie.
The ruthless yeomen / Valerie Anand.
p.   cm. — (Bridges over time; bk. 2)
ISBN 0-312-08884-1
1. Great Britain—History—Richard II, 1377–1399—Fiction.
2. Tyler's Insurrection, 1381—Fiction. I. Title. II. Series.
PR6051.N34R8   1993
823'.914—dc20   92-43172   CIP

First published in Great Britain by Headline Book Publishing PLC.

First U.S. Edition: March 1993
10 9 8 7 6 5 4 3 2 1

Sources

I would hate to attempt a definitive bibliography for this novel. I have collected information over so many years from so many different sources. But prominent among the works consulted are the following:

The Oxford History of England edited by Sir George Clark: *The Thirteenth Century, 1216 to 1307* by Sir Maurice Powicke, Clarendon Press, 2nd edition 1962 and *The Fourteenth Century, 1307 to 1399* by May McKisack, Clarendon Press, 1959;
English Society in the Early Middle Ages by Doris Mary Stenton, Penguin, 1983;
England and its Rulers, 1066 to 1272 by M. T. Clanchy, Fontana, 1983;
England in the Late Middle Ages by A. R. Myers, Penguin, 1979;
The Hundred Years War by Christopher Allmand, Cambridge University Press, 1989;
The English Rising of 1381 edited by R. H. Hilton and T. H. Aston, Cambridge University Press, 1984;
Medieval Technology and Social Change by Lynn White Jnr, Oxford University Press, 1964;
Seven Hundred Years of English Cooking by Maxime McKendry, edited by Arabella Boxer, Treasure Press, 1985;
English Costume by Doreen Yarwood, E. T. Batsford Ltd, 1952.

Author's Note

In the interests of a smooth narrative, I admit to having taken a few small liberties with history when dealing with the Peasants' Revolt.

I have gone in for some general simplification of the events of 1381, which were very complex indeed. Also, although it is generally agreed that Wat Tyler was not, in fact, present at the Mile End gathering when the peasants handed King Richard II their petition, I have put him there to avoid causing confusion by introducing extra peasant leaders, who would have vanished almost as soon as they appeared.

V.A.

Acknowledgements

The quotations which introduce each of the five parts in this book are all taken from *The Goshawk* by T. H. White, Jonathan Cape, 1951. They are reprinted by kind permission of David Higham Associates Limited.

Contents

THE RUTHLESS YEOMEN

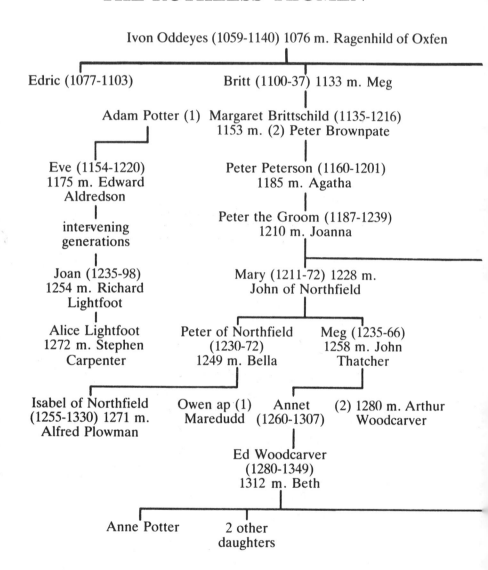

Ivon Oddeyes (1059-1140) 1076 m. Ragenhild of Oxfen

Edric (1077-1103)

Britt (1100-37) 1133 m. Meg

Adam Potter (1) Margaret Brittschild (1135-1216) 1153 m. (2) Peter Brownpate

Eve (1154-1220) 1175 m. Edward Aldredson

Peter Peterson (1160-1201) 1185 m. Agatha

intervening generations

Peter the Groom (1187-1239) 1210 m. Joanna

Joan (1235-98) 1254 m. Richard Lightfoot

Mary (1211-72) 1228 m. John of Northfield

Alice Lightfoot 1272 m. Stephen Carpenter

Peter of Northfield (1230-72) 1249 m. Bella

Meg (1235-66) 1258 m. John Thatcher

Isabel of Northfield (1255-1330) 1271 m. Alfred Plowman

Owen ap (1) Annet (2) 1280 m. Arthur Maredudd (1260-1307) Woodcarver

Ed Woodcarver (1280-1349) 1312 m. Beth

Anne Potter

2 other daughters

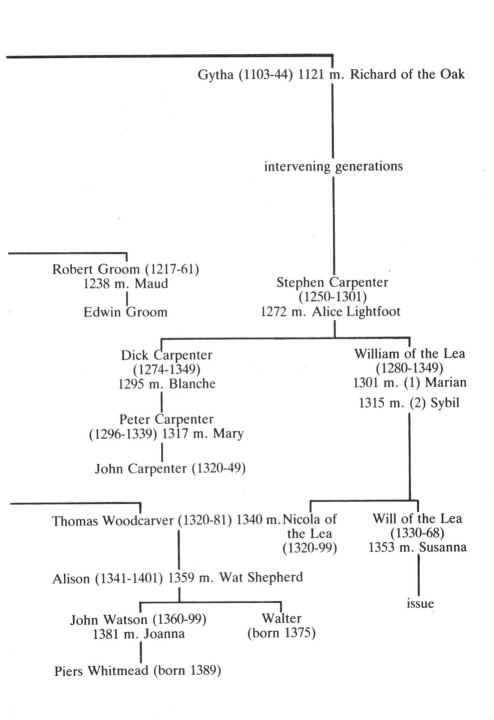

Gytha (1103-44) 1121 m. Richard of the Oak

intervening generations

Robert Groom (1217-61)
1238 m. Maud

Edwin Groom

Stephen Carpenter
(1250-1301)
1272 m. Alice Lightfoot

Dick Carpenter
(1274-1349)
1295 m. Blanche

William of the Lea
(1280-1349)
1301 m. (1) Marian

1315 m. (2) Sybil

Peter Carpenter
(1296-1339) 1317 m. Mary

John Carpenter (1320-49)

Thomas Woodcarver (1320-81) 1340 m. Nicola of
the Lea
(1320-99)

Will of the Lea
(1330-68)
1353 m. Susanna

Alison (1341-1401) 1359 m. Wat Shepherd

issue

John Watson (1360-99)
1381 m. Joanna

Walter
(born 1375)

Piers Whitmead (born 1389)

PART I

Isabel of Northfield:
The Mewed Hawk
1271–2

A wild and adolescent creature whose father and mother in eagles' nests had fed him with bloody meat still quivering with life . . . born to fly sloping sideways, free among the verdure of that Teutonic upland, to murder with his fierce feet and to consume with that curved Persian beak, who now hopped up and down in the clothes basket with a kind of imperious precocity . .

Chapter One

The Climbing Rose

On formal occasions, Sir Henry Rushley, the overlord of the three manors of Rushley, Oxfen and Redesmarsh, wore fur-trimmed gowns which hung nearly to his ankles, while his majestic wife Lady Judith and the well-bred damsels who attended her had dresses with bands of embroidery round the hem and shining crispine nets for their hair. Whether Sir Henry's fur edgings were squirrel or moleskin or sable or silver fox, and whether the ladies' embroidered hems were simple or elaborate and their crispines silver or gold, depended on the precise nature of the occasion. Their wardrobes contained garments nicely graded to suit any event, from entertaining untitled guests to attending a de Montalt christening at Castle Rising to dining with Roger Bigod, Earl of Norfolk.

People such as Master Herbert Grosney and Mistress Lucy of Normansland, the three-hundred-acre holding between Rushley and Oxfen, emulated their Rushley overlord as far as they could, although they were limited by the expense and in any case had a narrower social circle. It would be a long time before a Grosney dined with the earl, although Mistress Lucy, young and ambitious for her recently acquired husband and her prospective children, sometimes dreamed about it.

By contrast, Alfred Plowman, who lived in a reed-thatched farmstead on the banks of the Wend, owned four plough oxen and held ten acres of land from Sir Henry in return for the latter's annual ploughing, had one set of clothes for Sunday best and so had his young wife Isabel, and they considered themselves prosperous.

Alfred's Sunday best consisted of the sanguine-coloured tunic and green hose which his Aunt Griselda Potterswife, who lived in Rushley village, had made for him to wear at his wedding. Isabel had been married in a gown borrowed from her mother, but she had used a wedding gift of woollen cloth to make a dress for best. She had dyed it crimson, and she donned it for church each week along with a clean white coif.

She chose crimson because it made her skin look honey-toned instead of sallow, and she allowed a little dark hair to escape from the coif in front. Alfred admired the effect, which pleased her. She was pleased

3

too because although they were only a few months wed, there was already a bulge beginning under the generous dark red skirt.

But on this October Sunday they were not just leaving the dog to guard the house and setting out as usual to pole their flatboat down the nearby River Wend to the church at Rushley. They would be going on afterwards to a gathering in the village, and there were aspects to that gathering which made Isabel feel discontented.

'I wish I'd got something extra special to put on,' she said. 'A different sort of headdress or . . . or something.'

'What for? You look all right to me,' said Alfred, handing her the brown, hooded cloak which would keep out the weather as they made their way to Rushley. 'Here, put this on. Sharp, that wind is.'

'It's because of Rohese,' said Isabel. 'I daresay *she'll* have something special on. She always was a show-off, and *now* . . .'

'That was her parents mostly, or that's what Aunt Griselda always says,' said Alfred. 'She told me once, she reckoned Ralph and Isabel Shepherd set out to turn Rohese's head from the day she was born. But she's done well by them, there's no getting away from it.'

'I know. My folk never thought that wedding'd really come off,' said Isabel. 'my grandmother said she'd believe it when it happened. And now Rohese has been married three months and she's living right over in Redesmarsh! I've only been there twice in my life, to the fair.'

'And she's paying her first visit to her old home today and her parents have asked us to the feast and if we don't get a move on, we not only won't get to Rushley in time for church, we won't be there to see Rohese arrive either,' Alfred told her. 'Got those honeycakes you said you'd bring along? All right, then. Come on.'

Alfred was right about the sharpness of the wind. As they set out to the gathering which was to change the course of Isabel's life and send its repercussions on through time, the river was being whisked into wavelets. Leaves were whirling down on to the Wend from the alders on its banks, and rain was spattering. Alfred glanced upstream as he pushed off and remarked: 'I daresay the Pechers won't come out in this weather,' which made Isabel laugh. Tosti and Ufi Pecher were an anti-social father and son who held the land adjoining Alfred's to the west. However good the weather, they scarcely ever bothered even to attend Mass, in spite of repeated visits, exhortations and warnings of eternal damnation from Rushley's earnest priest, Father Benedict.

Ralph and Mabel would certainly not have thought of asking them to Rohese's homecoming feast and, if asked, they wouldn't have accepted.

'I don't like that Tosti, anyway,' Isabel said. 'It's something about the way he stares.

'Just as well. The only man who's got any right to stare at you,' said Alfred with a grin, 'is me.'

4

He steered them out into midstream. Isabel drew her cloak round her more tightly and did a little staring on her own account, watching her husband's deft handling of the punt pole. She knew quite well that she was fortunate to get him.

Her own family lived a mile and a half away, on a farmstead which like Alfred's stood apart from the village. Northfield was only a little smaller than Alfred's holding, Plowman's Acres. But its soil was poorer and although Isabel might one day inherit the tenancy, since she was the only one of Peter of Northfield's children to survive the ravages of childhood diseases and the marsh ague, that time had not come yet and Isabel's dowry consisted only of a little silver coin and a couple of cows.

And her doubtful charms. Alfred, sturdy and flaxen, with blue eyes in a broad face, met the Norfolk standard of beauty, as did Isabel's own mother, Bella. Acceptable too was the combination of fox-red hair and dark eyes which sometimes occurred locally. Her father was like that, and her grandmother, Mary, was said to have been thus as a girl.

But in Isabel's family there was also a thin, dark, sallow strain which was candidly regarded as plain and Isabel was an example of it. She had often stood looking down into the low streams and still pools of this marshy landscape, sadly admitting to herself that she had arms like sticks and that her dark hair was rough and wiry, and that the dark, slanting eyes which were so striking in conjunction with her father's fox-coloured hair, were set too close together in her small tight face.

There were a number of young unmarried men on Rushley manor but they had taken little notice of her, except, for some reason, Alfred. When she was fifteen, Alfred took to smiling at her across the church on Sundays and, presently, in his shy, slow fashion, he declared his liking openly, coming up to talk to her after the service, when the manor folk tended to cluster conversationally together in the churchyard before dispersing to their dinners. Isabel wasn't averse to the compliment. All right, she was plain. But she wasn't hideous, she didn't have a hunchback or a squint and she wasn't pockmarked. She had resented being ignored while the boys all clustered round that daft Rohese with her fair hair and her simper and the doting parents who overdressed her and called her their little princess.

'You ought to take Alfred,' said Bella. 'Besides, you're good with little ones. Better have some of your own. I doubt I'll be having any more. Remember that fever that your father caught off you and your little sisters, that made all your necks swell up and killed your sisters though not you, thank God? I think it did something to your father. I've not quickened since. So get your children while you can. You never know what's going to happen next in this world. You're turned sixteen and Alfred's a good catch for the likes of you.'

And so, she *had* taken Alfred and she hadn't been sorry. Except on that day last July, only two months after her own wedding, when Rohese

5

Shepherd, in the midst of astonished whispers, went to church to marry a Grosney.

If the gulf between the Grosneys and the real nobility was wide, that between the Grosneys and folk like the Shepherds was a great deal wider and it wasn't just a matter of money. The Grosneys were free. They could leave their birthplace at will, rent land where and from whom they liked. The Shepherds and the Northfields and Alfred Plowman and their kin were villeins, bound to the manors where they were born as much as were the barns and the livestock, and compelled by law and custom to serve the lord God had given them.

Freemen were always jealous of their status. No villein boy would ever raise his eyes to the daughter even of a poor freeman, and when a freeman looked towards a villein girl, marriage was not usually what he had in mind. And no family was more jealous than the Grosneys of Normansland. That any villein girl should extract an official *I will* from even a Grosney cousin of modest means in Redesmarsh was so wildly unlikely that the whole locality would have declared it impossible, until Rohese Shepherd managed it.

It was wrong to be discontented, wrong to be envious. Father Benedict said so. Isabel seemed to have been born with these unfortunate tendencies, and she knew it was her duty to fight them. And she also knew that she couldn't remind herself often enough: in winning the hand of Alfred Plowman, she had been very fortunate indeed.

She shifted her weight as the boat swung to the left, turning towards a narrow channel which at this point entered the Wend. Alfred put more back into it as he began to pole against the current. 'Your family'll be thinking we're late,' he remarked.

The River Wend, once hardly navigable above Rushley, had been deepened and widened on the orders of Sir Henry's father, Sir Reginald. He had had extra drainage ditches made across his land, using the dug-out soil to build stout dykes against the tides which had once regularly flooded the fields. He had brought acres of former marshland under the plough; Isabel's birthplace at Northfield had been a useless island surrounded by reeds until Sir Reginald set to work. The drained-off water now ran into the Wend and the Meadbrook which flowed through Rushley to the south, providing two serviceable waterways right up to Redesmarsh, the most inland of the three manors.

This had the paradoxical result that, although the district now contained more dry land than ever before, its people used the rivers more because they often provided the easiest route from one place to another. The improved system meant that by going a little out of their way up a channel called North Stream, Isabel and Alfred could reach Northfield and on Sundays they generally did so, to collect Isabel's parents and grandmother so that they could all go to Mass together.

But as they swung to the bank where the ground had been flattened

6

and planks laid to make a landing stage, only Bella came out of the house and down the little path to meet them. 'Your father's got one of his chesty coughs again, Isa. No, no, he hasn't any fever; don't worry. But I'm not coming to Rushley today and Grandmother Mary don't feel like going without us, so you and Alfred go along.'

'Is my father really all right?' said Isabel anxiously. 'Should I just go up and look in on him?'

'Not now, you're behind time as it is,' said Bella. 'Come over tomorrow. No, truly, Isa; he's just staying put out of this cold wind. It's one of his days for working on Sir Henry's land tomorrow and you know what'll happen if he don't turn up on time. We'll have Bernard Reeve here, wanting to know why and taking it on himself to decide whether a man's too ill to work or not. Go on, now. And mind you keep wrapped up, yourself.'

'I see to that,' said Alfred. 'Got to look after her just now.'

'The sin of envy,' said Father Benedict, deliberately making his Sunday homily longer than usual, because he knew perfectly well that the reason why his church was unusually crowded had nothing whatsoever to do with an outbreak of piety on the part of his flock, 'is one of the commonest of sins. But the fact that it's common, doesn't make it trivial.' He eyed his congregation disapprovingly. They fidgeted.

Rushley's church stood at one end of the straggling, muddy village street of daub-plastered, thatched dwellings, and although well-appointed, with stained glass and gargoyles and a small Lady Chapel, it was not especially large and did not need to be. It was big enough to contain its normal complement of worshippers comfortably. There were, after all, other churches on the three manors, including a splendid one at Redesmarsh, attached to the nuns' abbey of St Peter's, which one of Sir Henry's forebears had founded.

But today, some of those other churches evidently had more room in them than usual. People had come miles this Sunday to take the sacrament at Rushley. Many had not been invited to the Shepherds' party but had heard about it, and had come – just as they had on Rohese's wedding day – to stare at tall, thin Ralph Shepherd and his wife Mabel, with her rotund body and her amiable, slightly foolish face, and wonder yet again how this commonplace pair had managed to produce a daughter beautiful enough to make a Grosney marry her. There were also some who considered the said Grosney a fool, who would regret his bargain. Rohese had been popular among the young men, but young men didn't form the entire population and practically everyone else had thought her very silly.

'Envy is *far* from trivial,' said Father Benedict grimly. 'It is a sin against the natural order of things. What would happen if we were all wealthy and did not need to work at tilling the fields? Who then would till them? What would we all eat? God has arranged human society with care and wisdom, so that all tasks needful to be done, have someone to carry them out. To seek to change one's status is to rebel against the wise provisions of God and to verge upon heresy.' Very hot on heresy, was Father Benedict. He had once reported a parishioner – it was one of the Eelfisher clan on the southern edge of Rushley – for making a remark which he considered heretical. He'd gone all the way to Norwich to speak to the bishop. The bishop had overruled him but everyone knew he would do it again at any time he thought fit.

Father Benedict had disapproved of Rohese's marriage. He had conducted it under protest, failed to attend the marriage feast given afterwards by the Grosneys of Normansland and wouldn't be attending Rohese's homecoming party either. Herbert and Lucy Grosney were also absenting themselves, regarding it as a purely village affair, and Father Benedict would eat his Sunday dinner with them instead.

The homily droned on, to the annoyance of his flock. Whether one thought Rohese had deserved her good luck or not, she'd provided them with the biggest talking point they'd had in a twelvemonth and now they were longing to see how much her new life had altered her and, anyway, a party was a party. When their tiresome pastor at last ran out of words, they jostled eagerly out of the church, impatient to begin enjoying themselves. Outside, the wind had sharpened still more, and a fine drizzle blew into their faces. The wide Norfolk sky was a uniform dark grey and away to the west, where normally one could see that the land rose to a long, low crest with a line of trees along the top marking the boundary between Oxen and Redesmarsh, there was nothing but a grey blankness. The Shepherds' prospective guests set out instantly, heads down into the wind, for the shelter of their hosts' dwelling.

Ralph Shepherd, who cared for Sir Henry's sheep along with a small flock of his own, had left his charges safely pastured on a piece of well-drained land bordered by ditches so that he could be home all day, and had hurried on with Mabel to stand at his door and greet them. There was nowhere near enough space in the Shepherds' one main room for the cheerful crowd of Potters and Plowmans, Fowlers, Haroldsons, Hobsons, Wagoners, Carpenters, Smiths and Sixacres, but the neighbours in the adjacent dwellings opened their doors and made up their fires in hospitable fashion and the crowd overflowed good-naturedly into these havens, asking each other loudly where the guest of honour had got to, and poking their heads round the doors every now and then to see if Rohese were coming.

Isabel, being one of the many women who had brought along a gift of food, declined to be sidetracked from the Shepherds' house. Leaving Alfred at the door, where he had stopped to greet Ralph Shepherd and young Stephen Carpenter, who sometimes lent a hand with Sir Henry's ploughing, she pushed her way in with her basket of honeycakes, to find Mabel crouched by her stone-lined firepit, busily stirring pots and talking excitedly to aunt Griselda and Mistress Joan Lightfoot from the

8

cottage opposite. Beyond her, on a trestle table, prepared dishes waited. The cramped room with its soot-stained beams was full of inviting smells and Isabel's nostrils twitched in appreciation. She had suffered little sickness with her pregnancy, but she seemed to be permanently hungry. She hoped Rohese wouldn't be long, so that the eating could begin.

'I can't think where she's got to,' Mabel was saying to the other women. 'Oh, is that honeycakes, Isa? That's kind of you, dear. Put them by on the table there. She ought to be here by now. She sent word she'd go to early Mass with Gerald . . .' Mabel's voice was studiedly casual as she called Gerald Grosney by his first name without even putting *Master* in first because this Grosney was a relative and such familiarity was permissible. '. . . and ride over later. From where they live, it's straighter by land than water. He'll stay to dine with Master Herbert at Normansland and send her on here. Why *isn't* she here? I'm wanting to see her *that* much. She'd have sent word if she was ill, for sure. She sent to tell us she was coming, after all.'

Aunt Griselda sniffed. She was small and spry and, although she had reached her half century, had so far avoided the joint evil which afflicted nearly everyone on the three manors who lived past forty. Her tongue had a distinct touch of nimbleness, too. 'Most folk just turn up when they feel like visiting. Sending a serving boy with a message, indeed!'

'Well, it's what Gerald would tell her to do. She's got to live his way, now,' said Mabel rather sharply.

'I expect she stopped to pay her respects at Normansland,' said Joan Lightfoot in mild tones. 'After all, they gave her a fine wedding feast.'

'Yes, I know they did and Ralph didn't like it,' Mabel said. 'And nor did I. It was as good as saying we weren't capable of putting on a feast. Decent pewter we've got and Ralph has sheep of his own; we're not just cottars with nothing but a patch of ground to grow things on. They just took it all over and never even asked us what we wanted.'

Mistress Lightfoot's strong-boned and sensible face broke into a grin and she turned her head so that Mabel shouldn't see it. She winked at Isabel. Master Herbert Grosney and Mistress Lucy hadn't liked the match any more than Father Benedict had, but Master Herbert said frankly that being lately married themselves had made them a bit soft, maybe, and they were prepared to make the best of things. They weren't going to refuse to receive their cousin Gerald's bride or anything of that sort. On the contrary, since the bride's parents couldn't possibly accommodate all the guests who would have to be asked to the wedding, they were prepared to open their house for the marriage party.

And so they had and the village had frankly enjoyed being asked into the house at Normansland and presented with a wedding feast which included half a roast ox; stewed eels; heron sauced with vinegar, ginger and salt; spiced cabbage; pancakes stuffed with herbs and hardboiled eggs; three different kinds of sweetmeat, two of which contained real sugar instead of honey; and grape wine from France.

The affronted Shepherds, who had been given no choice in the matter at all, had smiled broadly throughout, seen their daughter and her groom conducted to the chamber which Herbert and Lucy had vacated for a night in their honour, and helped to tuck them up together under a fur coverlet strewn with rose petals. They had then thanked their host and hostess for their kindness and gone home speechless with fury, with the good red wine from Aquitaine so sour in their stomachs that they both had appalling hangovers next day – 'not because of the wine; just temper,' said Rushley gossip afterwards.

Ralph and Mabel were giving this feast for Rohese's homecoming as much as anything to recover their lost self-respect and everybody knew it.

Mabel gave a last stir to something meaty and aromatic and got to her feet, brushing her own best skirt of plum-coloured wool. 'She did ought to have come by now. I just can't think where . . .'

From the doorway, Ralph Shepherd and Alfred suddenly let out a simultaneous cry of, 'Here she is!'

And young Stephen Carpenter, lounging against the doorpost with his arm round Joan Lightfoot's daughter, with whom he was seriously walking out, observed, none too politely: 'And in style!'

'Well, what do you expect?' said Mabel tartly, shouldering her way to the door. 'She's a Grosney now. Don't expect her to come on foot or riding some old moke, do you?' She plunged out into the street, catching at Ralph's arm to pull him with her and then letting go, to run forward with a glad cry of welcome as Rohese dismounted at the door.

Stephen's rude remark had had some justification. Certainly, it was to be expected that Rohese would arrive on a decent-looking horse and with a servant in attendance. But sheer tact should have decreed that she should not overdo it and, regrettably, she had.

Rohese Grosney, née Shepherd, had been perched sideways on a pillion saddle with a footboard, behind a manservant, on a sturdy cob whose arched neck and dish face proclaimed valuable Barb blood on one side of his ancestry. With them, on a second cob, was another manservant and on his pillion was another girl who had sprung down at once to help Rohese alight and was obviously her maid.

Rohese herself, as the goggling womenfolk of Rushley observed, wore a gown not of good plain woollen cloth, but of thick, soft fustian with a nap like fur. It was a rich shade of green and over it was a hooded violet cloak in the same luxurious material. She put back her hood, and above her slender neck was a snow-white sketch of a barbette designed to show as much as possible of her pale hair, which was coiled over her ears and held there in a shining crispine of silver net.

Silver net, fustian, the pillion saddle, the attendants in the plural; these were gentry fashions. This was showing off and Isabel, following Mabel out along with Aunt Griselda and Mistress Lightfoot, heard Mabel's joyful cry of greeting ring out alone in the silence as Rohese alighted, resting her gloved hand in the hand of her maid and then standing while the maid adjusted the folds of her mistress's skirt.

But Mabel herself noticed nothing amiss. She paused only to let Rohese get her feet to the ground. Then she hurried forward again, arms spread wide to embrace her daughter. 'Rohese! Welcome home, dear, welcome home!'

'Dear Mother,' said Rohese. Her gaze went beyond Mabel and found Ralph. 'Dear Father. I am so happy to see you both again and I hope you are both well.' She made no move to run into those welcoming arms. Mabel stopped short where she was, looking slightly foolish, and her hands fell to her sides while Rohese, with the utmost gracefulness, curtsied deeply, rose to her feet once more, and observed coolly, in a voice which in only three months had grown sharper, leaving the blurred vowels of her native accent behind, 'These are my grooms, Eustace and Luke, and this is Goda, my maid. Could someone show the grooms where to put the horses?'

And that was the moment when the whole event, which from the start had been just a little off-colour, began to go decidedly wrong.

Mabel, her face puzzled and disappointed, stepped back. Ralph said in a hearty voice, 'We'd fixed for Matt Potter here to put your horse in his cow byre. I daresay he can manage two, hey, Matt?'

'I should think so.' Matt Potter was Aunt Griselda's husband and, in his laconic way had a manner nearly as edged. 'If them fine horses don't mind being crowded with my cows, I reckon the cows'll put up with the horses.'

'Come inside, dear,' said Mabel, recovering herself and taking Rohese's arm. 'We're having a feast for you and it's all ready.'

'And everyone's coming to it?' Rohese had now taken in the fact that there was a crowd round her home. She looked a little confused.

'Of course, dear. Everyone wants to hear about your new home and everything. Come in out of the wind, now.'

She and Ralph led Rohese indoors, Goda following. The men took the horses away. Behind the Shepherds' backs, the villagers grinned at each other, raised eyebrows and nudged each other in the ribs but they had their own code of good manners and no one said anything aloud except for Aunt Griselda who, as they made their way back into the cottage hard on the heels of the Shepherds, observed audibly to Isabel, 'She's not showing yet and she hasn't even got that look on her. I don't reckon there's anything under her girdle that wasn't there before. You had that look almost straightaway. Keeping well, are you? Not too much sickness?'

'No, I feel all right,' said Isabel. Rohese, now handing her cloak to Goda, was only a few steps ahead and she had heard. Her face had gone pink. She averted her silver-spangled head and let herself be put into a settle by the fire. Ralph, who had also heard, gave Aunt Griselda an irritated glance and began inquiring loudly who wanted ale.

11

Rohese recovered herself. Her newly elegant voice cut across him. 'What a very cold day it is. I have such an appetite after my long ride. Shouldn't we all eat?'

The serving of the food temporarily improved the atmosphere. As many as could possibly get into the cottage did so, and those obliged to eat in the next door houses had eatables passed to them on wooden platters, and a hum of cheerful talk arose. The maid, Goda, was made welcome by a group of Rushley girls, and when the grooms returned from the byre, they were greeted hospitably and urged to partake. Mutton stew and honeycakes, washed down with a draught of ale, softened Aunt Griselda to the point of questioning Rohese quite amiably on her new life in Redesmarsh, where her husband was one of the tenants of St Peter's Abbey.

Isabel who, after the first shock of disapproval, was grateful to Rohese for getting the food served promptly, was moved to edge over to her, admire her dress and crispine and ask where the materials had been bought and their price.

The result of this, however, was unsatisfactory. Rohese, who had known Isabel since they were both children, gazed at her as though she could hardly recall who Isabel was, and said lightly, 'Dear Gerald bought everything for me in Norwich. He said I owed it to my position to dress well. Of course, I didn't ask him about the prices.'

Isabel turned away and found that Alfred had detached himself from the Carpenter family and was just behind her. He took her arm and steered her away. 'Come and eat some more. Get outside of all you can while you've got the chance. Aunt Griselda,' he added in a whisper, as he drew them out of earshot, 'always said Rohese was a stupid girl and she's right. Owed it to her position, indeed! Here, let me cut you a bit of Mabel's mutton ham. I only hope she's left herself enough to get through the winter with, after this.'

There was a surge of voices at the door, and Matt Potter, who was drinking there with Rohese's grooms, called. 'Where've you got to, Mabel? Come and see this! The Eelfishers have brought you a pike!'

'And look at the size of it!' cried Stephen Carpenter. 'You come to feed the five thousand, Hilda Eelfisher?'

The Eelfisher clan held a few badly farmed acres on the edge of Rushley, and paid rent for it in the form of fish. Indeed, they paid for virtually everything they bought in the same manner. They were far better at fishing than at cultivation and depended on it. They resented anyone else even casually fishing on the stretches of waterway which they considered to be 'theirs'. There was a long-standing quarrel between them and the Pechers on this account, for the Pechers also took much of their living from the rivers and had no hesitation in trespassing on traditional Eelfisher territory or even setting traps in it. It was, no doubt, just as well that the Pechers were not at the feast.

12

But the Eelfishers were generous in their way. Now, led by their chief woman, Hilda, and enveloped in their usual aroma of marshwater and fish, they trundled their offering in on a handcart, shoving people out of the way. Hilda, a massive woman of unknown age, with a broad face burnished to a permanent red-brown by the east wind and a ferociously amiable grin full of broken teeth, saw Mabel tending the fire, brandished a couple of large pans at her and said, in her thick accent which the teeth did nothing to improve, 'Reckoned all your pans'd be full so brought these along. Pike'll go in 'em; he's gutted and chopped up ready!'

Mabel, exclaiming her thanks, stoked the fire in readiness as the handcart was pushed to the hearthside. Rohese twitched her skirt aside as Hilda passed, wrinkling her nose as Hilda's admittedly aromatic shawl brushed against her.

Which was unfortunate, for Hilda instantly recognised the symptoms of offended sensibilities, and the Eelfishers had their own ideas about what constituted good manners, and forbearance in the face of provocation wasn't one of them.

'What's wrong with you, my wench?' Hilda bawled. 'Can't stand the stink of good honest fisherfolk all of a sudden?'

There was a frightful silence. People who had been gossiping among themselves turned to stare. Mabel stopped stirring the fire and her lips began to tremble. Ralph moved up to her and put a hand on his wife's shoulder. He began to say, 'Now, then, Hilda . . .' but Hilda got in first. Putting her hands on her hips, the pans still jutting from her grasp like weapons, she looked Rohese up and down and let out a roar of laughter. 'Kill you, I reckon, living the way we do, out in the wet all day and cutting the catch by rushlight. You breeding yet, by the way? How long's it been? Three months? Only takes a night to get a baby started, if you're all there. Mabel, you got any oil for frying? I didn't bring that.'

There was smothered laughter from somewhere. Ralph glanced at his daughter and said quietly, 'You asked for that, my girl.' Mabel, with tears in her eyes, fussed with pans and oil. She glanced at Hilda as though she would have liked to take her to task but most people were slightly afraid of the big Eelfisher woman and Mabel had never been brave.

And Rohese, turning her head away from Hilda, said to Joan Lightfoot, 'I am so sorry dear Father Benedict couldn't be here. Father Ambrose at Redesmarsh dines with Gerald and myself twice a month, you know.'

After that, the gathering went from bad to worse. It seemed that behind Rohese's carefully tended, milky complexion and wide blue eyes, and beneath the ash-fair coils of hair in their silver net, was a mind incapable of grasping that her parents were hurt and her former neighbours offended by her airs.

She coughed when smoke from the fire blew into her face, waved it aside with a too-graceful gesture and said that at home they had one of the new flues built above their hearth, to draw the smoke straight up to the vent. She praised the flavour of her mother's ryebread and then spoilt the effect by adding that at home they had white bread all the time and she had nearly forgotten the taste of a rye loaf. Her voice was too high and clear and her manner far too gracious. Normally, a feast like this would have gone on late into the afternoon but, today, the drift away began early, even before the pike, which was a delicacy had all been eaten.

By the time Gerald Grosney appeared, accompanied by two menservants of his own, to collect his wife and her companions, hardly any of the guests remained except for Matt Potter, whose cow byre was sheltering the horses; Aunt Griselda because she was Matt's wife; Joan Lightfoot, who was fond of Mabel; Joan's daughter Alice and Stephen Carpenter because they were courting and this was a chance to be together; and Alfred and Isabel, because they were making the best of a windfall dinner and Isabel, however much she might disapprove of Rohese, was still fascinated by her clothes.

'Well, you're taking every care of her,' said Mabel valiantly to Gerald when the horses had been fetched and Goda had brought her mistress's cloak and the two girls were being helped on to their pillion saddles. The rain had stopped and everyone was out in the street to watch the guest of honour depart. 'They say,' said Mabel, 'that women don't come to harm so easily, riding sideways.'

Gerald was a quiet young man, rather thin of mouth and a watchful eye, but polite. 'There's no need to worry about that yetawhile,' he said, and it was impossible to tell from his face or voice whether he minded. 'We've not been wed that long.'

'If there's nothing by the spring,' said Aunt Griselda meaningly, 'you could go to a shrine or something. Take a pilgrimage to Canterbury. Folk say it's a grand outing, for them as are free just to go.'

'Perhaps we will,' said Gerald, either ignoring the sarcasm or unconscious of it. 'I hope to take my wife to London, too.'

'We've been to Norwich twice already,' said Rohese brightly. She smiled down at everyone and then said, 'Mother!'

Mabel went quickly to the side of Rohese's horse and stood with her face anxiously upturned. 'Yes?' Her voice combined caution with eagerness.

'I don't suppose I'll be able to come home very often,' said Rohese. 'But you must come to see us soon. Not next Sunday; the Abbess of Redesmarsh Abbey is coming. She is such a great lady. St Peter's is very wealthy, you know . . .'

'The abbess is a good bit sharper after turning an honest penny than a lady in her position maybe ought to be,' observed Matt to the air. 'And I've heard tell it's not always such an honest penny at that.'

14

Rohese ignored him. 'But perhaps,' she said winningly to her mother, 'you could come the Sunday after?'

'We'll see,' said Ralph from behind his wife. 'But with the sheep to see to, a man's apt to get too tired for traipsing. We'll send word. Safe journey home, now.'

As the little cavalcade rode away, Mabel said bitterly, 'You as good as said no, we're not going to call on her. Well, why not? She asked us, at least.'

'Yes, as long as we don't embarrass her by turning up at the same time as her precious abbess,' said Ralph. 'I ain't talked much today but I ain't missed much, either.' His voice was hard. 'I'd been looking forward to today, same as you,' he said. 'We was going to see our daughter happy as we've never dreamed of being, a credit to all we've taught her and all the gifts God gave her. We've been disappointed. Aye, she's happy enough. She's married into freedom and a fair bit of money. She won't want for anything. We're the ones who'll do the wanting, because we've lost her, for good and all, most likely. She's not our girl any more, and what she's turned into instead ain't welcome here, not again, and don't you go asking her behind my back, neither. And *we're* not going to her at Redesmarsh.'

'But if she has a baby!' cried Mabel.

'Oh, that'll be women's stuff. You can go and see the baby. But you can leave me behind. *If* she has one,' said Rohese's father savagely. 'Maybe she's a bit too nice for them sort of goings on!'

He went back into his house. Mabel stared at the road along which her daughter had vanished, looked at her remaining guests, produced an imitation smile and said, 'Well, well, young girls get their heads turned easy enough but they come round again.' She bit the last word off short and fled after her husband, not quite quickly enough to hide the way her mouth had twisted.

In the boat going home, Alfred was silent at first. Then he burst into sudden speech and Isabel saw that he was angry in a way she had never seen in him before.

'The little bitch! She wants smacking. She's got a fluepipe over her hearth! She's forgotten what ryebread tastes like! Don't come next Sunday, the abbess is coming! Did you ever hear the like?'

'Mabel Shepherd was hurt,' Isabel agreed slowly. 'I don't think Rohese understood.'

'Then she's stupid, like I said. All those fine things of hers are just wasted on her.' Alfred plied the pole with fury. 'They haven't done her much good, have they? She's not laying up any treasure in heaven like Father Benedict always says we should. We're luckier than she is. We've got food enough even if it's plain, and clothes enough to keep the wind out. And we've got each other and when we go into Rushley, folk are glad to see us. They won't be glad to see Rohese, not ever again,

I shouldn't think. And we've got a babby coming. I'm pretty well pleased with what we've got, ain't you?'

'Yes,' said Isabel.

She could hardly have said no. Alfred would have been hurt and probably angry again, with her this time.

But from the moment when she saw Rohese's silver crispine and the soft richness of her gown, something had been happening inside Isabel's mind. It ran alongside her dislike of Rohese's behaviour, like a tune being sung in counterpoint to another, as she had once heard a travelling group of minstrels sing.

Unlike Alfred, and in defiance of Father Benedict's homily today, Isabel had given way to envy.

It was unfair, after all, that stupid, ill-mannered Rohese should have a freeborn husband and could ride off the manor without asking permission, even to Canterbury if she liked, and had such nice things to wear while she, Isabel, had not. Why was it wrong to be annoyed by injustice?

She wasn't, no, she *wasn't*, pretty well pleased with what she'd got.

Which was unfortunate, because life was as it was and she saw no likelihood of change.

She went on sitting in the boat and thinking: a small peasant girl with rough little hands folded over her rounded stomach, and dark eyes, a fraction too close-set, which she kept lowered, because she knew that they were ablaze with thoughts which she must not speak.

In the morning, after Alfred had gone to his work, Isabel went to Northfield to see her father.

Alfred didn't like her using the boatpole just now, so she went on foot. As she reached the plank bridge over North Stream, Bernard the Reeve was just punting away, while Bella stood arms akimbo on the landing stage to watch him go. She saw her daughter and waved, and Isabel hastened to her. 'Is my father . . .?'

'He'll be up and at his tasks tomorrow,' said Bella reassuringly. 'Bernard's seen him and said all right, though he'll have to make the lost day up. It's a touch of the marsh ague, that's all. Bernard knows that when he sees it.'

'He's a bully,' said Isabel passionately. Once, not long after she and Alfred were married, Alfred had sprained his foot while ditching for Sir Henry, and Bernard had been there the next day, not to ask how he was, but to examine the foot to see if it amounted to an excuse for not working. He'd made some disagreeable jokes about newlyweds being prone to these minor indispositions, especially first thing in the morning. And it had been Bernard in person who had come to collect the cow which Alfred had had to pay to Sir Henry for permission to get married.

Being harassed by Bernard and his ilk, and compelled to pay for the right to get married or even inherit one's father's goods ('We're fined if we bloody well die,' her father had said once), were the natural conditions of life for such people as herself and Alfred and their families. There was no escape. Bernard knew everyone in Rushley by face and by name and, in her short lifetime, Isabel could remember only one Rushley man – other than an Eelfisher – trying to run off. He had been caught when halfway to Lynn, brought back and horribly beaten.

The Eelfishers were the only unclassifiable family in the district. Sir Henry probably considered that they were his villeins but, because of their continual intermarriage among themselves and with similar tribes who lived elsewhere in the wide fenland to the south, they all looked so alike that neither Sir Henry nor Bernard, nor even the despairing priests who were supposed to prevent cousins from marrying, had ever managed to sort out their number, or the names or relationships of any but the few who held farmland.

It was highly probable that among the Eelfishers, brothers and sisters cohabited as well as cousins and there was nothing whatever to be done about it. A further complication was that in a district where short lives were normal and people like Isabel's Grandmother Mary, who was now sixty years old, were exceptional, the Eelfishers were shorter-lived even than most. Some, like Hilda, looked hearty enough, but their horrific inbreeding and their waterlogged existences, fishing from punts and wading through the marshes on stilts, made them apt to succumb early to the fenland diseases, to rheumatism and marsh ague and a kind of premature ageing which could make a man go in appearance from twenty to fifty in a matter of five years. This, and the remote and scattered nature of their marsh-girt shacks, amounted to a set of circumstances which made keeping track of individuals next to impossible.

As long as the customary quantities of eels and lampreys, trout and pike were forthcoming for Sir Henry's table, he and his men left the Eelfishers alone.

Isabel knew about the premature ageing and did not exactly wish she was an Eelfisher. But sometimes, looking at Hilda, she had thought: what is it like to be so bold and free?

'You get along in and see him. I've a cowshed to clean,' said Bella, and marched away. Isabel went on up to the dwelling. Grandmother Mary was sitting at the door, plying a spinning wheel, and Isabel's father was seated by the hearth, with Joan Lightfoot keeping him company.

'I came up to see Peter and tell everyone about yesterday,' Joan said, after Isabel had asked her father how he was and received an encouraging report. 'That girl! I've never seen anything like it. Poor Mabel; she was that upset afterwards . . .'

Isabel, who had been looking forward to describing Rohese's party herself, said, 'Oh,' rather blankly, listened for a while and then wandered to the door and pulled a stool alongside her grandmother.

'Fine goings on in Rushley yesterday,' said Mary, jerking her head backwards to indicate Mistress Lightfoot. 'There she goes again. That's the third time she's been through it all. Nice woman, but don't she talk!'

Isabel laughed. Few people were better talkers than Mary of Northfield herself and she didn't like competition. She could remember every local event of importance, every scandal, tragedy, epidemic, gale and flood, for the last half-century and more. She could remember the free ale and roast meat given to the villagers at Rushley Hall by the lord of the time, when Queen Eleanor gave birth to Prince Edward, Henry the Third's eldest son. And she had a story that when she was a very small girl, no more than four years old, she had been taken to the feast which was held when her own great-grandmother, another long-lived woman, and a very exceptional one indeed, reached the age of eighty.

'I *can* remember it,' she would insist. 'Down in Rushley village it was, in that cottage Joan Lightfoot's got now. We're cousins of a sort. June it was, and warm, and we ate out of doors. That were the time some great charter or other were signed near London town, giving free men all manner of rights. My father knew all about it, 'cos he was groom to my lord and he'd gone south with him, to care for the horses. He was all eager about it: about the charter, I mean. And my great-grandmother told him he was talking nonsense, because it was only free people that would get any good by it. He said that it wouldn't always be like that, but I must say I ain't noticed much difference in my lifetime,' Grandmother Mary would finish.

Or sometimes not finish. There was, occasionally – if the family hadn't by then drifted quietly out of earshot of the tale they all knew by heart – a tailpiece to that story.

'Grandmother,' Isabel said suddenly, 'tell me again that story about your father's grandmother, that lived to be eighty and had a keepsake.'

'You got freedom on your mind, then?' Mary paused in her spinning and turned her eyes thoughtfully to Isabel. They were on closer terms than Isabel and Bella had ever been, for there was a curious mental rapport between them. To an outsider their conversation often seemed to have strange gaps, as though they had some means of communication which was not in words.

Isabel nodded in answer. Mary said, 'Well, that day she had a feast because she was eighty my great-grandmother said that our family would all have been free – like the Grosneys – if *her* grandfather hadn't been the stupidest man in creation. Seemingly, he was made a villein through some sort of accident, and he had a chance to prove it but somehow he threw the chance away. That's all there is to it, though. The keepsake was some old bone thing that was buried with her. It had his device carved on it – the device of the free family he was supposed to belong to. Wrong side of the blanket, most likely. I don't suppose there's much in the tale really. Many a villein's got good blood in him because his mother or his grandmother or whatever took the fancy of some lord or other and had a tumble in the hay at a harvest supper. I expect the story grew in the telling. Did Rohese make you jealous?'

'Yes, she did! She was horrible and she doesn't deserve her good luck. I wanted to tear that pretty dress off her.'

'And wear it yourself?'

'Not exactly. It was green,' said Isabel. 'I can't wear green.'

Grandmother Mary chuckled and then sighed. 'You're young, and you've always been one for wanting what you can't have. Used to worry your mother, that did. I recall she didn't like it your father went and taught you your letters, that he learned when he tried being a novice in a monastery for a bit. She said it'ud give you ideas. Reckon she was right, too. You've nothing to complain about if you've good health and a good man: you know that?'

'Yes. Yes, of course I know that.'

'I hope you do. I mind your Aunt Meg, our father's sister, that married the thatcher over at Redesmarsh. Just faded out of life, she did, because of the way he treated her. Died on her sixth childbed but it weren't the birth that killed her. She just didn't want to bother living any more.' Her gaze sharpened. Mary's dark eyes had faded very little with the years. Her glance was still keen. 'Alfred'll never make you feel like that.'

'I know he won't.'

'Stop where you are,' said Mary, and rose, slowly, for unlike Griselda she had not escaped the joint-evil. She hobbled inside. Presently she came out and placed in Isabel's hands a bronze medallion, strung on a thong. 'Before his grandmother was buried, my father had this made. He had the device from her old bone thing copied on to it. He gave it to me, later. See the pattern? Curved lines arching over wavy ones, sort of like a bridge over a stream.'

Isabel examined the medallion with interest, tracing the marks with her fingers.

'So this . . . this man we're descended from, came from a family that had a . . . a badge of their own or something? But only great people have that. Even the Grosneys don't have a badge. They just dress their servants in sanguine and grey, that's all.'

'Well, I told you what I heard, at my great-grandmother's do. My father repeated it all later on, so I know I got it right. And that's the device, yes. Take a good look, since you're interested. But I say again, I doubt there's much in it.' Mary sat down again and resumed her spinning. 'Like I said, it was probably a matter of some lord or knight amusing himself and maybe he gave the girl a keepsake but it wasn't worth much. An old bone thing: I ask you.'

'But it's interesting. Father Benedict was on about it yesterday, saying we all ought to be satisfied with what we are. But if there really was a mistake . . .'

Suddenly annoyed, Mary shot out a hand and seized the medallion

19

back. 'Mistake or not, it was all donkey's years ago and it's got nothing to do with us. No good people like us getting ideas. You watch it. That's what was wrong with Rohese, wasn't it? She's got ideas and forgotten where she come from. And you're not married to a Grosney. You've got to stop here with the rest of us. You'd better think like the rest of us, or you'll find yourself regretting it. Wish I hadn't shown you the thing now. I just thought you'd like to see it, be amused. Didn't think you'd be silly.'

'I'm not silly,' said Isabel indignantly. 'But . . .'

'I know, you've told me. You're jealous of Rohese and you wanted to snatch the gown off her back. Forget her, my girl. You've other things to think about. Your own home and your husband's dinner, for a start. Oughtn't you to be getting back?'

Isabel stood up. 'I'll just say goodbye to Dad. I'm *not* silly, Grandmother. It was only . . .'

'You say you're jealous again,' said Grandmother Mary, unfairly, since it was Mary herself, and not Isabel who had used the word, 'And I'll clout your ear for you.'

Alfred came home for his dinner, enjoyed the stew she gave him, asked after her father, and said, 'You're not doing too much, I hope. Your mother coming to see to you when the time comes?'

'I expect so. Her and Joan Lightfoot. But it isn't till March.'

Alfred's round blue eyes were amused. 'From what we saw yesterday, you'll be well over it before we find ourselves going to a feast for Rohese's first. If she does have one, Mabel'll make Ralph hold a celebration, mark my words, whatever he says now.'

'Oh, *Rohese*,' said Isabel dismissively. 'Joan Lightfoot'd been by when I got home today. She'd told them all about it. They don't think much of Rohese from what she said. My grandmother told me something interesting, though.'

'Oh?'

'Mmm. She's got a queer old pendant thing with a funny emblem carved on it and she says her father gave it to her. The emblem's supposed to be the badge of some great house or other that we're really descended from, only we were turned into villeins by some mischance or other. She said maybe the story's not true. But just imagine if it was.'

'Why? What's the point?' Alfred paused from eating, stew spoon in hand. 'I've heard that story,' he said abruptly. 'I heard your grandmother tell it once when I was over to Northfield, courting you. Isabel, that old tale matter to you? Does it?'

His blue eyes now were not amused but anxious. Alfred Plowman knew that just because he was himself so very solidly flaxen and conventional, he had been drawn to this thin, dark girl. She was different from himself and the difference had intrigued him.

It also made him, just a little diffident. For the difference lay not only in Isabel's appearance but in the sharpness of her mind, in the fact that her father had once taught her the alphabet, and in something questing and restless in her nature, which was not in his.

He was too inarticulate to find words for any of this, but he loved his Isabel in a way which made his bones seem to move deep within his stocky frame. It was right and natural that she should be a bit above him; he wanted to think of her in that way, as though she partook of some of the magic in the statue of the Virgin in the Lady Chapel in Rushley Church.

But he didn't want *her* to feel herself above him. On their marriage night, he had been gentle and careful as he led her into the ways of lovemaking but he had been glad to feel himself in command of her. That was how it should be. Nothing else would be right or natural and there had been something in her voice just then . . .

Isabel knew it. Quickly, she put down her own spoon and stretched out her hand towards him. 'It's just an old tale,' she said. 'Firesides in winter'd be dull without them.'

'That's all right then,' said Alfred.

Chapter Two

The Bitter Opportunity

At Christmas, Sir Henry gave the customary feast at Rushley Hall and all the villagers were welcome. His son, Sir Simon, who would be lord after him, would host similar feasts at Oxfen and Redesmarsh during the next few days but for this occasion he was his father's co-host and came over from Redesmarsh, where he and his wife, Lady Cecily, lived, making use of the lord's hall there. Each of the three manors had such a hall, for once they had had separate lords. They had come into the hands of the Rushley family through a series of adroit marriages.

The Rushley folk, as always, regarded Sir Simon with interest, and held whispered discussions over what the future would hold for them when Sir Henry was gone. The consensus of opinion was that it would be lively, because, according to the few old folk in the village, Simon resembled his grandfather, Sir Reginald, who had conceived the energetic drainage and dyke scheme, and was remembered as a man given to new ideas (not all of them as successful as the drainage scheme had been). The resemblance, said the gaffers, was more than just physical. Young Sir Simon was already trying out a new breed of sheep at Redesmarsh.

There was an eye-widening and stomach-distending selection of food and drink at the Christmas feast, to which everyone did hearty justice, because after this it would be salted meat and pickled beans and fish until Lent and then beans and fish without even salted meat until Easter, when the calves and lambs were born and there'd be milk and cheese again and a bit of fresh meat from the percentage of newborn stock which, every year, failed to survive. But just now, Easter was a long way off.

The hearth blazed, and the hall was decorated with evergreens. Sir Henry good-naturedly gave up his chair to the Lord of Misrule elected for the occasion. The Lord of Misrule this year was Aunt Griselda's youngest son, who was one of the kitchen boys. He sat in the chair of honour with a paper crown on his head, chose the games and songs and dances and called the forfeits for those who overturned buckets during the bobbing for apples, or whose riddles were guessed too easily.

He took visible pleasure in compelling Mistress Johanna, who was a freeborn widow and had charge of the maids and had an air of authority

22

which had been known to intimidate even her employers, to curtsy to him three times, and in making Bernard Reeve stand on his head, amid unanimous huzzahs.

But he was cautious when Sir Henry himself told a too-simple riddle which was answered by a dozen people shouting in a chorus, and merely ordered him to kiss the prettiest lady present. Sir Henry chivalrously kissed Lady Judith, and everybody cheered.

After those uneasy conversations with her grandmother and with Alfred, Isabel had not again mentioned Rohese to anyone. But she had gone on thinking, mostly about clothes. She had made a joke of it to her grandmother, saying that she couldn't wear green, but her private thoughts were serious. Clothes said something about you; people judged you by them. She wanted to know more and by determined pushing, she had got Alfred and herself into places near enough to the dais to see the ladies' dresses clearly. As well as his son Simon, Sir Henry had two daughters. They had been educated in and married from the households of friends and, in return, he was rearing the daughters of the said friends instead. The three damsels who attended Lady Judith were the daughters of these friends.

Isabel didn't know their names and if she should ever have to speak to one of them she would have to address her respectfully as Demoiselle and curtsy (she would have to curtsy to their tirewomen, come to that). But before this Christmas feast of 1271 was well begun, she knew their clothes and those of the Lady Judith and Lady Cecily by heart, so that she could close her eyes and instantly call up every detail of the embroidery on their cuffs and hems and the look of a woollen weave which was as smooth as calfskin.

There were some empty seats on the dais but Isabel did not notice these at first. Until, just as the Lord of Misrule was calling the first forfeit, Abbess Christiana of St Peter's Abbey in Redesmarsh arrived.

The abbess, late and unapologetic, swept through the hall with her two attendant nuns at her heels, to occupy the vacant places on the dais. Her personal presence swept before her like the bow wave of a ship so that everyone stopped eating and talking, in order to watch.

Isabel had seen her before, at other Christmas feasts, but had never before been so close to her. Abbess Christiana was a vision in flowing black draperies, white linen wimple as crisp and pure as new-fallen snow, with a five-inch high pectoral cross of gold, studded with garnets and amethysts, hanging round her neck on a golden chain. Jewellery was out of fashion in the secular world and the abbess's cross was easily the most spectacular ornament in the hall.

She gave Sir Henry and Sir Simon her hand to kiss, greeted their ladies with a graciousness just short of patronising, and took her chair as though it were a throne. The Lord of Misrule cried, 'A forfeit for latecomers!' but caught his lord's eye and subsided.

23

'An abbess,' said Sir Henry coolly, 'has higher responsibilities than that of punctuality at a frivolous celebration, even one in honour of the birth of Our Lord.'

'Indeed,' said the abbess, with slight impatience waving her two nuns to take the seats which awaited them at the rear of the dais, 'the cares of an abbess much resemble your own, Sir Henry. The abbey has lands, just as you have, which must be administered and above and beyond that, she must command a manor of the spirit.'

Isabel, gazing concentratedly at Christiana, thought with astonishment that in her black and white, with that one flash of colour in her pectoral cross, she made every other lady on the dais look tawdry and somehow smaller than usual. She wondered why, and how, and almost let herself be distracted from the Lord of Misrule's hilarious attentions to Mistress Johanna and Bernard.

She also talked about the extraordinary phenomenon of Abbess Christiana's elegance all the way home, until Alfred actually became irritable.

The twelve days of Christmas wore on. Sir Henry Rushley and his lady went to stay at Castle Rising; reportedly they were trying for a marriage alliance between a de Montalt and one of Lady Judith's demoiselles The villagers made merry in their own way and there was a gathering at Northfield. Isabel's father still had a cough but was a cheerful enough host, although Grandmother Mary was looking a little frail. She said repeatedly that this would likely be her last Christmas and in a fit of sentiment, presented Isabel with the bronze medallion. 'I don't want it buried with me; I'd sooner hand it on, and you were interested. You keep it to remember me by when I'm not here any more. Only don't you be silly about it. Don't go mooning over it,' she added warningly. 'People like us don't need that. You'll have enough to do, keeping alive and rearing your babies.'

'I wish she hadn't given you that thing,' said Alfred disapprovingly afterwards, when Isabel took to wearing it. 'You were funny-like, after she talked to you about it.' He lifted it and stared at it. 'What does that pattern mean, anyhow? Curved lines sort of arching over wavy ones. What's it all about?'

'I don't know. Nor does my grandmother, really. She thought it might be a bridge over a river, made simple.'

'Well, I don't care for it. And none of the other women wear necklaces, these days.'

'I'll put it away,' said Isabel, and did so, although not quite in the fashion which Alfred no doubt assumed, for she did not lock it in her personal chest but simply took to keeping it out of sight beneath her dress instead of on top. She liked to feel it there.

Work on the land resumed after the Christmas break, but then stopped again because of a heavy snowfall. The north wind whistled across East Anglia, freezing the waterways and crackling the frosty reeds in the marshes, sweeping the snow before it in a blinding, horizontal blizzard and piling it in drifts against dykes and walls.

It lasted a week. Then the wind swung to the south-west and it rained. The snow vanished and the water channels ran high between the muddy fields, and Alfred, inspecting the ground, said that in another day he'd be able to get the plough going again. 'I want to get that bit of scrub at the west edge turned over this year. I've got it scythed down but that's all and it annoys me, that land running to waste.'

The bit of scrub was on his own holding. In other parts of the country, farming was communal, with everyone, even the lord, holding strips of the great fields on which, of course, everyone had to plant the same crop.

But here in East Anglia, holdings had always been self-contained and an attempt by Sir Henry's father, the innovative Sir Reginald, to introduce the system on a few acres of newly reclaimed marshland in Rushley, was most definitely one of his non-successes, crashing as it did, head-on against a wall of tradition.

'My dad allus planted what he wanted and we ain't changing now.' 'Woad and madder and a bit of rye; they're our crops. Ain't at home sowing wheat.' And, with great indignation, '*Draw* for strips and have my acres scattered all over the place? I won't know where I'm at from one day to the next and what if I get one o' they feckless Eelfishers next to me? I'll have their dandelions in my beans. No thanks!'

When it came to the point, the land-hungry younger men of Rushley were not, of course, improvident enough actually to refuse the offer. But they traded strips vigorously and illicitly among themselves until, somehow or other, the land ended up as five self-contained holdings after all. The reeve of the day gave up the struggle to stop the process quite soon. 'If I tell a man he's on the wrong strip and he says he's doing a favour for someone who did the same for him when he was abed with the ague, how am I to know if he's lying?'

Eventually, Sir Reginald retired to a geriatric sickbed and Sir Henry quietly made the newly formed holdings official. Boundary markers, usually in the form of extra ditches and banks, appeared between them. Alfred's father had acquired the one now called Plowman's Acres, and had dug a ditch partway round it. He'd never quite managed to get it all under cultivation, though Alfred had had his eye on that last half-acre for a long time. It ran up from the edge of the Wend along the side of the new ditch and included the banked-up slope where the earth dug from the ditch had been piled. It was rough and uneven but potentially fertile.

Using that fertility, however, was a question of finding the spare hours, for the ground must be cleared before it could be ploughed and this took time. Alfred's father had never succeeded in finding enough.

'Tomorrow,' said Alfred, 'I'll get a full eight-ox team working on that bit of land. Sixacres'll oblige me as usual, I expect.' He was thought well-off, with four oxen of his own, but it was only half a team. Everyone in Rushley got their ploughing done by borrowing each other's animals. Even the Pechers, in their dismal way, lent their pair out sometimes in exchange for help when they did their own ploughing. But Alfred preferred to ask Sixacres, across the Wend, if he could. Tosti and Ufi were so damn glum, he said.

They always woke at dawn, whatever time dawn might be, sleeping longer in winter. The next morning, therefore, Isabel roused at about eight of the clock by the reckoning of the marked candles which Father Benedict kept always burning in the church. Alfred was still asleep, although he moved restlessly as she drew herself out of the crook of his arm and out from under the pile of fleeces which covered them.

Quickly, she pulled her gown on over her long woollen shift, and knelt, shivering, to take the clods off the fire and blow it into some kind of life. Then she put on her boots, threw a thick shawl round her, and went out to feed the hens and tend the cattle in their winter byre.

The sky was grey in the east but in the west it was still dark, with a few sharp stars. The grass underfoot crackled with frost. The cold was bitter once again, for the wind had backed east in the night. But it was blowing from the sea, and it brought with it something exhilarating, a smell of clean, wild distance. Before she had finished her tasks, the last stars had gone and the eastern sky had turned to pink and gold, barred with black cloud.

Pausing before she went indoors, Isabel saw a flight of geese pass across it, their V-formation hard and black against the glowing background. A hunting marsh harrier skimmed over the river, riding the wind currents, searching the cold reedbeds and the brown fields for any small living thing which might be good to eat.

Long ago, a forebear of hers, born in freedom and enslaved in middle life, had watched a hunting eagle glide and soar in the air of the alien valley where he was kept a bondman, and had known that he would never cease to hunger for his liberty. Now, his descendant, who had heard only a muddled legend of his existence and certainly knew nothing of the eagle, stood outside her mud-walled dwelling on this icy morning, and watched the hawk's free, menacing flight and, without warning, was seized with savage exultation and a desire to be like that too. For a moment, even the child in her womb was like a weight, a ball of solid clay, holding her down to the earth while, within her spirit, wings beat fiercely, struggling to take to the air.

The harrier plunged suddenly out of sight, earthwards. It had found prey, no doubt; some small bird of a kind which did not migrate south, perhaps, and was now dining on it. Isabel came back to herself, bewildered by the extraordinary sensations which had just overtaken her, and struggling to make sense of them.

The nearest she could come to achieving this amounted to: I'd rather

26

be a hawk than a scared little bird and that's all we are, Alfred and me and everyone like us, just scared little sparrows. We're frightened of Sir Henry, even when he's being jovial, like at Christmas. We always have to be careful not to forget who we are, not to go too far. We have to do what that Bernard tells us, or else. He didn't like it when Aunt Griselda's boy Sim made him stand on his head. He knocked Sim head over heels the other day, Aunt Griselda said, for getting in his way when he was coming out of Sir Henry's gate. But Rohese now, she's grown like a hawk, in a way. Maybe that's why she's lost her manners. Harriers aren't polite to little birds and frogs and things. They just eat them. Only it's funny; inside me, I *feel* more like a hawk than a sparrow. How is it that what you feel like inside and what other people see when they look at you, can be so different? It's like being two people at the same time and which one's real?

'Isa, where are you?'

Alfred was awake and missing her. She hurried back to him. 'Come back into bed for a minute or two,' he said invitingly.

Beneath the coverings he was warm and eager, nuzzling her with murmured endearments, patting the now very obtrusive bump which was their future offspring and anxious not to squash it, but equally anxious to draw her to him and slip affectionately inside her.

She cupped her hand round the back of his head and kissed him and, with a half-touching, half-comical mixture of enthusiasm and restraint, he pressed on. Isabel whispered reassurances and pet-names, and remembered that while they had been kept indoors, she had made and finished three crispines of coloured wool, red and yellow and pink. They would all show up well against dark hair and she had altered her barbettes, too, to show her hair at the back. When they got up, she'd put the red one on.

Alfred, once up, wanted to get at his half-acre as soon as he could and ate his breakfast at speed. Before he left, he lifted a mutton ham down from the roofbeam hook for her, and fetched a bucket of water from the well which his father had dug, with the help of neighbours, because the waters of the Wend turned brackish when there were storm tides. 'I got to see you don't strain yourself.'

Isabel thanked him, in a bright voice, and tried not to worry that, with his mind on his ploughing, he had failed altogether to notice the red crispine.

Watching him set off to Sixacres with his own oxen and his plough and his dog Shag trotting at his heels, she sighed, half in affection and half in irritation, before turning to her own morning's work. It was no good expecting Alfred to be more than he was, and she knew that. He was kind and hardworking and if he didn't look at her as much as he had when they were first married, and if he didn't understand her dreams and restlessness, well, her grandmother was no doubt right. One had enough to do without such things, just living.

She turned to her chores. Bread must be made and something hot prepared for Alfred at midday. She'd chop the ham with some onions, she decided, and make a pasty. They needed more rushdips, too. She had some candles, bought from the chandler in Oxfen, but they were too expensive to be used freely. Homemade rushdips had to do most of the time and making those was nobody's favourite business, being a smelly process of boiling animal fat down for tallow and then dipping trimmed rushes in it. She'd been collecting fat and would soon have enough . . . ugh, thought Isabel, pulling a face. How it would stink!

She set about making the bread, slightly hampered, when she squatted by the fire to make the dough, by her bulging middle. She wondered what giving birth would be like. Bella said there was nothing to it, but the truth was that women died sometimes. It would be a relief when this first one had arrived safely.

Well, it wouldn't do to go mooning about that, either. She put her mind to her work and by midday there were loaves baking nicely on the kerbstone of the hearth, and two hot, fragrant pasties ready, one for each of them. She went to the door to see if Alfred were coming, but there was no sign of him.

It was rare for him to be late. He liked his food and when he was working near enough to come back at noon, he usually came promptly. She looked out of the door several times in the next half hour and once or twice made a trumpet of her hands and called, 'Alfred!' But there was no reply although this was hardly strange, for the wind had become blustery and it whisked her voice away. She wondered if Bernard Reeve had wanted Alfred for anything. But he'd already given the instructions for the spring ploughing, and Alfred wasn't one for getting into trouble, taking fish or wildfowl on Sir Henry's land or anything of that kind.

At length, uneasily, she ate her own pasty. The baby was still making her hungry; sometimes she thought she was eating for twenty rather than two. The food warmed her and helped her to make up her mind. When she reckoned that Alfred was nearly an hour overdue, she banked the fire carefully, put on her thickest cloak, took a stave to help her keep her footing in the mud and set out, head down into the wind, along the track round the edge of their holding, to the half-acre which Alfred had said he meant to plough.

She was nearly there when she raised her head and saw the unexpected cluster of people just where the drainage ditch joined the River Wend. She began, clumsily, to run.

Nearing the cluster, she saw that it consisted, improbably, of Hilda Eelfisher and the Pechers. They seemed to be working together over something dark that lay on the river bank at their feet. Oxen stood at the water's edge and as she came closer she could see Shag crouched on the bank and hear him whimpering.

Only something immensely dramatic would ever bring the Eelfishers and the Pechers into any form of partnership. Shouting and waving, crying, 'Where's Alfred? What's happened?' she stumbled up to them and knew before they turned to her, what kind of answer they would give.

They had lifted Alfred from the river and Tosti Pecher was crouched astride him, trying to pump the water out of him while Hilda, stooping, chafed his hands and Ufi, his back to the others, was yanking at a dark hulk in the river. All three were wearing leather wading boots to the thigh and the leather streamed water. Hilda Eelfisher's skirts were kilted high above the knee, and they too were soaked.

Isabel threw herself down beside the sodden, unresponsive thing which had been her husband, had been kind and good and just occasionally grumpy and had sired the new life which now lurched within her. She pushed the lank wet hair out of his unseeing eyes and shook him and cried his name and clutched at the cold clay which had been his hands, the hands which had held her and caressed her. 'Alfred, Alfred! Come back, wake up, answer me!'

Hilda, at last, dragged her away and held her while they told her what had happened.

Alfred had been turning the plough at the corner where the ditch met the Wend. And the river bank, soaked from the thaw and the high water, had crumbled, tipping the plough and one of the lead oxen over the edge.

'We saw it happen, we was all down there . . .' Hilda, her brawny arms round Isabel, pointed downstream. Two flat-bottomed boats were drawn up on the bank, their poles flung down beside them. 'We'd met, out poling our boats and we was having a bit of a barney about who had the right to be on this stretch. We seed it all, and heard it. Heard the splash and Alfred shouting and the oxen bellowing and the dog there; he was barking fit to burst. We got here as quick as we could but it was against the current. Seemed to take for ever. Your Alfred cut the ox loose, the one in the river, before all the rest got dragged in, and he tried to save it before it drowned and we all tried too, but it was kicking and struggling; we couldn't get it out; we tried all ways. And then, in the middle of it all . . .'

'Think it kicked him in the head,' said Ufi Pecher. Although he and his father had joined forces with Hilda in the rescue attempt, he did not glance at the Eelfisher woman as he spoke. He was a dour, unemotional young man and there was little feeling in his voice even when he said, 'At any rate, he went under and the ox was on top. We got him on to the bank in the end but . . .' he shrugged. 'The ox drowned. We couldn't save it,' he said.

'I don't care about the ox! It's Alfred! *Alfred!*'

'It took too long to get him out,' said Hilda, holding her hard. 'When we did, it was too late. I'm sorry, love, I'm sorry, Isabel. That's what you're called, ain't it? But even if we'd been quicker, his head's that dented.'

She had seen that for herself already, the moment she pushed back the hair from his forehead. His temple was like an egg that someone had hit with a spoon. But it wasn't believable. It ought to be possible to turn back time and undo it. If she were to go home and start out all over again . . .

'We got to tell someone. Best tell Bernard Reeve,' said Tosti. He was shorter than his son and not prepossessing. He had lost most of his upper front teeth and the one survivor, the canine on the left side, stuck out like a fang. Some people called him Tosti One-Fang rather than Tosti Pecher.

'You'd best do that,' said Hilda. 'I've got to see to Alfred's wife here.'

'All right, all right!' said Tosti, affronted. 'Who're you giving orders to?'

'I ain't giving orders, I'm just saying what's obvious. Someone's got to look after Isabel here and it'ud best be a woman, so one of you'd better fetch the reeve.'

'All right, all right. I don't have to be told my duty by an Eelfisher that grudges me a few trout out of a river not half a mile from my home . . .'

'It ain't the odd trout we grudge, it's the traps that keep the trout from our stretch . . .'

'Oh, who cares about your silly feuds *now*!' Isabel cried, her head still pressed close into the fish-scented sheepskin jerkin which covered Hilda's upper half. 'What do the trout and the fish traps matter? The plough's got to be brought back,' she added hysterically, clutching at practical things as though they were talismans against reality. 'And four of those oxen belong to Sixacres and . . .'.

'It'll all be seen to,' said Hilda. 'Come on. I'd best get you to your mam. I'll take you in my boat.'

Something cold nosed at Isabel's legs and she looked down. Shag, shivering, was pressing himself against her and looking up at her with brown eyes full of mute bewilderment. She reached down a hand to his rough fur. 'We've got to bring Shag. I left the fire burning,' she added stupidly. 'Under clods.'

'I'll see to that after I've got you to your mam. Come on, now. Lucky we was around,' Hilda said, nodding towards the Pechers but not otherwise bidding them farewell. 'If you'd bin alone, no knowing what might of happened. You'd tried to get him out yourself, likely as not.'

'That's right.' Ufi Pecher had been nudging his father into silence. 'You go with Hilda, girl. We'll deal with the rest.'

She sat in Hilda's flatboat. Hilda had almost carried her into it because her legs had suddenly given way. They didn't seem to be hers any longer.

Nothing was hers any more. What seemed like only a few minutes ago, she had been in her home, making a midday dinner for Alfred.

30

Just that short time ago, life had been ordinary, too ordinary to please her, she recalled.

It had never occurred to her in her worst nightmares that in the space of moments, one's whole life could just fall to pieces.

In fact, it was impossible. It couldn't have happened. She couldn't, really, have knelt there on the muddy river bank and clutched at a cold, drenched, drowned thing and called it by Alfred's name. She could see Alfred in her mind quite clearly, stocky and flaxen, with his kindly smile, ducking his head as he came through their low doorway, wanting his dinner.

And she wasn't there to provide it for him. As the punt pulled in at last to the rough landing stage below the path up to the Northfield dwelling and her mother, who had seen them approach, came hurrying down to meet them, she realised, with a shock of distress which went through her body like a spear, that she had been quite wrong in coming here with Hilda. She had let herself be taken further away from her ordinary life whereas she should have gone back to it and made it real again by believing in it.

'I'm sorry,' she said, cutting in as Hilda began to explain what had happened, and her mother's hands reached out to help her ashore. 'I'm sorry, it's all a mistake. I must go home at once. Alfred will be hungry. I don't know what I'm doing here, I . . .'

The spear passed through her body again and she stopped, gasping, clutching her abdomen. There was blood on the flat boards of Hilda's punt.

There was a mooring post at the corner of the landing stage. With one smooth movement, Hilda rose and fastened the painter to it, stooped, lifted Isabel and stepped ashore. Hilda Eelfisher was as powerful as a man. 'I'll carry her up. You get on ahead, Mistress, and make ready.'

'For the love of God! She's not seven months gone yet! Is she . . .?'

'Aye,' said Hilda, grimly.

It would have been a girl. Not really what Alfred wanted or needed, but he had said he would be nice about it if they had a daughter and they might have a boy next time. He'd probably have said a girl would be company for Isabel as she grew up, and what should they call her?

She wasn't going to be called anything. She wasn't going to grow up. The poor bloodstained thing which would have been the daughter of Alfred and Isabel Plowman never drew breath. She, or it, was buried or somehow disposed of – Isabel never asked how – and Isabel herself lay on her old bed in her parents' dwelling, looking up at the reed thatch as she had done as a child and trying to understand that her short married life had been wiped out as though it had never been.

She could still see Alfred with perfect clarity inside her mind but in the flesh she would never see him again. He had been laid in his grave while she lay ill, being dosed by her mother and grandmother with various unpleasant-tasting concoctions guaranteed to be infallible remedies for bleeding.

'He's in the churchyard; when you're well enough, we'll go along there and you can put flowers or summat,' said Grandmother Mary, sitting at her bedside with Father Benedict, who had come to offer spiritual consolation to the bereaved, and assure her that her husband had had a properly conducted funeral, and that most of Rushley had attended it.

'Flowers? At this time of year?' said Isabel, turning her head away.

'There're snowdrops. We'll take a bunch of snowdrops.'

'All right,' said Isabel. It would be easier to do as she was told, she supposed. Taking snowdrops to Alfred's grave wouldn't do any harm.

They wouldn't bring him back to life, either.

And she wanted him brought back to life. Father Benedict said that this was wrong, that God for His own reasons had called Alfred out of the world and that to accept His will was not only her duty, but best for her, since that will could not be gainsaid. But there was no acceptance in her.

She was astounded at the strength of her longing for Alfred. She had married him because he was there, and everyone said she could do worse, and she hadn't loved him as far as she knew. She had regarded him, in fact, with something like kindly contempt. But his kind and solid personality, mind and body, had somehow filled a space in her life, like a door being fitted to complete a newly built house. And like the door, he had kept the winds out and the warmth in. And she had been discontented although she had at least not let him know that.

She lay there crying, day after day. At first, Shag would come and lie on top of her rugs and she would try to find comfort in stroking his rough coat and shedding tears on it, but Shag presently took to going off during the day with her father, beginning already, it seemed, to transfer his allegiance. Isabel then cried harder and more hopelessly and was unable even to talk to Lady Judith, who had come in majestic person to offer her condolences, or to the Lightfoots, who had come from Rushley to offer theirs. Bella, growing worried, sent for Father Benedict again.

He arrived with a swish of black priestly garments, and a severe expression on his square, blunt face.

'Now, my girl, this won't do. It's been a terrible thing that's happened to you and no one's denying that but your mother and your grandmother tell me that you're not even trying to look to the future again. It's your duty to do that, you know. Life's full of dangerous chances. It's a fortunate few that live as long as your grandmother. And having you in this state and not even trying to get up, though your mother tells me you're fit to rise now, isn't good for the rest of the people in this house. Your grandmother's getting frail and your father's coughing again; your mother has enough to do with taking care of them.'

Isabel was huddled under her fleecy rugs with only her face visible. The smell of a damp, misty February drifted into the dwelling through the slats of the unglazed windows. The slats were supposed to let in light as well as air, but at this time of year they were kept partly shuttered; Isabel's face was a white patch in the dimness until Father Benedict lit a rushlight and put it beside the bed.

'I see. I'm a nuisance here,' Isabel said. 'Well, I shouldn't be here, I suppose. It isn't my home. I think I'd like to go home. I won't bother anyone there.'

'And live by yourself on Plowman's Acres? No one would expect you to do that, child, not at your age. You sound,' said Father Benedict acutely, 'as though you're sulking. I don't know whether you're sulking at me or at God, but either way, you'll feel better as soon as you stop. You ought to get on your feet and start helping your mother about the place as best you can. If you can't carry water buckets yet, you can shape dough and twirl a spindle, I imagine.'

'What's happening at our – at Plowman's?' Isabel asked. She sat up a little and for the first time showed signs of interest in the outer world. She pushed a strand of damp, dark hair out of her eyes. 'Is it just being left? What about the crop? What about the planting where Alfred had started that new bit of ploughing? He meant to put beans in.'

'Yes, he'd mentioned that to your father,' Father Benedict said. 'Your father and the Pechers had a word with Bernard Reeve and they've been seeing to everything. The holding won't suffer too much though you're an ox short.'

'Your father told you,' said Bella. 'Only you wouldn't take it in.'

'Did he? I don't remember. But what about next year? I'll have to go back, won't I?' Isabel sank down again, suddenly overwhelmed by what felt like an impossible burden of responsibility. 'But even if I go back, what will I do? I can't do Alfred's ploughing or . . .'

'I said, there's no need for you to go back, or not yet. You stay here and give your mother some help. What's to be done about Plowman's will be settled before long, you'll see.'

'How?'

'I said,' said Father Benedict calmly, 'that you'll see.'

Not unkindly, although with slight impatience, he regarded the mutinous little face which the rushlight showed him. A few months of wedded life had been enough to give Isabel's sallow, slightly asymmetrical features that firm moulding which girls usually acquired after marriage, however young they might actually be. But there were lines round the mouth of which he did not approve. Yes. *Mutinous.* That was the word and it was a bad characteristic in a woman.

Perhaps it would fade as she adapted herself to the new turn in her life. She had lost a child as well; women always grieved over that and it was not surprising. Probably that was the reason why she found the will of God so hard to accept.

'All will arrange itself,' he said. 'You must put some trust in the people round you. While you have been recovering from your illness and going through your mourning, others have been busy on your behalf. You should be grateful. You will find out before long. For the time being, get up, my girl, and get strong. I shall expect to see you in church next Sunday. You have only to step into a boat, after all.'

Sir Henry Rushley was fifty-one years old and he was feeling his age.

The knee damaged in France thirty years ago when he had followed his namesake King Henry the Third across the Channel on what proved to be a disastrous attempt to reconquer the province of Poitou, had of late been giving trouble. He had been twenty-one when he was wounded, newly knighted and innocently full of a desire to win his spurs on the battlefield, and he'd made light of the injury afterwards. It had seemed to heal up well. But now, when he woke in the morning and began to climb out of the curtained bed he shared with his wife, the knee was usually puffy and reluctant either to bend or straighten.

Already, he had begun sending his son Simon, named for the great Earl of Leicester, Simon de Montfort, to represent him when Rushley was nominated to supply one of the two knights which Norfolk, like other counties, regularly sent to the parliament which de Montfort had first shaped.

It wasn't that he couldn't travel if he wanted to. He was still capable, thank God, of riding round his manor or travelling, occasionally, to Norwich. He owned three ships, and he could journey by water if he liked, instead of subjecting his knee to the strain of a stirrup. Sometimes, by means of his ships, he even went to London.

But he was beginning, nevertheless, to feel weary at the thought of taking journeys; conscious, every time, of the miles lengthening between himself and his home. He had, after all, such a comfortable home.

Rushley Hall had been partly rebuilt in his father's day, when the old house, after withstanding the easterly gales and marsh damps and the cracking frosts or a hundred and fifty years, showed signs of crumbling. Now, it was halfway between a house and a castle. It had a surrounding wall and gatehouse, a space within big enough to graze a few animals should the place be attacked, and only small slit windows at ground-floor level in the house itself. They kept stores and beasts down there, except for the kitchen at one end and what would eventually be a rather handsome chapel at the other. At considerable expense, Sir Henry had lately had the small original chapel demolished and was in process of building one more in keeping with the size of his household and his status in the shire. The bills for this kept mounting up, which depressed him. He had had to raise a loan and feared he would be in debt for years to come.

The bedchambers were on the second floor and they were well-appointed. Sir Henry, parting the bedcurtains in order to climb painfully

34

out into the dank air of February and shouting for his squire to bring him his fur-lined gown quickly, emerged into a chamber with an elegantly carved oak ceiling and two good windows equipped with shutters and oxgut membranes. It was cold, but in the first-floor hall below, where the central hearth was built on top of a massive stone pillar which rose through the undercroft, a fire would be blazing so that the household could hear morning Mass in comfort. He'd have to give some thought, he reminded himself, to heating arrangements in the new chapel.

He started rising before Lady Judith did but, as usual, by the time his squire had dressed him and shaved him and combed the hair which had once been brown and thick and was now getting grey and scanty, and he had limped down the stairs, Judith and her demoiselles were there before him. They were waiting politely, with faces washed, white headdresses in place and girdles neatly fastened, while Father Benedict, who acted as the household chaplain, stood with a patient air behind the small altar which lived in a curtained alcove. The assembled household was arranged in pious rows behind Lady Judith, hands clasped before them and eyes swivelling wistfully towards the sideboard on which covered dishes were slowly growing cold.

On this particular morning, Sir Henry noticed, the household had been augmented by the presence of Bernard Reeve. He raised his eyebrows at the reeve, and Bernard nodded, a silent and time-honoured exchange, which translated as, 'Do you want to see me urgently?' and 'Yes, sir.'

After Mass, the household broke their fast, casually, sitting or standing about, and helping themselves to food from the sideboard. Bernard ate with the rest; anyone who called at a mealtime naturally partook. But he did not approach his lord until Sir Henry had finished and the ladies had withdrawn to the adjoining solar. As soon, however, as the door had shut behind them, Sir Henry made a sign and Bernard came over to him.

Bernard was an institution. He was a widower, older than Sir Henry, who could barely recall the days when Bernard's father had been reeve instead, or bailiff as the office was sometimes called. On some manors, the two were separate, the bailiff being the lord's representative and the reeve the villeins' leader. But Oxfen, Redesmarsh and Rushley had one man each to combine both functions. Rushley's reeves were freemen, descended from an offshoot of the Grosneys and had their own holding, which they were allowed to sublet to a villein family who gave their work service to the reeves instead of Sir Henry. Bernard was gnarled and efficient and never turned up at breakfast like this without a good reason.

'So,' said Sir Henry, subsiding creakily on to a settle and motioning Bernard to sit down as well. 'What brings you here so early?'

Bernard took a stool. 'It's not a great emergency,' he said, using

French, as Sir Henry preferred to do, and as the Grosneys did at home. 'But there is some urgency and I have a deal of work on hand today. You've had flooding in your fields and I must get a squad together to repair one of the dykes. So I felt it best to get this other matter in hand quickly, before the day's work on your flooded cornfield drowns me.'

Sir Henry grinned, recognising this as one of Bernard's straight-faced jokes.

'Well, out with it, then.'

'Plowman's Acres,' said Bernard. 'We buried Alfred Plowman a month ago now. His land needs attention and next season, someone must take over his ploughing duties. The matter wants settling. The widow's only a girl of sixteen.'

'Ah, yes. Shocking accident, that. Trying to get the last inch of the land under the plough and trying too hard. Well, what do you suggest, Bernard. The widow has rights in the land. I gather that she was with child but lost it; my wife went to see her. She was with her mother then. Is she still there?'

'Yes, for the time being. She's recovering, I hear. But she can hardly go back to live on Plowman's alone and she couldn't run the place, anyway. So . . .'

'So? The answer, I take it, is to find her another husband, someone who can take the tenancy over.'

'Exactly.' Bernard glanced round and Sir Henry observed that Father Benedict, having tidied his altar and curtained it, was hovering. He came now to join them. 'Father Benedict and I have discussed the question,' Bernard said. 'A three-month mourning period must be permitted to the girl, of course, but after that . . . I am talking, Father, of Isabel of Northfield.'

'So I gathered,' said Father Benedict. 'Well, I commonly prefer a six-month mourning but in this particular case, I think the girl herself would be the better for a sensible arrangement as quickly as possible.'

'And you've thought up a new husband for her?' said Sir Henry, addressing both of them. 'It sounds as if you have. Well, who have you got in mind?'

'Ufi Pecher, the son on the adjacent holding,' Bernard said. 'It would be good sense to unite them and the land he's already working isn't so big that he couldn't manage the extra acres. His father's still perfectly active. They can take over Alfred's ploughing and maybe,' said Bernard drily, 'fish less. The Pechers have a feud with the Eelfishers which is causing trouble.'

'Ah yes. We had a dispute at the last manor court, did we not? It ended, if I remember rightly, bogged down in a muddle about where Tosti Pecher has always fished unchallenged, and where the Eelfishers have always fished unchallenged, and of why the two territories now, mysteriously, seem to overlap. At the next court, Bernard, please see that I have a plan of our waterways to hand and we will make a division

36

of the rights and never mind past history. I don't mind if the Pechers fish less, but I don't want them to stop entirely. They pay part of their rent in fish and very useful it is, too, especially,' said Sir Henry thoughtfully, 'when I entertain Abbess Christiana of Redesmarsh. She is a great stickler for keeping Lenten rules. If Ufi Pecher is agreeable and I don't see why he shouldn't be, you can tell the girl that she will marry him as soon as Lent is out. An Easter marriage for her. Poor little wench,' said Sir Henry, with unimaginative sentimentality, 'what a terrible thing, losing her husband and her baby like that. This will give her something to look forward to.'

Chapter Three

Redesmarsh Abbey

The deputation arrived at Northfield by water and Isabel, who was out of doors fetching kindling from the woodpile, knew what it portended as soon as the boat was close enough for her to see that in it were Father Benedict, Bernard Reeve, Aunt Griselda and Mistress Joan Lightfoot.

When Sir Henry ordered a marriage among his villeins, as he quite often did, Father Benedict and Bernard Reeve always had the task of informing the parties and, when they came to tell the prospective bride, they invariably brought female reinforcements.

It was Bernard's system. If the future bride were pleased, he maintained, she would want her women friends round her to chatter to about it, and if she needed persuading, women could talk sense into a woman's head better than a man could. Isabel, horrified, rushed indoors with the kindling and dropped it on the floor.

'Whatever's come over you?' said Grandmother Mary, peering at her. 'Seen a ghost?'

'No. I've seen the priest, the reeve, Aunt Griselda and Mistress Lightfoot coming here in a boat!'

'About time,' said Bella. She was cooking and went briskly on doing it. 'I wondered when they'd come.'

'You mean you *knew* they . . . that . . .?'

'Certainly. Father Benedict's spoken to me and your father and very sensible it is, what they're arranging. So don't you give any trouble, my girl. It's all for your good.'

'What is?'

'Oh, well, may as well tell you. I doubt they'll have changed their minds since yesterday when I saw Father Benedict last. Ufi Pecher,' said Bella, a little too loudly.

Isabel had left the door open. When the deputation arrived in the dwelling's smoky interior, they found her crouching behind her grandmother's chair while Bella dodged to and fro, trying to hit her daughter with a wooden spoon, and old Mary shouted for her to stop, to be calm, they'd have people here any moment.

'Oh dear me,' said Father Benedict. 'It seems you've told her already, Mistress Bella.'

'Well, it just slipped out, like.' Gasping, Bella turned her back on Isabel and began an attempt to greet her guests.

'You should have left it to us,' said Bernard reprovingly, interrupting her. 'We're official, from Sir Henry, and it shouldn't have been said before we came. Isabel, come out from there, now. We've good news for you, as you'll see in a minute. Come on, now.'

Aunt Griselda and Mistress Joan made soothing noises at Bella and Isabel alike. 'Isabel,' Bella said, 'you heard Master Reeve, now. Come along. I'm sorry I lost my temper with you but when my own daughter shouts at me like that, I don't like it.'

'Go on, girl.' Mary reached a hand behind her chair and caught Isabel's sleeve. 'Go forward.'

Isabel rose to her feet and stepped into the firelight. Her small face was more mutinous now than Father Benedict had ever seen it before. She held her shawl across her chest under crossed arms as though these things constituted armour.

She stepped right in front of the deputation and searched their faces for a moment and then she spoke.

'No,' she said. 'I am not going to marry Ufi Pecher *and you can't make me!*'

They tried, however.

'But what,' said Bernard Reeve in exasperation and also bewilderment, 'have you got against Ufi Pecher? He is a decent young man and you are acquainted with him already. It's a good match for you. Ufi is willing. He's going to pay the marriage fine for you.'

'I'm a widow,' said Isabel. 'Widows are supposed to be able to choose their second husbands.'

'You're a villein and you're a girl not yet seventeen, what's more. Since when do villein wenches defy their overlord's orders?'

'Isa, it's very good of Sir Henry to concern himself with you and you ought to be grateful,' said Bella, glaring at her daughter, bobbing an apologetic curtsy to Bernard Reeve, leaning on Aunt Griselda and wringing her hands all at the same time.

'Your mother's right,' muttered Mary. 'Best listen to her.'

'I don't like Ufi!'

'Why not?' demanded Aunt Griselda.

'What have you got against him?' inquired Mistress Joan.

'She's allus had ideas above herself,' said Bella.

'Isabel. Tell us why you object to Ufi Pecher.' Father Benedict said, waving down an indignant exclamation from Bernard that Isabel's objections were of no importance.

'I just *don't like him.*' The Pechers avoided other people and never laughed, and it mattered. If she had thought Alfred dull at times, Ufi Pecher would be a thousand times worse. Alfred at least had been lovable, had often been merry and was certainly sociable. 'He and his father just stay on their holding all the time except for fishing and never go anywhere or invite anyone.'

'Oh, you foolish girl!' cried Aunt Griselda. 'It's only because they have no women in their house! Why, when you're there, all that will change! We'll come to see you and you'll come to see us; of course you will. What a fuss to make all over nothing! The Pechers are good men. Look how they tried to rescue Alfred!'

'Yes, and Alfred's only been gone a month!' Half because of a genuine surge of grief and half seizing on it as an argument which these stern-faced and determined adults just might understand, Isabel let her voice rise to a wail and encouraged the tears to fill her eyes. 'I can't marry another man yet; I can't, I can't! I miss Alfred so much and it isn't right, it isn't respectful to his memory! Aunt Griselda, you're *his* aunt; how can you want me to marry someone else so soon?'

'Now, now. Why are we all standing up?' said Father Benedict. 'We should all sit down and talk this over quietly. Come here to me, my child, and sit beside me on this bench.'

There was one long settle in the Northfield living room. He sat down on it and patted the place beside him encouragingly. Isabel, whose knees were feeling shaky, accepted it. 'Now,' he said. 'No one is asking you to marry Ufi Pecher tomorrow. Of course it is too soon. Lent is approaching and, in any case, you have a right and a duty to mourn for three months at least.' Smilingly, he tweaked the pleated white linen which now shrouded Isabel's head completely, even covering her small chin. 'You are behaving with great propriety and we all approve. But it is sad to see the widow's wimple on a girl as young as you. Is it not, Mistress Griselda?'

'Yes, it is.' Griselda and Joan had found stools and drawn them up in front of Isabel, who now wished she had remained standing because they made her feel surrounded. They were older women, alike in their square, solid shapes, their durable brown woollen gowns and unbleached shawls, their tidy, if patched and not perfectly clean, headdresses and their decided expressions. They had come to tell her what was what and she didn't want to hear.

'My dear child,' said Aunt Griselda, 'Alfred was a good husband to you and I am glad in a way that you feel as you do, but nothing will bring him back and you have your life to live. His land must be tilled and you should have a baby soon, to help you forget your other loss.'

'I should be tilled as well as the land?'

'Isabel!' cried Bella, horrified. 'I shan't forget the way you're talking now. I'll make you sorry; you'll see!'

'She is upset,' said Father Benedict, quietly, shaking his head at Bella. 'Now, listen to me, Isabel. When Easter comes, the three months will be up and spring will be here and believe me, you will by then feel very different.'

'No, I won't!'

'And are you prepared,' inquired Bernard Reeve, who was still on his feet, and looking down at Isabel with an expression of chilly astonishment, as though, Isabel thought resentfully, she were a beetle he had found in his dinner, 'to say so to Sir Henry's face?'

'I don't want to marry Ufi Pecher! Why does it matter so much if I don't? You've said, or as good as, that I'm not important, just a villein girl, so why does it matter what I do or don't do?'

Bella, Aunt Griselda and Joan Lightfoot, all cried, 'Isabel!' at the same time but in differing tones of voice and burst into confused and simultaneous attempts to command, persuade and plead. Her mother's voice finally predominated. '. . . we've heard enough of this nonsense. You're to marry Ufi Pecher and you'll do as you're told, if you please.'

'Here's your father,' said Bernard Reeve, with relief. It was not, of course, the first time a message of this type had been badly received. He had known prospective brides burst into tears, and heard others mumble words of consent which were belied by an averted head and a veil tugged to a more concealing angle. But never before had he been defied like this.

Peter of Northfield came in slowly, wheezing a little as he always did these days. 'Oh!' said Bella crossly, 'Oh, Peter you will want your dinner and it's ready in the pot but meanwhile . . .'

'What's going on?' Isabel's father hesitated in his own doorway, looking from one face to another.

Several people at once set about enlightening him. When he understood, he laughed and went over to squeeze on to the settle beside Isabel and put his arm round her. 'So this is all about Ufi? I was going to tell her myself after I'd had a word with Ufi; you should have left it to me, Master Reeve. You've been crying, Isa; come along, dry your tears. It will be all right. I'm surprised at you women. You too, Bella. Master Reeve maybe is too much a man of business and Father Benedict is a man of God and so likely doesn't think of these things but can't *you* see what the trouble is with her? All of you standing over her, saying marry Ufi, marry Ufi Pecher. You're making him into just a name, a noise coming out of your mouths.' He laughed again. It turned into a cough but he shook his voice free of it. 'Poor little Isa. I was going to tell Ufi to come along and do his own courting. I'm still going to. That's all she wants; aren't I right, Isa? You want a bit of wooing.'

The trap was closing. The deputation went away, talking among themselves, nodding their heads sagely and giving Isabel kindly and knowing looks. Her father and grandmother dissuaded Bella from hitting her again and they did not talk to her about Ufi Pecher. But there must have been a good deal of talking going on behind her back because Ufi and his father fell in beside Isabel's family the next Sunday after church and it seemed to be taken for granted that they would eat their midday meal at Northfield.

They came along, in the dull dun garments which were their Sunday best, and sat round Bella's table and made comments about the crops and the fishing and the latest Eelfisher iniquity and after the meal, Ufi Pecher asked Isabel to walk with him.

She saw Bella's eye on her and was afraid to say no. Just walking with him didn't commit her to anything, anyhow. She went out beside him into an unpleasant grey and brown afternoon. It was very still and steely-cold and a thin mist lay over the fields and the marshes. They walked down to the river and along the bank, and Ufi told her stiffly that he understood that she knew what had been arranged for them. 'We're happy with the notion. We need another pair of hands at home. My father is lively for his age, but likely the time'll come when I'll want someone there to look after him. We live quiet and keep to ourselves.' Ufi imparted this dismal information as though he were saying, 'You take that track for Rushley.' That the prospect he was offering her might not please her had clearly not occurred to him. He wasn't even looking at her as he spoke and his voice was a flat monotone. 'We've no taste for gadding,' he said, 'but you'll soon settle in with how we live. You'll always be fed and clad warm, and the house is sound.'

That would be her life, though Isabel savagely. She would be isolated on the Pechers' holding, taking care of Tosti One-Fang as age took toll of him. Whatever Aunt Griselda might say, she'd be deprived of all company: there'd be no visits to the village and her women friends wouldn't be welcome. Ufi and his father didn't like gadding and they took it for granted that she would fall in with their ways entirely.

Once they were out of sight of her home, Ufi turned to her and kissed her. It was a grasping, humourless embrace. She decided not to resist, although her mouth was unresponsive and she could not have made it otherwise to save her life. Ufi, however, did not seem to notice it. 'We're promised now,' he said when he let her go, and walked her back to the house with one hand gripping her elbow. His fingers were hard; they wanted to possess, but not to please. She thought of Alfred, of the essential kindness of his touch, and wanted, then and there, to cry for him all over again. She went bleakly to her bed that night and when she got there, did not sleep.

She was afraid.

Solid and firm in her mind was the statement, I will not marry Ufi Pecher. But everyone was assuming that she would and she could feel the pull, like the current of the river dragging at the boat when one rowed or poled upstream. Nor had she ever heard of a girl refusing a marriage which had been made for her by parents or overlord and, although life with Ufi would be harsh and lonely, many girls would be glad of what he was offering: food, warm clothes and a dry house. What more could one want? Ufi wasn't even bad-looking, in a joyless kind of way, and she was no Rohese, with ash-fair hair and a lovely skin to bring to market along with her ten acres.

Restlessly turning on her pallet, she thought, well, I suppose there'd be children. But she did not want children by Ufi; and indeed, she was as yet afraid of being pregnant again. She had only to think of those awful hours to feel again the pain of torn flesh and of bereavement. Bella and the other women said one got over those feelings, in time. But she wasn't over them yet. And besides all that, besides detesting Ufi and being scared of childbearing . . .

Groping under her pallet, she felt the hard outline of the bronze medallion which Grandmother Mary had given her. In the morning, she took it from its place and went out with it, to look at it in daylight.

All that she knew about it was that the pattern upon it, of smooth lines arching over wavy ones like a bridge over flowing water, was said to be the device of a long-ago, freeborn family from which she might, possibly, be descended. But it was, to her, a symbol, and clear before her mind's eye were the things which it symbolised.

A silver crispine, a gown of green fustian and the right to ride to London or Canterbury without asking any overlord's permission.

If Alfred had lived, well, there would have been the baby, and Alfred had been a good man and she was grieving for him. But he was gone and wouldn't come back and now . . .

The thought took shape and put itself into words, etching itself as clearly on her brain as the arched and wavy lines were marked upon the medallion.

She did not want to marry again, not anyone, unless he was a freeman like Gerald Grosney and could confer free status on her.

More. She would marry anyone whatsoever, *anyone*, who would. She was surprised at the strength of her longing. She'd even consider Ufi Pecher, if he were free.

But he was not. She stared at the medallion in her hand and began to think, slowly and stumblingly at first (because she had had no training in logical thinking) but then with increasing confidence as step by step she completed the process tentatively begun at Rohese's disastrous homecoming, and one idea led on to the next concerning the true nature of freedom.

She now discovered that it was one thing to perceive a possible course of action, but quite another – and much harder – to bring oneself to the point of actually taking it.

It was hard, for instance, after Ufi and Tosti Pecher had dined with them for a second Sunday, and Ufi had taken her for a second tedious walk, to make herself sigh a little over some memory of Alfred and then say: 'But I suppose Ufi isn't so bad.'

It was not made easier by the fact that on that Sunday Tosti had taken it into his unprepossessing head – to give her a one-toothed grin, or leer, across the table and say how nice it would be to have a pretty little thing like her about the house. Even her parents had looked slightly startled at the tone.

Only by taking a deep breath and reminding herself that she was saying it to *escape* from the Pechers, and that by the look of Tosti, escape was not only desirable but imperative, could she get those lying words out.

Once she had said them, however, she had created a new level of urgency, which made it easier to say, a few days later when the sun chanced to be shining, 'I think I'll walk over to Plowman's and make sure all's in order. If I go down as far as the river, I might see Ufi.' No one hindered her. Bella looked relieved and Mary smiled knowingly. She knew they were thinking, 'There, her father was right. Nothing like a little courting to warm a girl's heart.' Since Sir Henry was sponsoring the match, they weren't letting themselves think about One-Fang's leer and what it might portend.

She set off wearing a cloak concealing beneath it a little bundle containing bread and cheese and a few belongings – a change of linen, a dark gown and some shoes – taken from her personal chest, which her father had fetched from Plowman's. Smuggling the bundle out was easy, too.

But it was hard again, very hard, once she was on her way, to keep to her plan. When she reached the plank bridge across the Wend just below Plowman's and walked over it, she felt as if her boots had leaden soles. She could only make herself go on by whispering, 'You haven't done anything yet that you can't go back on. It's a sunny day; you're tired of the house and the spinning and cooking. There's hardly any wind; the sun even has some warmth in it. You just feel like walking over the fields and you've chanced to go towards Redesmarsh.'

A little later, her feet slowed down again of their own accord. 'What am I doing here? What am I *doing*?' she asked herself. 'I won't get pretty things for my hair or rides to Canterbury this way. I'm turning my back on them for ever.'

Almost, she turned her back on her destination, and only managed not to by reminding herself that she was tired and a good way from home and would be best advised to eat her bread and cheese; maybe the food would put heart into her.

Finally, with her objective in sight, she decided – with an effort like a physical wrenching – that it would be silly and faint-hearted to have come so far and then run away at the very last moment. She had reached this point not only by the slow steps of her feet, but by an even more slow and difficult process in her mind, and she did not intend to retreat.

The process had begun at the Christmas feast, when the Abbess Christiana swept in and made all the smartly dressed and worldly ladies look trivial. She had begun to see it then: the Abbess Christiana had more power and respect than any of them, and she had not won it through fine clothes and the possession of a husband, but through wearing black and white and embracing chastity. She didn't even have to please a man. She had power in her own right.

Power, Isabel had thought, lying awake, with the bronze medallion gripped in her hand. Being respected, even feared by others instead of always having to fear them. Christiana in her abbey had far more of that kind of freedom even than Lady Judith, let alone Rohese. And in the end, the things that the medallion represented, such as costly clothes and journeys were themselves only symbols of that freedom, that power. She would rather be like Christiana than like Rohese or any of the other ladies.

And with that, she made her footsteps quicken. She would not, no, she would not, turn back. Indeed, what could she turn back to? If she were to go home, she would have to marry Ufi. It would be unavoidable; her pretence at yielding had already gone too far.

If at Christmas her close look at Christiana had told her more than she knew, she stifled the knowledge. It was too late now to listen to the little voice in the back of her mind which kept whispering, warningly: 'Christiana has power, all right.'

'I have to admit,' said Abbess Christiana of Redesmarsh, passing the sugared raisins to her guests, 'that I did not enter religion in the first place out of the love of God. But that is so often the way of it. People enter religion for all kinds of reasons, often worldly ones, and then find that they have come to the right place. I know that I have done so.'

Her guests were young Sir Simon Rushley, the son of Sir Henry, and Simon's wife Cecily, and Master Herbert Grosney with his wife Lucy. Simon and Herbert, who were friends in the careful way required by friendship between people of different rank, both ran thoughtful glances over the abbess's elegant habit and jewelled cross, not to mention the quantity of fine hangings, silver candlesticks, carved oak furniture and perfumed rushes which furnished her parlour and thought that Christiana's last sentence was ambiguous to say the least of it.

Sir Simon had an ingenuous, freckled face under a thatch of light brown, endearingly curly hair, but the mind behind it was not nearly so ingenuous as his face. Herbert Grosney's features, careworn at twenty-eight through the effort of always living slightly beyond his means, were keen as well as careworn and not at all ingenuous. He and Simon exchanged glances of faint amusement.

Lady Cecily said, 'Why did you enter, Mother Abbess? Or should one not ask?'

'It is a big thing, I think, to give up the hope of marriage and children,' said Lucy Grosney. The two women were no more alike than their husbands, Lady Cecily being a chubby bundle with a gurgle of a laugh while Lucy Grosney was carefully patrician. Lucy was conscious too of her married status. She now glanced sidelong at Herbert, with the air of one drawing attention to a prized possession, and slightly eased her position on the settle she was sharing with him. Lucy Grosney was not yet visibly pregnant but the shine of her big grey eyes and the moist pinkness of her cushiony mouth told their own tale to the knowledgeable.

Christiana dipped her fingers in the raisin bowl and smiled. Lent had

45

begun and no one was as punctilious as she in eating no meat and in weighing the quantities of bread she consumed, but raisins, she felt, did not count, and one must not embarrass one's guests by watching them nibble but not partaking oneself. One must be courteous.

'I was the eldest girl in a big family in Cambridge,' she said. 'My mother was one of two sisters. My aunt became a nun when she was young and rose to be a prioress in a house of nuns not far outside the town; we used to visit her. She was charming and always so calm and cheerful when she welcomed us. I enjoyed going there because it was so different from my home.'

The sugared raisins were expensive as well as delicious. There had been a time when English grapes had been dried to make raisins but summers had been warmer once, it seemed. Now, it was hard to grow good grapes in England and both the sugar and fruit were rare imported delicacies. Abbess Christiana paused to allow the tip of her tongue to explore her lips for an errant speck of sugar. She had a tight mouth. Her smile never showed her teeth and always seemed as though it referred to only the most ladylike amusements. Her eyes were always downcast but sometimes a gleam showed below her white eyelids, as though she were privy to some secret, satisfactory knowledge.

'Please continue,' said Lucy Grosney with well-bred politeness. She and Hubert had never been invited to the abbey before and she knew that the abbess had honoured them by asking them at the same time as Sir Simon and his wife. She wanted to be the kind of guest who is asked back.

'My family is ancient,' said Christiana. 'One of our ancestors came over with William the Conqueror. But we were not especially wealthy. My father was taken prisoner when he went with King Henry to France and it cost my mother – they were newly married, then – nearly all they had to ransom him. We had one home farm and one subletting left, of what had been a valuable manor, and there were so many mouths to feed. After my elder brother and I were born, there were many more children; indeed, they came along at such a rate, my dear, that one almost lost count of them. I can't remember most of their names, now. Because few of them throve well,' said the abbess, passing the raisins again. 'They'd live a few months, or even a few years, and then die, of an ague or the smallpox or the lung-rot. My mother broke her heart over every one of them and, in the end, continually bearing broke *her*.'

'Dear, dear,' said Lady Cecily. 'But how sad.' She and Sir Simon already had two children who were so far very healthy, and she had had no special trouble in producing them.

'I heard her, sometimes,' said Christiana gravely, 'pleading with my father to leave her alone but she was his wife and she had to do what he wanted. He said it was her duty. But she found it harder and harder at every childbed. The last one killed her. Then my father died too. I was just seventeen. My elder brother was nearly twenty. There were a couple of younger ones living then, both ailing – they died later. My brother

46

asked me what I wanted to do. He'd find a husband for me if he could, he said. He'd scratch up a dowry from somewhere. Or I could take it to a nunnery and enter as a nun.'

'So you decided to be a nun,' said Lady Cecily brightly. 'Well, no wonder.'

Lucy Grosney was sitting up straight and fiddling restlessly with her wedding ring. 'It is indeed a very sad tale. Your mother was most unlucky.' She gave Herbert another proud glance. 'I often thank God for my own happy married life.'

'I thought about my mother,' said the abbess simply, 'Having child after child and losing most of them and then dying of the last one, and I thought of my aunt, the respected prioress, the bride of God and therefore safe from men and childbirth. So I said I would enter religion. I didn't say it quite as calmly as that,' she added. 'To tell the truth, I was crying and shouting that I would never be any man's wife. You can hardly imagine what it was like, the way my mother died. It took three days and nights and all for nothing. I can remember sitting down in the hall with my father and my brother and others of the household, putting our hands over our ears to shut out her screams.' She spoke matter-of-factly, describing horrors while her face continued, improbably, to be the face of one who had never heard of such things, still less was in the habit of discussing them, and certainly not in mixed company.

Lucy Grosney was fiddling with her ring more restlessly than ever. She had gone rather pale.

'I can remember doing the same thing on previous occasions,' said the abbess, reminiscently. 'But . . .' Her voice dropped to a note of one who shares a dreadful confidence. '. . . this was the worst. The last baby was born dead, you see, and then she began to bleed. I ran in to her room when I heard her crying out for God to help her . . . the midwife and the other women there did all they could but it was no use. The bed was scarlet and the blood was in pools on the floor . . .'

'Please,' said Lucy Grosney. 'I don't feel well.'

Her small, dignified features had turned a light shade of green. She looked wildly round the room and Lady Cecily, rising quickly, went to her.

'It's all right. You're all right.' Cecily's voice acquired sudden authority. 'It happens at these times.' She glanced about her. 'A basin, quick!'

'There's a privy through there.' Christiana pointed.

Lady Cecily, with an arm round Mistress Grosney's shoulders, half lifted her, and swept her out.

'I'm afraid it was the raisins,' Lucy whimpered. 'All sorts of things upset me just now, because I'm . . .' She surrendered, miserably, to nausea.

'Yes, quite. And our charming hostess,' said Lady Cecily indignantly, 'knows it. I'd swear she does. You're not showing yet but, until this happened, you had such a bloom on you. She ought to know the signs, from what she says about her family life! Come on, up with it all. You'll feel better. And forget those lurid stories. My first just popped out when I'd only been lying in for two hours, because I happened to sneeze, and the second was even quicker than that.'

'You're very kind,' groaned Lucy. 'She frightened me,' she said, and clutched at Lady Cecily with a cold, clammy hand, all pretensions to dignity forgotten. 'I wish we hadn't come.' She didn't add that they had had the abbess to dine in order to angle for a return invitation. They wouldn't be inviting her again, not if Mistress Grosney could help it, and the last thing she wanted now was for Christiana, ever, to ask them back to the abbey. If she did, the reply would be a polite no, thank you.

'I'm not surprised. But don't be frightened, my dear. There's no need,' said Lady Cecily, grimly aware that it was now too late for that, and that Lucy Grosney would probably spend the rest of her pregnancy petrified and suffer all the more when her confinement came.

In the parlour, Abbess Christiana had gone to the door and given a message to the nun who sat outside it. 'Sister Julian will come,' she said, returning to the two men. 'She will bring a posset to help Mistress Grosney. You know of Sister Julian, our infirmarian, of course.'

They nodded. All the neighbourhood knew Sister Julian and most liked her much better than they did the abbess. She was younger than Christiana, with a pleasant, gentle voice. She had a wide knowledge of herbal remedies and a kindly reassuring manner, which could be a help even to sufferers who were beyond her simple medicines. Even Father Benedict, who was the district's physician as well as its priest and was not usually one to tolerate female invasion of what he considered to be his territory, approved of Sister Julian and occasionally called her to help with women patients.

Sister Julian arrived and hurried to the privy to help the sufferer. Christiana continued to make conversation to the men, while listening to the noises from behind the privy door, and thinking with private satisfaction that that would teach Mistress Grosney to patronise her by talking of marriage as though it were a superior state, and looking first at her husband and then at Christiana as much as to say that she had treasure which Christiana had not. It would be interesting to see if she felt the same in ten years' time. Or even six months.

As she embarked, however, on a civilised and informed description of the latest valuable illuminated manuscript to be acquired for the abbey library, Sir Simon interrupted.

'I think,' he said, 'that as soon as Mistress Grosney is somewhat recovered, we had all better leave.'

'Yes, indeed. My wife would be better at home,' said Herbert Grosney. 'Our thanks for your hospitality, Mother Abbess. I'm sorry to cut our visit short. But Sir Simon is quite right.'

'Such a pity that Mistress Grosney is unwell. I always enjoy a little gathering,' said Christiana sedately. 'It is an excellent thing, to find people so ready to call on the Redesmarsh house of nuns. It shows that you pay a proper deference to matters of the spirit.

'I hope,' said Sir Simon expressionlessly, 'That I will always be able to recognise true holiness wherever I meet it.'

The tap on the door annoyed Christiana, but she would not show annoyance before guests and called 'Enter!' in an accommodating voice.

Her doorwarden nun came in, a little timidly. '*Benedicite*, Mother. There is a visitor at the gate. She begs for audience with you. She has been there for some time. We told her you were occupied, but she will not go away until she has seen you.'

Supported between Lady Cecily and Sister Julian, pale of face but evidently better, Lucy Grosney reappeared from the privy. 'Please,' said Sir Simon and Master Grosney to Christiana, speaking virtually together. 'Don't let us detain you, Mother Abbess.'

The persistent visitor was in the general parlour, just a few yards from the gatehouse. Abbess Christiana swept in, surveyed the peasant girl who sat, clutching a bundle, on the low bench, observed the trail of smelly mud her boots had left across the stone floor, and thought, 'It's time I put fresh bags of dried lavender in my clothes chest.'

'You wished to see me?' she said. The girl put her bundle hurriedly down on the bench, rose and curtsied and Christiana now took in the fact that despite her youth, her headdress was a widow's wimple. Christiana also saw that she was tired and trembling. 'I am told you have insisted on speaking to the Mother Abbess. I am she. What is your name and what is your business and why could none of my deputies content you? It is the function of my prioress to speak for me with unexpected callers.' *Of your kind*, said her tone.

'I'm Isabel Plowman,' said the girl. She had a rustic voice but a pleasing one, except that it was slightly quavery with nerves. Her wary dark eyes made the abbess think of a small animal peering from a burrow. But they were intelligent, and what she said was straightforward, however tremulously she said it. 'I think . . . I thought that my business ought to be with you. I'm the daughter of Peter of Northfield, in Rushley, and the widow of Alfred Plowman of Rushley. I want to join the community here. I bring Alfred Plowman's land with me. He has . . . had . . . ten acres beside the Wend.'

'Sit down.' Christiana also sat, in the chair which was there for her alone to use. 'Now, tell me a little more. You wish to take the veil and you have a dowry of ten acres which to you no doubt seems a great deal. Are they yours to dispose of? You have no son or brother-in-law? No overlord with a claim on it? Your husband was a free man?'

The girl shook her head. 'No. Alfred was a villein.'

'In that case, my child, you cannot bring me his land. Whoever led you to think you could, misinformed you. But leave that for a moment,' she added, cutting Isabel off as she was about to speak again. 'Let us consider your wish to join my abbey. I would never turn away an applicant unheard. Why do you desire to enter? You have so great a love for Christ and for the estate of perpetual chastity?'

There was a fractional pause, as though the girl were choosing her reply. Then she said, 'I loved my husband Alfred. And they are trying to make me marry again. I don't want to be married again and certainly not to this man they've chosen. I'd rather marry God instead.'

'Who are *they*?'

'The overlord, Sir Henry, and Bernard the reeve. And now my family and the other village women. Everyone!' Isabel's voice rose.

Christiana studied her thoughtfully. The girl might talk of her husband but there was something else behind that, which she had not revealed. She kept avoiding Christiana's eyes. Not that the abbess was greatly concerned. The ten acres were of more interest to her than she chose to admit. Since becoming abbess six years before, she had vastly increased the abbey's wealth and encouraging people to bring it gifts was one of her methods. Some of the gifts were of much less worth than ten acres even of fertile land.

One must, however, go through the motions.

'What is it you hope to find here, my child, apart from protection from unwelcome male embraces?'

The girl seemed awkward. She looked away yet again and fiddled with the bundle.

'Come,' said Christiana. 'You can tell me. Many girls like you, and older women too, have sat where you sit and told me that they wished to come to Redesmarsh and some had very strange reasons for their request. I kept their counsel. I may not like your reasons. But if I send you away, I will not report what you have told me to anyone else. Do your family know you are here?'

'No. No one knows I've come. I could go back and . . .' The girl got to her feet, picking up her bundle. Their eyes met and for the first time Isabel endured the abbess's gaze. They held each other's eyes in silence for several long seconds and the experience was a shock to both of them.

For in Isabel's dark eyes was a hungry, questing look which Christiana knew, because it had once been in her own eyes. She knew what that hungry longing was for. It was for freedom and growth and, above all, for power.

And within this girl was not only the longing but the ability to win these things and use them. Christiana, staring into Isabel's eyes, knew it instantly. If this girl entered the abbey as anything more than a menial, she was quite capable, one day, of becoming its abbess. She might even oust the existing abbess in the latter's lifetime. Such things had been known.

Which meant she was a threat.

Isabel on her side saw the recognition as though it were an adversary's salute before a duel. She did not know what the abbess had recognised but she understood that here was a foe.

'I'd better go back. I think it was a mistake to come. I almost turned round halfway here and went home again and maybe I should have done. Only . . .'

'Only what? I shan't keep you here against your will,' said Christiana. 'But since you've come all the way from Rushley, you may as well explain fully what brought you. One moment.' She went to the door and called. Isabel, who had lost her nerve now that she was confronted with Christiana's somewhat overwhelming aura of authority, heard her utter the magical words *ale and pasties* and sank back on to the bench. She had in fact been sitting on it for an hour and a half, fending off offers of interviews with Christiana's subordinates, and that was after nerving herself in the first place to raise the iron knocker of the abbey's imposing gate, and actually make her presence known. Her noonday bread and cheese now seemed a long way off. She was ravenous.

'Wait,' said Christiana. 'And compose yourself. I will say a short prayer.'

There was a small prie-dieu in the room. The abbess knelt in front of it and began to murmur something in what Isabel supposed was Latin. Just as she finished, a nun appeared with a tray and put it on a low table.

'Take refreshment,' said Christiana. 'And when you have steadied yourself, let me ask you again. What do you seek here?'

Isabel ate a pasty and swallowed some ale. 'Even if you don't let me stay,' she said, 'you won't tell anyone what I've said? I could go back and no one need know?'

'Yes. I gave my word and you may trust to that. Now, what do you seek?'

Isabel stared into the abbess's inimical steel-coloured eyes for some moments and then, because she had come here to say it and because the abbess was the proper person to say it to, and because it was even possible that the foe might become a friend, if only one could make her understand, she answered.

'A *life*,' said Isabel, almost violently. 'A chance to . . . I'm ignorant, I know I'm ignorant! But I'm not stupid. My father taught me my letters; I know that much and I could learn more if I were taught and I want to learn; I want to be . . . I don't know how to say it. More than I am. If I marry this Ufi Pecher they want me to marry I'll never be anything; it'll just be ploughing and fishing, cooking and stitching and never going anywhere or even *thinking* about anything different. It wouldn't be like that here, would it? Well, you're not like that. I think I want to be like you. And I thought, if I brought you ten acres, it might make you want to take me in.'

'But you have no right to present me with those acres.'

'It's good land,' said Isabel. 'Well-drained but fertile because it hasn't

51

been under the plough that long. I thought a lady like you . . . might know of a way to . . . to claim it for yours, for the abbey.'

On the day that Rohese made her disastrous visit home, Matt Potter had said, 'The abbess is a good bit sharper after turning an honest penny than a lady in her position maybe ought to be. I've heard tell it's not always an honest penny, at that.'

It wasn't the first time Isabel had heard such things said of Abbess Christiana. She had gambled on them. She took a little more of the food and drink, and waited.

'Do you know what you're saying?' demanded Christiana.

Isabel stared at her. 'I don't know. I hoped. I want to come here and Plowman's Acres is all I've got, that's all.'

'Well, *well*,' said Christiana. 'Finish your meal, my child and let me think.'

Isabel obeyed. When the last pasty had been reduced to a scatter of crumbs and the ale beaker was empty, the abbess went to the door and called a second time. When the nun came, she said, 'Isabel, this is Sister Constance. Go along with her now. Sister, this is a new postulant, Isabel of Northfield. It is hoped that she will bring us a good dowry, so treat her accordingly. She has little education but she knows her letters, apparently, and we can soon build on that. Can you sing, by the way, Isabel?'

'Not very well, Mother Abbess.'

'Never mind. You will learn,' said Abbess Christiana, and departed, hands slipped into her wide sleeves, mouth primmed to a tight, pleased smile. There was no need, after all, to be afraid of a foe whom one had recognised while the said foe was quite at one's mercy. Indeed, in such a situation there were endless possibilities for amusement. She went on her way, her brain busily revolving alternative approaches to Sir Henry of Rushley on the subject of ten acres of first-class land, to which Redesmarsh Abbey had no shadow of a right.

'Why did she do that?' Lucy Grosney asked her husband protestingly. They had travelled to the abbey by water and, on the way home, he had settled her in the boat with a fur rug over her and told the boatman to make haste. The sooner she was home and in bed, the better. 'Why did she *say* those things?' Lucy asked, bewildered and hurt. 'Lady Cecily said she knew . . . about me, that she must have known.'

'Of course. She did it deliberately,' said Herbert.

'But *why*?' said Lucy. Her big grey eyes were frightened. Behind them the deep-toned abbey bell was ringing for the next division of the day. Lucy half turned her head, and shuddered.

'Because I suspect,' said Herbert, 'that she's a thoroughly wicked woman.'

'But she's an abbess,' Lucy protested.

'It can happen among any kind of people. She's influential but I think, in future, I'd rather keep away from her influence.'

Lucy Grosney, belatedly mindful that their attendants and the boatman, were all listening, sat up straight. But when she spoke, her voice was as heartfelt as it was calm. 'I think it would be best,' she said.

'I don't think we should drain this stretch of marsh,' said Sir Simon respectfully to his father.

'But why not? It shouldn't be difficult,' protested Sir Henry. 'Water could be channelled down into Duckwater Ditch which would carry it to North Stream. Simon, we need to make the most of our land. Nearly all our wealth is locked up in land and stock. I'm supposed to be a rich man but I've had to borrow to rebuild the chapel because I'm so short of silver. I need surplus produce to bring in more money. You should understand; all this will be yours one day and then you'll have the same worries.'

'I know,' said Sir Simon, 'But the produce shouldn't be grown just here. Why is the Duckwater Ditch called that?'

'Because ducks nest all along it,' said his father testily. Simon had this extraordinary knack of seeing things his father had missed and it could be useful, but he also had an irritating habit of making his parent play guessing-games instead of simply saying what he meant outright. 'You can see the old nests. But I don't see what . . .'

'And not only ducks,' said Simon. 'But avocets and coots and oyster-catchers; all sorts of marsh birds.' There were a few oyster-catchers wading about in the marshy flats in front of them, stabbing the mud with their beaks in search of food. 'It's a major nesting site,' said Simon, 'for birds that are good to eat. It would be a mistake to interfere with that. An acre or two at this end, perhaps, abutting on the north side of Plowman's, but apart from that . . .'

His father was no longer listening. He was staring in the direction of Plowman's, but his attention was now fixed on something on the holding itself. His fists were on his hips and his expression indignant. 'Am I seeing things?' said Sir Henry. 'Or is that Abbess Christiana? And if so, why is she tramping about in the middle of Plowman's Acres?'

The black-clad figure was a long way off, but the day was cold and clear and both father and son had excellent long sight. It was unquestionably Christiana. She had a long stave with which she appeared to be prodding the furrows. Two other dark figures beyond her were presumably satellite nuns, who seemed to be holding their habit hems distastefully clear of the ground. Beside Christiana was a man who was probably Osmund, the reeve of the Redesmarsh Abbey estates. At least, he was wearing green, as Osmund usually did.

'Either she's looking for a mislaid treasure or she wants to buy Plowman's,' said Simon. 'That woman should read her own Rule more often. Benedictine nuns aren't supposed to wander about as Christiana does. We'd better find out what it's all about.' He set militantly off on foot, followed by his father. They had come to the marshland by boat, but feet, now, were faster.

The abbess and her companions, engrossed in whatever they doing, and busily conferring, did not notice them and before Sir Henry and his son were even within hail, they moved off and were seen to be boarding a boat of their own on the Wend. But when it drew away, it travelled downstream, towards Rushley.

'She may be going to the Hall,' said Simon.

'Then we'll meet her there,' Sir Henry said, changing course back towards their own transport.

At Rushley Hall, they found Osmund taking a mug of ale by the fire, while the abbess and her nuns, said the butler, were with the ladies in the solar. 'The abbess wishes to see you, sir,' the butler explained. 'I told her that you were about the estate and might be some time but she said she would wait for an hour or so.'

'I'll bring her into the hall,' Sir Henry said. 'We'll sit with Osmund; he's obviously here for some reason.'

He strode across the hall and threw open the door to the solar. The scene that met his eyes had considerable charm. There was a bright wood fire in the modern hearth which his father had had built in one wall of the ladies' sanctum, and round it sat his wife Judith and her trio of demoiselles, all busily sewing. The eldest of the three girls, Eglantine, was shortly to be married, which represented a triumph for his own and Simon's diplomacy. The other two had been betrothed in infancy by their parents but Eglantine, who was Sir Henry's niece, had been orphaned as a baby. Finding a match for her had been a Rushley responsibility and since her portion was small it had been a worry as well, pretty though she was.

Their efforts, at Christmas, to marry her to a connection of the de Montalts of Castle Rising, had not been successful, but Simon had been to London since then and had made good use of contacts there. At Easter, Eglantine would marry a knight from the Welsh Marches, a relative of the famous de Braose family, and would go away to the other side of England. Her future bridegroom, Simon said, was decent and reasonably goodlooking and only three years older than Eglantine and had some land of his own, in Wales. They'd done well for her and they were going, furthermore, to send her off with a fine trousseau.

As long as they were allowed to get on with it. At the moment, Abbess Christiana and her two nuns were sitting empty-handed and talking church-shop in the midst of the sewing party like a false note in a lovesong. It was clear from the majestically upright way Lady Judith was sitting, and from her flat tone as she conversed with the abbess, and from the shy but determined whisper in which Eglantine was asking the girl next to her for the white silk thread, that the dressmaking was behind schedule and that callers just now were an unwanted distraction.

'My lady Abbess,' said Sir Henry formally from the doorway, giving his wife a nod which said that he understood the problem and was about to solve it, 'I believe you are looking for me?'

He held the door open and stood aside as Christiana and her companions filed out. Simon had already brought Osmund to the hall dais, where, since the central hearth was some way off, a brazier provided heat. A dish of oatcakes and a fresh supply of ale were on a table in front of them.

'Now,' said Sir Henry as they seated themselves. 'In what way can I serve you, my lady Abbess? Did we see you earlier, on Plowman's Acres?' He glanced thoughtfully at Abbess Christiana's feet. Her stout shoes had been roughly scraped, but a good deal of mud still adhered to them, as it did to the footwear of the nuns and Osmund. 'We wondered,' said Sir Henry, 'what in the world you were about.'

'I wanted to see the land for myself,' said Christiana.

'For yourself?' inquired Simon. His eyebrows rose.

'Yes. I have a claim on it, you see,' explained Christiana, and went into details.

Before she had finished, Sir Henry began to splutter, wanting to say so many things at once that he was unable to decide which one to say first. It was Simon who cut her short.

'Just a moment. Let us clarify this. The widow of Alfred Plowman has come to you asking to join your community and offering you her husband's land as a dowry? Do I have it right?'

'Yes, Sir Simon. That is perfectly correct.'

'Alfred,' said Simon, 'did not own his land. He rented it. It belongs in fact to us. In addition, Alfred was a villein and so is his widow, which means that she cannot leave the manor and enter a nunnery without our consent. In which case . . .'

'What she has done is quite outrageous! We'd have given consent if the girl had asked it properly!' Sir Henry barked. 'But she'd have had to pay for the privilege and the land wouldn't go with her. You know that as well as I do, Christiana!'

He had known her a long time. The forename slipped out on occasion, although there had never been an occasion quite like this.

'Isn't Alfred's widow very young?' said Simon. He had a good working knowledge of most of the tenants on the three manors. 'She is ignorant of the true position, perhaps. Have you not informed her, madam Abbess?'

'She is ignorant to some extent but not as much as that,' said Christiana. She spoke to Sir Henry rather than to Simon, because he was the overlord. 'She is anxious, it seems, to better herself. I admit that I doubt if this is a case of a true religious vocation. She made it clear enough that she hoped to buy an education and a position in my community with her husband's land. She was trusting to me, in a most touching way, I must say, to find a way to claim it. She knows what the legal position is. Her ignorance lies in the fact that she does not know how strong the law is.'

'We had arranged,' said Sir Henry, 'for her to marry Ufi Pecher on the adjoining holding.'

'Yes, she mentioned that too. She appears to have been very fond of her husband and to be reluctant to remarry.'

'One can sympathise,' said Sir Simon. 'And as my father has said, if she had asked consent, it would have been granted. Indeed, if she is already within your walls, we can scarcely snatch her out. But – Father, do you agree? – the fine for leaving manor service must be paid from her personal property. The remainder can go to the abbey as her dowry. But the land remains ours.'

'She owns cows,' said Sir Henry. 'We would claim the best of them as our fine.'

'Quite,' said the abbess. 'I've no quarrel with that. But as to the land . . . we were inspecting it this morning. I had Osmund with me as I wished for his opinion on it. Osmund?'

Osmund, called upon at last, nodded his head. 'That's good land, that is. Been cared for rightly, too.' With that, his contribution appeared to be over.

'And Redesmarsh Abbey,' said Sir Simon grimly, 'has *no* claim on Plowman's Acres.'

Sir Henry eyed the abbess with misgiving. 'What is in your mind, may I ask?'

'Your new chapel is coming on well,' said Christiana, delicately nibbling an oatcake. 'I hear you've ordered a fine silver rood and that you have master woodcarvers coming from Norwich to make a rood screen. The stained glass is already in place, I observe.'

It was proper for a knight and a gentleman to address and to look at an abbess with the utmost courtesy and respect. Sir Henry was now looking at Abbess Christiana as though he would like to kill her. Simon's face had become very cold.

'I imagine,' said the abbess, 'that the total cost is proving larger than anticipated? You must be badly stretched, Sir Henry and, of course, there is my loan to repay.'

'It will be repaid, interest included,' said Sir Henry.

'Yes. We shall honour our obligations,' said Simon. 'Even though it is questionable whether it is lawful for an abbey to charge interest on a loan.'

'One must be realistic,' said Christiana calmly. 'The fact may be that usury is undesirable, but business could hardly be conducted, or funds raised, without it. By lending to you as I did, I have at least kept you out of the hands of the moneylenders of London and Venice. Their rates of interest are higher than mine. Even at my rates, I imagine you will have some difficulty. I was going to say, I would accept Plowman's in part-settlement. It would relieve the strain on your silver.'

There was a furious silence from father and son alike.

'If it will help you to decide,' said Christiana, 'I could offer you one other consideration . . .' She glanced thoughtfully at the nuns, listening silently with downcast eyes. Her nuns, thought Christiana with irritation, twittered like sparrows whenever they got together in the common room. Normally she didn't mind but sometimes precautions were desirable. 'If I could speak to you privately, Sir Henry . . .?'

Life within the abbey was so different from her old life that Isabel still woke every morning with a sense of disbelief that she could really be here. It seemed so much like a dream.

The abbey was not in fact especially comfortable. It was stonebuilt, with high, vaulted rooms which were difficult to heat, and spiral stairs which weren't heated at all and it was often colder than the wattle and daub dwellings had been, with their filled walls and lively hearthfires.

Indeed, there were times, principally at dusk or when going into the church to sing the Offices which took place after dark, when the dream had something nightmarish in it. The shadows cast by stone buttress and round arch were so very black, and the whisper of the nuns' feet across the stone floors so much like the whisper of ghostly voices, and the echo of the wind on those winding staircases so mournful. There were times when Isabel, if sent on an errand which sent her through the abbey without the company of other nuns, found the place frightening.

But the white novice's habit she had been given to wear kept the draughts out remarkably well, and in the refectory and the dormitory and the common room there was indoor space of a kind which she had hitherto only glimpsed at Christmas feasts in Rushley Hall; and in the church there was beauty, in the carving of wood and stone, and the deep tones and glittering flecks of rich, flawed stained glass. The carvings and glass of Rushley church had been only a faint echo.

And if the meals were simple they were regular and she was only asked to work in the kitchen now and then. Her only regular task of a menial kind was to feed the rabbits which lived in pens inside the stable, across the courtyard from the kitchen. Isabel had never seen rabbits before. They were peculiar animals, rather like hares but more delicate. They came from a warmer country and had to be protected from cold, with plenty of straw. They were good to eat, and their soft grey fur made snug gloves, or trimmings for gowns. They bred fast and Abbess Christiana made quite a good thing for the abbey out of selling rabbit fur at Redesmarsh market.

Much of Isabel's time was spent in church or with the music mistress, learning to sing the Office, or else with the novice mistress, receiving lessons in reading, writing and Latin.

Her singing was off-key but her mind had sunk its talons into her studies like a falcon bringing down a dove. Already acquainted with her alphabet, she had in a week formed the beginnings of a fair hand, and at the end of a fortnight she could understand what cases were, decline

Mensa and conjugate *Voco*, knew several other Latin nouns and verbs and if shown them written down, could read them.

She was paying attention to her accent, too. She had grasped in a day that the way she spoke was rustic and that the other nuns would despise her for it. She spoke little but listened much and when obliged to speak, she tried to imitate what she heard around her.

Above all, there was the knowledge that Ufi Pecher couldn't get at her. She had defeated him and his beastly old father and she had defeated Sir Henry and Bernard Reeve as well. She had chosen her own path instead of having it made for her and although she could not speak openly of her triumph, triumph it still was, and it comforted her at the times when grief for Alfred and the baby rose up in her.

She did not know what had happened about Plowman's Acres, although she was aware that the abbess had called on Sir Henry. The nuns were not supposed to gossip but in fact they operated a highly effective grapevine in which Isabel shared. The other nuns, choir nuns and lay sisters alike were actually quite cordial towards her, even those who came from good families. The distaste she had feared showed in their eyes only when she accidentally let out some rough-spoken villein phrase.

Sometimes this puzzled her; it was as though the way they behaved to her and what they felt about her were not the same thing and somehow, she could not attribute the difference to the holiness of their calling. They were often bitchy enough towards one another. She redoubled her efforts to purify her speech. Full acceptance, she thought, would lie in conformity.

She longed to know the outcome of Christiana's visit to Rushley but although she was said to have offered to remit part of a debt owed by Sir Henry in return for Plowman's, no one knew what his answer had been. The abbess had returned and gone on with her abbey affairs as usual, sweeping between church and study and refectory, now and then appearing unexpectedly in the kitchen or arriving in the midst of a Latin lesson, to regard whatever was in progress with her tight smile, inquire if all were well, and then withdraw. She took no notice of her newest recruit and Isabel felt it best not to attract attention. She had not forgotten that moment in the parlour when she looked into Christiana's eyes and glimpsed a potential enemy. She worked hard in the hope of being reported on favourably and waited.

'Well,' said Sister Jeanne, the novice mistress, 'It seems, Sister Isabel, that you can say the first declension and the first conjugation correctly. We will therefore begin on the second declension, which is just as easy. The word we shall use is *Servus*, which means a slave. Listen carefully while I recite the singular cases . . .'

The lesson was being given in a room small by abbey standards but still quite sizeable by Isabel's. Three other novices, more advanced than she was, were copying out a Latin passage, sitting under a window, and sharing an original manuscript, veiled heads bent and quills busily scratching.

The three windows were glazed, and overlooked an inner courtyard. Down there was a square of grass with paved cloisters all round it, and in the centre of the grass was a little rose garden. How beautiful it would be in summer, Isabel thought. Would they, perhaps, be able to sit on the grass or stroll in the cloisters while declining Latin nouns? One of the Sisters had said that occasionally, in very warm weather, Sister Jeanne indulged her pupils in that way.

By then, correct speech would come naturally. She would have progressed in her Latin studies, would know her way amid the intricacies of the Office. She would be leaving her grief behind. At the end of a year, she would take her vows. She was beginning now to grasp some of the real life of this place, the devotion to God which had brought the best of the nuns here and inspired them still, despite their gossip and their petty feuds and snobberies. She was going to take to that too. Easier by far to love God than Ufi Pecher. And though she was mewed up in the abbey just as stringently as she would have been mewed up on the Pechers' holding, there was much more here for her.

She paid careful attention to Sister Jeanne and then began to say the declension after her.

'*Servus, serve, servum . . .*'

The door opened and there was Abbess Christiana on the threshold.

'*Benedicite,* Mother!' Sister Jeanne rose to her feet, motioning Isabel to stop. Christiana came near enough to have her ring kissed and then stepped back to survey the room.

'Are your pupils working well, Sister Jeanne?'

'Indeed yes, Mother. Sister Margaret . . .'

'I am especially interested,' said Christiana, 'in Sister Isabel's progress.'

Sister Jeanne, who was thirty-five but had a face as unlined and a manner as full of eager-to-please as though she were a somewhat gauche twenty, beamed at her most junior pupil. 'Sister Isabel is working marvellously well. We're all amazed at how fast she's getting on, aren't we, girls?'

There were murmurs of agreement from within the bent veils of the other novices.

'Good,' said Christiana. She stood still for a moment, looking Isabel up and down. 'You like your studies, Sister Isabel?'

'Yes, Mother Abbess. Very much.'

'Good. I thought you would,' said Christiana. 'I can usually tell with girls. I have indeed been anxious to encourage you. I have had reports of you from this quarter and that, and I have left you undisturbed till now deliberately, intending that you should advance in your work and settle into your new way of life and, I hope, begin to feel at home. That way, I decided, the lesson would be sharper when it came.'

Sister Jeanne looked bewildered, thus convincing Isabel that after all, she had heard aright, since the abbess's last sentence, although coherent enough, made no sense.

Then Christiana smiled at her, almost fondly, and proceeded, still smiling, to explain herself.

'I'm sorry to deprive you of an able pupil, Sister Jeanne, but Sister Isabel has no place here. She should be scrubbing the kitchen table or laundering wimples. You silly girl,' said Christiana to Isabel, still smiling. 'Did you really suppose that you, a villein wench, would be allowed to join this house as one of its ladies? My ladies come from well-bred families; did you really think you would be allowed to live as one of them?'

But . . . Mother . . . they've been nice to me,' said Isabel faintly, grasping at the only lifeline in sight.

'They were doing as they were bid,' said Christiana, solving a mystery and simultaneously snatching away the lifeline. 'They have taken vows of obedience and they keep them, without asking why. I ordered them to be pleasant, to make you feel at ease here. I told you: I meant your lesson to be sharp. And now *you'll* do as you're bid, and I'll tell you why. You've been foolish, Sister Isabel. You have no idea, have you, of humility and the virtue of keeping one's proper station in life? You left your bonded service without asking leave and you expected me to welcome you here and to take a gift from you of land which wasn't yours.'

Isabel's mouth was open. She was trembling.

'It is in fact abbey land now,' said the abbess with satisfaction. 'An arrangement has been made, pleasing to both myself and Sir Henry, who is a pious man. As for you: because through you the abbey has gained some valuable acres, I am prepared to keep you here and Sir Henry is pleased to allow it. You will have a roof, food and clothing and the opportunity to give your life to the worship of God. And also the chance to acquire some of the humility you so sadly lack. You should be grateful, girl. You are being treated more kindly than you deserve. But part of the agreement I reached with Sir Henry was that you should not be allowed to profit by your behaviour to the extent of rising above your station. Humble you were born and humble you shall remain. Now be off with you to the kitchen. The kitchen Sisters are waiting or you. There's work to be done there. Don't stand there looking at me. And don't look at Sister Jeanne, either. Be off!'

'But, Mother . . .!'

'I said, be off!'

Christiana never, as some abbesses did, struck any of her nuns. She had no need to do so. Her inherent authority was too great. Isabel's own feet seemed to take her towards the door, impelled by Christiana's will.

Head and shoulders bent, she found herself outside, going down the cloister, passing through the arch into the adjoining courtyard, entering the kitchen.

She was used to being in it for a couple of hours at a time. She had scoured pots here already, boned fish, shaped bread; everyone did at times. A certain amount of time each day had to be spent in manual tasks, either indoors or out. Caring for the rabbits had been part of that, too.

But from now on, she saw, as the kitchen Sisters, greeting her with cold faces (Christiana, clearly, had been talking to them), handed her an apron, some silver sand and a grease-encrusted cauldron to render shiny inside and out, these tasks would be not just part of her day but would fill the gaps from Office to Office, day in and day out.

There were over a hundred nuns in Redesmarsh and the kitchen was a steamy cavern in which the tasks involved in feeding them began before dawn and did not end until midnight.

It would be much worse than life in a villein's dwelling, which one could sometimes leave to walk across the fields or go to the village. Even from the Pechers', she might have made the occasional illicit trip to Rushley. Life in the abbey on these terms would be far worse than life with Ufi and Tosti.

But if she left the abbey, where could she go? She was trapped here. Her captivity would be for ever.

Hilda Eelfisher, poling her flat-bottomed boat briskly round a bend, ducking under the alder boughs and fending them off with a muttered oath as the sluggish current tried to bump her into the bank, saw Ufi Pecher and his boat in front of her, and turned scarlet with fury on the spot. Plunging the pole into the mud in a series of savage jabs as though she were stabbing a number of deadly foes to the heart, she thrust her way towards the intruder.

'Hey, you, Pecher! This here's our bit of the Wend, lord hisself said so, last week at the manor court! What in hell's name . . .!' Her boat, coming up to his, bumped against it and now, at close quarters, she could see what he was doing. 'Mother of God, that's our eel-trap you're robbing!' yelled Hilda and raised her punt-pole menacingly.

Ufi neither shied back nor raised his own in self-defence. Instead, he sank limply down on to a thwart and looked up at her. Surprised, Hilda lowered the pole and peered at him more closely.

'Sorry,' said Ufi, which in itself was epoch-making, for never before had a Pecher apologised to an Eelfisher, no matter how blatant his offence. His voice sounded odd, husky and thick. 'Must have food in the house. Needed to get summat easy. Not feeling well.'

Then she saw that his face was grey, with burning red patches on it and that he was shivering all over, from head to foot.

'You're sick!' said Hilda accusingly. 'You ought to be laid up. Why can't your father get the food and all?'

'He's sick too,' said Ufi in a blurred voice. 'Not as bad as me but it's cold and he's not so young. I wouldn't let him come out. It's *that* cold,' he added, 'but I keep feeling so hot. It's the marsh fever, I think, but I ain't ever had it like this before.' He dropped his head between his knees. Then he fainted.

Chapter Four

The Monster of the Law

Abbess Christiana knelt in her stall in the abbey church, and prayed for forgiveness. She asked too that when, very soon now, she informed Sister Isabel of certain developments in the world she had left behind, she would not take active pleasure in hurting.

She also knew quite well that she hadn't told Isabel sooner simply for the pleasure of saving the news up, because the potential for hurt in this kind of news was so very great.

'Please forgive me,' she whispered to the Saviour, whose presence she could feel so acutely in the quiet, dim church, whom she could see illustrated in the gold and ivory rood and the stained glass passion in the north window. 'I do not know why I do these things. I do not know why I was cruel to Mistress Lucy Grosney when she visited me. I was not jealous; I have no desire for a child. It was hurting for the sake of it. There is a devil in me sometimes.'

Her contrition was entirely real, and her tendency to say unkind things was something she confessed regularly and for which she had said innumerable Paternosters and Hail Marys. There was no pretence in Christiana's piety; when she said she had come to the abbey for the wrong reasons but stayed because she found it was the place for her, she spoke the truth.

But the devil of unkindness, which had taken hold of her long, long ago, when she was still a child, refusing to become fond of her small brothers and sisters because she could see they were all going to die soon, and distancing herself from the mother whose example she did not intend to follow, had never been exorcised. It had grown as Christiana had grown, gaining power as Christiana gained it. Now that she was head of a rich abbey and held in awe by every family in the district and a good many beyond it, it had developed new tentacles. She did worse things sometimes than simply indulge in unkindness, things which she dared not confess. Father Ambrose, though often irascible, had a degree of innocence; he had never seen through her yet. But if he ever did, heaven help her. Or Lucifer. Heaven might not oblige.

If only, she thought, rising from her knees, she could conquer temptation just this once, over this small matter of Isabel, then perhaps she would have taken a first shaky, tiny step back towards redemption.

And she knew, before she had passed through the low door out into the cloister in order to go to her private office, that if ever that step were taken, it would not be now. The pleasure of baiting Sister Isabel was too great to forgo.

The summons to the abbess's office found Isabel in the kitchen courtyard, squatting on the paving stones beside another novice. They were killing rabbits for the refectory.

The other sister, who was gently reared and squeamish, held them and looked the other way while Isabel, who had been brought up to kill chickens when required, wielded the chopper.

'You're to come at once,' said the nun who brought the message. 'I will take over your task.'

Isabel was wearing a shroudlike garment, originally white and now stained with blood, with a hole for her head and slits for her arms. She dragged it off. 'I've still got blood on me,' she pointed out. She had pushed up the sleeves of her habit, but they were splashed with red just the same.

'The abbess will not mind,' said the nun. 'But hurry. She expects you now.'

Let her! thought Isabel privately, and set off for the abbess's office at a pace which was just fast enough to qualify for obedience, but did not suggest a sycophantic level of it. When admitted, she knelt by the abbess's chair as custom dictated and kissed the ring on the carefully manicured hand which was extended to her and spoke the formal greeting. '*Benedicite.* Mother.' She turned her face upwards and Christiana looked down into dark eyes full of the most intense dislike.

Isabel, she knew, had suffered the bitterest grief and resentment over her banishment to the kitchens. She had tried to get the other novices to pass on details of their Latin lessons in secret and been caught practising her letters after she had been expressly forbidden to do so. The kitchen sisters said she did what they told her but with compressed lips and angry movements. She had been obliged to perform penances for her lack of obedience. She had since taken to an attitude which was always near the edge of it, although rarely over. She hadn't appeared in Christiana's presence *quite* as quickly as she should and the abbess knew it.

Oh, indeed, it was beyond Christiana's powers to miss the chance of being unkind to Sister Isabel.

'I called you here,' she said, 'to give you some news. You are aware that there has been an outbreak of the marsh ague, of course.'

'Yes, Mother.'

It would have been somewhat difficult not to be aware of it. Isabel had been killing easily digestible rabbits in quantity because sixty per cent at least of the nuns were ill.

The marsh ague was endemic at some level most of the time. A few people were always down with it. They shivered and ached and ran fevers and a really violent attack could be fatal even to a young victim, since it could turn to lung congestion and a form of the fever which raged like a fire and consumed the sufferer's flesh and strength.

From time to time it seemed to gather extra power and attack in force, knocking people down by the hundred, killing half of them outright and leaving many others permanently damaged in lungs or joints. When this happened, it might well be months before the epidemic subsided. This one had been rampaging for eight weeks now, outwearing the winter, constantly finding new fodder among people who had just decided that after all they must be immune, and casting them into sickbeds which as often as not had to be tended by shaky kinsfolk who were still in the midst of a slow recovery.

The state of the three manors showed it, at least as far as the villeins' holdings were concerned. On the home farms of Redesmarsh, Oxen and Rushley, and that of the abbey, if a villein were too ill to perform his weekly manor service, it simply had to be done by someone else, and neither would have much chance to tend his own fields. Over all the smallholdings, an air of neglect now lay heavily, with weeds amid the sprouting corn and ditches blocked by debris.

Within the abbey, the task of covering for the duties of the sick also had to be confronted. Isabel, who had continued well, had never worked so hard in her life, and was only glad that the Lenten fast was now over. You needed food to keep you on your legs when in addition to the continual attendances in church, including those at midnight and before dawn, it was also necessary to do the work of three in the kitchen and rush at times to help Sister Julian brew herbal possets and change bedding and rub stiff joints and deal with sick-bowls and bedpans and the thousand and one duties of an overburdened infirmarian in such times as these.

A month ago now, Sister Julian herself had succumbed. She had not been among the severely stricken ('I spend too much time among the sick to be an easy target,' she said cheerfully) and she had now been out of her bed for a week. But she still could not do as much as she had before, so Isabel, who by virtue of simply remaining healthy, had now become her chief assistant, conversely had to do more. She had learned to admire Sister Julian and toiled far more willingly in the infirmary than in the kitchen, even when exhausted but . . .

It would have been *very* difficult, she thought, kneeling by Christiana's chair, not to notice that there was an epidemic. Why did the abbess talk to her as though she were a fool? She was young, yes, and ignorant and rough in her ways but she was not stupid. Sister Julian certainly didn't think so. She lowered her eyes to hide the hatred in them, unaware that Christiana had already, grimly, registered it.

'My dear child. I'm sorry to have to tell you,' said Christiana, knowing that she did not sound in the least sorry, 'that I have learned . . .' – there was no need to admit precisely when – '. . . that your former betrothed, Ufi Pecher, and also your father Peter of Northfield, both died at the beginning of the outbreak, two months ago . . .'

'My . . . my father?' Isabel did not care about Ufi Pecher. 'My *father?*'

'He had no strength, I gather,' said Christiana solemnly. 'He had weak lungs; he had had a persistent cough for a long time. And you know yourself that he had suffered worry and sorrow over you. Your illness first, after your husband's death, and then your disobedience and desertion.'

Isabel's mouth had lost its usual firm line. It was tremulous. Christiana observed this with delight.

'I should have been there,' said Isabel. 'Mother Abbess, I should have been there, with my mother, at the burial. Why was I not sent for? I ought to go to my mother now. I have taken no vows!' She came sharply to her feet. 'There is no reason, is there, why I shouldn't visit my mother?'

'Your diction has improved since you came here,' said Christiana. 'So much, in fact, that you must have been trying hard to improve it. You still dream of bettering yourself, don't you? Perhaps you now feel that since you have fewer opportunities here than you hoped for, you might yet return to the outside world? There's no place for you out there now, my dear child. I haven't told you everything yet. Sir Henry, you understand, has been concerned, as a good Christian and a good manor lord, to do something for Tosti, who has been bereaved of his son, and who, through Ufi, was regrettably mistreated by you. Sir Henry has therefore approached me with the suggestion that Tosti should become the abbey tenant on Plowman's Acres, which now belongs to St Peter's. After all, the holding should have gone to the Pechers with you. I have agreed. In addition, he has arranged a useful marriage for Tosti. There is no need for you to go to your mother, Isabel. She has your grandmother for company still and in four weeks' time, she will have a husband. She is to marry Tosti, and Northfield goes with her as her dowry.'

'North . . . Northfield?' faltered Isabel.

'Yes, indeed. It is after all in Sir Henry's gift. No doubt you thought that it would one day be yours? Not now, my child, not even if your mother has no children by Tosti. If she does, your half-brother or sister may in time inherit his tenancies. But if Tosti has no new heir, his tenancies will all be awarded as the abbess of that day and the lord of that day, decree, but they will not come to you. Never you. You do understand, I hope?' Christiana leaned down to gaze into Isabel's horrified eyes. 'You've lost everything, my dear. If you thought there was still a way out, still a way back to the world, you were wrong.'

Isabel tried to speak, but failed. The tenuous villein right to

65

Northfield, which might, just might, one day be hers, was something she had rarely thought about, for it lay beyond her father's death. But some part of her, she now found, had remembered it all along. Somewhere within her, she had seen it as a way – perhaps – of ultimate escape from Christiana. She had already decided, without quite knowing why, to avoid taking vows if she could. She knew why now, but it was too late. Her father was dead, and the door of escape had been slammed in her face. Her mouth opened and shut, speechlessly.

'I did not suggest any of this to Sir Henry,' said Christiana, reading in Isabel's eyes the accusation which her tongue dared not utter. 'These were his decisions and his alone. But of course I agree with them. Humble you must stay, for your soul's health.'

There was silence.

'Well,' said Christiana briskly, 'That is all. You had to be told. I am sorry if it comes as a shock. But you yourself, of course, are provided for within these walls. You are assisting Sister Julian, are you not? I am sure that she will give you leave of absence from your duties if you wish to pray for the souls of your father and Ufi Pecher. I should remind you, however, that we are in the midst of a crisis and that hard work, especially in the care of others, is the best cure ever invented for grief. You may go.'

Isabel went.

As she stepped out of the abbess's office on to the cloister outside she had the illusion that the paving stones beneath her feet were made of mist. There was no stability left anywhere in the world. The home she had left behind, where her kindly if detached father was, and the mother who was sharp-tongued but loved her nevertheless, had vanished. Her father was dead and her mother was about to join forces with Tosti One-Fang. (How could she? How *could* she?)

Bella had not sent for her and that, presumably, was because her mother didn't want her. Bella, bereaved, had turned – or allowed herself to be offered – to Tosti One-Fang instead. Alfred was gone, and the baby. She, Isabel, was alone now except for the abbey where she was welcome to stay, provided she kept her place and did not seek to grow beyond the humble, the menial, the unlettered. Provided she continued dutifully to kneel and kiss the ring of Abbess Christiana, who had taken pleasure – oh yes, she had seen the pleasure in Christiana's eyes – in telling her that her father was gone, and trying to make her believe that somehow it was Isabel's fault.

She had seen Alfred lying dead by the river. Suddenly her imagination recreated that scene but this time it was her father who lay there and now she knew how much he had loved her and how greatly, in return, she had loved him: his vague kindliness, his gentle sense of humour. His well-meant and not entirely mistaken suggestion that a girl needed to be wooed. If Ufi had gone about it differently, her father might have been proved right. And she would not have run away and perhaps it was true, that her father might then have been able to throw off the ague.

Might have been. Might have been. If Alfred had been more careful as he turned his plough team round the corner by the river. If Ufi had been pleasanter. If . . . if . . .

Blind with tears, she faltered against the wall and leant there for a moment, longing for a kindly voice, a gentle hand; someone to ask her what was wrong and offer comfort.

There was no one. Except perhaps Sister Julian. Sobbing wildly, oblivious of the rule which enjoined that Sisters should proceed from one part of the abbey to another at a sedate walk, she ran to the infirmary, to seek her only friend.

Who was exceedingly preoccupied. Leading out of the infirmary on the far side was a small room where Sister Julian kept supplies of dried herbs, a brazier for concocting her medicinal brews, and shelves of ready-made medicines, the ones that would keep. Sister Julian was there, busily packing a selection of remedies into a satchel. A stranger was with her, a worried-looking elderly woman in a brown working dress with an unbleached shawl round her head and shoulders. Her expression and way of standing by the door revealed impatience.

'Oh, Isabel, there you are!' Sister Julian looked up. 'I have to go to the Grosneys of Rushley. I must take another Sister with me, of course, and I think you . . . my dear child, whatever is the matter?'

Isabel threw herself into Sister Julian's arms and, in brief and broken sentences, blurted it all out.

Her words were muddled with crying and Sister Julian had to ask several questions before she could understand, by which time the woman by the door was fidgeting from one foot to another.

'My dear child,' said Julian again, meaning it, which was more than Christiana had done. 'I am so very sorry. Of course you need not come out of the abbey with me unless you choose. I can find someone else and you can go to the church or whatever you wish. But for the moment, I have to go to the Grosneys. Mistress Lucy is desperately ill and Father Benedict has sent for me to help him. This is Annota, Mistress Lucy's woman. Hush, hush, Sister Isabel. Now, tell me what you want to do because I have no time to lose and if I need to take a different companion, I must . . .'

'No . . . no.' Native toughness reasserted itself in Isabel. At home, when her brothers and sisters had died, everyone, including Bella, carried on. Food must still be prepared and wool spun and cows milked, no matter what life-and-death tragedies might be in progress all round. Isabel, collapsing after the loss of Alfred and the baby, had failed to meet this demand for resilience and had been lectured about it. She could hear Father Benedict saying: 'Now, my girl, this won't do.'

And she was sick of the sight of the abbey walls, sick of being imprisoned within them. She had learned to hate them now.

'It is all right, Sister Julian.' She stepped back, wiping her eyes roughly with the backs of her hands. 'I'll come.'

'Good girl. You'll feel better for it, I promise you,' Sister Julian said.

They went by boat. Herbert Grosney had sent his own, with two boatmen to row and pole and get them downriver as quickly as possible. Annota, who had brought the message, sat in the bows of the boat, staring ahead and apparently trying to make it go faster by an act of will. Sister Julian, accustomed to trust in the will of God, sat serenely at Isabel's side and did not talk, and Isabel also sat without speaking, engrossed with her own private grief. She was not thinking about the Grosney household. The shock when they arrived at the landing stage, and Annota rushed them up the path to the house, was therefore all the greater.

Isabel had seen the house before, at Rohese's marriage feast. While there, she had seen Master Herbert Grosney. She remembered the house as it had been then, decorated with flower garlands, sweet with the rosemary and lavender which had been strewn among the rushes underfoot, and with tables set for feasting, the top tables adorned with fresh white linen and burnished silver, the lower boards scrubbed white and set with pewter and earthenware.

Similarly, she remembered Herbert Grosney as he had been then, a dignified figure in a formal murrey gown, his jaw-length hair neatly trimmed, mousey in colour but with the sheen of cleanliness just like his silver. She had seen him close to when he came round the tables to ask if his guests were all content with the fare. If the expression in his hazel eyes had been a little disdainful – as though it pained him to see so many common people in his hall – his viands had been generous.

Today, she could hardly recognise either the house or the man. The Grosney hall was cold and untidy, the fire almost out and the rushes a trampled mess underfoot, while Herbert Grosney came hurriedly to meet them, dressed in old clothes, with a grimy smear on his chin and a face deeply scored not this time with disdain but with worry. There was a redness in the fine, dry skin round the hazel eyes, as though he had been crying.

'Sister Julian! If anyone can help, you can, Father Benedict says. My wife . . . it's the marsh fever but now . . . the baby's coming early and I think . . . oh my God,' said Herbert Grosney desperately, 'I think she's dying!'

'Who's with her?' Sister Julian inquired briskly.

'Mistress Lightfoot; well, you know her, she has some skill in midwifery. Griselda Potterswife has more but she's down with the fever too.' Grosney sounded distracted. 'Half my people are down with it. We can't get things done. We can hardly get food cooked or firewood brought in. Lucy needs fresh bedlinen but there's no one to wash the dirty stuff and . . .'

'Before we go, we'll boil some linen for you,' said Sister Julian calmly.
'Ah. Father Benedict.'

Father Benedict hurried down the last few steps of a nearby staircase.
'You came quickly, Sisters. I will take you up. It's a bad business,'
he added, ominously.

He and Herbert Grosney came up with them but did not enter the
room. Isabel, following Sister Julian and Annota, walked into a boxlike
chamber hung with tapestries, and was at once surrounded by such
horror that her own distress was thrust out to the edge of her mind.

The room smelt of blood and ordure and was full of a wretched
inhuman whimpering which clawed at one's heart. The curtains of the
big bed were tied back to let Mistress Lightfoot work. She was leaning
over the bed, sleeves rolled up and a big basin of water on a table by
her side. White cloths were piled on another table, beside a wine flagon.
A tangle of used cloths lay on the floor. On the bed itself was the
twisting, moaning, sweat-soaked thing which Lucy Grosney had become.
As they approached, her eyes, wide with pain and fear and luminous
with fever, peered at them through a tangle of saturated hair. She opened
her mouth and screamed.

'Hush,' said Sister Julian gently, as she came to the bedside. 'Hush,
hush. We have come to help. I have some medicines with me
which . . .'

'Go 'way!' shrieked Lucy. She heaved and tossed and Mistress
Lightfoot cried: 'Easy, now! Steady . . .!'

'Don't want nuns!' Lucy wailed. Her breath was coming short and
fast and rasping hideously in her lungs. 'Don't want abbess . . . you're
the abbess!' She half lifted an arm and pointed accusingly at Sister Julian.
'You're *her*, go away, go away, go away . . . oh, *oh* . . .!'

There was frenzied activity from Joan Lightfoot and Sister Julian
together. They had worked in partnership before and did so now without
pausing to talk about it. They snapped orders to Isabel. 'Another cloth!
Another! Here, wrap this in something . . . it's dead, just *wrap* it
somehow . . . wring this out in the water . . . more cloths . . . sweet
Mary have mercy on us . . .'

Isabel obeyed orders, darting hither and thither. Redness was
spreading swiftly over the bed. Mistress Lightfoot was struggling to
staunch the flow. Sister Julian was trying to offer the patient wine, but
it was knocked out of her hand. 'No! It's poisoned! Lemme alone, stop
pulling me about . . . oh stop it, stop it!' wailed Lucy. 'Stop pestering
me, I'm so sore, I ache so much, I . . . tell you I know you, I know
what you're after!' Lucy's voice was a hoarse croak of terror and
suspicion. 'You want me to die, you're *her*, you're Abbess Christiana,
you . . .'

She began to rave, her voice still hoarse but nevertheless
comprehensible as she babbled a stream of fear and rejection and
accusation which made the hair prickle on Isabel's scalp. From what,

Isabel wondered in shaken amazement, had such wild and ugly imaginings sprung? If Father Benedict were to hear Mistress Grosney now . . .

'It's all right,' said Sister Julian calmly, turning away to rummage in her satchel. 'She is delirious. I'll make her up a draught, Mistress Lightfoot, and perhaps you can give it to her. It can be mixed into the wine. Here we are . . .'

Isabel ran to the door and called down the stairs for Father Benedict and Master Grosney. She did not know what the outcome would be but Abbess Christiana had rejoiced in telling her of her father's death, and anything that might make life even a little unpleasant for Abbess Christiana was worth trying.

'I didn't tell you to call them!' said Sister Julian, harassed and slightly annoyed, as male footsteps sounded on the stairs. 'So why did you?'

'She says she's dying! Maybe she is!' whispered Isabel urgently, and truthfully. 'Her husband and the priest ought to be here.'

'Yes, well, but you should have asked me first . . . I suppose you meant well,' said Sister Julian, flustered, as the priest and Herbert Grosney hurried into the room, in time to hear Lucy Grosney say, once more, that she was dying because Abbess Christiana had put the evil eye on her and ill-wished her baby, and she was terrified, because she had seen the Abbess Christiana here in this very room, just now, laughing at her torment.

She was only half in the world when she said it and she did not recognise those to whom she spoke and her voice came from a throat and chest so inflamed that the larynxes of those who heard her throbbed in sympathy. But she made herself clear enough before, in spite of the cloths which Joan Lightfoot and Sister Julian were packing so desperately into her, the haemorrhage surged and her life went out while the scarlet stain spread like a tide across the bed and dripped to make a puddle on the floor.

'This is appalling,' said Bishop Roger de Skerning candidly to his chaplain. 'It is embarrassing. It could create confusion, even argument between the church and the secular authorities. I shall have to put up with having my hall packed with the sheriff's men waiting to pounce if I declare her excommunicate. And worst of all,' said the bishop somewhat plaintively, 'there is no *precedent*. I have never had to deal with such a situation before and I know of no one who has. We're on very shaky legal ground altogether. The charge of murder on such evidence is extraordinary. Is this the correct procedure? What *is* one supposed to do?'

'I feel sure, my lord, that no one could say it was incorrect to hold a special inquiry as you have decided to do. There may prove to be nothing in the charge but, if there is, it is such a serious matter that to deal with it at a special court sitting such as this would seem to most people quite proper.'

'All of which,' said de Skerning, 'is another way of saying that in the absence of a precedent, I must simply set one. And that's something I don't like doing.'

'Let us hope, my lord,' said the chaplain diplomatically, 'that it proves to be nothing but a great storm about a triviality.'

'If it does, I shall have some sharp words for Father Benedict, and not for the first time. I do expect my clergy to use their commonsense. It's abdicating their responsibilities if they don't. I shall bring it up at the next Synod. It's not,' said de Skerning, 'that I don't believe in the existence of witchcraft, Maurice. But in my experience, very few people, even the ones who actually believe themselves to be witches, actually have any power whatsoever, and even if the abbess has, she must still be proved to have used it harmfully. Unless someone actually saw her sticking needles into a wax image of Mistress Grosney, or heard her pronounce a curse after reciting the Lord's Prayer backwards, she can't be found guilty. Benedict has the body of a man and the mind of a beldame. This is a case, I am convinced, of terror and delirium in a woman at the point of death. I detest,' said the bishop, 'cases involving women. I feel that there is always something . . . squalid about them.'

'At least, my lord, you insisted that the abbess should be brought to Norwich. You have not wasted your time in riding to Redesmarsh.'

'No, but two archdeacons and three canons are wasting their time attending this inquiry instead of completing other business. I had better,' said de Skerning, 'go and robe and make sure we begin promptly. That way at least I can make sure that no more time is wasted.' Walking towards the door of his office in the bishop's palace, he glanced at his chaplain with an almost piteous expression on his otherwise somewhat immobile features. 'Never before,' he said, 'never in my lifetime, have I heard of an abbess committing murder, least of all by witchcraft . . . If she *is* found guilty, what would be done with her?'

'The sheriff will take charge. It will go to the lay court,' said Maurice de Winburgh comfortingly.

'They may not know what to do either,' said Bishop Roger bitterly. 'They may even ask me! And I don't *know*. There have been cases on the continent of murder by witchcraft . . . I'm a kindly man by nature, Maurice. I don't like the way opinion on these matters is running on the continent. Canon de Harland, who will be with us today – ' the bishop was far too discreet to insert the word *unfortunately* at this point, but his tone implied it ' – has visited France several times and I fear has imbibed some of their more extreme ideas about heresy. He talked to me yesterday evening for an hour on the subject before I could get away from him. I can't accept the attitude he holds and I don't want to be the man who introduces it here. Just at this moment, I rather wish,' remarked the bishop, 'that I were safe in bed with the ague!'

This, thought Abbess Christiana, is a nightmare. Soon I shall wake up in my chamber at Redesmarsh and everything will be just as usual. I shall attend Lauds and Prime . . .

All I did was answer a question. Well, that *is* all I did. Lady Cecily and Lucy Grosney asked what had brought me to the life of religion and I told them. I didn't know the Grosney woman was pregnant . . . well, I wasn't sure, anyway . . . and if I had been sure, what of it? Why all the to-do? Why should she suppose that what happened to my mother was going to happen to her? Why not assume that she'd be like Lady Cecily who never has any trouble with her babies? Why imagine I wanted her to be like my mother, or think I was capable of making her so? . . . Oh dear God, I'm not dreaming, this isn't a nightmare, it's real. *I'm in a cell in Norwich Castle and I'm going to be tried for witchcraft! And murder!*

It had happened at unbelievable speed. She had been preparing for Sext; in the very act of brushing a little dust off her skirts and settling her crucifix in the middle of her chest, when Sister Jeanne brought word that the Bishop's men had ridden in and that de Skerning's representative was waiting in the parlour.

And so, clicking her tongue, she had swept off to the parlour to be confronted not by an archdeacon or any other normal episcopal emissary, but by six men-at-arms and a mail-clad sergeant with the badge of Norwich diocese embroidered on his surcoat who stiffly recited that she was charged with procuring the death, on 20 April, of Mistress Lucy Grosney of Rushley, through the agency of witchcraft and was required to accompany him forthwith to Norwich to appear before His Grace the Bishop, who wished to inquire personally into the allegation.

Half an hour later, she was on the sergeant's pillion. She had been given just time, under surveillance, to hand over the care of the abbey to her prioress, ask for a change of linen to be packed, and appoint another nun to come with her. She'd chosen badly in her haste, moreover. She'd been distracted and bewildered. Her angry protestations had bounced off the sergeant's imperturbable determination to carry out his duty like poor quality arrows off his hauberk, and it was a long time since Abbess Christiana had encountered anyone on whom she had so little effect. She didn't know how to deal with him or with herself and her judgement had gone askew.

'One of your nuns may accompany you for propriety and support,' said the sergeant stonily and Sister Jeanne had been there. She'd also been gaping in horror, eyes and mouth as round as coins and . . .

I should have known she'd be useless, thought Christiana savagely. Stupid, over-hearty, much too anxious to please and they're always the ones who can't please anyone. She's spent too much time teaching the novices; she's as childish as they are. Just look at her now, sitting on the bed staring at me with big wet eyes, as scared as though she were the one on the charge. Not one word of help or comfort has she had for me, just constant snivelling and *Oh, Mother, how could this happen?* and *Oh, Mother, it's so awful: I can't believe it's real!* How does she think I feel, I wonder?

When we get back to Redesmarsh, Christiana decided venomously, I'll change all the offices round and she can have a spell as assistant cellarer. That'll make her grow up. She'll have to learn to keep accounts, for one thing.

Oh, sweet Jesu, *when* we get back. *If* we get back. If I ever see Redesmarsh Abbey again. If . . .

There were mailed footsteps somewhere outside, approaching the cell. Christiana's head came up sharply and Sister Jeanne let out a sob.

'Pull yourself together!' snapped Christiana. 'And do remember that you're supposed to be here to help me. I shouldn't have to be encouraging *you*. Wipe your face and straighten your wimple; you look like a drunken mummer. They're coming.'

If the summons to Norwich seemed unreal to Christiana, it was just as unreal to Isabel. She had not, of course, been accused of anything. She had seen that Mistress Lucy was dying and called out in a panic for Father Benedict and Herbert Grosney to come. Strictly speaking, Sister Julian should have called them, of course, but no one could say that Isabel had really done wrong. Only Isabel herself knew that she had not summoned them out of fear, but because she thought that it might somehow hurt, or cause trouble for, Abbess Christiana, if the priest and Lucy's husband heard that deathbed accusation.

But I only meant it to cause a little trouble she moaned inside herself, horrified, when she learned that Father Benedict had ridden to Norwich to report Mistress Lucy's last words to the bishop, and that the abbess had been taken away and that she and Sister Julian were to follow in the company of Herbert Grosney, Sir Simon and Lady Cecily, Joan Lightfoot and Father Ambrose, the parish priest of Redesmarsh and also the chaplain to the abbey, as witnesses summoned to the inquiry at Norwich.

She had been told all this by Father Ambrose, who had interviewed her in the abbess's office, or rather, talked to her while she stood there speechless with shock. She wanted to cry out, 'I never meant this to happen! I thought it would make gossip, that people might be a bit nasty to her, make remarks, not invite her at Christmas, something like that!' But in the face of this legal monster which she had somehow roused from its lair, she dared not utter any such words. The monster would eat her if she did.

So there she stood, dumb, while Father Ambrose explained that she would have to testify in the bishop's court. 'Which means that you must repeat what you heard Mistress Grosney say when she was dying, and tell the court anything else you heard or saw at the abbey which may bear upon this matter.'

Testify? Her, Isabel of Northfield, villein of Rushley manor? Stand in the middle of some great hall, in front of a bishop – a *bishop* – and answer questions, point the finger at Abbess Christiana in public?

And what, inquired a grim little voice within her, if the abbess is acquitted? What will she do to you if you speak against her in that hall?

'Do you understand?' said Father Ambrose impatiently. Father Ambrose, so the nuns' grapevine said, although heaven alone knew how they had picked it up, was furious because he considered that he should have been consulted first. Father Benedict had ridden back with the men who fetched Abbess Christiana and summoned the witnesses and not until then had he called upon Father Ambrose. There had been a shouting match from which Father Benedict had retreated looking pale.

'Yes,' said Isabel, quailing before Ambrose's irritable gaze, and finally forcing her reluctant tongue to move. 'Yes, Father. I understand.'

She set out to Norwich, trapped amidst a squadron of fears, of the abbess and Father Ambrose and the bishop, and made the journey in a terrified daze.

The cavalcade was large. It was led by Sir Henry and Lady Judith, partly to accompany Simon their son, who was a witness, and partly too because they were bringing their ward Eglantine on the first stage of her journey to the Welsh borders for her marriage.

'She should have left before, but she had the marsh fever badly,' said Sister Julian, who had gone twice to help Father Benedict minister to Lady Judith and her demoiselles. 'Now that she is well, she must set off at once. Her bridegroom is sending an escort to meet her in Norwich. We are going on horseback as it is faster than water. So we shall be riding in a wedding party as well. I think, Sister, that we should try to keep that in mind and not sadden the bride with our unhappy faces.'

As far as Isabel was concerned, it was a vain instruction. She could take no interest in the bride and indeed scarcely saw her, since Eglantine was an elegantly dressed figure always at a distance from her and always in the company of Sir Henry and his family or with the other demoiselles. Nor could she find any glamour in the size and importance of the cavalcade, the caparisoned horses and brightly coloured scalloped reins, the men-at-arms supplied by Norwich, Rushley, Redesmarsh and the abbey and adding up to a force of thirty, and the train of laden baggage mules. To Isabel, they were only a foretaste of the horrible grandeur of the bishop's inquiry.

She travelled mainly at the rear of the party, mounted sideways behind a man-at-arms, on a pillion with a board for her feet. It was the way Rohese had ridden back to Rushley, Isabel remembered wryly. Now that she was trying it for herself, she found it hard and uncomfortable. She was jolted at every stride and by the end of the first hour she was aching badly. She wished very much that she could fall off the horse and die.

But the horse was stolid and the saddle, however hard, was well-designed. They brought her, shrinking with dread, safely into Norwich.

Norwich was a welter of noise and crammed buildings; of lanes, so dirty underfoot that people wore clogs to keep their shoes clean, and so narrow that the crowds were pushed back almost into the doorways of the houses as the cavalcade went by. Street vendors shouted and somewhere a bell was tolling for the death of some local resident. Isabel thought of Abbess Christiana and shivered on her pillion.

Most of the party was lodged in the castle, whose great square keep, rebuilt in stone in the previous century, overlooked the town. Joan Lightfoot went with them, in the company of the ladies' tirewomen. But Isabel and Sister Julian were accommodated overnight in an abbey, although they were lodged apart from the other nuns. 'That's so that the others won't ask us questions,' Sister Julian said. Since Lucy Grosney's death, Sister Julian had remained pleasant, but there was a trace of coolness now in her manner towards Isabel. *She knows*, Isabel thought miserably. *She knows I did it on purpose. Or suspects, anyway, and that's nearly as bad.*

In the morning, an escort fetched them and took them on foot to the bishop's palace. There was a gatehouse, huge and crenellated (the gatehouse of Redesmarsh Abbey, which had once intimidated her, was a miniature by comparison), and guards who stood to attention with raised pikes as they marched through, and then there were steps up to a gaping arch and a hall with no rushes on the cold, flagstoned floor. Sunlight streamed in through stained-glass windows and everywhere Isabel looked there were banners and richly coloured robes, and the calm, judicial faces of men, men of power and rank.

Who would question her and might, if they thought fit, weave her answers into a rope to strangle a living neck. If that was what they did to abbesses who killed people with the evil eye. She was too bewildered and frightened at first to see where the focal point of the hall was. Finally, she grasped that opposite the door was a raised dais with an empty chair on it. She stood beside Sister Julian among the other witnesses in a somewhat untidy cluster to one side. Only Sir Henry and Lady Judith, because they were not witnesses but onlookers, had been given seats on a bench. The rest, even Sir Simon and his wife, had been left to stand.

Trumpets sounded and there was a stir in the hall. A loud bass voice cried, 'Pray silence for His Grace Roger de Skerning, Bishop of Norwich!' and through a side door came a man, in splendid robes thick with gold and silver thread, carrying a crook and wearing a mitre. To Isabel's alarmed gaze, he looked about twelve feet high.

He mounted the dais and stopped before the chair, turning to face the gathering. He thumped the end of his crook three times on the floor and sat down.

'Are all present who have been summoned?'

His voice was light but carried well. He could easily be heard the length of the hall. A clerk stepped forward and began to read out a list of names, pausing expectantly after each so that its owner could say 'Present.' She heard Sir Simon and Lady Cecily declare themselves, and then the other witnesses, but when it came to her own name she had to be prodded by Sister Julian before she realised that she too must speak, and managed to gulp out: 'Here, master!'

'Good,' said Bishop Roger. 'Bring in the prisoner.'

There was another stir, and then Abbess Christiana came in through another door, flanked by two mailed guards and followed by Sister Jeanne. If the bishop looked unnaturally tall, Isabel thought, then the abbess, mysteriously, seemed smaller than usual, although she walked firmly, which was more than could be said for Sister Jeanne, who shuffled along with bent shoulders and an air of resistance as though she were being dragged forward by an invisible hand.

There were preliminaries. A chaplain asked a blessing on the proceedings, and the clerk who had called the roll of the witnesses read out the charge, that the accused, known as Christiana Abbess of the Abbey of St Peter in Redesmarsh, had feloniously procured the death of Mistress Lucy Grosney of Rushley through witchcraft.

Abbess Christiana was asked to confirm that she was indeed herself and no one else (don't they *know*? Isabel wondered). She said something which Isabel couldn't hear, and was then given a stool and allowed to sit down.

The stool was on the floor below the dais and once seated on it, Christiana looked more dwindled than ever, like a black-clad dwarf with a pale, upturned face. Sister Jeanne was given a stool too, but near the wall. She was not close enough to Christiana to whisper to her or touch her.

'Oh,' breathed Sister Julian, 'the poor soul! Our poor abbess is almost alone at this moment. I wish I could go to her!'

And Isabel, turning to look into Sister Julian's face, saw that as well as throwing Abbess Christiana to the legal monster, she had also made Sister Julian, whom she very nearly loved, shed tears.

'Let it be clearly understood,' said de Skerning's cool, uninflected voice, 'that the gravamen of this charge is murder. Witchcraft is a form of heresy and both are serious sins in the eyes of the church, since they tend to lead to the challenging of accepted authority and if unchecked could disturb or even overturn society. But neither is against the law of the land unless and until harm is caused through their practice.' At this point one of the canons in the row of seats which flanked the dais, moved sharply and de Skerning gave him a repressive glance. 'In some

76

countries,' said de Skerning, 'the most severe penalties are being proposed for any kind of unorthodoxy, but this inquiry is being conducted according to English law. Today we must establish not only whether the accused has practised witchcraft, but also whether she may have committed murder by that means.'

'One can almost,' muttered Sir Simon, 'hear the squelching of a metaphysical bog round His Grace's feet.'

'Witnesses may not speak until summoned,' said an official sternly.

'I will hear the evidence now,' said de Skerning. 'As a matter of propriety, I first call the husband of the deceased woman Mistress Grosney. He has been bereaved and it would be ill-mannered to make him wait. Summon Herbert Grosney.'

And with that, the monster which Isabel had inadvertently awakened, acquired a voice.

'. . . Yes,' said Herbert Grosney bleakly, standing in the centre of the floor in front of the dais. 'It is true that Lady Cecily and my wife both asked Abbess Christiana to tell her story. To the best of my recollection, Lady Cecily asked first and my wife, later, requested the abbess to continue.'

'Had Abbess Christiana attempted to encourage them in their questions? Had she led the conversation round so as to invite them?'

'No, sir, not to my recollection.'

'And had anyone told the accused of Mistress Grosney's condition?' asked de Skerning distastefully. The human race had to be continued, of course. But only the doctrine of the Fall could explain why the process had to be so unpleasant, rooted in secretive snugglings and achieved in a violent and dangerous catharsis.

'No, sir,' said Grosney.

'What was your own opinion, when you heard your wife accuse the abbess?'

Grosney hesitated.

'Come, Master Grosney. Did you at once think: yes of course? Or did you think: poor soul, she is so ill?'

'I didn't know what to think,' said Grosney helplessly.

'Very well. The court realises that this is a time of great distress for you. Thank you for your testimony. You may step down.'

'She didn't have to give all those details,' said Herbert Grosney, suddenly angry. 'What the abbess told us was disgusting. And that *was* how my wife died. The same disgusting way.'

'I said, step down, Master Grosney. Will Mistress Joan Lightfoot come forward?'

Joan Lightfoot, self-possessed enough at home in her own sphere was here so overawed that at first they could get nothing from her but alarmed curtsying and a lather of 'Oh, sir, I hardly know . . .' and '. . . oh, my lord, I wouldn't presume to say . . .'

Persuaded at last to cease bobbing up and down as de Skerning put it, 'like a potlid on the boil', and that she had only to promise to tell the truth and then repeat the words she had heard Mistress Grosney say when she was dying, she finally faltered out that Mistress Grosney had thought that Sister Julian was Abbess Christiana, and had cried out, 'You put the evil eye on me and ill-wished my baby!'

'Thank you, Mistress Lightfoot. You see, there was nothing to fear. You may step back. Sir Simon Rushley, please.'

Simon, as Herbert Grosney had already done, repeated the conversation in the abbess's parlour but could not be restrained from commenting in forthright tones, 'My lord, I don't know if the Abbess Christiana has had dealings with the devil or not but I think she spoke in malice when she talked of her mother's experiences in the presence of Mistress Grosney.'

'Sir Simon, I asked you to repeat the words that the abbess said, but not to comment on them. In any case, malice is a sin but not a crime. I wouldn't have ordered this inquiry to investigate mere ill will. One moment.' De Skerning leaned from his chair and beckoned his canons to his side. They conferred in low voices. 'Perhaps this is relevant after all,' he said at length, turning back to Sir Simon. 'Why did you conclude that the abbess spoke in malice?'

'Master Grosney was right when he said that her words were disgusting. And I have known Abbess Christiana,' said Sir Simon, 'for a long time. I believe her to be malicious.'

'Can you give other examples of this malice?'

'I think, my lord, that an expression on someone's face, glimpsed now and then when they were saying something that just might have two meanings, or a look of too much triumph after getting the better of a bargain, wouldn't be evidence. But it might be an indication, as the direction of smoke indicates the direction of the wind.'

On her stool, Christiana seemed to shrivel. 'Oh!' whispered Sister Julian. 'It is cruel, cruel. Mother has her little faults as we all do, but those who know her, know her worth.'

'On the other hand,' added Sir Simon blightingly, 'I agree that malice is one thing and witchcraft is another. I doubt if she's a witch. I think she's simply nasty.'

'I repeat, you are not required to comment on the evidence, Sir Simon. That will be all. Lady Cecily, if you please.'

Lady Cecily did not comment on the evidence but she was as blunt as her husband to the point of causing embarrassment.

'Yes, sir, in the presence of Mistress Grosney she did give details of a tragic confinement . . . no, no one told the abbess that Mistress Grosney was with child but the fact was perfectly clear to anyone who knows about these things and the abbess did know. She had seen her mother through many pregnancies. There are signs that appear quite early. Mistress Grosney's eyes were lustrous and her lips were full. I believe that the abbess should have guessed, at least.'

De Skerning looked revolted, as though the mere mention of such things had somehow polluted his hall. 'You may step aside. I will now hear . . . no, on second thoughts, I wish to confer.' He rose to his feet and collected his clergy with his eyes. The sheriff, who was seated opposite to them also rose but when he made to accompany the clergy out, de Skerning shook his head. 'This is purely ecclesiastical.'

In the quiet of an ante-room, he surveyed his archdeacons and canons and said, 'Frankly, I think we've heard enough. It's as I thought. The whole thing is turning out to be a mare's nest. What does any of it, so far, amount to? Spite, that's all. Female spite on the part of the abbess.'

'I must say I agree.' The older of the two archdeacons nodded. 'Women are often thus. They are weak creatures. Men are scarcely talented when it comes to combating the sinfulness with which all humankind is born, but women are worse. Their drive towards sexuality is so strong that nuns often do envy women who have husbands and children.'

'That is true.' Canon de Harland spoke up. De Skerning regarded him warily. De Harland was a short, swarthy man with fierce dark eyes and the vibrance of suppressed energy, perhaps suppressed anger, about him. 'No doubt God ordained it so, for unless men and woman come together to create the next generation, there would be no human beings on earth to worship God. Indeed, what was so extremely offensive about the Cathar heresy on the continent is their belief that men and women shouldn't come together at all, and that if they cannot forgo sexual relations, they should have them with their own sex. But it is just because of that offensiveness, that here in England, we should strive in every way to keep heresy of any kind from taking root. I realise that if any heresy has a grip on Abbess Christiana, it is certainly not Catharism but . . .'

'The Cathars were quelled over fifty years ago,' said de Skerning irritably, 'and I must say that my own observation of my fellow creatures long ago convinced me that, amid such lustful beings, Cathar ideals never had the slightest chance of becoming popular. This is completely irrelevant. You're obsessed with heresy, de Harland. This inquiry is not concerned with heresy; only with murder. King Henry outlawed inquisitions into the private beliefs of his subjects twenty years since.'

He had indeed, to the accompaniment of a rude suggestion that his prelates were so well-fed and proud that they had become insane. De Harland, perhaps thinking of this, had flushed. 'But we *are* dealing with heresy,' he said obstinately. 'Abbesses are in a different category from ordinary people; they can be excommunicated for it. And this particular heresy is *witchcraft*, which may have been used to commit the murder of which you speak. My lord, I beg you: the court should

79

hear the other witnesses. In particular, we should hear Father Benedict, who laid the original complaint.'

'I've heard him already,' said de Skerning. 'He won't add anything useful, believe me.'

'It would complete the inquiry if we heard all the witnesses rather than stopping now,' said the elder archdeacon peaceably. 'No one could then say that the inquiry was not thorough.'

De Skerning sighed. 'The sitting,' he said with reluctance, 'will resume.'

It resumed with Father Benedict, and even Isabel, waiting fearfully to know if she would be called or not, could grasp that Father Benedict was a most unsatisfactory witness.

'. . . but *why*, Father Benedict, were you so sure that the matter ought to be reported?'

'I wasn't sure, my lord. But I felt it was more correct to do so and leave the decision whether there were a case to answer or not, to more learned heads than mine. A sin of omission is as grave as an active sin, after all, my lord.'

'But why did you feel so strongly that there was more here beyond a few foolish and perhaps unkind words, remembered by a woman on the point of death, when her mind was disordered? It is a serious thing, to bring an accusation against someone so highly thought of as an abbess.'

'I can only repeat, my lord, that I did not know what to think, any more than Master Grosney. That was the very reason why I sought this inquiry. So that witnesses could be heard and the truth given a chance to emerge.'

Beldame! thought de Skerning exasperatedly. *A stickler for detail but terrified of responsibility when it really comes to the point.*

'Enough, Father Benedict. I will now hear the witnesses who know the accused best. Will the abbess's confessor, Father Ambrose of Redesmarsh, kindly step forward.'

Father Ambrose, who had been growing increasingly restive, bounced out with alacrity to take the floor. He was a stocky little man, red-faced from exposure to the east wind as he went about his parish, and possessed of a warm-hearted but impatient temperament. He often admitted that when he got angry he *got angry*, and the wrath which had already caused him to conduct an unseemly wrangle with Father Benedict, hadn't subsided. He gabbled the oath and then, before de Skerning could begin to question him, burst straight into a speech of his own. Father Ambrose was somewhat given to walking into rooms without knocking. This, as those who knew him realised, was another version of the same characteristic.

'This entire inquiry is an outrage and an insult. I am chaplain to the Abbey of Redesmarsh and if anything were out of order there, I would know. The abbess is a holy woman, devout and conscientious in all her observances, aware of her faults and in constant strife against them . . .'

'Father Ambrose . . .' began de Skerning.

'. . . this absurd accusation is a reflection on myself as the abbey chaplain as well as on the abbess and all her nuns. A few casual words, distorted in the brain of a dying woman . . .'

'Father Amb . . .'

'. . . it is monstrous that Father Benedict did not see fit to consult me before rushing to Norwich like a madman. In similar circumstances I would certainly have consulted him and . . .'

De Skerning pounded on the floor with the butt-end of his crook. 'Father Ambrose!'

The diatribe stopped.

'Unless you contain yourself, I shall have you removed and fined for contempt. I wish you to tell the court without further ado whether you have ever heard the Abbess Christiana express an heretical opinion of any description and if so, what it was.'

'No, my lord, I haven't.'

'Stop and think. Are you quite, quite sure? Remember you are on oath.'

Father Ambrose, boiling, said nothing for about twenty seconds and then repeated, 'No, my lord,' more than a little pugnaciously.

'Has she ever shown hesitation or reluctance to take the sacrament? Ever made an excuse not to take it?'

'Certainly not, my lord.'

'Have you ever had reason to remonstrate with her – outside the confessional, of course – about her behaviour in any way?'

Father Ambrose paused, belatedly cautious. After all, although de Skerning was talking about the abbess as though she were a total stranger to him, this was not true. She controlled an abbey in his diocese and he must know a good deal about her.

'The abbess sometimes has to leave her abbey to conduct its business. I have occasionally commented that she leaves it perhaps more often than is strictly necessary.'

'All right,' said de Skerning resignedly. He was well aware of Christiana's wandering tendencies. He deplored them but they were nothing to do with heresy or witchcraft or even malice. 'No more questions.' He had memorised the witnesses' names up to now but at this point lost track and consulted a clerk. 'Ah yes. Sister Julian.'

Sister Julian was calm, clear-voiced, and was a daughter protecting her mother. Yes, she had heard Mistress Grosney say the words alleged. No, she did not believe they meant anything more than the delusions of a dying and delirious woman. 'There was nothing extraordinary about her illness. We were having an epidemic of the marsh ague. She'd caught it and her fever was very high. It was the ague that brought on the miscarriage and the combination of the two killed her . . . no, I have never had cause to look on my abbess as anything other than a holy and devout bride of Christ . . .'

She was allowed to move aside. De Skerning spoke to the clerk again. And then, 'Sister Isabel, come forward.'

The moment was here, for which Isabel had been waiting with damp palms and a thumping heart. Someone gave her a push. She was walking out across the flagged floor, towards that terrifying, iridescent, episcopal figure on the dais. Everyone was staring.

In particular, Abbess Christiana was staring. Glancing sideways, Isabel saw the glitter of Christiana's eyes watching beneath the shadow of her veil.

'There is no need to be nervous, Sister Isabel,' said de Skerning. 'If you would first take the oath . . .' She obeyed, and was asked to speak more loudly. 'The court cannot hear you and the oath must be heard.'

'. . . now,' said de Skerning briskly. 'Tell us in your own words what happened when you went with Sister Julian to attend Mistress Grosney. You are Sister Julian's assistant?'

'Yes, sir, at that time, anyhow.'

'Well, tell us what happened.'

She could feel the abbess's eyes on her. She tried hard to remember the upper room at the Grosneys' house. She'd got to get through this somehow. She'd got to use her wits. All villeins had wits; people who hadn't any power needed them. She'd got to be careful what she said. She mustn't contradict anyone else but she mustn't, daren't, say any words against Christiana, either. If she had to commit perjury, she would. Christiana never struck her nuns but Isabel now discovered that as well as hating the abbess, she feared her even more than she feared the bishop. 'Mistress Grosney was very ill, sir. Mistress Lightfoot was tending her. I handed towels and water and things.' She stopped, losing her way.

'Yes? And?'

'Well, I reckoned Mistress Grosney was dying. She was very frightened and so was I. I'd never seen nothing . . . anything like that before, sir.'

'Was she afraid only of her illness, of death? Or of any other thing or person?' said de Skerning helpfully.

This was the difficult bit. It was like walking over marshland, testing every tussock before you put your weight on it.

'I think she was frightened of us, sir, me and Sister Julian.' She had reverted instinctively to her natural accent. 'She seemed to think . . . well, she seemed to think Sister Julian was someone else. I couldn't make it out, quite.' That was perjury. Well, she couldn't help it.

'And then what happened?' De Skerning was unable to prevent himself from sounding bored.

'Then the baby come, sir. It was awful.'

'I'm sure it was and you needn't give us the details. Tell us what you did next.'

'Well, she shouted at Sister Julian to leave her alone . . . Sister Julian was trying to give her some wine. And then she started, well, just raving and she was bleeding, and . . . I lost my head, sir!' said Isabel, producing the age-old villein excuse for error, and now embarking on perjury with a will. 'I said afterwards to Sister Julian that I was sorry, I know I should have waited for her to do it . . .'

'Do what?'

'Well call down the stairs for the Father and Master Grosney to come up.'

'You say Mistress Grosney was raving. Did you hear her say any words in particular?'

'I . . . well . . .' Christiana's eyes were boring holes in her. She knew it without looking round. 'I heard something about ill-wishing, sir. She said someone had ill-wished her. But I didn't get it clearly, I don't think I was listening. I was so panicky, sir; there was all the blood, you see, and . . .'

'Quite, quite. Tell me, Sister Isabel, do you like and admire Abbess Christiana? Tell us how she seems to you?'

'To me, sir? Well . . .' Villein cunning came to her aid again. 'I'm a bit scared of her, sir.' There was faint amusement from the clergy. 'We novices all are, sir. And she's so high above me. I'm villein-born, you see, sir . . .'

'You may step aside.' She curtsied and turned away thankfully, feeling the sweat run down her temples. Her eyes met Christiana's.

And, at the glaring rage in the abbess's eyes, she felt terror leap into her own. If Christiana had not previously known the sequence of events round Mistress Grosney's deathbed, she had learned it at this hearing. She now knew exactly when Isabel had chosen to summon the men to the chamber. And – Isabel was certain of it – she guessed why. She knew that the cringing, humble Isabel who had just taken refuge in her villein birth and testified to losing her head was a liar. She knew that the real Isabel hated her. Oh no, she had not fooled Christiana.

Back in her place, willing herself not to faint at the memory of Christiana's eyes, she watched the clergy gathering round the bishop to confer. One of them, a dark, intense man, seemed to be dissenting, but the rest were nodding their heads at whatever de Skerning was saying.

The clergy returned to their places. De Skerning spoke.

'I feel there is no need to prolong this investigation further. I find that there is no case to answer. There is no evidence of anything questionable in Abbess Christiana's beliefs or religious observances, no deliberate attempt to cause harm to Mistress Grosney, no reason to assume that these unhappy accusations were anything more than delusions in the poor lady's mind. The case,' said de Skerning, 'is dismissed.'

'Thank God,' whispered Sister Julian.

Isabel thought, 'I knew she'd get off. Well, I didn't say anything against her. But she knows. She can see right through me. She'll take it out on me somehow.'

'And you,' said de Skerning, finding Canon de Harland close to him as they left the hall, 'think I'm wrong, don't you?'

'I'm afraid I do, my lord. On two counts.'

'Two?'

'Yes, my lord. Firstly, I think the woman is guilty. And secondly, I take the whole concept of heresy more seriously than you do. At the start of the proceedings today, you said that it tended to lead to the challenge of accepted authority and could disturb or even overturn society, but – forgive me, my lord – do you really know how true that is?'

'I don't think it would happen very easily,' said de Skerning. 'I believe it to be possible in theory, but . . .'

'No, my lord,' said de Harland earnestly. 'It is a fact. Allow authority to be challenged, and we will end with the natural order of things turned upside down, with the devil at large and the law set at naught, with men defying their overlords and blood running in the streets.'

De Skerning, relieved to be rid of the inquiry, was inclined to humour. 'I rather think that the danger, although real, can be averted by permitting a degree of challenge, and allowing one's orders to be modified sometimes by those who are expected to carry them out. If you dam a river too ruthlessly, it may break the dam and cause a disastrous flood. It is wiser to provide a safe channel and a regulated flow. Which is why, my dear de Harland, I am now allowing *you* to challenge *me*.'

'My lord! I wouldn't presume . . . naturally, I have accepted your verdict. This is a private expression of opinion, nothing more.'

'Sophistry!' said Roger de Skerning blandly.

Chapter Five

The Devil and Christiana

Between the menacing inquiry in the bishop's hall and this sparkling and joyous occasion in the outer bailey of Norwich Castle, there could scarcely have been a greater contrast.

The hearing was over, the abbess was vindicated and free, and Sir Henry Rushley had come to Norwich for another purpose besides that of attending the court. He had come to hand over his niece and ward the demoiselle Eglantine to the escort who would take her to her husband. 'Abbess Christiana is a disagreeable woman, to put it mildly,' he said to his son, 'but whatever she has done, she must have paid for it in these past days. They must have been a most unpleasant experience. It would be correct for us to ask her party to ride with us on the way home. She and her nuns and the other witnesses can be present for Eglantine's little ceremony.'

It was a glittering morning: sun alternating with showers, and a brisk wind to shake the banners which flew from the great square keep above, and the pennants which danced on the spears of the knights. As he had been Sir Henry's host, Roger Bigod, the Earl of Norfolk, was present in person, a tall figure in bright ceremonial chainmail which had never seen a battlefield, a gauntletted hand resting casually on a swordhilt that flashed with gems, and a long purple cloak streaming to his heels.

Isabel stood meekly behind Christiana, not far from the principals, eyes lowered and hands folded and swore secretly that never again would she make trouble, or fight for any sort of notice or status. The experience of giving testimony had finally unnerved her. Humble Isabel was the real one after all. The world of power was too frightening, even on an occasion of peace and well-wishing such as this. In its presence, her lowliness felt like an incurable disfigurement, as though she had been born with a club foot.

Christiana had been lodged in the castle last night, well apart from Isabel and so far this morning had ignored her completely although she had talked to Sister Jeanne and also to Sister Julian at some length, quietly, so that Isabel could not hear what she said. She was silent now, however, for the ceremonial handing-over of Eglantine had now begun and was proceeding with immense dignity.

Sir Henry's household was drawn up facing the representatives of the prospective bridegroom whose name, apparently, was Sir Hugh le Hale,

85

lord of a place called Cwmanog, in northern Wales, otherwise known as Gwynedd. All this was formally announced by a man who declared himself as Sir William FitzWilliam, half-brother to Sir Hugh.

Standing forward of the formidable row of mounted knights who would have the task of guarding Eglantine as she travelled across England to her wedding in Wales, he declared that his brother was making his castle ready to receive its new chatelaine. He said that the name Cwmanog meant the Valley of the Immortals. 'My brother bade me say that he hopes that the love between himself and his bride will also be immortal. He bids me promise on his behalf that every love and care will be given to the demoiselle Eglantine when she becomes his wife.'

Behind him, the knights raised their spears in a salute. Sir Hugh had sent a standard-bearer and the le Hale device, a fierce-looking pike with an elongated jaw, argent on gules, rippled as the breeze caught it. There were murmurs of approval and Sir Henry and Lady Judith led Eglantine forward.

She was arrayed in blue: a hooded mantle in a deep and vivid shade and a gown of lighter blue beneath it. She put back her hood in order to receive William FitzWilliam's kiss of welcome and, for a moment, Isabel had a clear view of her face. She was miraculously lovely, with the polished look which no mere Isabel of Northfield could ever hope to achieve. Glossy brown braids framed a charming face, with faint hollows under the beautiful cheekbones, and a perfect skin. How she must treasure that skin, Isabel thought, and how she must fear the smallpox. All fine ladies feared smallpox and were much more prone to it than their villeins. There was a theory that caring for cows somehow provided a protection.

In a clear, sweet voice, Eglantine was declaring her willingness for the match and her gratitude to Sir Hugh for honouring her with such a splendid escort. She then took leave of Sir Henry and Lady Judith, thanking them for their care of her and embracing them. The farewell embraces began formally and then turned into fierce hugs, as Eglantine clung to both of her foster-parents at once and buried her face in Sir Henry's shoulder in order to sob. She pulled herself back after a moment, wiped her eyes, and apologised to FitzWilliam.

'There is no need to be sorry, demoiselle. An affectionate heart is a virtue. Carry such affection to my brother and he'll be a happy man. But it is time we set out.'

A horse was brought for Eglantine. She was not to ride pillion, it seemed, but in the usual fashion, astride, on a mount of her own. But the mount was a dapple-grey ambling palfrey and the saddle and bridle and the scalloped reins were of scarlet leather. For a moment, something renegade and envious stirred within Isabel again. She quelled it quickly.

Sir William helped Eglantine to mount. Her tirewoman came forward and was also given a horse. The baggage mules were led out and got into line. There were cheers, a few tears and some farewell waving from Lady Judith and the other demoiselles, who until now had been Eglantine's daily companions. The Earl of Norfolk raised his hand in a signal and trumpets spoke. The cavalcade moved off towards the gate.

Sister Jeanne sighed romantically. And Abbess Christiana, who had stood upright and silent throughout, gave her a sharp look. 'Well,' she said in a low voice, 'we have had a treat, after our alarming day yesterday. But for us, remember, all such things as this are worldly mummery. Now, God be thanked, we shall return to our abbey and to the resumption of our spiritual lives. Some of us have far to go to achieve any kind of holiness, I fear.'

With that, her eyes, for the first time that morning, fixed upon Isabel's face. The two of them stared at each other. Isabel saw, with the clear and unforgiving perceptiveness of youth, that although Christiana was not yet old, she wasn't young either, was in fact just on the turn and that it was showing. She saw too that her own youth made Christiana's hatred stronger.

And she saw how strong that hatred was.

After they were back in the abbey, Christiana wouldn't go on ignoring her. The terror which had invaded her stomach yesterday when she had finished her testimony and the abbess had looked at her, swept over her again. The abbess *knew*. Not just guessed, but *knew*. And she, Isabel, was in her power.

On the homeward road, they broke their journey to eat an alfresco meal by the wayside. A shower began just as the packets of bread and cold meat and the flasks of wine were being given out, and Sir Henry waved them all into the shelter of a small wood. Isabel found herself beside Sister Julian.

She needed kindness from someone.

'I'm glad,' she said hesitatingly, 'to be off the horse for a little while. Those pillion seats jolt such a lot.'

'Yes. I used to ride as a girl, but I always preferred my own mount,' said Sister Julian absently. She was not looking at Isabel, who followed her gaze and realised that she was staring at Christiana. The abbess was watching while Sister Jeanne and one of the men spread a cloak under a tree for her to sit on. Father Ambrose was at her elbow. Christiana's back was towards Julian and Isabel, but something in the very line of it seemed to Isabel to be ominous.

Sister Julian's expression was worried. 'Mother Abbess is very angry with you,' she said suddenly. 'She believes that you meant Father Benedict to hear what Mistress Grosney said. I myself hope that that is not true but I admit that I fear the contrary. If it *is* true – and only you can know for sure, Sister – you must understand that her anger is natural. This has been a dreadful time for her. Do you realise what could have happened to her? They are saying in France, these days, that witches should burn.'

'But I didn't mean . . .'

'Didn't you?' asked Sister Julian.

'She hated me before that,' said Isabel miserably. 'That's why I . . . why I gave way to temptation. It wasn't fair. She had no reason to hate me.'

'I think she thought you presumptuous,' said Sister Julian carefully.

'Sister Julian . . .'

'Yes?'

'When we are back in the abbey, if the abbess is angry with me . . . please don't be angry with me too. I shall need a friend.'

'We are not allowed to have particular friends. You know that.'

'Not a particular friend! Just a friend. I mean, talk to me sometimes, smile at me. Not dislike me. Why did she think I was presumptuous?'

'Well – weren't you? I don't want to hurt your feelings,' said Sister Julian. 'Come, sit here under this oak and have something to eat. Sister, I found you an invaluable help in the infirmary. There is so much good in you. But a girl born in your circumstances cannot expect to be a choir nun, and be taught calligraphy and Latin, or hope one day to take a seat in Chapter. And you did seem to expect these things.'

'But why not? *Why* not?'

'Oh my dear. We are born into the positions God thinks best for us. It is presumptuous to argue with His will.'

'Then can't anyone ever try to become more than their parents were?'

'Sometimes it may be given as a gift. Those who give good service or show great merit may have advancement given to them. But it is wrong, yes, to seek it deliberately.'

'Were you well-born? You're a choir nun.'

'My father was a knight, yes.'

'It's easy to say it's one's duty to be content with what you've got, when you've got *that*,' said Isabel bitterly.

'What do you mean by *that*?'

'Freedom,' said Isabel. 'Position. A nice home to live in, nice things, horses to ride and people respecting you. The right to learn. I wanted to learn. From the moment when my father taught me my letters, I wanted it. And when I came to the abbey and began having lessons in Latin and theology and figures . . . it was like . . . I can hardly find words . . . it was like beginning to grow! Why can't I want that? Why *do* I want it, if it isn't natural?'

'Perhaps it is your opportunity to make a sacrifice for God?'

'But why should I have to sacrifice it when you don't? Why are we so different?'

'Oh, my dear,' said Julian again. 'Listen, Sister Isabel. You were a wonderful help in the infirmary, and after Mistress Grosney died, when we boiled all the dirty linen in the Grosney house, I would never have got it done without your help. You're quick and strong, even though you're so slight. You're gifted at those tasks. You should let yourself be valued for them. Accept what you are. How can we expect to understand God's intentions for us? That's bound to be beyond our powers. Excuse me a moment.' She rose to her feet but paused to smile down at Isabel. 'I must just slip out of sight behind a tree. I'll be back.'

Isabel gazed after her. 'I'd have been gifted at Latin too, if I'd had a chance to prove it,' she muttered resentfully. And despite her resolution as she stood behind Christiana in the bailey of Norwich Castle, never again to seek notice, old longings and an old bitterness flared anew.

As they mounted again to continue their journey, Abbess Christiana caught sight of Isabel's face, observed that upon it was a discontented frown, and was at once swept by such a gust of fury, like a blast of heat from a burning building, that she almost reeled off Father Ambrose's pillion. The mare actually sensed it and laid back her ears.

So Sister Isabel looked discontented! Earlier on, she had looked afraid which had pleased Christiana, but discontent was an impertinence. Oh, wait till they were back inside the abbey! Christiana would make sure that Sister Isabel was so very discontented that she'd wish herself dead.

'Are you all right, Sister?' inquired Father Ambrose courteously.

He was an obliging confessor, the abbess thought. He knew that the bishop had taken her to task, privately, for malicious talk and that the penances she must perform would take weeks to discharge and, no doubt feeling that that was enough, he had himself uttered not one word of rebuke. He was travelling with her, back to the abbey, to present her to her nuns as utterly vindicated and clean, fit to be received once more as their Mother and their head, and he was not on speaking terms with Father Benedict, any more than she was.

He must not know of the storm of fury and hate which possessed her because he would call it sin. Which it was, of course, only it was also, in its ghastly way, so very enjoyable. She thought of the trouble Sister Isabel had brought upon her: the fear and the disgrace and those damned penances, and the mere act of recounting them to herself produced a hideously pleasurable inflammation of wrath.

She sat on the pillion as they rode at a steady walk, along the track across the first outlying fields of Redesmarsh, and her rage was like a being, a hot, red demon, which had lodged in the pit of her stomach. Oh, just let Sister Isabel wait . . .

'I said,' said Father Ambrose, 'Are you all right?'

'I . . . yes, oh yes, thank you. Your mare's pace is very easy.'

'You are distracted,' said Father Ambrose. He did not turn his head to talk and all she could see was the back of his tonsured head and the folds of his brown hood. She couldn't tell if his eyes were anxious or friendly or displeased. 'I have been thinking,' he said.

'Yes Father?'

'Did Sister Isabel call the men into that room on purpose?'

'I think so, Father.'

'I thought as much. I saw you look at her when she had finished testifying, and I saw *her* look at *you.*' Father Ambrose, clearly, had missed very little. 'Will you listen to my advice?' he asked.

'Yes, Father. Of course.' She would not dare do otherwise. She had just skirted the edge of an unimaginable abyss and the memory of fear was still strong in her, alongside her anger.

'She hasn't taken any vows. Get rid of her,' said Father Ambrose. 'If you keep her, her presence will be a constant irritant. If you are to put this dreadful affair safely behind you, you must be free of her presence. She will only tempt you.'

'Tempt me, Father?'

'To wrath and bitterness and perhaps to revenge. I imagine that you will always be a little afraid of her, and that,' said Father Ambrose astutely, 'will surely make a woman of your temperament angry.'

'Yes, Father . . . I see,' said Christiana.

'Think about it,' said Father Ambrose tersely.

They plodded steadily on. Christiana brooded. It would be very , very difficult to let go of her chance to make Sister Isabel's life into a foretaste of hell. Various deft and subtle ways of going about this had occurred to her already and more would come.

On the other hand . . .

Another memory which was likely to stay with her for a long time was that of her very first encounter with Isabel, when she had looked into those dark, hungry, challenging eyes and been not only angered, but chilled.

Christiana was not one to underestimate an enemy. Even kept-down lay sisters had been known to acquire power. She had seen it happen, in her predecessor's day. Sister Amicia had never learned her alphabet but she hadn't let that restrict her. She had had a pretty face and a manner both modest and hard-done-by and she had also had that indefinable thing called magnetism.

Before Sister Amicia was done, she had gathered a court around her, of nuns who would do anything for her smile, and champions who became indignant every time Sister Amicia implied that she had been slighted or unjustly penanced. Sister Amicia had no seat in the Chapter but her adherents argued forcefully there on her behalf, getting her into posts of responsibility and finally into the position of confidante and companion to the ageing abbess. Once there, she controlled access to the abbess and acted as her mouthpiece until the other nuns began to say that, to all intents and purposes, Sister Amicia *was* the abbess.

That was her downfall, naturally. Even her champions began to grow cold towards her then and when the old abbess died, they voted Christiana into her place largely because they felt that Christiana could deal with Sister Amicia if anyone could.

And so she had. Sister Amicia, like Isabel herself, had been demoted to the kitchens and the yard. She had also been given such penances of fasting and extra duties, mostly damp ones out of doors, that she had very quickly caught the lung-rot and died of it. Christiana had enjoyed watching the process and helping it along.

But she had been younger then. Now, she was beginning to notice twinges and failures of energy which only a year ago had not been there. And in Isabel's face at that first meeting had been not only a leaping hunger and a frightening force of will, but youth. Time, already Christiana's foe, might prove to be Isabel's friend.

Father Ambrose was uncomfortably right. She had understood Isabel, presumptuous, hungry Isabel, from the beginning. Now she had indeed begun to fear her. Yes, it was true. The abbey would be better off without such a dangerous influence.

The cavalcade, with Sir Henry Rushley and his son Sir Simon leading it, escorted the Abbess Christiana to the gate of her abbey where the Rushley party pulled up, leaving her to ride through with her nuns and retainers and Father Ambrose. Her retainers were quartered outside the abbey, on its lands but half a mile outside its walls; but they would see her into the outer courtyard before taking their leave.

From the moment when the abbey came into sight as they topped the low rise of land which curved round it to the south and east, Christiana had not taken her eyes off it.

There it stood: St Peter's, which she had feared she would never see again. She did not know what manner of welcome would await her inside it, but the dignified escort which had brought her home should be proof enough that her character was clear.

And before she entered, she would have done something towards regaining and maintaining her authority.

Outriders had gone on ahead to announce their approach and the gates were open. But in the gateway, Christiana cried; 'One moment before we enter!' and Father Ambrose reined in too. The entire cavalcade came to a halt.

Christiana twisted round on the pillion. 'My thanks, Sir Henry and Sir Simon, for your company and you especially, Sir Simon, for your testimony in my favour at Norwich!' she called. Neither Sir Simon nor Sir Henry replied, but she had not expected it. At least the porteress must have heard and would probably repeat it.

Now for that girl.

'There is one more thing to do before I re-enter my abbey! With me to Norwich came three of my sisterhood, Sister Jeanne, Sister Julian and Sister Isabel. But only two will return. Sister Isabel is under no vows and is free to depart and I herewith order her to do so. You are insubordinate and a troublemaker, Sister Isabel, and there is no more holiness in you than in the horse that carries you. Probably,' said Christiana punitively, 'much less! Dismount!'

Isabel looked nonplussed.

'Dismount, I say! You may wait in the porteress's lodge and those belongings with which you entered the abbey will be sent out to you. Then you may go where you will. Which had better be back to Rushley, to return to your villeinage there. It is only because Rushley has a claim on you,' said Christiana untruthfully, 'that I allowed you to come back from Norwich at all. If it were left to me, I would have turned you loose in Norwich to make your living in the stews where the seamen go who bring the ships up the river. Why have you not dismounted as I bade you?'

Slowly, Isabel slithered down from her own pillion. Her man-at-arms stared blankly ahead. He was a partisan of the abbess and hadn't spoken to his passenger once on the journey.

Sister Julian began, 'But, Mother Abbess . . .' caught Christiana's eye and fell silent.

Father Ambrose clicked his tongue. 'I didn't quite intend . . . My child, I advised the abbess that you should leave the abbey but I trust you have somewhere to go? Perhaps . . .' He glanced towards the Rushley party. 'My lady Judith . . .' he began tentatively.

Father Benedict interrupted. He had been made to look a fool at Norwich and mostly by Sister Isabel, who had started the whole thing – possibly on purpose, according to the abbess, out of resentment at some matter of abbey discipline – but had proved weak and unhelpful during the inquiry. 'My lady will hardly wish to be troubled with the girl. Isabel has a mother in Rushley. Bella Pecher. She had better go there.'

Lady Judith had begun to ride forward but now reined in and nodded. 'Yes, that would be best. The girl has never belonged to my household.'

From their faces, it was all settled. Isabel, standing there on legs which did not seem quite steady, did not know whether the recently remarried Bella would welcome her and feared not. Bella had made no attempt to get in touch with her since her father's death; she was sure of that. Nor did she want to enter a Pecher household. But she must seek shelter somewhere and these people were leaving her no choice.

She looked at Christiana and knew that any sign of distress would give the abbess pleasure. 'I shall be glad,' she said clearly, intending her voice to carry to the Rushley people, 'to see my mother again. I am afraid that after all I have no vocation for the religious life. I make mistakes and then indeed I must appear ill-behaved. I thank you, Mother Abbess, for releasing me. I will pray for you always. Now I will wait in the porteress's lodge for my belongings as you suggest.'

She curtsied, straightened up, and then walked on through the arch, turning aside into the lodge door.

Sir Simon, in the act of departure, wheeled his horse close to Christiana and laughed. 'She got the better of you there, Madam Abbess,' he said.

The little bitch. *The little bitch.* Fuming, Christiana entered her abbey. She gave a brusque greeting to the deputation of welcome, headed by the Prioress, which met her in the vestibule, She then announced that she wished to be alone, left everyone, including Father Ambrose, standing where they were and, like a black cloud in a strong wind, swept off through archway and cloister to the shadowy spiral stair which led to her private room. The nun whose duty it was to sit in the little ante-room outside and guard her superior's privacy, was at her post. She half rose as Christiana went past, and then sank back, ignored, as Christiana strode on into her sanctum and slammed the heavy oak door behind her.

Once inside and out of sight of anyone else, she stood in the middle of the floor, too furious to sit down, or pray, or touch the pasties and wine which had been set ready for her.

She had meant to dismiss Isabel with ignominy before them all and what had happened? Isabel had received dismissal as though it were a blessing, turned a curtsy into an insult and made Sir Simon laugh at *her*, Abbess Christiana.

And now, Isabel was going to her mother who might possibly be glad to see her even though she'd run away from home. You could never tell with villeins. They had a mysterious, tribal solidarity. Villeins who hated each other would lie for each other in the manor court rather than side with the lord. Isabel might very well escape into happiness. She might remarry. She might even, thought Christiana, her imagination running out of control, present herself at the abbey one day, perhaps to visit Sister Julian, with a baby in her arms, and patronise its abbess as Lucy Grosney had done.

'You dare, my lady!' thought Christiana grimly. 'You dare!'

From her desk, she fetched a small knife used for sharpening quills, and from a chest she took a key, and her abbess's crook. She carried them to the back of the office and there unlocked a small wooden cupboard let into the stone of the wall.

Inside, was a box containing one of the abbey's treasures, a very beautiful and costly copy of the writings of Bede. If the bishop's men had searched her office, as was very likely, and had found both key and cupboard and duly investigated, there was nothing here to arouse comment. A precious item had been safely locked away, as was natural. They would have examined the book, put it back, locked the cupboard and returned the key to the chest.

It was most improbable that they would have done what Christiana now did, which was to lift out the box and use the knife to prise up a strip of wood at the very back of the cupboard's floor. And even if they had, and someone had wriggled a hand down into the cavity, which was only six inches wide by eighteen inches long, they would have discovered nothing but space. Only Christiana, who had found the loose piece of wood by accident on the day she became abbess, when a protruding nail in the book-box caught it just as she was lifting the box out to examine it, knew the cavity's depth and that the bottom of it could be reached with the aid of her crook.

It was the sort of secret, she had thought at the time, which might come in useful. And so it had, especially when dealing with Sister Amicia. It had been Sister Amicia who had started Christiana on her path of unforgivable sin.

Now she pushed the crook down into the cavity, hooked end foremost. When her arm was at almost full stretch, she was able to hook the ring attached to another box, lying at the bottom.

She had used wax to fix the ring upright so that it was easy to catch. She drew the box up and brought it to the desk, blowing the dust off it. It was small but more elaborate than the book container, shaped like a hooped chest in miniature. She opened the catch and put back the lid.

Inside, lay one of the secret methods she had used to dispatch Sister Amicia. At least, she didn't know for sure that it had any power. Making certain that Sister Amicia got wet through several times while suffering from a cough had probably done more. But it had given her such satisfaction to use this. She enjoyed hatred as women like Lucy Grosney, she thought with disgust, no doubt enjoyed sex.

Carefully, she lifted out the contents of the box. First came a little doll, six inches long, made of woollen cloth stuffed with bits and pieces, its face a white patch on which features had been roughly painted, its hair made of bits of wool stuck on with the glue that was used to attach gold leaf to vellum. Then came a phial and a long steel needle in a case.

She had had holy water in the phial but there was none left now. Not that it mattered. It was hate that she wanted to discharge; she was no true witch. Going through the motions would content her. She would use the wine which had been left for her to drink.

She dipped her fingers into the wine and dabbed it on to the doll's forehead.

'I baptise thee Isabel Plowman, born Isabel of Northfield. In the name of the Father, the Son and the Holy Ghost.'

The wine was red and made a nasty-looking patch on the doll's forehead. Just like blood, thought Christiana with savage contentment. Holy water hadn't been nearly so pleasing.

'And now, dear Isabel,' she said softly, although the oaken door was thick and the nun outside couldn't have heard even a raised voice clearly, 'let me make it plain to you. You will never have any luck. For what you have done to me and for what you have tried to do, be accursed for ever. Be accursed in life and in love and beyond the grave. With this needle, I transfix thee . . .'

She held the doll down on her table with one hand and drove the needle home through its heart with the other.

She was standing there like that, looking down at her cloth and wool victim, her face suffused and her heart pumping with fulfilled hatred, just as it always had when the doll was called Amicia and she had done this to it, when Father Ambrose, having been assured that the abbess was alone, brushed aside the guardian nun outside, knocked, and then in his usual careless fashion, without waiting for a summons, raised the latch and walked into the room.

Chapter Six

An Unfamiliar and Exotic Room

So here she was, Isabel thought, walking back to Rushley from Redesmarsh Abbey, retracing the walk she took when she fled from home. And returning with less than she had taken. I set out with hope, she said to herself as she plodded past Oxfen village. What hope have I now, of bettering myself?

She'd never be a freewoman now. Faced with the episcopal majesty of Roger de Skerning, she had even taken refuge in her villeinage. *I'm a bit scared of her, sir. We novices all are, sir. She's so high above me. I'm villein-born, you see, sir . . .*

She couldn't remember that without feeling sick, and she couldn't forget it, either.

The walk seemed long and she was confused, in any case, over where she ought to be going. Bella had evidently gone through with her marriage to Tosti Pecher. But were they living in the Pecher house or at Northfield or had they moved to Plowman's Acres, which was strategically placed in between? Grandmother Mary wouldn't have wanted to leave Northfield, but she couldn't be left there alone, either. The Northfield house was a good one; perhaps Tosti had been agreeable to moving there. If so, she was in for a long walk.

There was no hearth-smoke from the Pecher homestead, but a cheerful thread of it from the roof of Plowman's. The sight of it sent a stab of misery through her. Plowman's had been *her* home, where she had lived with Alfred, and whoever was there now, using her hearth and cooking pots, was an intruder, even if that someone should be her own mother.

It was a relief when, as she neared the house, a woman came out who was obviously not Bella, but a woman she recognised as the wife of a Rushley cottar.

'Susannah!'

'Why if it ain't Isabel! But we all thought as you'd gone into the abbey.'

Susannah was stout and easygoing, her headdress and apron always grubby but her temper amiable. Her husband, as Isabel remembered, had had no land beyond a tiny plot attached to his Rushley dwelling. It looked as though they'd had some good luck.

'You living here now?' said Isabel, and instinctively reverted to her original accent.

'Aye, that's right. Tosti couldn't manage all the land he'd got after he married your mam and Northfield with her, so he's sublet to us. Chance of a lifetime!' said Susannah with a grin. 'Oh, I'm sorry, duck. Never could watch my tongue. All very nice for us, but you've lost your man and I take it the abbey didn't turn out right for you. Left it, have you?'

'Yes.'

'Well we heard this and that,' said Susannah. 'The abbess is back, they say, but if you spoke against her, well, maybe you're best out of there.'

It was a question disguised as a statement. Isabel answered it. 'I didn't speak against her exactly, but it was me that called for Father Benedict just as Mistress Grosney was dying and . . . and saying things . . . and the abbess thinks I did it on purpose. So I've left. I'm going to my mother. Where are she and Master Pecher living? Northfield?'

'Aye, that's it. It's a fair step. You want to come in for a drop of ale?'

'No thanks. It's kind, but I'd better get on; the days aren't that long yet.' She couldn't bear to sit in the cottage which had been hers, and watch Susannah play hostess. 'I'll be on my way. Susannah . . . my mother is all right? And my grandmother?'

'Far as I know. But your gran's getting frail, I fancy. She don't come to church these days. Before he went off to Norwich, Father Benedict was poling out there now and again to see her. You sure you won't come in?' said Susannah, hospitable and tactless. 'I've altered things around in there, you'll be surprised. Don't you want to see?'

'No, no, I must hurry if I've to get all the way to Northfield. Goodbye, Susannah.'

The last thing she wanted to see was what another woman had done to the home which had been hers and Alfred's. Her life with him now seemed, in retrospect, much more contented than it ever had while she was living it. Besides, the wind of the morning had dropped and the bright, showery weather had changed during the afternoon into a brooding, overcast stillness. Far away to the east, the gleaming line of the sea had a steely glint. It would rain soon. There were good reasons for making haste.

She was very tired before she reached Northfield. It had been a day of so many changes that it felt more like a week, or a lifetime. There were plank bridges to cross over the Wend and the North Stream. Coming over the latter brought her within sight of the house. It looked solid and welcoming, its reed thatch in good condition and its hearth-smoke rising steadily into the grey sky. When she reached the door, she found it unlatched. She rapped, and then pushed it open and went in. Bella was seated on a stool by the fire trench, where the light could fall on the garment she was stitching. She looked up, needle poised above the green dyed stuff across her lap. 'Oh. It's you.'

'Yes, Mother. I've come home,' said Isabel unnecessarily.

'So I see. We were expecting you, considering what we've heard about how you got the abbess accused of witchcraft. That'll never stick, a lady like her, that's what Tosti said. And we'll see that girl of yours back here with her tail between her legs; he said that too. And here you are.'

Isabel came right into the room and found another stool. 'How are you, Mother? Are you all right? I mean, with Tosti.'

'Why shouldn't I be?' said Bella aggressively. She resumed her stitching, rather jerkily.

'Well, the Pechers . . . you can't have wanted to marry him, Mother. Did they make you?'

'No. Tosti offered and I said yes. And why not? You listen to me, my girl. Tosti's not your father, no, and I loved your father, don't you make any mistake about that.' Bella's hard face softened for a moment. But the softness soon vanished and her voice was aggressive again as she said, 'But I'm a woman and I ain't old yet. Well, it was a waste, that's all. Tosti was no beauty but he'd got his own land and your old holding and added to Northfield, it made a tidy bit of ground. We'll have some youngsters, with luck. You were a fool, turning down Ufi. Well-off widow you'd have been by now.'

'I didn't know that,' Isabel pointed out.

'You were a fool,' Bella repeated. She tied off a thread and neatly cut it with a little knife. 'And I can tell you this, my girl. You're my daughter so I'm not turning you out into the night. You can stay for a while. But . . .'

'How's Grandmother Mary?' Isabel interrupted. 'Where is she?'

'In the back room. She don't leave her bed much these days; we've put a brazier in there for her. You can make yourself useful while you're here, taking her food and drink to her and cleaning out her slops. It won't be for long.'

'Not for long?'

'Shouldn't think so.' Bella shrugged. 'She's been failing since your father went and you had a bit to do with him going, let me tell you.' She looked up, grimly. 'It'll be a help, if you look after her while she's still here. But you'll stay with her, out of sight in the back room, as much as you can, do you hear?'

'Yes, but why . . .?'

'And when you're not needed there any more, you'd best find employment somewhere else. I don't need help in this house otherwise and I wouldn't want yours if I did. As for why: I fancy,' said Bella, 'that you'll soon find out.'

The door was pushed open again. Isabel, who had been looking at her mother in surprise, turned to see Tosti on the threshold. He grinned

97

at her, showing his one fang He was decently dressed in brown, with long boots, and he had a net over his shoulder and a basket of fish in his hand.

'I got us a good supper,' he said. 'Lucky I did, seeing we're one extra.' The grin changed into the leer she had seen across her parents' table, in this very house, a few days before she fled. But she had always known, she thought, that it was there under the surface. It had been part of her dread of marrying Ufi. And Bella knew about it too. Tosti, forecasting Isabel's return, must have let her see it.

She said, rising politely to her feet, 'I was sorry to hear about Ufi.'

'Oh aye. Well, that's how it goes. I've lost others; he warn't my only son, just the last of 'em. With luck, I'll have others yet. I'm capable,' said Tosti with satisfaction. 'Well, well. We've bin expecting you home, you know. I was certain you'd be along.'

He grinned once more, not at Bella his new wife, but at Isabel, and there it was again, unmistakeably. He was looking at Isabel blatantly, as though she were something to eat.

Grandmother Mary died twelve days later. Isabel had been expecting it, for the moment she saw old Mary lying in the little room which had been made for her by hanging up a blanket curtain, she knew that her mother was speaking the truth and that Mary would not need her, or anyone else, for long. She was bedridden, too weak to sit up without help, and often confused.

She emerged from her confusion for a day or two after Isabel came home, partly because she said she found Isabel's young face refreshing, but also, it appeared, because she had a strong urge to deliver a warning.

'I'm glad you're back, but you've got to be careful and when I'm gone, girl, you'd best not stay.'

'That's what Mam says.'

'She's right,' said Grandmother Mary, and spelt it out. 'I didn't know much about them Pechers before Bella went and married one, and now I see you were right to turn Ufi down. You know what would have happened if you'd gone there? Ufi and his father would have shared you. Tosti's said as much. And he told Bella that if you came home, he didn't see why she shouldn't share *him*.'

'He said *that*? Said it openly, to my mother?'

The old head was nodding and nodding, trying to drive the meaning home. 'Reckon you smelt it, too. I thought you was wrong at the time and being awkward but by God I don't think so now. Bella's kept saying you'd be a well-off widow by now if you'd agreed, but that's just Bella trying to pretend things ain't what they really are. She knows you were right. She told you to keep with me and out of Tosti's sight, didn't she? I heard her. Well, you stick beside me and you'll be safe. But when I'm gone, you get out and fast. Reckon you'll have to,' Mary added with a faint echo of her cantankerous days. 'Because,' she said,

'Bella'll throw you out, mark my words. She may not think much of Tosti but he's hers. He's got a wildcat by the tail there, and he don't know it.'

'But where am I to go?' Isabel asked blankly. Since Alfred died she felt as though she had been rootless, belonging nowhere, a lodger at Northfield and at Redesmarsh Abbey alike.

'Oh, a lot of people were finished off in this last outbreak of the fever,' said Mary, who had never had it in her life. Isabel's family, though generally as prone to illness as any, did sometimes, her father had once said, throw up individuals who seemed impervious to anything. Mary, and Isabel herself, were of this fortunate breed. 'Ask for work at one of the great houses, Sir Henry's or Sir Simon's or something,' Mary said. 'They'll find you a place. You're a Rushley villein and it ain't always a disaster, being a villein. They got to look after you, up to a point.' She settled back into her bed and sighed. 'I'm tired now. Want to sleep.'

When she woke, hours later, she was once more confused and from then on, remained so. Tosti, during Mary's last days, did not approach Isabel in any way, and Isabel had little time to worry about Tosti, since Mary occupied all her attention. She weakened day by day. Isabel helped her to turn in bed, supporting her grandmother's shoulders while she held cups for her to drink or fed her broth from a spoon. Isabel fetched pans in which Mary could relieve herself and then, as Mary worsened, Isabel and Bella together lifted the incontinent old body out so that the soaked bedding could be changed. They did their best to protect the pallet, laying old rugs under their patient and soaking them in the nearby river afterwards, but the work grew steadily harder.

Isabel, however, had learned a good deal from Sister Julian in the infirmary and besides, as Bella said once, 'You was always good at looking after my little ones, as long as we had them with us. Seemed to bring out the best in you.'

This was true. Confronted by sickness or helplessness, Isabel became kindly. It was the powerful and the superior who aroused her resentment.

On the twelfth day, as usual, she took porridge to Mary at first light. Mary did not want it, but, confusedly anxious to please, tried to take a little. But after she had swallowed two small mouthfuls, she gasped and her eyes widened. She jerked upright without aid, lurched forward, knocking bowl and spoon from Isabel's hand, vomited and collapsed over the edge of the bed. When Isabel, crying out in alarm, caught hold of her grandmother and lifted her up, Mary's head flopped back. And Isabel saw that the stare in her old eyes was fixed.

She was buried three days later, in Rushley churchyard. As they stood round the grave to listen while Father Benedict recited the last prayer, Tosti edged close to Isabel and nudged up against her.

'Reckon you'll miss your gran,' he muttered into her ear. 'But don't you worry; I'll comfort you. You can rely on old Tosti.'

On the way home, sitting in the boat beside her mother while Tosti poled, Isabel said quietly, 'Tomorrow I shall go to Rushley Hall to look for work. I'll leave the house as soon as I can, Mother,'

'You've made me angry many a time,' Bella whispered. 'But you've sense, at heart.'

'Yes, certainly, tell Stephen Carpenter that he and Alice Lightfoot can marry, when they like.' Sir Henry Rushley was dealing with routine affairs, glad enough to do so by the hall fire. He had found the journey to Norwich a great effort. He could now ride only by using the longest possible stirrup and even that made his knees and hips throb. He'd ached for a week after he came home and spent most of it in bed. This morning he had managed a short ride round his fields but, although there were bluebells and anemones under the elms which one of his ancestors had planted as a windbreak along the eastern edge of the home farm, and the air was full of the bleating of lambs from the marsh pastures where the ewes were grazing, the wind had an edge on it, and, presently, something else besides.

He had been on his way home when, in the belfry of Rushley Church, the funeral bell began to toll. It went on and on. He knew what it meant. He was glad to get inside his hall, where the sound was faint.

'They were talking of a month's time,' Bernard Reeve was saying. 'To give time for Mistress Joan to put a feast together. They didn't like to mention it until she came back from Norwich.'

'That poor woman,' said Sir Henry, 'was scared out of her wits all the time she was in Norwich although God knows no one was accusing her of anything. This will be nice for her; she'll be able to forget about Norwich if anyone can. What a hideous business it has been. Well, Mistress Joan'll have a grandchild in a year, with luck; Alice is a bonny girl. It's a pleasure, Bernard, to be able to deal with happy business once in a while. Anything else?'

'Your groom says your mare is flourishing and he thinks we can expect a sturdy foal before the end of May.'

'Good, good. If it's a colt foal, I may present it to my son to train as a destrier later on. Destriers come expensive and . . .'

An opened door sent smoke spiralling from the fire, and Sir Henry's squire appeared. Eustace would soon become a knight; he was already more young man than boy, confident as well as deferential. He caught his master's eye, received unspoken permission to deliver whatever message he was carrying, bowed and said, 'Father Benedict and Master Grosney are here. They wish to speak with you.'

'Good morning, Sir Henry.' Father Benedict came briskly up the hall, with Herbert Grosney behind him. The priest, like Eustace, had a confident step these days. 'I have had a letter from Roger de Skerning. I think I should read it to you. Don't go, Bernard. The letter will have to be made public; you may just as well listen.'

'Sit down. No need for ceremony,' said Sir Henry. 'Is the letter about . . .?'

'Yes, Sir Henry,' said Herbert Grosney. He had not come in confidently, but drearily, as though Father Benedict were towing him against his will. His eyes had the dulled look of a man who is not sleeping. He took a seat more slowly than Father Benedict and more as though he were too tired to stand than in obedience to Sir Henry's gesture. 'I never really believed it, you know,' he said. 'I hated her. I was bitter against her but now . . .'

'Eustace,' said Sir Henry, 'shut that damned door, will you? It's letting in the sound of that accursed bell and *I don't want to hear it.*'

So here I go again, Isabel thought, setting off across the fields on the shortest route to Rushley Hall. I seem to have done nothing for years and years except go from one place to another. I lost my home with Alfred and I've never found another.

If she couldn't get work at Rushley Hall, she must try elsewhere and meanwhile look for lodging in the village. Aunt Griselda would take her in. She wasn't popular; no one had approved of her running away to the abbey, or approved either of her behaviour at Mistress Grosney's deathbed, but if she explained about Tosti, perhaps people would understand.

Failing Rushley, there was always, though as a last resort, a chance of sanctuary with one or other of poor Aunt Meg's children. Her father's unhappily married and long-dead sister had married John Thatcher of Oxfen and their children all still lived there, although Isabel scarcely knew them, since the thatcher had never encouraged contact with their mother's kin.

That really would be a last resort, though. She wanted work, not charity. But one thing was sure: she couldn't go home. Her few possessions, most of them things returned to her when she left the abbey, including some clothes and Grandmother Mary's bronze medallion, were bundled up in a spare cloak under her arm. That made it definite. She had moved out.

As she went, she heard the bell of Rushley Church tolling. It seemed to be going on for a very long time. She wondered who had died. Mary's funeral peal was long since past.

The gate to Rushley Hall was open, as was usual during the day, when people were constantly in and out. She had come here for Christmas feasts of course, but this was different. She had to ask the gatewarden where to go to ask for kitchen work.

'Round there. That's the kitchen, at that end. There's a small door there and you ask for Mistress Johanna.'

Isabel duly went round there and in at a low door to find herself in a steamy cave not unlike the kitchen at the abbey. There was a high, vaulted stone ceiling and two hearths set into the wall in modern fashion. A majestic female figure at the far end was in consultation with a leather-aproned but very dignified man who was probably the chief cook, though neither could be clearly seen because of the clouds of steam in the air. A boy was turning a spit and another leather-aproned man was chopping meat. A girl was slapping dough about at one end of a table while at the other end, a second girl was breaking eggs rapidly into a bowl. An older woman was going from pot to pot and hearth to hearth, stirring pots and snapping at the girls to work faster. There was a marked feeling of stress in the room.

The girl with the eggs was nearest. Isabel went up to her. 'Can you tell me where I can find Mistress Johanna? She glanced towards the majestic, steam-wreathed lady. 'Is that her, there?'

'Is that who? No, course not. That's . . .'

'What is it, Peg?' The majestic lady came mightily across the room. Emerging from the swirls of steam, she turned into a lady of substance in both senses of the word, complete with gown of fine blue wool, costly leather shoes, and white, well-cared-for hands. Turned, in fact, into Lady Judith in person.

'This girl's asking for Mistress Johanna, my lady, but she ain't here. She's off to Oxfen to her sister today.'

'I came to look for work, my lady. I was told to ask for Mistress Johanna. I'm Isabel Plowman,' Isabel said nervously.

'So I see. Since our memorable visit to Norwich, I could hardly fail to recognise you. And you want work here?'

'Yes, my lady.'

'You entered Redesmarsh Abbey but were sent away. Although, perhaps not justly . . .' Lady Judith studied her thoughtfully. 'But I imagine that when the abbess accused you of disobedience, she had a certain amount of right on her side. You would not obey Sir Henry when he made most wise provision for you. A vow of obedience would come hard to the likes of you, I daresay. I thought you'd gone to your mother.'

'I did, my lady. I helped look after my grandmother. But now she has died and there's no place in that house for me.' She did not mention Tosti's dishonourable intentions. The disparaging eyes examining her from amid their folds of flesh belonged to a woman who would at once say that she must have encouraged him.

'And now you want employment,' said Lady Judith. 'Do you know kitchen work?'

'Yes, my lady.'

'This is the kitchen of a big house, not a villein's cooking fire.'

'I worked in the kitchen at the abbey, my lady.'

'Did you indeed! Maybe that was more than you bargained for,' said Lay Judith keenly. She had talked to Abbess Christiana on the way back from Norwich, Isabel remembered. Christiana had no doubt made some pithy comments on her latest novice's character.

'Well, I can't have you in the house without speaking to Sir Henry,' said Lady Judith. 'In fact, I'm not sure I want you anyway. Come with me. He's in the hall.'

'Sir *Henry*, my lady?' said Isabel, taken aback. When seeking work in a humble capacity in the kitchen, one did not expect to be interviewed by the lord in person.

'Yes,' said Lady Judith shortly. 'Come along.'

Lady Judith, though built like the destrier mare whose foal Sir Henry was now awaiting, could move rapidly. Isabel almost had to run to keep up with her as she surged out of the kitchen by way of the stone steps which descended into it in one corner. She led the way up into the first-floor hall, where they were greeted by the smell of wind-swirled hearth-smoke, and the sound of masculine voices from where Sir Henry, Father Benedict, Herbert Grosney and Bernard Reeve were sitting, not on the dais, but on settles round the central hearth.

'Ah, Judith, my dear.' Sir Henry rose as his wife came towards him.

Lady Judith paused. 'I did not know you had anyone with you but Bernard,' she said to her husband. 'I wanted to consult you on a minor domestic matter but it can wait if . . .'

'If it will only take a short time I'll settle it now.' Sir Henry believed in being accessible. 'What is it? And who's this?' Isabel, reluctantly, came out from behind Lady Judith. 'But this,' said Sir Henry, 'is Isabel Plowman. Caused all the Norwich business. Is it about her?'

'Yes. It appears that there's no place for her now at Northfield. She's asking for work here in our kitchens. We're short-handed since the ague took off three of our kitchen people, and it seems she knows the work as she did it in the abbey. But in view of her past history, I felt I should consult you.'

'Why?' said Sir Henry. 'The kitchen's your province, you know.'

'Because we need the extra help but I've doubts about the advisability of hiring *her*. I thought I should not do so without asking your opinion.' Lady Judith spoke of Isabel as though she were deaf. She did not seem to mean this as an intentional insult, but to regard it as natural. Isabel, gripped by an old rebellion which she must not show, clutched her bundle tighter and rose from a curtsy to stand as straight as possible.

Sir Henry considered her with no very friendly eye. 'You refused Ufi Pecher and ran off to the abbey, which you then set by the ears by getting the abbess arrested. Intentionally, in her opinion, I may say. As things turned out . . . but you didn't know how they'd turn out. My son accused the abbess of malice but it seemed to me that there was a fair amount of that in you. In my judgement,' said Sir Henry, 'the abbess was right when she called you a troublemaker. Father Benedict?'

'I fear that I'm obliged to agree, despite later events,' said the priest.

They were all, Father Benedict, Sir Henry and Lady Judith, looking at her with distaste. Only Master Grosney's face continued to wear its usual worried expression as he gazed at her in silence.

'Well, my lady,' Sir Henry said, talking past her to Lady Judith, 'I'd have accepted any decision you made about the kitchen; I've always said running the household is your province and I respect that. But since you've brought this to me, I'd say no, we don't want her. You're a villein of this manor again, now that you've left the abbey's service, Isabel, but you'd best contribute by serving someone else. Go and find someone on the three manors who'll hire you to cook or wash or look after the goats. I shan't arrange another marriage for you, by the way, although if you find a man I won't refuse consent. But I rather hope you don't,' said Sir Henry candidly. 'Children bred from you might be more trouble than they're worth. Now clear out.'

'But, sir . . .' She found herself reduced to pleading. 'I've no home to go to. That Tosti . . .' She stopped. They *would* blame her; she knew it without speaking.

'You have kinsfolk here and there. Go to them,' Sir Henry said.

It was another dismissal, another casting-out, as blighting as anything Christiana had done to her.

'The fact is,' said Lady Judith, 'That you've shown time and again, Isabel, that you don't know your place. There's no room in the world for people who don't know where they belong.'

Isabel shrank. She wanted to get away from their disapproving faces and accusing eyes but did not know how. She wanted to bolt out of the hall but she was still gripping her bundle and she could feel, through the material of the cloak that swathed it, the hard circle of the bronze medallion. According to the legend that went with it, she had freeborn ancestors and that meant dignity. She'd lost all her dignity in Bishop Roger's hall when she quavered out those nauseating words *I'm villein-born*. She had regained it a little when she thanked Abbess Christiana for dismissing her. If she now ran away, it would be lost once more.

She opened her mouth to bid them a polite good day instead and then realised that she couldn't get it out without a humiliating sob. She stood there, trying to force her mouth not to quiver. And then Master Grosney finally spoke.

'When Sister Julian and Sister Isabel, as she was then, came to tend Mistress Grosney, they did all they could for her,' he said. 'And when it was all over, they still wouldn't leave my house until all the linen was boiled and set to dry. There was linen for the whole house. We'd had nearly everyone down with the ague. You did a lot of work, very heavy work,' he said to Isabel, 'and did it well. I'm short-handed, too. Two maids I lost in the epidemic. I need someone to have charge of the linen. Now that my wife is gone, I have to think of these things myself. Would you come, if Sir Henry allows?'

'I'll allow,' said Sir Henry with a snort. 'As long as I don't have her here. I warn you, Herbert, you may be taking on a source of trouble but that's your affair.'

'Well?' said Grosney to Isabel. 'All found, feast-days off in the usual way, and there'll be a wage.'

'Unnecessary!' snapped Lady Judith. 'Villeins work for their keep.'

'But, Lady Judith, she isn't *my* villein.' Grosney's voice was mild, but firm. 'I pay a small wage to all who work for me and some of the others come from your villein families, too. It amounts to very little,' he said to Isabel, 'but you'll have a few pence to call your own.'

'I'd be glad to come, sir. Only . . .'

His face was so worried and he looked as though he really minded about her. Widowerhood must have changed him; he was different from the fastidious man who had been careful not to get too close to the humbler guests at Rohese's marriage feast. Isabel gripped her hand round the outline of the medallion once again and discovered that she owed it to the dignity she now knew was so precious, to meet consideration with consideration.

'I'll be very glad to come and I'll work my best. But I think, sir, that there is something I should tell you first.'

'And that is?' said Grosney. Father Benedict stirred sharply. 'No, Father,' said Grosney. 'Let her speak.'

Isabel looked at Grosney. 'Father Benedict thinks I called you and him into Mistress Grosney's room because I wanted to get the abbess arrested. In Norwich, I said that wasn't so. Well, it wasn't, not quite, because I didn't think she'd be arrested, exactly. But I hated her and I hoped she'd get into trouble. Yes, that *is* true and I'll say so now and say I'm sorry, though not that sorry because I still think she – Abbess Christiana – deserved it. If you'll still employ me now I've said that, I'll do my best to work well. That's all.'

'*Well!*' said Lady Judith, not knowing what to make of this. Sir Henry and Father Benedict looked too bemused to say anything at all.

But Herbert Grosney was nodding. 'Have you heard any news from the abbey since you came home, Isabel? Because I notice you don't mention it if so.'

'News from the abbey, sir? Why, no. I've been nursing my grandmother; she died a few days ago and she was buried yesterday. I've heard no news at all.'

'Then I think I should tell you.' said Herbert Grosney, 'That after Abbess Christiana returned to Redesmarsh, she was caught red-handed by her own confessor, in the act of performing a devilish ritual. She was carried back to Norwich again the following day. And this morning, we received word from Bishop Roger de Skerning that Christiana of Redesmarsh was hanged in Norwich yesterday.'

'Hanged? The abbess? Is that why the bell . . .?'

'Yes, it is!' said Sir Henry. He added, in a mutter 'Damned bell! It's like gloating.'

'It's a funeral bell, not a paean of joy,' said Father Benedict, with assertion. He had been proved right after all and had very nearly had an apology from the bishop. 'It's ringing not for a passing spirit but for a lost soul.'

'Hanged!' said Isabel, appalled. 'Abbess Christiana!'

Herbert nodded. 'But only hanged. There was an outcry for burning as would have been done in France but de Skerning objected and the secular authorities heeded him. But she is dead, convicted of murder by witchcraft and of laying a curse by the same means . . .'

'Who . . .?' blurted Isabel before she could stop herself from interrupting.

'Who did she curse? I don't know,' said Grosney. Father Benedict also shook his head. He did in fact know but saw no reason to give this tiresome girl any more importance. 'But,' said Grosney, 'when you called me and Father Benedict into my wife's room, Isabel, well, perhaps it was because you hated the abbess, but I would rather think that you knew by instinct that she was an evil woman and a witch and desired to see her brought to justice. At any rate, you are welcome to join my household. You will have a roof, and work and a chance to earn back the good name I fear you may have lost. You can come with me now.'

'I'll be happy, sir.'

Isabel made him her curtsy. Rising from it, she looked up into his lean, worn face, and into the worried eyes which now seemed to her more friendly than any she had seen, she thought, in months, and said to herself he wants comforting and looking after.

And with that, as though the floor had given way and precipitated her without warning into an unfamiliar room, where all the furnishings were strange and exotic, decorated with gold and silver leaf and glittering embroidery and perfumed with roses and sandalwood, Isabel Plowman, born Isabel of Northfield, fell in love.

PART II

Isabel of Northfield:
The Lure
1274–6

Gos regarded me with tolerant contempt. He had no doubts about who was the slave, the ridiculous and subservient one who stood and waited.

Chapter Seven

Accession of a Hero

King Henry the Third was dead, and it was difficult for anyone to believe it.

He had reigned, after all, for fifty-six years, a contradictory king with a drooping eyelid. He had performed no spectacular feats of valour; his attempts to win back English possessions in France had been calamitous and his grandiose effort to bag the Sicilian throne for his second son such a costly failure that his own throne shook. But he had loved his wife and he had been a conscientious father; he had created no scandal, left no trail of royal bastards. And he had been pious, taking Edward the Confessor as his personal saint, naming his eldest son Edward in his honour and, like the Confessor, rebuilding Westminster Abbey.

He had also known when religious enthusiasm had gone far enough. King Henry's piety had skidded to a halt with ears flat to its skull whenever his own power or that of the royal justices seemed threatened by the church. King Henry the Third, who had heard three Masses a day, had also kept the Inquisition out of England.

Henry had been sometimes naive, sometimes petulant; he had sometimes had to be taken in hand, or to task, by his barons, even to the point of warfare.

But when he died in 1272, the country which he had once run into debt had a currency which was the envy of Europe and the realm was so stable that Prince Edward, his heir, who was far away, crusading, felt free to amble home by easy stages, imperilling his neck by jousting at the court of Burgundy, settling a revolt in Gascony, England's last remaining continental fief, and finally sailing into Dover on 2 August 1274 in the certain knowledge that the Archbishop of Canterbury would be waiting to crown him in London in the presence of a loyal baronage, as he began, officially, the first new reign England had seen for over half a century.

It would be a strange new world. Few were left who could remember any monarch but Henry. His father King John belonged to legend now, to stories told by ancient dames like Mary of Northfield. A legend too was the crowning of the young Henry who, aged only nine, had had his coronation at Gloucester instead of Westminster and had a simple circlet from his mother's jewelbox placed on his head instead of the crown of the realm because that part of the royal regalia which was not under the mud of the Wash with the rest of the baggage lost on his ailing father's last journey, was in London, which was in the hands of the barons who had been rebelling against King John.

The rival claimant they were promoting was Louis of France, who had married King John's niece. John had been struggling round his country, relieving one hard-pressed castle after another when seized by the dysentery which killed him.

Far away in time though they were, those vanished days still had echoes. In that time, when even the mighty stronghold of Norwich had fallen to Louis' backers, Lincoln Castle had held out. The defence of Lincoln was a story for stirring songs and the drinking of toasts, for its hereditary castellan, whose bold spirit kept the defenders in heart till help arrived, was a woman. The valour of Nicola de la Hay would never be forgotten and girl-babies were still being baptised Nicola in her honour.

Sir Henry Rushley's father, Sir Reginald, held his land of the Earl of Norfolk but he had not been in Norwich Castle, having been one of the men sent by the Earl to represent Norfolk county at the young King's court. He had been one of the force under the mercenary leader Falk de Breaute, which went to Lincoln's aid.

The relief of Lincoln meant the end of the movement for Louis. And because Sir Reginald had stayed by his youthful ruler when, with Norwich Castle in enemy hands, he might well have thought his best interests and the secure tenure of his three Norfolk manors lay in making haste to support Louis, he had been valued by King Henry, had held offices at court, and so in turn, had his descendants.

Which was why his son, Sir Henry, and his grandson, Sir Simon, were in due course invited – or commanded – to attend the coronation of King Edward the First.

'I can't get out of this,' Sir Henry said unenthusiastically to his wife and son and daughter-in-law. 'I'll have to go. We'll have to go, that is.'

'But it will be a great occasion!' Lady Judith was already mentally planning a new wardrobe for herself and her demoiselles. She had two bolts of fine wool cloth put by and half a bolt of murrey silk and some unused fur trimming, though she would need to buy more white linen and ready-embroidered silk in a hurry. It would be a rush but every female pair of hands in the house could be co-opted, and the summer evenings were light. Thinking of her demoiselles brought something else to mind, too. 'Will Eglantine's husband be there? I'd like to hear news of her.'

'Or perhaps even see her. She might come too, unless of course she can't travel,' Lady Cecily said.

'The last we heard, there was still no child,' said Lady Judith.

'That's a pity.' Lady Cecily was sincere. She was sympathetic towards any woman whose middle did not thicken each year as her own did, although admittedly she was pleased that the news of the coronation had arrived just as she had completed a lying-in. Her three elder offspring, Reginald, Eleanor and Henry, were in the care of a nurse and her latest, Petronilla, was comfortably accommodated with a wet-nurse. She could set off to London with a free mind.

'Eglantine may attend. I wouldn't know,' Sir Henry was feeling harassed. He hadn't travelled beyond the three manors since he went to Norwich to see Eglantine off and to attend the inquiry into Abbess Christiana's activities, and he vividly remembered how exhausted he had been after that. The prospect of the journey to London made him miserable.

'We can go by water, Father,' Simon said. 'Our ships are all home.'

'By sheer good fortune!' said his father testily. 'I seem to remember buying them so that I could transport my household by sea but, since you took to hiring them out to merchants, they're hardly ever here.'

'It pays well,' said Simon calmly. 'One day we'll be able to afford to drain another stretch of the marsh between here and the sea and build a proper sea-harbour for deep-sea trading vessels and give ourselves some importance as a port. We can't get major shipping up the river, in spite of all my grandfather's improvements.'

'I'm satisfied with things as they are but there, you young men always have ideas,' said Sir Henry. 'I daresay the three manors will be unrecognisable before I've been in my grave a year.'

'You're a long way from your grave yet, Father.'

'Am I? I don't feel it sometimes.' Sir Henry groaned and stiffened his back against the settle on which he was relaxing after dinner. The least exertion these days made him ache all over. 'We shall certainly have to go by water, because if I went any other way, I don't think I'd get there. In future, Simon, please make sure that at least one ship is always available. For this journey, we'll need them all; I must take a respectable following. I'll want representatives of all the main free families on the three manors, and they'll bring servants. We shall be a crowd.'

'Herbert Grosney will be included, I suppose. A pity he hasn't married again,' said Lady Judith. 'He's a lonely man in my opinion. But it's no good mentioning re-marriage to him; he just changes the subject. He was too fond of Lucy for his own good.'

'Possibly.' Sir Henry was not especially interested in Master Grosney. 'Now . . . we can take sixteen horses and twenty people per ship . . .'

Lady Judith said: 'Cecily, I think I shall go myself to Lynn or Norwich to buy new dress materials. Would you like to attend me?'

As usual, Isabel woke at daybreak. It was summer, so the shutters of the upstairs chamber which she shared with the other women servants,

111

were not closed and the thick green window glass could let in the dawn. She lay still for a moment, savouring her excitement.

Today, they would finish packing all the sheets and garments which, over the last two weeks, had been so painstakingly washed and mended, and she, along with the rest of the fortunate few who had been chosen, would board a ship for London. She'd have to work when she got there, of course. Her duties in London would be the same as here: to wash and mend the household linen. She would have to cope with unfamiliar washing and drying arrangements in an unfamiliar place and stitch the repairs in any corner she could find which was sufficiently out of her employer's way and supplied with sufficient daylight.

But she'd be travelling, seeing London! When she went to Norwich, she'd been too frightened to enjoy it or even take it in. And best of all, she had been picked out as essential; Herbert Grosney did, after all, remember that she existed. There had been times during the last two years when she feared that he didn't, even though he saw her virtually every day.

Because she was under the same roof as Herbert Grosney and seeing him often, she had been, generally speaking, happy.

But it was a feverish sort of happiness, without fulfilment, like being permanently sharpset, mouth watering in expectation of a dinner which never materialised. Every time she came face to face with him and bobbed the obligatory curtsy, every time she saw him in the hall, his profile remote and absorbed, studying the tallies where the bushels of corn from his fields or the weight of the fleeces at shearing time were recorded, or reading for pleasure (something she had never seen anyone do before), she hoped that he would speak to her, notice her, look into her eyes and see the fire that burned for him within. Only, the hope had never been realised.

His face and voice had been kind when he offered to employ her. But having done so, he seemed to set her aside, as though she were a task completed, a book read through and closed. She had come to Normansland as a passenger in his boat, which was poled and rowed by two of his men. Grosney had asked if she were comfortable, nodded when she said she was, and thereafter sat gazing out over the marshes, lost in his own thoughts. On reaching the house that first day, he had handed her over to a middle-aged couple whom he said were Jenkyn his steward and Jenkyn's wife Anna, with the words, 'This is Isabel who has come to be our linen-maid. She's done the work here before so she knows her way about already, but show her where she can sleep and put her things.' With that, he walked off and apparently dismissed her from his mind. Jenkyn and Anna were new, a couple from Lynn, who at first knew nothing of Isabel's previous visit to the house or what had come of it and when informed by Aymer the cook (who had been laid out by the ague but had been among the lucky ones who recovered) could see nothing in the story to become excited about. 'So she's been a novice and it didn't work. Well, it doesn't always.' said Anna, and Jenkyn added, 'So the girl was frightened when she saw the poor lady was dying and called for the priest and Master Grosney. Don't see any need to go whispering about it as if it was some scandal. Turned out to be true anyhow that the abbess was a witch, didn't it? You'd do better to put your mind to your work instead of gossiping like a woman, Aymer Cook, and while I'm on the subject of your work, there was too much marjoram in the stew yesterday. The master asked me to speak to you.'

Jenkyn was a small man with rough grey hair. He was very proud of being a steward, spoke of Herbert Grosney in tones of hushed respect which would have made Sir Henry envious, wore long, formal gowns all the time unless obliged to ride, and walked with a measured, authoritative stride from the hip. Anna wore a clean wimple every week, had a flat back and large bust and a way of supervising the other servants by standing to watch them with hands folded at her middle and her square chin raised, which her underlings found very intimidating.

They had defended Isabel from gossip and she could not therefore dislike them, but they persistently stood between her and personal contact with Herbert Grosney. She daydreamed sometimes about further epidemics of the ague, in which they and Herbert Grosney alike would be stricken, and she would care for them all, Anna and Jenkyn with patronising efficiency, and Herbert with a tenderness which would win his heart and, after his recovery, his body, including his hand in marriage.

Unaware of her feelings about them, Anna and Jenkyn were pleasant enough towards her. She was competent. In Redesmarsh Abbey, she had helped to cook, wash and mend for one hundred and fifty nuns and the experience showed.

It was in fact needed, for Master Grosney, as he gradually grew away from his grief and became his old fastidious self again, was exceedingly pernickety. Before sitting down on a bench or settle, he would dust it with the palm of a dry, long-fingered hand, and Isabel had seen his mouth curl in pure revulsion at the sight of a mark on a shirt. Bedlinen was changed oftener in Master Grosney's house than in any other house she'd ever heard of, Anna said. Isabel achieved and maintained the necessary high standard.

Yet although she was sure that Master Grosney had never in his life had shirts so clean and carefully mended, or sheets so tenderly boiled and dried and smoothed, he seemed to take it all for granted. Isabel was still just another maidservant, who slept on a pallet in a room with Marian and Nell the serving girls and the elderly widow Mald who wove cloth and mended the hangings and fifteen-year-old Tilda who swept the house and put the rushes on the floor.

The wide pallet which she shared with Marian and Nell was against the wall which divided the room from the one where Herbert Grosney lay alone in a great curtained bed, with his manservant Rob in a truckle bed beside it. Sometimes, through the wall, she would hear Grosney speak to Rob, or hear his curtain rings rattle. The great bed, like her pallet, was close to the wall; the spare body and careworn face she loved, the long-fingered hands she longed to feel on her own skin, were only three feet away.

He was a sweetness she could feel through the timber of the wall. He was unattainable. He was heaven and by not noticing her, he condemned her to live in hell.

But now, this very day, things might change. Isabel pushed off her rugs and reached for her shift. Around her, the other women too were waking up, yawning. Mald was poking Tilda who was always the last to stir; Marian had her head in her hands and was shaking it from side to side to get the sleep out of her brain; Nell had got straight to her feet and reached for the ewer of water which the last to bed brought to the chamber each night, ready to be poured into a basin for laving hands and faces in the morning.

They must all hurry, even those who were not travelling. Every last item must be packed ready for departure the moment Mass and breakfast were done. They would then board small boats and go down to Rushley to embark on Sir Henry's vessel *Archangel*. Today she, Isabel, would be on a ship with Herbert Grosney.

She would still be under the orders of Jenkyn, who was coming too (though Anna was not), but she wouldn't have to wash linen on board ship or drag carefully packed garments out of their chests to mend them. For hours together, her employer would never be more than fifty feet way from her and, if she had anything to do with it, would usually be much closer. She would not have to engineer meetings on the stairs or in doorways and she would not be tied down by tasks. She would be waiting for her chance. Somehow or other, before they came home again from London, she would make him notice her.

The *Archangel* was not large but she was well-designed, and seemed more spacious than she really was. Her great square sail could make use of a cross-breeze as well as a following wind; she could carry horses in her hold and she had a deck with a small deckhouse fore and aft. The deckhouses were shaped like little castle towers, complete with crenellations but their purpose was to shelter the important passengers from the weather.

To her annoyance, Isabel discovered, soon after they were aboard, that these included Rohese Grosney, looking more elegant than ever, and her husband Gerald. To her even greater annoyance, Herbert Grosney immediately retired into one of the deckhouses with them and remained in their company throughout.

Her disappointment, however, was swiftly overtaken by a more pressing sensation. Even if Herbert Grosney had been outside on the deck, within her reach, she would not have been for long in any state to bid for his attention. As soon as they were out of the river and on the sea, she was overtaken by seasickness, which lasted most of the way to London.

King Edward landed on the 2nd of August and was crowned on the 19th but the notice wasn't as short as it sounded; he had sent his messengers ahead. There was time for lords and knights, even from the most outlying parts of the realm, to hear of his arrival and get to London to see him crowned. In addition, he brought with him his own immense train of the men who had been with him on crusade and a whole additional court collected in Sicily, Paris and Gascony.

As a result, London was jammed to the last corner and the ultimate garret and so many tents were pitched outside the city walls that the place looked as though it were under siege, except that it was rare for fat sheep and cattle to be driven unhindered into besieged cities, and ships and mule trains and bullock carts laden with flour and fruit, spices and wine, poultry coops and rabbit hutches and pig pens, would also have been ruthlessly excluded.

As things were, the gates stood wide, the guards were jovial, banners waved, church bells pealed and trumpets blared and the butchers and vintners and stallkeepers whistled cheerful tunes as the coins rolled in. The sellers of foodstuffs weren't the only happy people, either. Purveyors of cloth, be it wool or fustian or silk; sellers of gold and silver thread, white linen, needles, gloves, ready-made cloaks and fur trimmings and jewellery were doing the trade of a lifetime too.

And so were the innkeepers. Earl Roger Bigod of Norfolk, who had flung the hall of his London house open to as many of his lords and their households and friends as could wedge themselves in, remarked out loud that he must be mad not to charge them for the privilege.

Sir Henry had taken advantage of his earl's hospitality and on the strength of having married Sir Henry's ward Eglantine and brought her with him to London, so had Sir Hugh le Hale, up from his Welsh castle of Cwmanog for the occasion. Roger Bigod's house also had the advantage of being beside the river, which meant that getting to Westminster and the scene of the coronation was considerably eased.

The house however had only three bedchambers and these were already full of Earl Bigod and his family and his more exalted guests. The de Montalts of Castle Rising qualified, but Sir Henry Rushley, lord of only three modestly sized Norfolk manors, and Sir Hugh, the castellan of a small Welsh castle did not. For them and theirs, it was a matter of sleeping wherever they could find space. Most people had their own bedrolls and the house was well supplied with spare straw pallets. Hall and solar were turned into dormitories, with the sexes roughly segregated, although there was a certain amount of midnight prowling as husbands and wives and the partners in a few other, less legal arrangements became seized with the desire for each other's company. Daybreak usually found a percentage of abandoned rugs and other contentedly sleeping heaps which had acquired two heads in the night.

Sir Hugh le Hale and Gerald Grosney, however, did not seek out their spouses, and the spouses in question, although they were both beautiful, knew that they would not be particularly welcome if they sought their husbands out instead.

Neither Rohese nor Eglantine, however, would have dreamed of saying so. Both had decided long ago that neglect was best ignored if one was to maintain one's dignity in the face of it. Instead of gazing wistfully after their husbands, they chose, since they were on adjacent pallets, to introduce themselves to each other. Rohese realised at once who Eglantine was, and realised too, with delight, that Eglantine, who had never when she lived at Rushley taken any interest in the village, had no idea of Rohese's origins. It was hard work, sometimes, maintaining the appearance of a lady when among women who knew where she had been born. Eglantines were rare in Rohese's life and, when they did appear, were very very welcome.

She wasn't likely to give her origins away herself. She had worked hard on her accent and now no one could tell anything more from her speech than the fact that she came from the east of England. But she hoped that no one would blurt out the truth in Eglantine's hearing. She was horrified, when she woke on the first morning under Earl Roger's roof, to see Isabel of Northfield staring at her from a pallet six feet away.

Even when they were children, she had never really liked Isabel, with her thin taut body and her hungry dark eyes. Isabel, Rohese thought, always looked at you as though she wanted to rob you, or eat you. She decided to pretend that she hadn't recognised her. She turned away her head.

In the course of the day, when she glimpsed Isabel hurrying about with a pile of linen, and noticed the redness of her hands and arms, she knew she had been wise. Isabel, clearly, was someone's linen-maid. She certainly wasn't the sort of person a friend of Lady Eglantine would be expected to know.

'It is quite amusing, isn't it,' she said to Eglantine as they prepared for the second night, 'to travel about and mix with all manner of people? Although one has to be careful. There are always some presumptuous people about.'

'There's always a risk of infection, in such gatherings,' Eglantine said. 'It's as well to be careful. One should safeguard one's health, and one's looks.'

Rohese's maid Goda had brushed her mistress's fair hair a few minutes ago, and Rohese was complacently aware of its gilded-silver flowing down her back. She regarded Eglantine's beechnut brown braids with admiration, however. Eglantine's hair was longer and thicker than her own, and her complexion even better. Rohese had been shocked, that morning, to discover a pimple on her own forehead. It was a rare event but she would have preferred it never to happen at all.

'Tell me something,' she said to Eglantine. 'Do you use anything for your complexion?'

'Crushed strawberries when they're in season,' said Eglantine. 'The rest of the time, oatmeal and milk. I'm lucky; I don't really need it. But it makes me feel as though I'm taking trouble.' They settled themselves under the rugs, Rohese with her back carefully turned towards Isabel. Eglantine lowered her voice. 'Rohese. You said yesterday that you had no children. How long have you been married?'

'Three years now.'

'I've been married for two. I've never had a sign of a child, either. Does your husband mind?'

'He is always courteous. I'm very fortunate,' said Rohese carefully. 'But he minds, of course.'

If there were a child in the care of a nurse back at Redesmarsh, she would be able now to go to Gerald's pallet, or else he would be finding his way to hers. But everything they had once had, the warmth and desire between them, the way he had once protected her and given her presents, had begun to fade six months after their marriage, Gerald growing a little more distant after each month's disappointment.

'But what hope is there of anything ever being different, if you never come to me any more?' she had said to him once. But he hadn't answered, just gone on washing a muddy greyhound and, after a few minutes, asked her to pass him a towel, as though she had never spoken at all.

'They always mind,' said Eglantine, still quietly, but with suppressed violence. 'However kind they are; however much love they promise at the start. And no one, no one knows how to put it right. There are wise women in Wales, clever women. I've consulted three of them. They've given me things to take at this phase of the moon or that, and I've prayed; oh God, how I've prayed. I've lit enough candles to illuminate a palace. It makes no difference. Nothing happens, nothing. And Hugh is just going further and further away from me. He wasn't like that at first; we were merry then, always laughing together. But now . . . you've not found anything that might help, have you? I mean, I know you've no children, but perhaps there's something you've just begun to try, some potion or other, that I could try as well?'

Rohese shook her head, startled and somewhat embarrassed because even if Eglantine didn't know of the difference between them, Rohese did, and secretly regarded her new acquaintance as a higher form of life. She hardly knew what to do with these confidences.

'It's why I take trouble with my skin,' Eglantine said. 'I feel I must try to be sure I please him in every way I can, to make up for the way

I can't. Oh, you're wondering why I'm telling you all this, when I hardly know you. But that's just it. We probably won't meet again after we leave here. With people you know well, you have to pretend all the time, or else they pity you and you can see them doing it.'

'Yes,' said Rohese. 'Yes, I know.'

Eglantine stretched out a hand. Rohese's hand came out to meet it and for a moment they clasped each other in mutual fellow-feeling and the giving and receiving of consolation.

To slacken the tension of emotion, and to stop herself from bursting into tears over her own loneliness, Rohese whispered brightly, 'You said you came from Wales. Is it a Welsh accent that your maid has? What is Wales like? I've travelled, of course; we even went to a tournament in Paris last year and we saw the King there. But I've never journeyed to Wales.'

'Mountains,' said Eglantine. 'With their peaks lost in cloud, half the time. Steep dark valleys, rushing rivers, people who have their own language and their own ways. Most of them hate us. Oh, not Bronwen – that's my maid – and yes, she has a Welsh lilt. Bronwen is a good girl. She has been in my mother-in-law's household since she was a baby. And my husband's squire, Geraint, is trustworthy. But for the most part,' said Eglantine candidly, 'I loathe Wales and I loathe the Welsh.'

'Oh. I'm sorry,' said Rohese inadequately.

'There's nothing to be done. But thank you for being sorry,' said Eglantine. 'I think we share some of our sorrows, Rohese. I wish you a happy delivery, in both senses of the word, from yours. Good night.'

She turned over and closed her eyes. Rohese watched her for a moment and then turned over as well, to find herself gazing through the summer dusk, once more straight into the eyes of Isabel.

Judging by her expression, Isabel had not overheard their low-voiced conversation. She had only seen a girl who was once no more than she was herself, talking intimately with a knight's wife, who had once been among Lady Judith's demoiselles. And her face was fierce with jealousy.

The maids had moved away and were in talk together while they folded their mistresses' clothes. Eglantine seemed to be going to sleep. There was a bedroll between Rohese and Isabel but its owner had not yet claimed it. Rohese raised herself, leant across it, and addressed Isabel in a whisper.

'Were you listening? Not that it matters. One word from you about where I come from, just one word and I'll say you stole my purse. I'll see it's found among your things. I'll be believed and you won't.'

'Don't worry. I shan't spoil your games,' Isabel whispered back, with equal aggression. 'Mistress high and mighty,' she added viciously.

Rohese threw herself over and lay once more with her back to Isabel and her face towards Eglantine. During the night, there were, once more, stealthy comings and goings among the pallets. She pulled her rugs over her ears and tried not to listen.

In the morning, both she and Eglantine dressed in their finest clothes, with silver crispines for their hair, and smiled at each other, commiserating, because they were alike and knew it. They were like shining, empty shells, from which the heart and the substance were gone.

That Isabel should be so patently jealous of her was, Rohese thought, very nearly comical.

Earl Roger was in the abbey for the crowning of King Edward but the Rushley family and Sir Hugh le Hale and his lady were not. They did, however, have front row places along the silk-canopied and carpeted path that led from the palace of Westminster to the abbey, along which King Edward and Queen Eleanor would walk. The Grosneys, Gerald, Rohese and Herbert, were just behind them, able to see over their shoulders as the royal pair came past.

Isabel was right at the back, squashed against the wall of a house and wedged between Rohese's maid Goda (who hadn't recognised her, which would no doubt be a relief to Rohese) on one side and Eglantine's maid Bronwen on the other. Sir Hugh's squire Geraint was on the other side of Bronwen, grasping her elbow as though afraid she would run away, as if anyone could run anywhere in such a crowd. Isabel had already gathered that Geraint was sweet on Bronwen and regarded London, with its hordes of well-dressed men, as a hotbed of seducers. Bronwen, highly amused by her swain's anxieties, had said as much.

Geraint had black hair and wild dark eyebrows which began low over his nose and thereafter swooped up and out like the flightpath of a falcon. Isabel thought he looked handsome but unpredictable. Herbert Grosney was still her choice, with his worry lines and his civilised air.

Hemmed in as she was and without even the benefit of height, Isabel's view was limited to the bulk of the abbey rising to her right, a glimpse of pennants waving from the tops of the innumerable marquees which had sprouted wherever there was space – no one had been able to tell her what they were for – the heads of the people in front and, beyond them, the scarlet of the silk canopy with its trimming of yellow silk fringes and small silver bells.

But she could not catch even a glimpse of the procession except for the glittering tips of upraised ceremonial spears and only knew when the royal pair were approaching by the surge of cheers that accompanied them, quivering the yellow fringes and tinkling the bells.

Geraint's voice broke in on her. 'Here, you girls, don't you want to see, indeed? Bronwen I can hoist up but not the three of you, but there's a coping on that wall at your backs, look you; get one foot each on there and hold on to the sill above and you can get enough inches. Come on and try!'

She turned round, put a foot on the coping in question, caught hold of the sill as bidden and hoisted herself up.

And so, for the only time in her life, she saw King Edward and Queen Eleanor in the flesh.

Everyone had kept on calling them the new young King and Queen. Edward was a hero of the crusade and the tournament, Eleanor the angelic partner who had gone to the Holy Land with him and borne him a daughter in Acre, and sucked the poison out of the wound when an assassin attacked him with a poisoned dagger.

In fact, they were not so very young, either of them. Eleanor was nearly thirty and Edward thirty-five. The Queen, for all the magnificence of her coronation clothes, had lost her waistline through having children and, while she was away in the Holy Land, two of the children she had left behind had died. Above her dumpy body, her small face with its straight nose and carefully plucked eyebrows and sad dark eyes with the pouches beginning under them, was touching but not beautiful.

But thirty-five or not, Edward, who paced beside her holding her hand aloft, was unquestionably superb. For a moment, Isabel forgot even Herbert Grosney in admiring that tall, strong figure whose powerful shoulders had no need to cock forward against the drag of the heavy purple coronation cloak, and whose sword lesser men could scarcely lift.

'See him?' Geraint shouted up to her and Goda. He was standing on tiptoe, and had heaved Bronwen on to his shoulder, where she sat giggling and clutching at his hair.

An elderly man in the crowd twisted round and grinned at them. 'Something worth seeing, eh? Ah, there'll be some fine doings now that young cockerel's on the throne. There'll be all the chances you young men want for winning your spurs under that one. He'll be leading us to war and victory before we know where we are. There are new times coming.'

'He's not *my* King,' Geraint remarked, though good-humouredly. 'I'm Welsh.'

'Thought I heard you talking funny. Well, well, your Prince Llewellyn'll have to watch his step, with that one on our throne. Hah, I wish I were twenty years younger!'

Geraint lifted Bronwen down. 'And I should watch your tongue, old man. Others besides you have a pride in their princes'

'Now, give over,' scolded Bronwen, hitting him in the ribs with a reproving elbow. 'And you the squire to Sir Hugh, indeed, and him so proud of you. This is a holiday and we're all here for rejoicing, or that's what I thought.' Geraint continued to eye the old man with disapproval, but Bronwen elbowed his ribs again and said something in Welsh, which made him laugh.

Isabel looked at them, engrossed in each other, and thought of the dumpy, grave-faced woman whose hand that splendid King held up so proudly, and of Herbert Grosney who would rather look at his wife in memory than look at Isabel of Northfield at all, and of Alfred whom she had never appreciated while she had him. Even in the days when she had wept for both Alfred and their baby, she had not known so deep a despair.

Coming up the Thames, on the last leg of the journey from Norfolk, Isabel's seasickness had subsided but the pounding headache which went with it had lingered until well after they were under Roger Bigod's roof and she had at first looked on London as distractedly as she had looked at Norwich.

Vaguely, she observed that the ship was gliding past walls and warehouses. She saw overpowering battlements and someone said that that was the great Tower. The galleys of Mediterranean merchants manoeuvred in the river, and her nose twitched to curious smells drifting from the shore: exotic spices mingled with the stink of a tannery; charcoal smoke and cooking; animals smells and boiling glue.

She caught sight of narrow lanes, crowds and confusion, and recalled dimly that Norwich had been similar in this respect, although there seemed to be much more of London. But, through the hammering of her head, none of it seemed important.

It wasn't until the day after the coronation, when she went out in the morning with Bronwen, Geraint acting as escort, to look round a nearby market, that the size of the place and its atmosphere, which was heady with excitement as well as with peculiar smells, suddenly reached her.

She had an errand. 'While we're in London, the master says to buy some fresh linen for the household. Get a couple of bolts,' Jenkyn told her. 'The stallholders'll deliver if you buy enough. Here's some money, and here's some extra for buying gewgaws with. The master's giving us all some silver to spend; this is yours.'

She was still in the grip of the depression which had fallen on her the day before. She hated Jenkyn for being there, like a buffer between herself and Herbert Grosney, for passing his master's message to her when she longed to receive messages from Grosney's own mouth and tips from Grosney's own hands, and for a miserable moment she almost hated Grosney for his impersonal generosity.

In a voice on the edge of impertinence, she said, 'Where's Master Grosney today then? I've not seen hide nor hair of him. He wasn't even at Mass in the chapel.'

'Not surprising, is it?' said Jenkyn, unconcerned. 'He was at the coronation feast yesterday. Great big banquet it was, spread out through all those marquees we saw. All the great folk in London and some of the not-so-great. Our master's still in his bed, whimpering about a posset to relieve his head and saying something must have disagreed with him. Too much strong red wine, more like! Didn't you hear the racket when they all came back yesterday evening? Now you be off, but don't be late back. There's a reason.'

She forgave Herbert Grosney at once. She would have liked to minister to him, to put wet cloths on his head and hold a comforting posset to his lips but she certainly wouldn't be allowed to do either, so she might as well go out as bidden.

So, with Bronwen and Geraint, she set off into the streets of London.

In Norwich, she had not merely failed to notice detail, but had actually been insulated from it, for she had gone everywhere with an escort, and only in main thoroughfares, just glimpsing the alleys from a distance. Now, in London, she entered such alleys for the first time. The overhang of the upper storeys, which almost shut out the sky, the washing lines strung across, the garbage underfoot, the jostling and the smell, came as a shock.

Within the first ten minutes, Geraint had been splashed by the contents of a chamber pot being emptied out of a window, and outraged because when he shook his fist at the woman responsible, she only laughed; and Bronwen had clouted a grinning urchin who, she said, was certainly hoping to pick her pocket.

The noise was incredible, too. Stallholders bawled the virtues of the wares displayed under the awnings on their portable stalls or in front of their workshops; stray dogs fought, snarling, over scraps thrown from a pie-stall; the horses of knights and merchants clattered by, shoving people haphazardly out of their way; church bells seemed to be constantly ringing.

The crowd was a varied selection of humanity. The three of them pushed their way amid housewives, apprentices, a group of young bloods, an archer with a girl on his arm, a couple of grey-clad figures which Isabel recognised as Franciscan friars like those she had sometimes seen preaching in the street at Redesmarsh Fair. And then, just as Bronwen exclaimed, 'Look!' and began to steer them all towards a cluster of people round a dancing bear and its handler, she felt sunshine on her back and, ahead, saw it glittering on a segment of river visible at the far end of a narrow alley; and the sights and sounds and smells, startling her senses from every side, suddenly began to sparkle in her blood. Depression dissolved, lost like a handful of salt in a river and she was seized by its very opposite, a wild, ecstatic joy.

The world was glorious after all. She was young, wasn't she? She was only nineteen! She had years ahead and anything could happen. Her body was strong and her will powerful; she would *make* things happen! She would make Grosney look at her yet!

Impulsively she caught Bronwen's arm. 'Isn't it wonderful? What a place London is! I've never seen it before; have you?'

'Yes. I came when Sir Hugh sent his brother to fetch my mistress. We rode all across England to London and then on to Norwich. Yes, indeed, it's exciting. But I like my mountains better. If you think

122

London's wonderful, you should see the mountains!' said Bronwen enthusiastically. 'Wild and mysterious, they are! Armies can hide in them and swoop down on an enemy out of the mist and be there before the sentries can open their mouths to shout. My mountains are like living things. They have moods like people. They smile in the sun and frown under cloud, and oh how they can beckon. Our bards put the sound of their waterfalls into their harp music!'

Rohese would hardly have recognised this description of the Welsh mountains. Isabel responded to it at once. 'Oh, how I'd like to see!'

Bronwen laughed, showing good white teeth in her sun-browned face. Her eyes were as dark as Isabel's and deeper-set and she had a sharp nose which gave her face a look of decision. 'We never know what the future'll bring although there's some will read your palm and make pretence to tell you.'

'I'd like to see everywhere and everything. I'd like to see the Holy Land and watch a tournament and . . .'

'Hold the moon in your hand? Well, I said, who knows?'

'*You* know,' said Isabel, surprising both of them. 'I mean, you know what your future's going to be. You'll marry Geraint and live in Wales among your mountains and maybe you'll travel to other places sometimes and maybe not but either way you won't mind. You're . . . you're *satisfied* with who you are and where you're going.'

'Of course I am. Why shouldn't I be? There's funny you are,' said Bronwen cheerfully. 'Here we are at the front, where we can see the bear . . .' Suddenly, her smile faded and she turned her head to look at Isabel. 'I forgot. Stupid, I am. Goda said you were crying last night. I won't pry, but if you're unhappy about something, I'm sorry.'

'What? Did Goda hear me?' She had indeed cried in the night but now, this morning, she didn't want to be reminded of it. She wanted to keep this new mood of gaiety and hope. 'Oh, I hope I didn't disturb her. I wasn't feeling well, that's all. I'm all right now.'

'That's good,' said Bronwen. 'Because there's a lot of nice things still to come. Oh, the show's over. They're moving off. Where's Geraint?'

'I don't know. He was here a moment ago!'

'Here I am,' said Geraint, emerging from a press of people. In his hands, skilfully balanced, was a stack of sweet smelling pasties. 'Apple, raisins and chopped lamb, the man said. I thought this would keep us going. But they're not too big or heavy because we'll want our appetites later on, indeed we will.'

'Will we?' said Isabel. 'Why?'

'Aha!' said Geraint, and caught Bronwen's eye and grinned.

In the afternoon, she found out the answer to her question. Jenkyn was waiting when they returned to Earl Roger's hall. 'You have ordered the linen?'

'Yes, two bolts of fine white. It should arrive soon.'

She had also bought a length of red ribbon with silver embroidery. She would make a trimming with it for her best dress; it could go round cuffs and hem. Perhaps she might find time to put it on today. It would make the dress quite striking.

'You'd better change. Put on your best things whatever they are. The boat'll leave in an hour.'

'Boat? Where to?'

Jenkyn laughed. 'You'll see.'

She managed to stitch the trimming on to her dress just in time. Presently she found herself in a boat containing herself and Goda, Bronwen and Geraint and a number of people like them, servants of Earl Roger and his guests. There were some other Welsh folk along with Bronwen and Geraint and, for some reason, they had brought on board a number of mysterious bundles done up in cloth and a small oak chest. The Welsh talked together in their own tongue and seemed to be chortling at some secret joke of their own. Clearly, they all knew where the boat was going.

They went upstream, as they had done yesterday when they set out at dawn to take their places for the coronation procession. They tied up at a stage near the main Westminster landing and on the shore they found a path defined by a temporary fence of rope, with banners on tall poles here and there, and some official-looking persons, who said 'Good day and welcome!' and shepherded them along the path towards the marquees which had puzzled Isabel the day before. Presently, she found herself inside one of them.

The marquee was full of the smell of the trodden, brown grass underfoot, and sun-heated canvas and food. It was set with tables and benches, and they were invited to sit.

When every place was full and the ushers outside could be heard directing arrivals to another marquee, a trumpet sounded and a very dignified individual in a long gown and gold chain stood up to announce that it was the pleasure of the King's grace, for this day and fourteen days henceforth, that dinner would be served in the marquees to all comers, high and low, even the poorest, at the King's expense. 'God save King Edward. So fall to with a good appetite, one and all!'

Bronwen, Geraint and the rest of the Welsh had disappeared. Isabel had slid on to a bench beside a boy she didn't know, who was dressed in a kitchen hand's leather jerkin. On her other side was a girl she didn't know either. Goda was opposite. She was carefully dressed in what was probably one of Rohese's cast-offs and looked just a little prim.

The marquee was garlanded inside with roses and broom flowers which were wilting in the heat, which was considerable, as the sun beat down and the people crammed together at the tables gave off their own concentrated body heat. They also gave off noise: talking, laughing, scraping benches, shouting, whistling.

Some of the arrangements looked as though they had been put together in haste. The sauce-dishes and bowls and spoons and the enormous tureens on the long trestles were a mixture of turned wood, pewter and earthenware in a wild variety of colours and shapes, as if the store-rooms of every house in London and Westminster had been plundered and every tableware vendor bought up.

But there was nothing makeshift about the food and drink. London and Westminster, Isabel soon concluded, must be full of exhausted butchers, overworked cooks and empty cellars.

Ale and wine were brought in great flagons and dumped on the tables by the royal-liveried servers. Then a stew was ladled from the monster tureens into individual bowls and turned out to be rich with peas, beans, onions and chewy lumps of meat, all in a thick gravy flavoured to sting humble palates on to new high levels of awareness.

Dishes of fish followed, whole mackerel and herring, and gigantic codfish chopped into segments and set along the centres of the tables for the guests to help themselves. Rounds of bread were issued to act as absorbent plates. All this was presently followed by more bread and large pasties.

The bread was white, an amazing luxury, and if the ale was ordinary enough, the wine was good quality, and red. Isabel ignored the ale and imbibed the wine joyfully, incurring a shake of the head from Goda, who leant across the table to remark, 'A woman shouldn't drink so deep. Mistress Rohese was quite sober when she came in last night from the great banquet. Her husband weren't but she was.'

'Oh get on with you. We'll never have another chance like this,' said Isabel and wished she hadn't mislaid Bronwen, who was better company. The Welsh, she supposed, had been directed to another marquee.

The trumpets shouted again, bringing down the noise level. One of the Welsh appeared, a young man whom Isabel remembered seeing on the boat. Geraint had called him Owen. He was very like Geraint to look at; stockier in build but with the same flyaway eyebrows and the same dark hair and eyes. He strolled into the marquee, dressed in green and yellow, a hat with a turned-up brim cocked sideways on his black head, and a small harp in his hands. He ran his fingers over the harpstrings and began to sing to the rippling music. The silence was anything but complete, but his voice was strong and as he sauntered among the tables, he got a fair hearing.

He sang a romantic song about Queen Eleanor and how she had saved her husband from the assassin's poisoned dagger in the Holy Land, and a warlike song about King Edward's feats on crusade. There hadn't actually been many but the verses made the best of a truce which guaranteed the Christians of Jerusalem the right to go on pilgrimage to Nazareth. The young bard then followed this with a very slightly less than respectful but gloriously funny song about King Edward's feats in tournaments on his way home, for which he had been rebuked

125

by the Pope, who said that royalty shouldn't endanger its life for fun.

After three songs, he bowed, swept off his hat and passed it for largesse, and then departed presumably to amuse the diners in another marquee but the entertainment wasn't over, for there was another fanfare of trumpets and a small horse pranced into the tent.

The head was so realistic that at first sight it looked like a genuine horse and only after a moment or two did it become clear that its eyes were deep hollows, its coat was made of painted cloth and its hocks bent the wrong way. When this became evident, there were cheers and laughter and the horse stopped, tilting its head comically as though it were shy. Then it tried to perform a sort of bow, crossed its front feet awkwardly and fell over. When it got up again, it began, with all four legs wildly unco-ordinated, to dance.

It was hilarious. When its front legs wanted to go one way, its back legs wanted to go the other. When the front legs broke into a high-stepping trot, the rear end slithered to its knees as though it had been taken by surprise. It turned its head and gazed wonderingly at its uncooperative back legs. It tried to perform a full *passage* sideways along one of the aisles, crossing its feet from right to left, and tripped itself up again. An indignant argument, between a man's and a woman's voices, was heard to begin inside it.

Isabel, laughing helplessly, was obliged for the second time to clamber over the bench and retreat to the buckets thoughtfully provided outside the marquee. When she came back, the horse was cavorting close to her place and as she put a foot over the bench to climb back, it became evident that the view through the eyesockets was somewhat restricted. The horse tripped over the foot she had not yet lifted over the bench, and fell over again amid more roars of laughter.

But it had some difficulty in getting up and from its stomach, a female voice exclaimed, 'There's my ankle twisted now!'

The word *ankle* was preceded by a rich and, to an English tongue, unpronounceable adjective, and the voice, to Isabel, was familiar.

'Bronwen!'

'Hello,' said Bronwen. The horse's flank convulsed and Bronwen's face, rather red, poked through its belly. 'Is that you, Isabel, and was that your foot that I have fallen over? Why must you leave your feet about so carelessly? My ankle is hurt, I tell you. And I'm hot enough to die and starving hungry and we can't eat till we've done another two marquees and why we ever agreed to give this show I don't know. Sir Hugh asked us. We should have said no.'

'Who's that in front?'

'Geraint,' said the horse's head hollowly. 'Bronwen, what's in it with you? Can't you get up?'

Bronwen's head vanished. The diners had begun to lose interest and the babble was increasing again. The horse heaved once more and stood up but on only three legs. One hindleg, after a single attempt to stand firm, was raised hastily off the ground. 'I have done my ankle right in, I tell you,' said Bronwen's muffled voice from inside.

The wine had made Isabel reckless. 'Is it difficult, what you're doing? Did you practise much beforehand or could Geraint manage with a stranger if he just calls out what to do?'

'Easy enough but who'll volunteer to be the hind legs?' said Geraint. 'We've a couple more teams but they're being horses in the marquees we're not doing.'

'If you can get out of that horse and let me in,' said Isabel, '*I'll* be the hindlegs.'

'All right,' said Bronwen, before Geraint could answer, 'unhook me, then.'

There were hooks and loops all along the horse's belly. Bronwen had peered between two of the fastenings. Isabel helped her to get free. 'You can have my place and my piece of pie.'

'You won't enjoy it,' Bronwen warned her, hopping gingerly to the bench to take Isabel's seat. 'It's as hot as hell in there. Oooh! Thank God to sit down and not be bent in half like a fish-hook any more. Oh, my poor ankle. Purple it'll be by tomorrow and all the places where I hit the floor. We do this at home sometimes but we do it gentler. You'll regret this, I tell you.'

'I'll do it for a friend,' said Isabel blithely, all the more so because Goda was eyeing her with considerable disapproval. Goda had clearly been affected by the airs and graces of her mistress Rohese.

'I hope we'll get by,' said the head and forelegs grumblingly. 'I'll have to mutter to you to fall down or cross your legs or this and that. Then afterwards when I shout that you've done it wrong, you just answer back any way you like.'

'Shout the instructions too! Then when I get them wrong, everyone'll think they're part of the show as well. They'll laugh till they burst,' said Isabel.

What seemed like a very long time afterwards, Bronwen helped her out of the horse again. Isabel was tousled, sweating, and so hot that she was dizzy. Her back ached from being bent double so long and she was bruised all over from falls which had connected with table corners nearly as often as with the floor. Her mouth was so dry that, as she shook down the skirts she had bundled round her waist in order to get into the horse's legs, the only speech she could manage was a single croaked word, 'Wine!' Merriment and applause were echoing in her head and she had never been so happy in her life.

Bronwen handed goblets to Isabel and Geraint, who extricated himself from the other end of the horse, remarking that he was husky with shouting instructions, but that it had worked, they had made people laugh. 'When we do our horse at home, Bronwen,' he added eagerly, 'we'll try it this way, with the front end calling orders to the back end all the time, see, so that when the back end gets it muddled, it's funnier. Isabel here could make a living at this sort of thing, indeed.'

Smiling, Bronwen made room for both of them on the bench. 'Come and eat, Geraint. What is in these pasties, Isabel? Marvellous, they are.'

'It was rabbit,' Isabel said. 'I've had it before.'

'Rabbit?'

'Little animals rather like hares, but they're bred in hutches. They come from the south somewhere.'

'They taste like magic,' said Bronwen fervently.

The whole day, to Isabel, had tasted like magic. She went home in the boat with the Welsh, counting as one of them, sitting beside Bronwen on the chest which contained the cloths and head for the horse, giggling, exchanging toasts in the wine which someone had brought aboard, enjoying the horrified expression on the face of Goda, who had withdrawn to the other end of the boat, as though a talent for being the back end of a horse were a disease one might actually catch.

As Isabel, with Bronwen and Geraint, stepped chattering into Earl Roger's hall, they came face to face with Herbert Grosney, strolling out of it with Gerald and Rohese.

'So they have enjoyed their dinner as the guests of the king,' said Herbert. 'Look at them; they're as merry as jesters. All you ladies will have to brush your own hair tonight, Mistress Rohese.'

'I am perfectly sober,' said Bronwen indignantly and inaccurately. 'But it has been a grand day and a grand dinner and what the King is spending, if this is going on for a fortnight, I don't dare imagine. There won't be a bite to eat left in southern England and you will all be invading Wales, looking for food, next!'

'Hush, Bronwen,' said Geraint, quickly.

The Grosneys, however, laughed. 'You have had a good dinner too?' Herbert Grosney said amiably to Isabel, and she saw that he had recovered from his hangover of the morning, and was probably well on his way to another. Clearly, wherever he and his kinsfolk had eaten their own dinner, theirs too had been good and well supplied with wine.

'Yes, oh yes!' She looked up into his eyes. He was actually looking at her and speaking to her. This is it, she thought. It's beginning at last.

'There was rabbit pie,' said the irrepressible Bronwen. 'I have never tasted rabbit before!'

'We should have it sometimes at home,' said Isabel boldly to her employer. 'It is so tasty; Bronwen is right.'

'By all means, if you can tell me where to purchase rabbits,' said Herbert Grosney amiably.

'Oh, that's easy!' Warm with wine and enjoyment, Isabel, laughing, spoke as freely as though he were an equal. 'We used to have them at the abbey when I was there. I helped look after them. I expect that they still have them; when we go home, I could ask. It is Abbess Julian now, isn't it? She was nice; I'm sure she'd sell us some.'

'Then, when we get home again, you will have an errand to the abbey,' said Grosney politely and, with his companions, walked on.

That was the way to do it! Not looking and longing and arranging accidental meetings on the stairs, but cheerful and easy and outspoken, offering to help and putting herself bravely where he must see her and speak to her and look into her eyes.

When they were home again, she would get rabbits for him. He would be grateful. He would think, the first time rabbit pie was served, oh yes, it was that girl Isabel who arranged for us to have these. An interesting girl; useful, with good ideas and really, so pretty . . .

He would make occasion, himself, to talk to her alone. Their eyes would meet. Then a silence would fall between them, for their eyes, then, would begin to do the talking for them. And then . . .

Hopes and dreams buoyed her up, all through the rest of their stay in London and all through the journey home, although the weather was bad and she was ill again on the voyage, and several of the others had picked up some sort of fever in London and were very gloomy company as a result.

Chapter Eight

The Wavering Flame

After they returned to Rushley, Isabel waited some days for Herbert Grosney to remember that she had offered to get him some rabbits. He said nothing so she accosted him one morning in a doorway. He seemed to be thinking of something else, and gazed at her as though he hardly understood what she was saying. He must be tired, Isabel thought, and as usual when she saw him looking tired, something inside her lurched. She wanted to go to him and put her arms round him and draw his head on to her breast.

'Rabbits?' he said vaguely. 'Oh. Yes, I recall you said something . . . you can go to the abbey tomorrow and inquire about them. Ask Jenkyn for some money in the morning.'

The next day, she set out on her errand with eagerness. It was a joy to be doing something for Master Herbert, and besides, she might see Sister — no, Abbess now — Julian again. She did not feel diffident about going to the abbey, not now that Abbess Christiana was gone, vindicating her in the process. Abbess Julian would surely be her friend again now. It would be nice, seeing her.

But the abbess was not there. It seemed that even though she now had such heavy responsibilities, Julian was still occasionally called to minister to the sick. 'Lady Judith at Rushley Hall is ill,' the porteress explained. 'Sir Henry is unwell, too. They fear smallpox. Picked up in London, no doubt. You had better warn your master. If anyone at Normansland gets it, they should be wrapped in red cloth and have red curtains hung round them. The abbess says it helps the rash to heal. Have you had it yourself?'

'No. But I used to look after cattle. My grandmother always said people who milked cows mostly didn't catch the pox.'

'That's true, Abbess Julian says.' The porteress nodded. 'At least — did you ever have to care for a cow with a sore udder, and did you have any fever with a rash about then?'

'Cows with sore udders I can remember more than once. Fevers with rashes, different sorts of rashes, I can remember having too. Come to think of it,' said Isabel, 'I do recall being indoors once with some illness like that, and my mother grumbling because she had to see to the cows and one of them had inflamed teats and kicked her. Anyhow, one of my little brothers died of smallpox and I looked after him and didn't get it.'

'Then you'll likely be all right,' said the porteress. 'But if we have a big outbreak, pray for the folk who aren't.'

The atmosphere of Redesmarsh Abbey had altered since Christiana's going. The shadows seemed less gloomy, the stone less heavy. There was light behind the arched doorways which had once looked like dark and yawning mouths. A number of walls had been limewashed which had been bare stone before and perhaps this was why. But most of all, Isabel thought, it was a thing of the spirit. Christiana had taken the darkness with her.

The prioress received her somewhat coolly. Her manner seemed to say that Isabel might have done the abbey a favour in ridding it of Christiana but that Isabel herself was remembered as, well, questionable. She would never come back here again, Isabel decided privately. But she was permitted to buy a pair of rabbits for the pot plus a pair of breeding rabbits, however, and the prioress, echoing the opinion of her abbess, suggested that she also purchase a pot of red dye, in case there was a sudden need for crimson cloth at Normansland. Isabel accepted but the dye and the rabbits between them cost more than she had expected; she would have little change to give back to Jenkyn. The rabbits were heavier than expected, too, and she was glad she had come by flatboat.

On her return, she carried them straight into the hall, hoping to evade Jenkyn and find Herbert Grosney in person. It was time to eat and with luck he would be indoors.

There was no sign of any food being set out, which was a disappointment because she was extremely hungry. There was, instead, a curious hush. She brought her purchases into the empty hall, and set them down, relieving the ache in her arms. She stood, head cocked, wondering where everyone had got to.

Then Anna came hurrying out of the kitchen, drying wet hands on a towel, looking uncharacteristically flustered and busy. 'Oh there you are; where have you been? Here we all are, looking for you and . . .'

'Did Jenkyn not tell you? Master Grosney sent me to Redesmarsh Abbey to buy some rabbits. I've brought them back with me. Was I wanted for something? I thought I left everything finished that ought to be.'

'We needed clean bedlinen and I had to get it out of the store myself. No, Jenkyn didn't mention it; he's had other things on his mind. Now, get along into that kitchen and lend a hand; we're all in a muddle and people have to be fed and . . .'

'But what about the rabbits? They need a proper pen and some food, and I ought to show them to the master. Where is Master Grosney?'

'You can't see him now. Taken ill, he was, an hour ago. Come to think of it, he's been looking queer these two days, and not eating right.

And I've got my own ideas what's wrong with him, too, and so has his man, Rob. Out in the stable, very very busy with his master's horse, Rob is. Says the horse may be throwing a splint. He just don't want to go near his master, that's what it is!' Anna's voice was shrill with nervous annoyance, and she cast an uneasy glance towards the stairs to the bedchambers.

The fear which jolted through Isabel was not for herself but for Grosney. It was followed almost at once with a most unworthy joy as she saw an unrepeatable opportunity, far better than that offered by the rabbits, come within her grasp.

'Is it smallpox?' she said.

Anna eyed her suspiciously. 'How do you know?'

'I've just been to Redesmarsh Abbey and it seems they've got it over at Rushley Hall. The abbess had gone to help. Look, while I was there, I heard what Abbess Julian is saying people ought to do for it. She says people should be wrapped in red and have red curtains hung up and I've bought some crimson dye, just in case. Anna, if you haven't had it, you oughtn't to go near him. But the chances are I'll be all right!' She explained about the cows and Abbess Julian's theories. 'Let me nurse him, Anna! You keep yourself safe.'

And saw, with more of that unholy joy, the relief in Anna's eyes.

Despite all that followed, Isabel in after years remembered the time of Master Herbert Grosney's illness with gladness. It was a time separated from all other times. During those days, she had the man she loved to herself, to care for as devotedly as she wished; and also, gently and affectionately, to chide and to command.

She did a good deal of chiding and commanding of others besides Master Grosney and enjoyed it. It was one of the few times in her life when she exercised authority of any degree, and it was like exercising hitherto unknown muscles.

Master Grosney was not at first glad of her ministrations. His worried face, flushed now with fever, regarded her doubtfully when she came up, carrying milk and chicken broth, and said, 'I take it Anna sent you? She should have given that tray to Rob.'

'He's in the stable. He thinks your horse might be going lame.'

'He thinks I've got something contagious you mean,' said Master Grosney. 'And so I might have. It could be just a touch of the ague, but I feel very ill and I don't think you ought to come near me. You're young. Your life's ahead of you.'

'I'm not worried sir. And in case it isn't the ague, but . . . well, I know what's best to do. You just take your milk and broth, and leave it all to me.'

'I forbid it. Looking after me isn't your work.'

'I was trained in the abbey infirmary. I'm very good at nursing.'

'I'm aware of that. I'm unlikely to forget that you were the girl who

132

came with Sister Julian to my wife! I still say if Rob won't come, then Anna must.'

Isabel smiled at him kindly, arranged the tray on a stool beside him and put a spoon into his hand.

'You mean,' said Master Grosney, 'that Anna's afraid to come as well?'

'I might be safer than she is, sir. I don't get ill very easily. But don't you worry. Whatever's wrong with you, I'll care for you and bring you through as right as rain.'

Master Grosney made a helpless gesture and sank back. Isabel gave him another smile, and set about removing his bedcurtains.

There was only one length of crimson cloth in the house, a roll of material put aside by Mistress Lucy for making a gown and never used. Isabel fetched it, insisted that Master Grosney should wrap himself in it, and then went down again to order that huge cauldrons of water be put to boil in the kitchen and that every set of bedcurtains and half the linen sheets in the house should be dyed red.

She succeeded in getting the dyeing done and the sheets and curtains out to dry just in time, before her fellow servants, in swift succession, began to fall ill like Master Grosney.

Thereafter, she together with the elderly Mald, and two kitchen lads, all of whom had already had the disease, coped as best they could. Rob had moved into the loft over the stable and would let no other person approach him but did at least look after the animals.

In the intervals between draping beds and swathing people in scarlet, she brewed possets and made easily digested meals for those who could manage them, carried trays and reassured those who were sufficiently aware of what was happening to be frightened, and sent to Redesmarsh Abbey for advice on fever-reducing possets and cooling lotions for the rash.

She was also obliged to build a pen for the rabbits and look after them. She was useful with her hands, as capable with hammer and nails as with a needle, and did the job well. Later, when Master Grosney was recovering, she killed two of the rabbits and stewed them for him.

There was one day when she feared he would not recover, when his worsening fever reached the point of delirium and no rash had yet appeared, although most of the others, all of whom had sickened later than Master Grosney, were already erupting hideously. During that day, and the following night, she never left his side.

But the following morning, the rash broke out and the fever began to abate. He was safely encircled by red cloth by then, by bedhangings as well as wrappings for his body.

'You will be all right,' she said, when she saw from the expression in his eyes that he could recognise her. 'The worst is over. You'll get well and you won't be scarred, either, not if I have anything to do with it.'

'You're a good girl, Isabel.' His voice was weak, barely loud enough to hear, but at least, she thought thankfully, he was now talking sense. 'I'm grateful for all you're doing. I don't know why you should take such trouble.'

'It's no trouble,' said Isabel, smoothing his coverings. 'If you think you could take a little bread soaked in wine, I've got some ready. Also I sent to the abbey for advice, and Abbess Julian sent back a potion she said might help.'

'You're a good girl,' whispered Master Grosney again.

In the hall at Rushley, Sir Simon stood on the dais, looking down at the table, on which he had laid down his latest new idea.

It was an enormous elmwood bow. Hugh le Hale had given it to him when they met in London for the coronation. 'It's as tall as a man!' Simon had said, awed, when Hugh handed it to him to inspect. 'How does one draw it?'

'To the ear, and it takes strength and knack,' said le Hale. 'But the southern Welsh are using it and it's made them into formidable warriors. In trained hands, its range is tremendous. Go on, take it. I brought it for you; I thought you'd be interested.'

He was interested. Very. He had experimented with the weapon himself, privately, out on the marsh and now he intended to have some identical bows made and to train his own men in using them.

And he had been looking forward to talking to his father about his plans.

But he had just come from his parents' bedchamber, and he knew now that he would never talk to either his father or his mother again about anything.

He did not fear infection for himself. He had come through the smallpox long ago as an apprentice knight in someone else's household. Cecily had had it too as a child and, at the first news of the outbreak in Rushley, they had sent their children away with their nurses and a good supply of food and drink, to an outlying house, recently fallen empty because its tenant had died of old age. His own family ought to be safe.

But the sheet had already been drawn over Lady Judith's face, and his father . . .

He had knelt by the bed where they both still lay, taking his father's hand, regardless of the oozing pustules with which it was covered, and holding it tightly. And Sir Henry had been saying farewell.

'I ache all the time even when I'm well. I shan't get over this and don't want to. Don't want to stay without your mother. Just wish it was finished. It's a young man's world now, anyway. New young King . . . you'll follow him to war, I expect. War with Wales, that's what it'll be first. Llewellyn'll try it on, with the new King, mark my words, and Edward'll want to show his mettle. Give a good account of yourself. I was always proud of you. Hope I'll be proud of you in heaven.'

'Father . . .'

'Is Father Benedict here?'

'Yes.'

'Then send him in to me.'

Benedict was with Sir Henry now, conducting the last rites which would prepare him for eternity. Simon was alone in the hall. The sickness had thinned the household; there were several sufferers upstairs as well as his parents, and two of the serving men had been buried already. He had ordered the rest to leave him to himself. They were all huddled now in solar and kitchen, or out in the courtyard, or tending those hideous bedsides upstairs. In a moment he must return for the last horrifying vigil. The human body in dissolution was a terrible thing to behold.

By tomorrow morning he would be an orphan, and the lord of the three manors of Rushley, Oxfen and Redesmarsh, and he would train his father's men as well as his own in the use of the Welsh longbow.

Simon of Rushley sat down at the table and laid his boyish face down on his arms and cried.

'What's all that crying and wailing about?' asked Herbert Grosney weakly. He was making his shaky way back and forth across his bedchamber, while Isabel remade his bed. He paused, leaning on a bedpost, as the sounds of desperation from the floor below escalated into alarmed shouts and a scuffle.

'It's Tilda, sir. She got hold of a silver mirror that must have belonged to Mistress Grosney, and saw herself in it. She had the red wrappings and the cooling lotion but she scratched her spots and she's badly scarred. She first saw herself yesterday and she tried to kill herself with a kitchen knife. By the sound of it, she's had another look at herself and tried again.'

Tilda's voice came shrilly up to them. '. . . leave me alone! I'd sooner be dead like Nell and Rob! Leave me alo . . o . . one . . .!' The cry tailed off into hopeless sobbing.

'Poor child,' said Herbert Grosney. 'Maybe she's right. It's a hard thing for a young girl to be so marked. Though she won't be the only one and the boys will be as bad. She'll marry in spite of it, I daresay. At least she's alive. Poor Rob's in his grave, in spite of all his panic-stricken hiding in the stables.'

'That's very true, sir.'

'You haven't let me see my own face yet,' Grosney said. 'Perhaps it's time I did.'

Isabel finished her task and turned to look at him. She studied his face and smiled, the kindly smile which was no pretence, but which appeared effortlessly whenever her eyes rested on him. Even when he had been covered with spots, the smile had been there for him.

She had hung the window as well as the bed with crimson and the light in the room was still a shadowy red, but it was clear enough to tell her that his rash was drying up well, that many of the spots had lost their scabs and that they had left only faint pink marks which would soon fade entirely. The weakness which the illness had left was her present concern. He was regaining his strength very slowly. He was trying hard and walked about in his room now each day, but he had not ventured yet to leave his chamber.

'You can see yourself if you want to now, sir. You've got marks, mind, but if you look carefully you'll see that they won't last. A few weeks and no one will know you ever had the pox.'

'It doesn't really matter,' Grosney said. 'I'm not a young girl like Tilda.' He pointed towards a chest under the window. 'There should be a mirror in there. Get it out and give it to me.'

Presently, having examined his face, he gave her back the mirror and said, 'I wouldn't have worried much about scarring but still, I am in debt to you, Isabel.' He sat down on the edge of the bed, a thin figure in the bedgown into which Isabel had fashioned his crimson wrappings. 'You have cared for me in a way beyond my power to repay. And for others, so I gather from Mald. You did your best for poor Rob, she tells me, and Tilda's distress now may well be partly her own fault. That lotion you got from the abbey was very soothing and she should have been more self-restrained.'

'You've repaid me very well,' Isabel said. 'You're alive and you'll be fit to be seen. I just wish you'd pick up strength a bit faster, that's all. You're not getting your appetite back quickly enough. Is there anything you specially feel you'd like for supper? I'll get it for you somehow if there is. You just tell me.'

Grosney shook his head. 'There's nothing in particular. Bring me what you think best; I'll try to eat it.' He began to get back into the bed and Isabel hastened to help, steadying his elbow and drawing the moleskin rug over him. Her patient needed warm coverings. The autumn was setting in and the day was chilly. A sharp wind buffeted the house and a draught was lifting the rushes on the bedchamber floor. 'Why are you taking so much trouble?' Grosney asked. 'You sat here with me all night, once at least, Mald says.'

It had come, the moment towards which she had been working with infinite care, watching him, listening to him, her whole mind open and sensitive for the smallest clues to his state of mind and body.

She settled him against his pillows, smiled at him again and said, 'You want to know why I'm taking so much trouble. Well, I can tell you, only I'll have to be careful how I say it because I wouldn't want to give offence.'

'Offence? I doubt you'll do that. Tell me, Isabel.'

'Well, sir, I think you're lonely and I'm sorry for that, that's all. I wanted to comfort you.'

'Lonely.' Grosney repeated the word as though it were a new object which he did not recognise. He seemed to be examining the shape and sound of it.

'Yes, sir. You've got your household all round you, of course. But no one properly close to you, if you know what I mean.'

'I had my wife once, and we hoped to have a child. Since they've been gone, I haven't wanted anyone else.'

'Well, that was natural, sir. But . . . I want to say something more – only again, I'm scared of making you annoyed.'

With a glimmer of humour, Grosney said, 'Isabel, I'm as weak as a five-minute-old calf and in no position to be annoyed. I daresay, however bad-tempered I was, you'd still go on bringing my food and making my bed and I'd be thankful for it. I'd have to be remarkably ungrateful to let the offence outweigh the gratitude. Say whatever you want.'

'Well, sir, it's been more than two years now. Time mends all, as I know myself. I was married to Alfred Plowman once and expecting a baby, but he died in an accident and then I lost the baby too. So I know what you've been through. You mustn't think for a minute that I don't. Only, after a time, I got to feeling better. Things slip away into the past and it's best to let them, as far as I can see. It isn't right for you to go on being alone. You ought to let someone, well, be company for you.'

'You mean I ought to marry again?'

Oh no, thought Isabel passionately. What's the matter with you, can't you see it's me I'm talking about? No, I don't mean marry again, not unless you marry me and you weren't thinking of that; I can tell. How can you be so slow? I've been bringing you your food, wearing my good dress with the red and silver trimmings on it and you never notice. Oh won't you look at me properly, even now?

'Not that especially,' she said carefully. She sat down on the side of the bed, also carefully, judging her distance: not too near him, not too far away. 'But just . . . let someone keep you company, like I said. Get close to you.'

Upright against his pillows, Herbert Grosney gazed at her and then at his own thin hands with the drying rash on them. 'Isabel, are you making me some kind of offer?'

Isabel stood up, and once more smiled at him, and this time her smile had in it more than a trace of coquettishness. 'I'd be glad to offer anything you wanted to ask, sir. It's for you to say.'

And then, lightly and quickly, she leaned forward, kissed the very tip of his nose and withdrew, going away and not glancing back.

She did not return until nightfall, when it was time to bring him his supper. She had made it herself, choosing it with great care. In the abbey, Isabel had learned a good deal about cooking for invalids, and

137

since Aymer Cook and Anna were still ill, though recovering, she was now in charge in the kitchen.

For Master Grosney she had made a white bean soup containing almond milk, honey, raisins and some of the white wine which was stored in the cellar under the kitchen. With it was a small portion of trout, which she had grilled and then simmered gently in white wine, ginger and the verjuice which Aymer Cook made from fermented crab-apples and of which he kept a good supply. There was also a goblet of red wine, to give Master Grosney vitality, and a little dish of bland custard.

She gave him the tray, curtsied, smiled again and went away once more without speaking. She returned later, to find that on the tray, which he had put aside on a small table next to the bed, was an encouraging display of empty bowls and a drained goblet.

'Come now, that's better. Tomorrow maybe you'll fancy something more filling. I got those rabbits, you know, and two are ready to eat. A bit of creamed rabbit tomorrow, how about that? And apple fritters?'

'Don't go too fast,' said Master Grosney. But as she came close to pick up the tray, he reached a thin arm out of the bed and put it round her. He pulled her towards him and then hesitated. 'I know I'm improving, but I'm not very handsome yet and I know it.'

'You've no spots at all round your mouth, sir,' said Isabel sedately. Grosney laughed, and for a brief and marvellous moment, pulled her head down to his. It was a very short kiss, not much more prolonged than Isabel's momentary salute to the tip of his nose had been. Then he let her go and said, 'That's to say thank you for everything. Take the supper things away now.'

Further than that, she knew instinctively, he would not go unaided. She had touched her flame to damp tinder and it was wavering on the very edge of life. But she would rouse it to a blaze if she could. At least she had lit it. The rest was up to her and what had she to lose?

She put the tray down on a table, and came quietly back to him. The resolution and fear and hope pounding in her veins were nearer to pain than joy but her smile showed nothing of this as she once more sat down on the bed, this time as close to him as she could. 'I'm not Lucy, sir, and you're not Alfred. But it's a bitter, frosty, night. Suppose I came in with you and we just kept each other warm?'

As she spoke, she was loosening the gown with the careful trimming which he had never noticed. But he noticed the neatly shaped form within her shift; she saw it in his face. She did not quite dare to raise the rug and slip beneath it until he gave his permission, but she looked at him with the question in her eyes.

'Isabel, I can't . . . I mean, you shouldn't . . .'

There was a pause. Then she said gently, 'I've been lonely too, sir. I've thought you were in need of companionship but it's me as well. Time does make things better but maybe not as fast as I pretended to

138

you today. Can I stay? Please.'

He said nothing in words, but he lifted the rug and then put out a hand and drew her to him. She rested close to him, feeling desire surge but checking it, knowing that the prize was within reach and that impatience might lose it. She put her head into the hollow of his shoulder. Around them, the house settled. After a time, she slept.

They woke at first light. They were lying folded together and as the daybreak filtered slowly through the crimson defences of the bed, he took her hand and guided it. 'Only I've no strength yet,' he said. 'I can't do much. But if you use your hand . . .'

Isabel pushed back the bedhangings to let in a little more light and then thrust back the rugs. She drew her shift off, ignoring the cold bite of the air. She saw his eyes widen at the sight of her nakedness. She shook her loose dark hair to make it spread over her back and fall forward over her shoulders, and slipped astride him.

'I'll do it all, sir. You just lie back,' said Isabel.

It was the most triumphant moment of her life.

It was also quite a new experience. Weak though he was, so that of necessity she took the lead, when his neat, long-fingered hands reached up to her, his touch was dry and exact. He played deftly on her senses and knew precisely what he did. He was like a cat treading delicately through a garden, an utter contrast to Alfred's eager, puppyish snugglings.

But when, at the height of it, Isabel released the words she had kept locked inside her for so long, and whispered, 'I love you,' although he did it kindly, he laughed.

Sir Henry's deathbed prediction that the new King would launch his reign by going to war with Wales was almost correct but not quite. King Edward the First's first swashbuckling enterprise after his accession was actually in the field of kidnapping.

Chapter Nine

The Valley of the Immortals

In the castle of Cwmanog, the room which the Lady Eglantine used as a solar was set in one of the towers. From its windows, the view was a breathtaking vista of soaring mountain and plunging valley, of dizzily sloping pasture and wooded ravine, of the argent streaks which were distant waterfalls and the grey cloud-wreathed mountain crests and beyond all these, vague with distance, the outlines of yet more mountains, marching away for ever upon all sides.

Eastward, the outlook was especially staggering for there the hilltop on which the castle perched swooped down four hundred feet to a river in a narrow wooded valley and away to the north where the head of the valley was, the river poured into it over a fall which could be heard from that side of the castle, a faint unending murmur which at close quarters would be a deafening roar.

The valley was the Cwmanog itself, the Valley of the Immortal Ones, and there was a flat place like a shelf beside the falls where one could stand and look straight down into the pool below, and it was said that if you threw a stone into the pool and wished for your heart's desire, it would be granted. At a price.

There were legends, of a woman who longed for a son and was granted one and saw him grow up to slay his father, and of Prince Gruffyd long ago, who asked the Immortal Ones to make his young wife, to whom he was an alarming stranger, fall in love with him. This too had been granted, for a time, until he was betrayed and murdered by men he trusted, and died in his princess's arms, and her final declaration of her love for him was no act of love, but of violence, for she stabbed his killer.

Eglantine hated the mountains and the castle on its precipitous eyrie and hated the Cwmanog valley most of all. Much as she longed for a child, and pined for Sir Hugh's affection, she had never tried any heathen experiments like tossing stones into the pool and making a wish. Though, as she stood in the solar and listened to what Bronwen was telling her, she thought she might as well have done.

'I might have had something worth having before I lost it all,' she said, speaking part of her thought aloud. Bronwen broke off in surprise. 'Madam?'

'It doesn't matter. I'm wandering. Oh dear God, I can't believe Sir Hugh is dead!'

'Geraint saw him fall. Madam, please to sit down. The shock . . .'

'Why did Geraint live to tell the tale? Why did he not protect my husband? Where was he?'

'Pinned under his own fallen horse, Madam. Oh, my dear lady, *please* sit down.' Bronwen took her arm and guided her to a fleece-covered couch. The junior lady, Myfanwy, put a fur round Eglantine's shivering form. 'Madam,' said Bronwen, 'I'm afraid there's more. Myfanwy, fetch some wine.'

'More? There can't be more. What can be worse than this? Oh, why must there be these everlasting wars?' Realisation was taking hold of Eglantine. Sir Hugh hadn't been the best of husbands, not after those first few ecstatic months. But he'd never been actively unkind. Once he had decided she was barren, he'd taken to finding his sex elsewhere but when at home he'd usually slept beside her even if all he did was sleep and he was courteous in public. He'd even, eventually, defended her from his bad-tempered old mother who wouldn't have considered even a winged angel good enough for her son and at first had criticised every single thing about Eglantine, from her choice of clothes to her embroidery and her East Anglian accent.

Eglantine's failure to produce a baby had been a backhanded source of delight, a glorious pretext for criticism and nagging. At her mother-in-law's funeral, Eglantine had rubbed her eyes to make them red and strangled with difficulty a great desire to dance behind the coffin on the way to the churchyard.

But before that day, Sir Hugh had, however belatedly, insisted that his mother at least go through the motions of politeness. He'd been disappointed in his wife and let her know it, but in this strange wild land, he had represented a kind of security, and now . . .

From somewhere in the lower regions of the castle, there was a confused noise, like someone hammering and shouting. She herself felt like shouting – or better still, screaming.

'What if Prince Llewellyn wouldn't pay homage to the King?' she demanded, pointlessly and rhetorically. 'Why should he? It was true that the King was sheltering Llewellyn's brother who once plotted against him. Why couldn't the King just let things be?'

'We'd all agree with that. Thank you, Myfanwy. Madam, you must drink and put some heart into you . . . but as things are . . .'

'Tell me the rest!' Eglantine commanded.

What she already knew was bad enough. Only yesterday, the castle had been full, with not only Sir Hugh there, but his men as well, who were a mixture of English and loyal Welsh.

Then he had set out on a sortie, to clear the hills of enemies, he'd said. The King and his men were at Rhuddlan and Flint and if they meant to push south, which he'd thought they would, then he felt bound to help clear a path for them. He had left a skeleton garrison behind him, all of them Welshmen. 'When it comes to fighting their own people in the field, I only take those that volunteer willingly. But fighting their own is one thing; defending you from them is another. I can ask that of them, sweetheart,' Hugh had said, using the endearment because they were in the hall where others could hear them. It was part of his public courtesy towards her.

Now Hugh and all the men who had gone with him, except for Geraint, were dead; ambushed, overwhelmed and slaughtered while she stayed here, because Hugh had said at the start of the hostilities that she would be safer in his castle than trying to get through the mountains of Gwynedd to reach England. 'The valleys are crawling with armed Welshmen,' he'd said.

Quite. And now Hugh was dead at their hands, and not only the valleys, but the whole damned castle was crawling with them. The ones in the castle were supposed to be Hugh's loyal men, but except for a few, like Bronwen and quiet little Myfanwy, and Sir Hugh's minstrel Owen who was Myfanwy's elder brother and, yes, Geraint, she found them alarming and mysterious. 'When they talk to each other in their incomprehensible language, they're talking *at* us as well,' she had once said to Hugh, and she knew that the people outside the castle mostly lived weird nomadic lives, doing little cultivation but roaming incessantly through the mountains with their flocks of sheep and goats, living in makeshift huts and ready at any time to carry on hit and run warfare against the English.

Here in the north, in Snowdonia, which in the Welsh tongue was Gwynedd, the spear by which Hugh had died was the traditional weapon. But the Welsh bowmen of the south, which they called Deheubarth, were terrifying. She'd seen their bows; immense affairs of wild elm, as tall as a man, more dangerous even than the high-velocity crossbows for which King Edward had bolts manufactured in gigantic quantities at the Castle of St Briavell in the south.

The deadly archers of Deheubarth were currently on King Edward's side and if they stayed there, then the King would surely win this war. But he wouldn't win it tomorrow or even the day after and, meanwhile, what would happen to her?

'Madam, swallow that wine,' Bronwen was saying urgently. 'I am sorry to be so slow getting to the point, but there's ashamed I am to tell you some of it . . .'

'Ashamed?' Eglantine sounded terrified.

'. . . and Geraint won't face you himself, the great booby. Brave enough on the field – for that he is; it wasn't his fault his horse was killed. But when there's hard things to say . . .'

'*What hard things?* My husband's dead and I don't know what will become of me; aren't those things hard enough? Will you tell me what you're talking about? Tell me at once!'

'Well,' said Bronwen, sitting down beside her, 'you remember how all this started, not quite two years since? When Prince Llewellyn was to marry the daughter of the English lord Simon de Montfort of Leicester, and the King . . . forbade it?'

'The King,' said Eglantine frantically, 'kidnapped her when she was on her way to Wales by sea and ever since then she's been in honourable custody in Windsor, until Prince Llewellyn agrees to do homage. What about it?'

'When Geraint's horse fell on him, he was knocked out for a while and when he came round; well, Sir Hugh and the rest were lying there dead and beyond his help. I suppose the enemy had thought Geraint was dead, too. Anyhow, he crawled out and started back here with the news but he was taken and questioned. With a dagger to his throat. Madam, a man is apt to tell lies if that's what's needed to save his life.'

'And what did Geraint say?'

'Well, from the direction he'd come from, they guessed he'd been with Sir Hugh. He said he owed Sir Hugh's family some old debt but that at heart he was true Welsh and had been planning to leave his master, now that there was war, in fact that he'd been searching for Welshmen to join, and he was glad to see them and he wanted to be one of them . . .'

'How resourceful,' said Eglantine faintly. 'Did they believe him?'

'Madam, he sat round a fire with them up in the hills, and talked of how desperate it is for Llewellyn here in Gwynedd, with armies all round, along the north and south Marches and coming up from the south. He talked of the perfidious Deheubarth nobles in the south, who've made terms with the King of England and he . . . well, no, indeed, they didn't believe him. They said it was more likely that he'd been Sir Hugh's true man and was just trying to talk his way out of it – as he was, indeed – so in the end . . .'

'Yes, and? Bronwen, you're frightening me to death!'

'They were going to kill him.' said Bronwen. 'But one of them said, well, let him prove his good faith.'

'H . . . how?'

'Sir Hugh left ten men here,' said Bronwen reluctantly. 'Geraint came to the gates with thirty and announced them to the gate-guards as friends, volunteers come to give their help to Sir Hugh's people. Until they were in, and then . . .'

'In? In the castle – *this* castle? Are you telling me that Geraint has handed this castle to the enemy?'

'He didn't want to die. And they were getting other ideas besides a clean dagger thrust.'

'But wasn't there fighting? I didn't hear any fighting!'

'There was no skirmish.' Bronwen shook her head. 'Mother of God, wasn't I on the hall steps with your clean barbettes in my hands? I saw it all. They came in, they bent their bows to hold the men they found in the courtyard and guardroom while they searched out the rest. They've locked them up; that's the banging and shouting you can hear. The castle has been seized in the name of Prince Llewellyn and you are a hostage. They hope to use you to force the King to retreat.'

'*What?*'

'They say it is fair, since the King is using Prince Llewellyn's intended lady against him.'

'But I'm . . . I'm not important enough . . . no one would withdraw an army or jeopardise a campaign for me! What will happen to me if the King's forces won't . . .?'

'Nothing will happen to you, indeed it won't.' Bronwen, whose voice had been carefully expressionless as she told the ghastly news, suddenly slipped to her knees and put a beseeching hand on Eglantine's arm. 'We are not savages. I know that you think we are all just that, with our lax ways and our language that to you sounds like someone gargling . . . oh yes, that's how it is, so don't deny it . . . but no one will harm a good, innocent lady like yourself; it will be only a bluff . . .'

'But they'll keep me here! Oh, my God!' Nightmare visions of rape and dungeons raced through Eglantine's brain and she clutched at Bronwen's hand. 'And what of you and Geraint and Myfanwy? And Owen the Minstrel? Whose side are you on? Geraint is your lover, and Myfanwy and Owen are kin to him!'

'Our lax ways,' said Bronwen, trying to make Eglantine smile. Eglantine made a choking sound halfway between a laugh and a sob. The haphazard Welsh attitude to morality had always bewildered her. They divorced if they wanted to, regardless of the laws of the Church, and bastard children could inherit. Owen, Myfanwy and Geraint all had the same father, a minstrel once employed by Eglantine's mother-in-law. But Geraint had a different mother from the others and, although the minstrel had acknowledged and supported them, both he and the women servants who had borne his children remained unconcernedly single. As, so far, had Bronwen and Geraint themselves although they had somehow, as yet, avoided having offspring.

'Madam, please don't distress yourself too much. Except when they are angry, my people are not so eager to kill. They have imprisoned the garrison but no one has been slain . . .'

'A bloodless capture!' said Eglantine. 'But I'm still a captive. Look at those mountains!' She pointed with a shaking finger at the view beyond the arched windows. 'I'm trapped here in the middle of them. I was frightened from the day I came, when I realised that we were *inside* Wales instead of on the border. I want to go home! If the devil himself were to appear this instant, and told me that if I sold him my soul I could be whisked straight home to East Anglia, where the land is flat so that you can see where you're going, and people speak my own tongue, I'd accept, I tell you!'

'Madam, don't say such things. Listen to me!' Bronwen spoke pleadingly. 'We are all on *your* side: me, Myfanwy, Owen and Geraint too . . .'

'It is true, Madam,' said Myfanwy in her soft voice.

'. . . and Geraint is that ashamed. We have a regard for you, as we had for Sir Hugh and even for his mother. She was a hard woman but honest and when my mother died bearing me, and no man came forward to say he was my father, she saw that I was nursed and reared. Geraint wasn't altogether lying when he told his captors he owed the le Hales a debt. He does. He owes them for me! And besides,' Bronwen added in a practical tone, 'for all our songs about our warrior ancestors and the great Welsh princes of the past, Llewellyn has no chance of winning. Gwynedd is ringed all round with enemies. He must make peace or die. And *we* must get you away from here and I've told Geraint that the least he can do now is to help. I said, if he won't, he can kiss goodbye to me. There's plenty more where he came from,' said Bronwen with spirit.

'You have been kind to me and to Owen,' Myfanwy said. 'We are with you, Madam. Believe me.'

'But *how* can you get me away?' Faint hope appeared in Eglantine's voice, but her eyes went to the door. 'They'll be up here any minute, won't they? These men who have taken the castle; they'll come to look at me.'

'Not yet,' Bronwen assured her. 'Geraint had sense enough to tell them the news must be broken to you kindly and you must have time to quieten your mind, and he came at once to me. That was when I warned him he must help you out of this mess he has made for you, or else. Be brave, Madam, and you'll see your home in East Anglia again.' It puzzled Bronwen that Eglantine wanted so much to go back there, since to her, a flat country with no mountains sounded peculiarly awful. But there, the English *were* peculiar although some, like Eglantine, could be lovable. 'Madam,' she said, and knew from the startled look the tearful Eglantine gave her, that her own eyes were dancing, 'one thing we know already is that they intend to have a feast tonight, and they'll want entertainment . . .'

'A feast? Oh, God! They'll get drunk!'

'The problem,' said Bronwen, as though her mistress had not spoken, 'will be getting you out through the hall. This tower of yours leads straight down into it. Even dressing you as a maidservant won't do. They'll take a good look at anyone female coming out of this tower and you're right, of course; they'll be coming to see you soon. They'll know your face. But could you, do you think, contemplate being the back legs of a horse?'

Eglantine had no illusions about herself. Living here, in a hollow marriage and a wild and frightening land, she had learned in self-defence how to make the occasional tough-sounding joke, but it was only pretence, for at heart she was timid. In one way, she thought, it was as well that the castle of Cwmanog had been taken by stratagem for she did not see herself as a Nicola de la Hay, masterminding its defence while it was under seige.

Now, challenged to put not only grief but fear aside and play a part for considerably longer than it took to make a wry witticism, she could only manage it by detaching herself from reality. Only by continually saying to herself: this is all a dream; it isn't happening, could she hope to come through.

The first part of the plot was easy enough, because Bronwen said that she had best seem helpless and prostrate when the enemy came to inspect her, and ought to be found huddling in bed, and this was the thing she instinctively wanted to do most.

Clothing felt like a sort of armour, so she shed only her outer garments before creeping under the rugs. Myfanwy stayed with her and Bronwen, after nodding in approval, went away, to return presently with a strange man. 'This is David ap Hywel, who commands our new . . . guests, Madam,' she said.

David ap Hywel was a discouraging sight. He carried a five-foot spear like a badge of office and he was dressed in tunic and hose of brown and green which were none too clean. He had an unkempt beard and a rough head of hair, both ginger. He looked to Eglantine like a complete barbarian. His words, however, spoken in slow and heavily accented English, were intended to be reassuring.

'This castle has been taken in the name of Prince Llewellyn of Gwynedd but no harm is intended to anyone in it who behaves wisely. No ill will come to you, my lady. But you are Prince Llewellyn's prisoner, in my care, and you must keep to your quarters. Food will be sent up to you. Your chaplain is downstairs, if you are wanting to see him. It's bereaved that you are, I think.'

'Tomorrow,' said Eglantine weakly. 'I'll see him tomorrow.' She tried to take courage. 'If you want to use me to bargain with the English, you'll be wasting your time. I'm no one important.'

'Sir William FitzWilliam, your brother-in-law, is with the Earl of Chester, who is one of the King's chief barons, and Sir William has some prominence now. He may have something to say in the matter. So may Sir Simon Rushley who is also there and is, I believe, your cousin and the son of your former guardian.'

Clearly, this horrible man knew all about her. It gave her a feeling of having been watched and discussed without her knowledge. On top of that, the mention of her guardian brought Sir Henry into her mind, kind and lame, coming late to Mass in Rushley Hall. She could see Lady Judith, too, and the solar where the Rushley ladies had stitched on bright mornings, as clearly as though they were before her in reality. Though Sir Harry and his wife were gone now, but the longing to be back in the house where she had lived with them was so strong that she did not know how to bear it. Her enemy's face swam behind a haze of tears. 'Go away,' she whispered.

'Food will be sent,' he said again. 'There will be feasting downstairs later. I control my men, you need not fear, but you may yourself feel safer if you bolt this door.'

Bronwen said pertly, 'We will fetch the food, Myfanwy and I, if we are free to come and go. There may be other things my lady needs. You will want some clean linen, Madam, and your prayerbook, perhaps.'

She stared significantly at Eglantine who said quickly, 'Yes, and some mulled wine, Bronwen, if you will. The way you know how to do it.'

Bronwen turned to David ap Hywel, who said shortly, 'By all means. Come now and identify yourselves to the guard in the hall.' He bowed to Eglantine, banged his spear-handle on the floor apparently as a species of salute, and strode out.

Bronwen winked at Eglantine and she and Myfanwy went after him. Presently they reappeared and Bronwen said, 'So far, so good!'

'Bronwen, I don't . . . I don't think I can . . .'

'Madam, you must. Or I'll never be able to forgive Geraint.'

'That's the maddest logic I ever heard!'

'There, I've got a smile out of you. It is just as well,' said Bronwen cheerfully, 'that Sir Hugh's mother, God rest her, didn't get on with your English tirewoman and sent her home. I thought she was harsh at the time but, after all, it was best. We'd have had hard work to rescue *two* of you and get you through the mountains to the English lines.'

'Bronwen, if we're caught, they probably won't do much to me beyond keeping me closer. But what of you and the others?'

Bronwen looked at her mistress steadily, and glanced at Myfanwy. Myfanwy's eyes were very large. Neither of the Welsh girls spoke.

'They'll be angry enough to kill you, won't they? I can't agree to this. The risk is too great for all of you. What if I make a mistake, and we're all discovered because of me?'

'What if I make a mistake, or any of us?' said Bronwen. 'Madam, Geraint owes the house of Le Hale something on more than just my account. So does Geraint. He was Sir Hugh's squire and he should now be defending you, not selling you to your husband's foes and well he knows it. As for Owen and Myfanwy, they are true to you, and they will act with me and Geraint as they always have.'

'I am not afraid,' said Myfanwy. The big eyes belied her, but she held her chin up. She made Eglantine feel ashamed.

'Listen, Madam,' said Bronwen. 'It will be easy. You have only to do as Geraint will tell you and we will all be safe.'

Later, as dusk fell and the sounds of merrymaking began to drift up from below, she sat on the edge of the bed, wearing old clothes of Bronwen's, and waited for Geraint to come with the horse costume.

He had promised the revellers an entertainment, Bronwen said; everything was in hand. Eglantine, listening for the sound of feet on the stairs, thought that Bronwen was an optimist. She could not begin to imagine how she would carry this through. She found herself longing with incredible violence for Hugh. Even snoring and unresponsive with his back turned to her in this bed which they would never share again, he now seemed not only a symbol of safety, but beloved beyond words.

There was a tap on the door and Geraint's voice said, 'I'm here, my lady.' She drew back the bolt and let him in. He at once knelt at her feet. 'My lady. I have to ask your pardon for . . . for the castle and everything. I didn't want . . .'

Eglantine heard herself say sharply, 'It's too late to worry about that now. I suppose I must be grateful that you're still willing to help me. Where's this horseskin we're supposed to be getting into?'

Geraint stood up. 'It's in a little room off the tower steps, down near the foot. There would be no getting down the steps in the costume; it's falling down them we'd be. But Owen is in the hall now, singing ancient lays of war which should keep them quiet for a while. We must slip down the stairs and into the little room, and dress there.'

'Very well,' said Eglantine. 'Lead the way.'

Myfanwy and Bronwen had gone before the feasting in the hall began. They had preceded their final departure by some artistic dashings up and down the stairs and through the hall and out across the courtyard and back on the planned excuses of fetching food, linen, a prayerbook and the mulled wine for Eglantine. Bronwen said that they must scurry confusedly about so that people would cease to notice them, and therefore wouldn't realise that they hadn't returned to their mistress before the feasting began.

But the last thing that Bronwen did before setting off was to thrust a sheathed dagger into her mistress's hand. 'Just in case.'

'In case of what? I couldn't . . . couldn't *use* this.'

'This is war. Take it,' said Bronwen fiercely. 'Hang it on your girdle.' She did.

Sunset still shone through the windows of the tower rooms and the arrow slits on the stairs lower down. Passing the solar, Eglantine glimpsed it turning the fleeces on her couch to pink. But on the stone walls of the tower, it was the colour of blood.

She mustn't think of Hugh, ambushed, pulled off his horse and run through with a spear or of his men butchered round him. And she mustn't think of the awful mountains, under the mists and the half-moon, through which she and Bronwen must adventure when night had fallen.

Especially, she mustn't think about climbing down into the Cwmanog.

'I now a quick way to reach Rhuddlan – that's the nearest place to find the English,' Bronwen had said. 'We'll be there just after dawn. Provided we don't slip on the way down into the Cwm.'

And provided they didn't run into any enemy patrols, and that Bronwen and Myfanwy would succeed in hiding until full darkness fell and then slipping across the courtyard and setting the postern ajar without being seen. There was a guard, but the men were above the gatehouse, Geraint had said, with their attention on the hillsides. They were watching for the beacons which would warn them that the enemy was coming south.

The little room had only one window slit, which faced east. It was almost dark. The noise in the hall was very close to them now. She could hear Owen singing. Some of the audience were singing with him. The hall was always gloomy at the best of times; they would be lighting the cressets by now. But how far away, she wondered, was the true darkness they needed? Surely this was too soon to act?

Geraint, however, was pulling the horse's head on without more ado. She climbed into the rear end of the costume and struggled with the fastenings. 'Are you all right?' said Geraint's voice, hollowly.

She didn't feel in the least all right. Her heart was hammering so much that she could hardly breathe, and the inside of the horse was stuffy. She was bent double behind Geraint, holding on to his belt. She could see nothing. Only Geraint could see where they were going and that none too well. She must follow him and hope for the best.

Bronwen had told her what she would have to do. Now, in a whisper, Geraint added a few extra details. 'When we get into the hall, Owen will be singing. We shall interrupt him, cavorting. He will snatch up a spoon or something and hit out at the horse with it . . .'

She achieved one of those deceptive, tough-sounding jokes. 'If he hits me, I shall kick him.'

'Do, if you can. It will get a laugh.' Geraint, who in her tower chamber had knelt at her feet in self-abasement, was now the one in control. 'He'll chase us out into the courtyard but we shall come back in and give a show. Then we shall let him chase us out again and in the foot of the other tower across the bailey, Myfanwy will be ready to change places with you.'

'And then I steal out through the postern and Bronwen will be waiting. Will you and Myfanwy . . . be all right?'

'I trust we will. We will go back to the hall inside the horse and do some more fooling and then we shall climb innocently out of it, in full view of everyone, and she will say she is going to join you, and she will give the alarm that you have gone, but by then you will have had a long start and I do not think they will suppose you have taken the route that you have, down into the Cwmanog.'

'Bronwen says there is a possible way down. But . . .' She could hear the uneasy doubt in her tone.

'Steep it is, and you need to know it, but Bronwen does. We were great ones for climbing as children; we found it then. It is a blessing there is no moat here. You will have only to edge round the foot of the castle until you are above the Cwm. Now then. We can start, I think. The light's fading quickly and it will be dark by the time we have finished our performance. You have seen me and Bronwen being a horse to amuse you and Sir Hugh so you know what we are aiming for. I will give you signals. When I whinny or snort, cross your right foot over your left and fall down. Otherwise, just prance and galumph.'

She was Lady Eglantine, who had once stitched altar-cloths with Lady Judith in the solar at Rushley. Now, her husband had been killed, and she was a prisoner of war and she had never been so frightened in her life, and she was expected to . . . to . . .

She followed Geraint blindly into that hall full of dusk and torchlight and lusty, singing, drunken Welshmen, and pranced, and galumphed.

David ap Hywel had looked to Eglantine like a barbarian but he was not. David ap Hywel regarded himself as a man of culture, far more highly bred and sensitive than any of the terrible Saxons and Normans who were lumped under the title of the English and were in his opinion a collection of uneducated philistines who considered minstrelsy, the noblest calling on the earth, to be the province of travelling entertainers of low degree. The English had red, meaty faces, no wit, no imagination and believed themselves to be superior for no reason whatsoever that David ap Hywel could see.

He did not think that Llewellyn should give his fealty to the King of England, whether or not the said King were harbouring Llewellyn's enemies and he was horrified that King Edward had interfered in Llewellyn's marriage plans. The Prince had been making lovesongs to sing to Eleanor de Montfort at their marriage, and it was a sin, in David's opinion, to keep Llewellyn from his lady.

He was quite prepared to fight until all the blood had been spilled from his body or to kidnap a hundred Eglantines in order to demonstrate his disapproval of these things.

But he was also aware that Eglantine's situation was wretched and, as a cultured and imaginative man, he wished to alleviate it. Also, by the time the feast was halfway through, he was in a great good humour. The boy Owen had played his harp and sung excellently, and the performance with the horse was hilarious. When it first came prancing in, Owen had pretended to be very angry and hit the horse across the rear end with a wooden ladle, and whoever was playing the back legs had managed to kick his assailant with both feet at once and toppled him neatly backwards, causing him to knock a bowl of soup and a lark pie on to the floor.

It was all quite splendid and it was a pity that the poor lady upstairs should be left brooding over her grief, and missing the fun. Her women were missing it too. He ought to fetch them all down. They'd be safe enough from his men while sitting with him at the top table. The performance seemed to be ending, but when Geraint and whoever was his partner were out of that horse-skin, David would have a word with them and get them back into it for a second show later. Meanwhile, he'd go himself to collect the women. Lady Eglantine might, just, trust the word of the leader that she'd be safe, but she most likely wouldn't trust anyone else.

His friend and first lieutenant, Rhys ap Griffith, was beside him. 'I'm going to fetch the women down,' said David. 'Get some places made ready for them at this table while I'm gone.'

It was almost dark now. He took a cresset from a wall bracket before entering the tower and climbing up to Eglantine's chamber.

No one answered his knock and when he tried the latch, the door yielded. The foolish girls hadn't bolted it, then. He called, 'It is David ap Hywel and I mean no offence,' waited again, heard nothing and walked in.

The curtains of the bed were drawn back on one side and as he tilted the torch to cast light this way and that, he saw that the bed, and the room, were empty.

He strode to the windows. The solar and this bedchamber had windows of reasonable size for the excellent reason that they were out of reach of any siege ladders. One glance at the yawning drop outside, just visible in the very last of the light, assured him that the women had not gone that way.

'He went quickly back down the steps, checking the solar on the way and the little room near the foot of the tower, but these too were empty. He paused for a moment, thinking. He was the leader of his men as much because he could think fast and imaginatively in a crisis as because he was skilled with sword and spear.

She had left the tower. The only way out of the tower was through the hall. She certainly hadn't walked through the hall in the usual way. Her women had come and gone, but openly, their faces clearly seen, and she did not resemble either of them.

But neither face nor sex were apparent when their owner was inside a painted cloth horse.

Cresset in hand, David ap Hywel sped back to the hall.

But the horse, which he had left performing its antics there, had gone. The boy Owen was singing again and the door to the courtyard stood open. He did not want to shout to the whole hall that his most valuable prisoner had vanished. Efficient leaders didn't let their prisoners vanish. But he could trust Rhys ap Griffith, who was now looking at him, a little puzzled, from the midst of three freshly laid places at the top table.

David strode to the table, caught Rhys by the upper arm and jerked him to his feet. 'Come with me, quick, *bach*. We have to arrest a horse.'

Eglantine was not only tired but out of breath as Owen drove them out of the hall for the second time, and all but did an unscheduled fall on the steps down to the courtyard.

'Careful,' muttered Geraint. 'My arms are trapped in this thing; you almost caught me off-balance.' He cavorted them into the courtyard, pranced across it and in at the door of another tower. 'Quick!'

Hands were already fumbling at the hooks. Eglantine helped from inside and then, thankfully, scrambled free. The moon was out now, shining through the tower door and in it she saw that Myfanwy was there, kilting her skirts in readiness to climb into the horse. 'Hurry,' gasped Eglantine.

And then came feet, running, grating over the paved courtyard, and the light of a torch replaced the moonlight as two powerful forms loomed up in the doorway.

'Well, well, what have we here?' inquired the voice of David ap Hywel.

They turned to him in horror, Myfanwy now half in and half out of the hind legs, Eglantine in the old clothes which Bronwen had hoped would be a disguise from a distance, if they were seen on their journey. The horse's head, which was made of wood and tin, turned on Geraint's shoulders, with an air of comic inquiry. David, while his companion held up the torch. seized the head in both hands and wrenched. Geraint's face, running with the sweat of exertion and fear, was revealed.

'Traitor!' said David ap Hywel. He threw the horse-head aside, gripped Geraint by the throat and drew and used his dagger in a movement so smooth and swift that Eglantine did not understand what had happened until, as David tugged the blade free, she saw the blood come after it, and saw Geraint's eyes in the torchlight distended with terror and then rolling upwards and changing horribly, as his knees gave way. David let him fall and turned to her.

'And now, my lady, if you will take my arm, I will escort you to your chamber. You should not be abroad in the dark; there are drunken men about. Rhys, bring the other girl.'

It was as though someone else had taken possession of her. It could not, surely, be Eglantine who was reaching for the dagger Bronwen had given her, was pulling it from its sheath and driving it into David ap Hywel's chest just as he had driven his own blade into the helpless Geraint: slaying the slayer, as Prince Gruffyd's lady had done, more than two hundred years before.

He had had a good deal to drink and he was not expecting an attack from such a harmless-looking quarter. In the torchlight, she saw disbelief and amazement in his face before he suddenly let out a gurgling cry and his hands came up to clutch at the dagger hilt. He dropped his own weapon. At the same moment, Myfanwy, who had just been dragged clear of the horse's costume by Rhys, kicked him where it would do most harm and Rhys went down, gagging and clutching himself. The torch fell and Myfanwy stamped on it. In the fleeting moment before the light vanished, Eglantine saw that Myfanwy had a knife and was going to use it. In the darkness, David was making hideous choking noises. He was still on his feet, but he was lurching at the end of the dagger, like a gigantic fish on a line.

'Quick, Madam, help me kill this one!' Myfanwy cried.

David was falling, falling, and she felt the dagger come away as the weight of his collapsing body dragged him free of it. In the moonlight she could see Myfanwy on top of a dark and heaving heap. She saw the flash of upraised steel. She flung herself down on the heap and used her own weapon again, and then again.

There was a filthy struggle, an awareness that the dark, hot, frantic thing she straddled was fighting in terror and agony for its life. Fingers closed round her forearm and she bit them, savagely, like an animal. And then there was a gasping moan which faded out, and a final, violent convulsion and something warm, with a sickening smell, sprayed into her face. As she got to her feet, she retched.

'There's no time for that.' Myfanwy was there beside her. 'Come, Madam. Bronwen is waiting. Run!'

In East Anglia, they were having a hot summer.

For two weeks now there had been no wind; only a breathless blue sky, day and night, and from the small flat-roofed tower which was part of Herbert Grosney's house, the twinkle of the distant sea made the eyes ache if you stared at it too long.

The marshes had shrunk, leaving stretches of cracked, dried mud where once there had been swamp, and clumps of withering reed, and here and there stagnant pools which bred midges in clouds. One of Sir Simon Rushley's ships had been damaged, running aground in the abnormally shallow Wend.

Sir Simon himself was away in Wales, a volunteer in the King's forces, by permission of the Earl of Norfolk, but Lady Cecily had been in touch with him by messenger and was now on his behalf obtaining quotes for the construction of the deepwater harbour her husband had been planning for so long. 'We should have seen about it before,' she told Master Grosney, encountering him when both of them were out surveying their irrigation channels, with some anxiety.

At night, the huge East Anglian sky was a marvel of stars. Isabel, crossing Master Grosney's courtyard with an armful of linen washed in the late afternoon and effortlessly dried by nightfall, stopped and craned her head back to marvel at them. She had never seen stars so bright, so blazing. The Milky Way wound across the sky like a silver river. What *were* the stars, she wondered. They shed little light, served no purpose that she knew of. They were simply there, beautiful beyond bearing. A gift from God, perhaps, and a demonstration of His majesty.

She had never thought about such things before but love, even unsatisfactory love, deepened you. She had discovered that.

Especially in summers like this, when the nights were so warm and melting and full of soft scents and the call of the nightingale, and after dark she would lie on her pallet in the little room which had once been Mistress Grosney's robing room, and wait for the tap on the wall which meant that Herbert Grosney desired her company.

Only, there were many nights when he did not, when she lay awake, yearning and languorous, in vain.

It had been three years.

As Isabel sometimes put it to herself, what was between her and Herbert Grosney had stuck, like a calf caught in a bog. She had him and yet did not have him. When he wished it, she shared his bed and they made love. In the secret darkness they whispered *sweetheart* and *darling* to each other; she called him Herbert and he called her Isabel.

But by day, in the eyes of the household, nothing whatsoever had changed. She was still just Isabel Plowman, the villein daughter of the villein woman Bella of Northfield; Isabel who looked after the household linen and sometimes, since at the time of the smallpox epidemic she had proved to be an able cook, acted as Aymer Cook's second-in-command.

She had been rewarded for her services at that time. She had better wages and the privilege, for ever, of sleeping by herself in the one-time robing room. Only she and Grosney and one other person knew that this also enabled her to visit his bed unseen. The third person was the manservant Grosney had hired to replace Rob. John Fenn came from Ely, had no friends in the neighbourhood and no living relatives anywhere. Complete silence on the subject of his employer's love-life was a condition of his employment and his own generous pay, and he observed it.

So did Isabel, for Master Grosney had made discretion a condition of her employment too. No one must know, he said. It caused jealousy in a household if one member were picked out and made much of. 'You are a dear, good girl,' he had told her, 'and I can't be too grateful for your goodness in this terrible time. But if you ever reveal to anyone that you are my mistress, you must leave my house that same day.'

And so, in public, she called him Master Grosney and at dinner, sat far away below the salt. He occasionally gave her presents but only one was of any value. He gave her this openly but pretended that it was part of the reward for nursing him through the pox. He had noticed that she often wore a bronze medallion and had asked her about it. It was worn and discoloured, he said, but it clearly meant something to her. What was it? When she told him that it was a keepsake from her grandmother and that she thought of its pattern as lucky (instinctively, she did not speak of freeborn forebears), he offered to have it copied in silver for her. 'The device on the old one will be worn away soon,' he said.

The new silver medallion was beautifully made and had a silver chain, which threaded through a ring at the top, whereas the old bronze pendant had only had a hole, which meant that it hung awkwardly. Isabel, touched, had thrown the old one away and now wore its replacement constantly.

It was a very worthwhile present indeed, but all the rest were things like gloves or shawls. A girl on a small wage might reasonably buy such things for herself, and Isabel was forbidden to tell anyone that they were from him.

The only other thing he had given her consisted of some remarkable instructions. After that first night he had said, worriedly, that he hoped she was not with child, and then to her amazement, he had presented her with a sponge. She was to cut it into pieces. She was also to take a flask of vinegar from the kitchen, and she was to insert a piece of vinegar-soaked sponge before coming to him the next night.

It would prevent pregnancy, he said, and he only hoped it wasn't too late.

It wasn't, which was fortunate. If she had conceived, he told her later, she would have had to go elsewhere, although he would have supported her, he said.

And so, for three years, they had gone on. And it wasn't enough. She had known that after the first few months. It wasn't enough to have his body, in secret. She wanted his heart and mind; she wanted to be acknowledged by him before all the world; she wanted his child.

She wanted to be his wife, to share his board as well as his bed, to be Mistress Grosney, as Rohese was.

And to share her husband's free status. The old hunger, the old ambition, had leapt up in her again, and would not be assuaged.

But when, just once, she had hinted that she wished she could be his wife, he had been so angry that she thought for a moment that it was all over and that he would cast her off the next day. He had not, but she had never dared say it again.

'It is natural for you to want marriage,' he said, when his first wrath was over, and he had finished telling her that if he had not spoken of such a thing, it was not for her to do so, and that he would never replace Mistress Lucy. With an effort she could actually see, he made himself sound reasonable. 'If any man of your own degree asks you to marry him, then take him, with my blessing. I will miss you, but I would not stand in your light.'

But she never would take any other man, she thought, craning her neck to gaze up at those astonishing stars and wondering if Grosney would summon her tonight. She wanted only this man. That was the other side of her intense and hungry nature: this fierce fidelity to the one whom she had chosen. She wanted to stay with him and love him and care for him and defend him from all ill, for ever. Only Grosney, with his worried face and long, fine hands could please her. No one else.

She went indoors, picking up the candle she had left burning near the hall door. She was the last to bed. She left the clean linen on a settle, to be sorted and put away in the morning, and went quietly to her little room. The sponge and vinegar flask were ready in a small wall-cupboard.

She lay down on her bed and waited. Presently she heard the sound she longed for, the soft tap-tap on the wall. Rising, she prepared herself, and went quietly through the door to Grosney's chamber. John Fenn was a dark shape on his truckle bed, pretending as usual that she didn't exist. She passed him like a shadow and slipped through the curtains round Herbert Grosney's bed, into the humid darkness beyond, and the heat and sweat and precision and delicacy of Grosney's body in the act of love, and the shining, expanding ecstasy at its core.

Which would be all that she desired, until the daylight came, and then it would be *yes, sir, no, sir* and *Master Grosney* once again and beneath it all, hunger and anger and resentment with which she would simply live, because she did not know what else to do.

The next day was as bright and blazing as the one before. Isabel took a pile of mending into the courtyard and sat in a shady place to sew. Tilda sat with her. Tilda's face was not, in fact, as seriously marked by the pox as she imagined. But she would not be convinced of this and had become very timid and retiring. She did not like leaving Normansland even to see her mother in Rushley, and would hide away from visitors.

It was Tilda who alerted Isabel to the arrival of unexpected guests, by uttering an exclamation of alarm, jumping up and running off with the napkin she was mending, into the shelter of the house. Isabel, who had been holding a needle up in order to thread it against the light from the dazzling sky, lowered it and looked round to see why.

She could see through the open gate to the path that led down to the landing stage. Some small boats seemed to have arrived, and a number of people were disembarking. Then she saw that one of them was Sir Simon Rushley, and that he appeared to be carrying a woman in his arms.

The boy who was on duty at the gate came running. He dashed shouting, up the hall steps and in a moment Anna and Jenkyn came out, followed a few seconds later by Herbert Grosney himself just as Sir Simon, striding ahead of his companions, came through the gate-arch.

'Sir Simon! We all thought you were in Wales! I'm happy to see you, sir, very happy to see you safely back. But what brings you . . . and what, I mean who . . .?'

Grosney was looking in bewilderment at Sir Simon's burden, who had her arms round his neck but whose head sagged against his shoulder as though she were barely conscious. She was young, with brown hair in a white headdress which was now slipping off. Her face would in health have been pleasantly rose-tinted and browned with sunshine.

Now the sunburn lay like a stain over a frightening bloodlessness.

'This is Eglantine le Hale,' explained Simon. 'She's my cousin – she was my father's ward. I've brought her back from Wales. Her husband was killed there and she's been through terrible times. I got her right across England on horseback and she bore up through that,' he said worriedly, 'but no sooner did we get to Redesmarsh, last night, than she seemed to collapse. Relief, she said it was, relief at getting to a place she knew. We set out again this morning, to cover the last few miles to Rushley, and to make the journey easier, I decided that we'd travel by flatboat. But just as we were passing your landing stage, she fainted. I thought it best to come here for help. I don't think she's seriously ill; only exhausted. I know, it's absurd, when we're so close to Rushley but if you would be indulgent . . .'

'But of course, come in, come in! Has the young lady a maid with her?'

'Yes, indeed,' said a voice which Isabel, who had hurried inquisitively forward, at once recognised. There, sure enough, was Bronwen, hastening to catch up with Sir Simon and her mistress. 'I will see to her and take care of her if she can just rest in a bed for a few hours, maybe. She was that homesick in Wales and she has seen and done such things! Seeing her home country has overset her but she will be all right with a little care. *Cariad*, you will be all right now,' she said, leaning over anxiously to smooth her mistress's hair. 'Dear lady, can you hear me? You are safe among friends in your own place now, and Bronwen is with you.'

'Bring her in!' said Grosney. 'Isabel, fetch fresh linen and make up my bed for our guest. I will sleep in the hall tonight.'

'Yes, sir.'

'Isabel! *You're* here!' cried Bronwen, suddenly recognising her.

'You know each other?' said Grosney, glancing at them and clearly wondering vaguely where they had met without being interested enough to ask. 'Excellent. Isabel, you must help this girl, show her where things are and fetch whatever is needed.'

'Give that sewing to me,' said Anna, slightly affronted because Grosney was giving his instructions to Isabel instead of to her. 'On rare occasions, Grosney did this absent-mindedly and Anna always noticed. Sometimes, Isabel wondered if she had guessed about them. 'I'll take it inside,' said Anna, in slightly officious tones, 'and Tilda can see to it.'

'If water could be made hot,' said Bronwen, 'I know my lady would be better for a fresh steaming napkin for her face and hands.'

'Follow me,' said Isabel.

'Oh, I feel so silly,' whispered Eglantine, from the depths of Herbert Grosney's bed. 'To let myself collapse like that, after the things I've seen and done! Not two miles from home! But I was thankful, so thankful to be in Norfolk. There are mountains all round one in Wales,' she said to Isabel. 'But when we were riding east, bit by bit the hills fell away and the sun seemed to grow warmer. I never felt warm in Wales. And something inside me began to loosen and loosen . . . and then today my knees loosened too and I couldn't even sit upright in that boat. Oh, how foolish you must think me.'

'You have seen and done enough to send some women off their heads, indeed,' said Bronwen briskly.

'And what of the things *you've* seen and done, Bronwen?' said her mistress.

'I've never had to stab a man,' said Bronwen.

'No. But you risked your own life. They would have killed you, Welsh though you are.'

Isabel, busy folding Grosney's used sheets, glanced at Eglantine with interest. Stabbed a man? It was difficult to imagine it. Eglantine, lying in the bed, seemed as fragile as a daffodil stalk. Her hair, loose and not yet combed, was surely too heavy for her slender neck and her hands, though browned by the sun on her ride from Wales, were surely too slim and fine of skin to be capable of such a thing.

'You need to sleep, my lady,' Bronwen said. 'That has been your trouble. For all the riding and open air, which would make most ladies sleep sound at night, you have not rested an hour in peace since you did what after all you had no choice but to do.'

Eglantine looked unhappy. 'But I did have choice, Bronwen. David ap Hywel was not trying to kill or violate me. He treated me honourably, in his fashion. He was only holding me prisoner. And I . . .'

'He had killed your man and he had put the dagger into *my* man, my Geraint, and killed him too, before your eyes. And he would have used you as a hostage. It was war,' said Bronwen in a strong voice. 'As I have said before, and as I will say again. You have confessed to a priest, you have had absolution. Now you should sleep.'

'Anna has a recipe for a soothing draught,' said Isabel. 'She buys things for it in Lynn. There is a kind of poppy seed in it, some foreign poppy. That would help her to sleep.'

'Would you ask her to make some, then, Isa?' Bronwen said.

'If I can leave her in your charge for a day or two, I will be glad,' Sir Simon said to Herbert Grosney, over the wine which had been served to them in the hall. 'I have other worries. I must go back to Redesmarsh, for one thing. There was a message I should have delivered except that I was worried about Lady Eglantine and wanted to see her safe into my wife's care.'

'A message? My dear Sir Simon, I have half a dozen people I could send on your behalf if you will entrust me with it,' Herbert Grosney said.

'Not this one, though I thank you. This message is the kind I must deliver in person. Your cousin Gerald Grosney rode with me to Wales, as one of my men, you'll recall.'

'Yes, indeed,' said Herbert, without commenting further. He was no warrior and when Simon sent out a request for volunteers to follow him, Herbert had chosen not to answer it. He had felt slightly ashamed of this when Gerald went, though not ashamed enough to change his mind. Wales was a long way off in his opinion and nothing to do with Norfolk.

'He won't be returning,' said Simon. 'And it is I, and no one else, who must tell Mistress Rohese that.'

'Killed?' ventured Herbert.

Simon nodded. His face still had some of its former boyish roundness and his light hair was still as curly as ever. But there were harder, straighter lines now round his mouth and a few grey strands near his temples. 'We're winning,' he said. 'No doubt about that. South Wales is ours. We've regained all the border lands where Llewellyn was trying to establish his rule, and we've claimed and are building castles in the north at Flint and Rhuddlan. There's to be a landing soon in Anglesey, to close in on Llewellyn from the north-west and he'll be suing for terms before the summer's out. But in any war, there are casualties. Well, I've told you now how Lady Eglantine's husband died. We were relying on him and a few like him to hold their fortresses within the borders of Gwynedd and frankly he was a fool to ride out. He had no need to, and he paid with his life.

'But the main army did need to make sorties. We had so many mouths to feed and we wanted to find out if we could where the enemy were lurking in the hills. Those damned Welsh mountains,' said Simon. 'They are like a maze of ravine and precipice. An army ten thousand strong can be within a half mile of you and no sign of it visible. Gerald Grosney was on a sortie, and it was attacked and he died.'

'Poor Rohese.' Herbert frowned into his wine. 'Gerald was an abbey tenant and there is no son to take over the tenancy. Rohese will be dispossessed, I suppose. The abbey may offer her a pension or a small tenancy but I think I shall have to do something for her. I might build her a house. I know of a suitable site. It could be built quite quickly. One must discharge one's responsibilities. I would find her another husband if I could, but . . .'

'Quite,' said Sir Simon.

'. . . there are things I don't want to remember, Eglantine said. Pleasingly clad in mulberry, with her brown hair brushed and neatly confined in a lattice of silver studded with amethysts, and refreshed after a sleep induced by Anna's poppy draught, she had come to the hall for dinner.

She was still pale beneath her sunburn but she was, she insisted, almost herself again. She was seated on Grosney's right, well away from Isabel. But she had a clear voice, which carried, and most of the household were candidly listening, because what she had to say, was interesting.

'. . . and there are things that seem too incredible to believe when

159

I do remember them! Being the back legs of a horse! It seemed so . . .
inappropriate. It was like a piece of music with a false note in it, or
a pattern with a flaw.'

'You put it wonderfully well,' said Herbert Grosney.

'Without Bronwen and Myfanwy, I would have been lost. I never
thought I could kill anyone. They gave me courage. And I *know* I could
never have climbed down those rocks into the Cwmanog, but for
Bronwen.'

'Some ladies couldn't have done it, even with ten of me,' said
Bronwen, who was beside her.

Herbert Grosney said, 'Cwmanog was the name of your husband's
castle, was it not? Does the name have a meaning?'

Eglantine shivered. 'It means the Valley of the Immortals and there are
all manner of legends about it. A waterfall plunges into the head of it, near
the castle. The sides are very steep except near the bottom, where the slope
is easy enough to let trees grow. But we went in from the top. Bronwen
said it was the only safe way to get us out of the district, the only way that
we could be sure of not meeting the enemy because they wouldn't think
it possible to climb down the sides of the Cwmanog. And it *wasn't* possible,
not really,' said Eglantine earnestly, 'except that somehow, with Bronwen
to help me, I did it. She knew a way. We climbed down backwards,
holding on with fingers and toes, and there was moonlight . . .'

She stopped, quite unable to describe how it had felt, the sense of
the drop below and the way the rocks tore at her palms, and the din
of the nearby waterfall, which was far louder on the sides of the valley
than within the castle, and which seemed to muffle all her senses.
Fortunately, it had even numbed the sense of fear. Bronwen, sometimes
beside her and sometimes below, said, 'Set your foot here,' or 'grasp
this piece of rock,' and 'it isn't as hard as you think; I've climbed down
this way many a time, for the fun of the thing,' and guided her now
and then with a firm hand on ankle or wrist.

Later, there had been the long, stumbling night walk along the boulder-
littered path by the river, the noise of which was still loud enough to
drown speech even when they had left the waterfall behind, and the
stunted oak trees leaning over them and closing them in so that . . .

'When we were at the bottom and going along the valley, I felt as
if the trees were watching us,' she said. 'And sometimes we glimpsed
the moon overhead, peering through the branches. I felt as though the
moon were watching us, too.'

'Everyone who goes through the Cwmanog says something is watching
them,' said Bronwen. 'But it is the Immortal Ones, not the trees or
the moon. They let us pass safely, at least.'

'Yes. Yes, they did. And we reached Rhuddlan where some of the
English army were and from there we were sent to Flint where the King
was — on horseback; there was an easy route; the King's forces have
been felling trees and driving roads. King Edward was so *kind* . . . he

had us brought straight to him. What we must have looked like! We'd just had a few hours' sleep at Rhuddlan, in a tent. We'd had a wash, but we had grazes from the climb down the Cwmanog and our clothes were torn . . .'

And there were bloodstains all over hers, but she didn't want to remember that.

'. . . the King sent someone to Chester where the Queen was and got clothes and things for us. I was given this.' She put up a hand and touched the silver and the amethysts. 'But oh, Master Grosney, Bronwen and I escaped safely but my other maid, Myfanwy, she went back because her brother was in the hall playing the harp. We could still hear him playing and we thought that perhaps, when David and his man pursued us, they hadn't told the rest of our escape. Myfanwy said she would wait a little and then rush in and pretend to have found the bodies, to have got blood on herself trying to see if they had any life in them and needed help, and to be innocent and terrified . . . but it was a terrible gamble. If she or her brother Owen were suspected after all, then they must be dead by now. She was so brave. I'm not brave at all. And I don't suppose I'll ever know what happened to her, or to Owen.'

'You should not think of it too much,' said Herbert Grosney kindly. 'You must eat and drink and sleep well again tonight and tomorrow, perhaps, you can finish your journey to Rushley Hall. Once you are there, Lady Cecily will look after you.'

'Yes. You sent me a message that Sir Simon wouldn't be here for dinner because he has gone back to Redesmarsh. Has he gone to see Mistress Rohese, Gerald Grosney's wife – I mean widow?'

'Yes. Poor soul,' said Grosney. 'Though perhaps, as things were, it won't be the tragedy it might have been.'

Eglantine nodded. 'Sir Simon talked to me about them on the journey. Poor soul indeed. She must wish doubly now that she had a son or daughter to be a support to her.'

'We never see Mistress Rohese these days.' Tilda, who was next to Isabel, nudged her. 'Funny, that.'

'Not so very. She probably knows I'm here. I'd remind her of things she'd rather forget,' said Isabel.

At the head of the table, Eglantine was still talking. '. . . I used to dream of Norfolk, all the time I was in Wales. And when I saw the flat country again, and the marshes and the lovely wide skies, well, as you know, I just came over weak with thankfulness,' Eglantine smiled at her host. 'I can still hardly believe I'm back. When I see Sir Simon and Lady Cecily, I shall implore them: don't send me away from here again. I'll marry anyone they say or enter Redesmarsh Abbey, if only, if only, I need never leave Norfolk again.'

On a sultry August morning, two weeks later, Master Herbert Grosney sent for Isabel.

She was sitting in the courtyard again, patching the elbows of a favourite tunic of his. Although he was usually smart in his dress, there were a few aged garments to which he was attached. He only wore them privately, at home, but he liked them kept wearable for as long as possible. She put the work aside when Anna came to tell her that the master wanted her in the hall. She was puzzled. Grosney so rarely singled her out in public, and on the rare occasions when he did, Anna usually looked annoyed. This time, she seemed rather pleased.

Nevertheless, Isabel was glad as well as puzzled, for there had been no tap on the wall now for fourteen nights. She went quickly.

In such hot weather, the hall was usually deserted during the day. Those who could, found occupations outside. Master Grosney was alone, standing by the empty hearth, holding an open book in his hands and frowning at it. He looked as dear as if they had been lovers last night, and as remote as though he were his own effigy. She made her curtsy. 'Sir?'

'Good morning, Isabel. Another very sticky day, isn't it? I think we shall have thunder soon.'

He couldn't have called her in here to discuss the weather. Isabel waited. He put the book down on a nearby table. 'Isabel, I have something to tell you. I thought it best to tell you quietly, before I made an open announcement to the household. My news will come as a surprise to you and perhaps upset you somewhat. Believe me, you will always have a place in my employment and indeed, in my thoughts. I have been grateful for your kindness in comforting my loneliness . . .'

What in the world was he talking about? Isabel's stomach felt strange, hollow. 'Sir?'

'I shall be making the announcement at dinner today. There is no sense, I suppose, in wrapping it up in a great many words. At Christmas, I am to be married, to the Lady Eglantine, widow of Sir Hugh le Hale and cousin to Sir Simon Rushley.'

Isabel said nothing. The hollow where her stomach had been was a great yawning pit and she felt as though she were toppling into it.

'And so,' said Grosney, ploughing on, 'our . . . our arrangement must naturally now come to an end.'

Eglantine. That pretty, silly, *barren* creature, with her pathetic airs. Five years married and no children. While she, Isabel, who would so gladly have given children to Herbert Grosney, had been ordered to use a vinegar-soaked sponge to prevent it.

She had loved Herbert Grosney and served him devotedly for all those five years, and then Eglantine had been carried under the gate-arch, to take away everything, *everything*, for which Isabel had yearned.

'Oh, for the love of God,' said Master Grosney, 'Don't cry!'

'I can't help it! After all this time . . . I loved you from the moment I first came here, even before we . . . I . . .'

162

'Loved me? Stop that. Stop crying, I say! We shall have half the household buzzing round like gnats. You desired me, yes.'

'More than that! Much, much more!'

'Isabel, please remember that we belong to different stations in life. There could be no question of anything, well, lasting between us and . . .'

'Why not? Why not? Look at Rohese and Master Gerald Grosney!'

'Well, that was a mésalliance. But . . .'

'Why? Why?'

'Because,' said Herbert Grosney coldly, regarding her tear-streaked face with distaste, 'Rohese was born a villein, and had no dowry to speak of, no connections, nothing except her beauty and, among people of my sort, a bride is required to have dowry and connections . . . *brides*? Isabel. I remember that once before you made hints about marriage. I told you then that between us, such a thing was not to be mentioned.'

'I love you.' Isabel wiped her eyes with her hands. 'Please don't talk as if I were just a kitchen slut.' Into the shocking silence which followed, Isabel said tightly, 'That's what you do think, isn't it?'

'My dear girl, you said it. I didn't.'

But it was true. The signs had always been there. The insistence on secrecy; the sponge, her unchanged place below the salt, his small, mean gifts; and, most of all, that frightening anger at even the whisper of the word *marriage*.

'No,' she said. 'You didn't say it. But you think it, right enough. I can tell.'

'Isabel, I'm a man, with a man's needs. I took what I was offered and yes, I was glad of it, and I hope that I gave you something, some pleasure, in return. But when all is said and done . . .'

'All this time, I've been thinking we were lovers and you've been thinking you were amusing yourself with a slut.'

Grosney was angry now. 'It was you who threw yourself at me, if you remember. And before that, well, I had noticed things. All the times you accidentally bumped into me or had to squeeze past me in doorways: the way you'd look at me all through dinner. Every time I glanced along the table, I'd see you staring . . .'

'I'm not a slut! You look at me and that's what you see?' An errant memory, long submerged by time, surfaced in her mind. A marshland dawn, back in the days when Alfred still lived, just after Rohese had paid that memorable visit to Rushley. Herself, watching a marsh harrier and thinking: *how is it that what you feel like inside and what other people see when they look at you can be so different?*

'You're cruel,' she said. 'And you're wrong. I never had any man but my husband until you and . . .'

Her voice broke, in hurt and misery, and she began to weep. 'Hush, hush . . . stop that . . . *Isabel*, stop it!' Grosney said, and when she didn't stop, seized her shoulders and shook her. Her sobbing went up

163

and down the scale but still continued. He pushed her into the nearest settle, grabbed a cushion, rammed it over her face and held it there, muffling the noise. Then he removed it. Isabel, scarlet, gasped for breath. They were no longer alone. Interested faces, drawn by her crying, were peering round the doors.

'Out!' roared Master Grosney. The spectators vanished, though with an air of reluctance.

'Thank you,' said Grosney furiously. 'Thank you very much. You have made a din and a disturbance and undoubtedly started gossip in the house; the one thing I hoped would never happen.'

'Because you're ashamed of me?' said Isabel bitterly.

'Perhaps because I have sometimes felt ashamed of myself. I have never approved of men who make use of their maidservants in such a way. I have been aware of my own weakness.'

'And that's all I've been? Just a weakness?' The hurt was beyond tears now. It burst suddenly into a wild and useless threat. 'What if I go to her, your lady Eglantine and tell her all about us? What then?'

She knew as soon as she had spoken just how stupid those words were. Even if Eglantine then refused the marriage, Grosney would not return to her, to Isabel. He would hate her all the more. And Eglantine would not refuse, in any case. Lonely men often consoled themselves with their maidservants; what of it? She would ask only that the maidservant should not remain under this roof. And Herbert Grosney would not deny her.

She looked at him, and saw what she had done, saw the fastidious lines deepen to a horrifying disgust, saw her own exile in his eyes.

'I could have given you children,' she said hopelessly. '*She* can't, from all I hear. If only I'd been freeborn, you . . .'

'Be quiet! My children are not your concern. How dare you?' He paused, then continued in grimly measured tones. 'Well, Isabel, you have shown yourself plainly to me this morning. May I ask, has anyone ever told you how it came about that Abbess Christiana was finally condemned?'

Isabel gaped, bewildered.

'No, perhaps they didn't. I didn't know myself at the time when I brought you here, or I wouldn't have brought you. I didn't find out till much later, when I chanced to dine with Sir Henry and Father Benedict was there. He spoke of it. Abbess Christiana was caught in the act, my dear, of cursing *you*, and she said a good deal at her second trial, about the way you didn't know your place and the hard task she'd had to keep you in order, and it seems that she repeated, over and over, that she was sure that when you called me and the priest to my wife's bedside, it was an act of spite. When I offered you work, I'd believed otherwise but when I heard the details of that second trial, well, I started to wonder. I started to think, maybe, that witch or not, when she cursed you, she had had provocation.'

Isabel remained silent.

'I won't deny,' said Master Grosney, 'that in a way, it was part of your attraction, that streak of badness. You were such a mixture. So kind and good during my illness but with that badness there just the same. It was attractive; like a meal with spice on it, I suppose. I came to you, my dear, like a hawk to the lure. But those days are over now. They would never have begun if I'd known just how far the evil in you went. If you had accepted my marriage gracefully, I meant to treat you well. You could have continued in your present work, or I would have recommended you to another household, or I would have found you a marriage in your own degree . . .'

I don't want another marriage. I only want you. The words kept drumming in her head. For five years he had been the desire of her life and she would have followed wherever he led. If he had been cast out of his home and driven to live in a fetid alley in Norwich or London, she would have gone too. She would have followed him to war and risked death at the hands of the most savage enemy; she would have gone to fabled Cathay with him, or to hell.

That hideous moment of physical contact just now, when he had thrust her into the settle and used a cushion to silence her crying, was the last time she would ever touch him. In her whole life. In all eternity.

'But as it is,' he said, 'I see that I am at risk from your spiteful tongue. I shall see that you have as little chance as possible to spread your poison. If the future holds scant happiness for you, the fault is yours.'

'This is the place,' said Father Benedict, and pushed her through the door. 'Wait here, and I will fetch your new mistress. She is hiding herself away, which I fear is a habit of hers.'

The house was on Normansland, but out on its border with Oxfen, a good two miles from any other habitation. It was stout enough, newly built and dry, made of wattle and daub, but double-walled and thickly thatched with reeds. It had two ground-level rooms, one for use as a byre, and a loft above. It was essentially the dwelling of a well-off villein.

She was to live here, Father Benedict had said in the flatboat which had brought them up the Meadbrook to the nearest landing point, and serve the woman who was the only tenant, and look after her two cows. She stood in the main room with her bundle at her feet and waited.

It was only a day after that ugly scene with Grosney. She had not seen him since. She had hidden in her room all the rest of that day, going without her dinner, for then, he would announce his marriage plans. She had cried all night in her little room.

But with the morning, a numb acceptance had taken hold of her. Grosney had not said what was to happen to her, but she would know soon enough and when it came, she would have no option but to endure it. Behind her were generations of villeins who endured whatever burdens their masters laid on them because they could do nothing else.

When Father Benedict arrived and said she was to come with him, she had obeyed, putting her few belongings together and accompanying him without speaking.

Father Benedict, now, had vanished up the ladder to the loft. Isabel stood looking at the aperture through which he had gone, awaiting events without even curiosity. Presently, he came down again, followed by a woman. She wore a dark gown and a concealing widow's wimple and she descended the ladder with her head averted. Not until she reached its foot did she turn and face the girl who had been brought to serve her.

They stared at each other in shock.

'Of course,' said Father Benedict, 'you must know each other a little. Mistress Grosney, you surely remember Isabel of Northfield. And Isabel, yes, this is Mistress Rohese Grosney.'

It was clear now why, at dinner on the day Eglantine came, Master Grosney had made that cryptic remark that perhaps Gerald Grosney's death wasn't the tragedy it might have been. Isabel had thought it referred to their childlessness but she had been wrong.

She understood now why Rohese hadn't been seen in Rushley for three years and perhaps why Gerald Grosney had volunteered to serve in Wales.

Rohese had had the smallpox, and no one had wrapped her in protective crimson. Her face was a ruin, a hideous, pitted mask, which looked as though the coarsened skin had been bombarded with pebbles or attacked by woodworm. Only her blue eyes retained their beauty, looking out from her dreadful face as though the pockmarks were the bars on a cell window.

And the size and nature of this house, thought Isabel grimly, were no doubt the result of oh, such nice judgement on the part of Herbert Grosney. Rohese had married his cousin Gerald and was therefore, by marriage, a member of the Grosney family. Now that she was widowed, Herbert, as head of the family, had a responsibility towards her. He was discharging it, providing her with a house and a servant and probably with an allowance. Gerald had been a tenant on Redesmarsh Abbey land and it was, Isabel knew, the abbey's custom to pay pensions to tenants' widows, but she also knew that such pensions were usually very small. Very likely, Grosney would choose to augment it.

But he had not forgotten that Rohese was born a villein of Rushley. It was not the sort of thing that he forgot.

'Mistress Grosney's maidservant Goda is soon to be married,' said Father Benedict briskly, 'and she did not wish to live in so remote a place, in any case. But your new mistress, as I'm sure you understand, would rather live secluded. She will see no visitors and prefers to be where casual passers-by will not come. This house is well away from any track and you will have noticed, Isabel, that it can't be seen from Meadbrook, although the stream passes it quite close. You will be not only Mistress Grosney's servant, but her only company.'

Rohese stared at her defiantly, daring her to laugh, to point a finger. Blankly, Isabel said, 'I'm sorry, Rohese. I'm very sorry.'

166

'Thank you, Isabel.' Rohese's voice was a flat monotone. 'It's kind of you to say so.'

Rohese had been rude to her when they met in London, but she had also been afraid of her. Isabel knew that quite well. She wouldn't have wished this on Rohese. Her misery would be lifelong, as endless as Isabel's own.

Father Benedict spoke once more. 'Isabel, you are to serve and look after Mistress Rohese. You are to remain at all times with your mistress. She must not be left alone. You must be kind and attentive; let me hear no complaints of you from her. May God pity you if there are. You're to talk to her about everyday things and encourage her to do everyday tasks, to spin and stitch and to help you with the cows and the butter and cheese. You will have to live as much like sisters as mistress and servant. You must encourage her all you can; otherwise she'll just sit and cry or stare at the wall. You must try to overcome your despair, Mistress Rohese. It is a sin so to rebel against the will of God. Three years, and still you are repining! It is not even your husband's death which has done this to you. In your old home, you have kept to your chamber ever since you were ill.'

'And ever since my illness, I have been as good as a widow,' said Rohese, still in that flat voice. 'My hold on Gerald was poor enough even before that. Afterwards, I had nothing. He averted his eyes if he saw me. Do you wonder that I hid from the world? Here, at least, I can take the air sometimes.'

'You have a life to live. You have refused to enter the abbey, so you will live it here. Isabel will help you, but you must make more effort. Isabel, I trust you understand? This is your work and there's to be no neglecting it, no running off to Rushley village or Redesmarsh Fair. I will come frequently, to celebrate Mass and to find out what needs to be bought for yourselves or for the house. I shall expect to find you here, every time. If you are once found absent, I assure you, you will weep for it. Your mother may visit you occasionally, of course.'

'You won't stay,' said Rohese, looking at Isabel. 'You'll go off and get married. Like Goda.'

'I shall stay,' said Isabel shortly.

She had sat silent in the boat on the way, but Father Benedict had done some talking, while she sat dumbly listening. He had told her then that she was to be a servant to a woman in a lonely house, and he had made it clear that the task would be for always.

'I know what has passed between you and Master Grosney and although he is a sinner, you are much worse, Isabel. You tempted him, and you are in addition beset by the sin of pride and possessed of a vicious tongue. I fear, as does Master Grosney, that the Abbess Christiana was right about that. And so, Isabel, we have decided that for you, and your salvation, the right to seek new employment or another marriage on your own initiative, must be withdrawn.

167

'You once wanted to enter the abbey. That would have been lifelong. So will this. It is no more confined and maybe it'll save your soul which I fear you've placed in jeopardy. Nor can you appeal to the lord of Rushley. Master Grosney will tell Sir Simon everything. I have no doubt that Sir Simon will support our decision.'

Isabel had no doubt of it, either. They were all men and they were all men of status. They would stand together against any challenge from the outsider who was both a villein and female.

She stood there, looking at Rohese but not seeing her. She saw instead, the years that stretched before her, desolate as the flat marshes themselves, empty of human society except for, occasionally, Father Benedict and her mother, and, not occasionally but day after day, of all people, Rohese.

Herbert Grosney, whom she loathed now as much as loved but still − because the body apparently had an obstinate mind of its own − desired, would be only a couple of miles away, but she would never see him. Grosney would make sure of that.

Her old friend Bronwen would be there too, but she would not see even Bronwen. He would make sure of that, as well.

And so it would be; until age took hold of her and all desire, for love or friendship, faded away; until either she or Rohese died.

Isabel of Northfield, who had once hungered for freedom quite as fiercely as she had hungered for Herbert Grosney, would stay here, cut off from the world, with no choice, with even the limited rights of the villein taken from her.

It was almost funny. She had always been good at looking after people. It had been her best virtue in the eyes of her mother and of Abbess Julian. It had won her, for a short time, the body of Herbert Grosney.

Now she would have to devote the rest of her life to looking after . . . Rohese.

To the alarm of both Father Benedict and Rohese, she began to laugh. Then she felt the bubbling up of hysteria and forced herself to stop, gasping and clutching at her throat.

Her fingers touched the chain on which she wore, hidden under her dress, the one valuable gift her lover had ever given her: the new silver medallion bearing the motif passed down to her by a freeborn forebear.

If Christiana had really cursed her, the curse had worked. She, Isabel, was less now than a villein, and her own one and only claim to effectiveness was that she could, in a manner of speaking, be said to have killed the Abbess Christiana.

PART III
Thomas and Nicola:
Flying Free
1330–50

It was like death in a way, something too vast to hurt much or even to upset you. I saw the end of the twine lying loose, with no leash tied to it. It had snapped quite clean. Gos was gone . . .

I searched for him with an electric torch for two more hours, but he was gone.

Chapter Ten

Reaching High

Nicola of the Lea was in the smokehouse behind the cottage, gutting eels and making a neat pattern of sloping cuts in them, so that the smoke would penetrate when they were hung up over the peat fire in its stone-lined bed.

She worked quickly, being used to the task, but if her hands were efficient, her expression was nevertheless slightly tinged with distaste. She had tied a scarf over her hair, to keep out the smell of fish. Nicola had hair of a pretty honey colour, which matched her eyes, and she often wasted time (*wasted* was her mother's word) gathering scented herbs to add to the water when she washed it. She washed her face in buttermilk too, whenever she could get hold of some. Her hair and her eyes and her pleasing, rounded features were worth looking after, in her opinion. They represented most of her fortune.

Running feet and a bang as the door was flung open announced the unwelcome arrival of her ten-year-old brother Will. 'Mam says aren't you finished with that basketful yet? There's another still to do. She says if you must send Dad all over the place on wild-goose chases for you, you could at least get the work done while he's gone.'

'I'm nearly done. It might be as well if you lent a hand instead of running about with messages and then lounging in that doorway with your hands idle.'

'I'm not idle. I've been up the Meadbrook and got us perch for supper. I had a look downstream as well. No sign of Dad coming back yet. It won't be any use, you know,' said Will in a lofty voice.

'What won't?' Nicola impaled an eel on a hook and picked the last one out of the basket.

'What he's gone to Osbert Smith for?'

'You know nothing about it. You're too young.'

'And you'll be too old soon,' said Will smartly. 'You're already twenty. You've fair worn our Dad out, Mam says, going here and there and worrying over you and trying to please you. You've wasted years, she says.'

Nicola applied the gutting knife angrily to the final eel and snapped, 'Will you mind your own business?'

171

'I think what happens in the family is my business as much as yours. You want too much,' said Will maddeningly. 'You'll end up not marrying anyone and scrubbing floors in Redesmarsh Abbey instead. That's what happens to girls who won't wed. They get pushed into the abbey to be lay sisters. Everyone says so.'

Brother and sister regarded each other inimically. 'You listen a lot too much to what your elders say with those jug ears of yours, and you don't understand even half of it,' said Nicola offensively.

'Don't call me jug ears!' Will had the same hair and eyes and the same round face as his sister, but Nicola had always been devoutly grateful – to the point of whispered prayers in church – that her ears were not large and obtrusive like his.

'I'll call you what I like. You're a pest,' she snapped. 'Go away.'

Will continued to lean casually against the doorpost. 'I saw Thomas Woodcarver while I was out,' he said. 'He was walking along the bank. I poled over to say hello. I like Thomas. He made me a whistle once, with sort of leaves carved on it. He asked after you.'

'Did he now?' said Nicola furiously.

'You ought to take him. He's willing. Dad won't get anywhere with Osbert Smith any more than he did with those people at Oxfen or the ones at Redesmarsh. What have you got that they'd want?'

Nicola turned on him. 'I'd have got that boy over at Redesmarsh but for you! If you hadn't been born, I'd be in line for this whole place and if I'd married a freeman he'd have had it to sell or let. But you had to come along and spoil it all, didn't you?'

'You're silly,' said Will, undisturbed. 'Sir Edward wouldn't let it go just like that. Mam says you just don't know what the real world's like.'

'If you quote Mam just once more, I'll . . .!'

'You'll what?'

'Cut your jug ears off!' screamed Nicola, and ran at him, brandishing the knife. Will folded his arms and grinned. Nicola threw the knife down and advanced, empty-handed but menacing. Her brother, recognising that while the knife was not a serious threat, the flat of Nicola's strong palm most definitely was, stuck out his tongue and then fled.

Nicola picked up the knife, stared at it blankly and then turned to look out through the open door, across the vegetable patch to the Meadbrook and its muddy, wandering course downstream to the marshes. There was still no sign of her father's boat.

The blustery late September wind blew in and sent a cloud of smoke swirling from the firepit. The smell of smoke and fish seemed to pervade the whole world. Nicola turned to go on gutting the eel and then, abruptly, burst into tears. She dropped the knife again and her hand went to her breast, and through her brown working dress, her fingers grasped the round, hard outline of the medallion she wore concealed there, which had been given to her by her aged relative Isabel Plowman, of whom Nicola now wished with all her heart that she had never heard.

'I'm sorry,' said Osbert Smith to Nicola's father, William of the Lea. 'But there it is. I've a duty to do my best for my son. I don't want to give offence, William. But . . .'

Osbert bore the name Smith but he did not keep a forge, although his grandfather had. This was happening more and more nowadays. Whole families had become known by the callings or nicknames of just one forebear. There were still Smiths, cousins of Osbert's, in the Rushley forge but their various kinsfolk were now farmers and fishermen and Osbert had a hundred and twenty acres on the seaward side of Rushley and the right to take shellfish and wildfowl on the marsh between his land and the sea, in return for handing Sir Edward Rushley a share. No lord of Rushley had ever tried to drain that stretch of marsh. It was not only too extensive; it was also rich in tasty food.

Osbert paid rent in fish and fowl but not in work. His time was his own. He was free, and no villein. There always had been a sense of mystery about smithcraft and a special respect paid to it, and when, forty years ago, Osbert's grandfather had walked into Sir Simon Rushley's hall followed by his two sons each carrying a box of silver, and requested to be allowed to buy himself and his family out of villeinage for all perpetuity, Sir Simon hadn't argued.

The Smiths were people of consequence in the district now and Osbert, indeed, had special importance. Edward the First had made a law that every district must appoint two constables, to organise the hue and cry if a crime were committed, and to make sure that all able-bodied men possessed and could use weapons of some sort, so that they could be summoned in time of war. Osbert was a constable of Rushley.

Though separated from the forge by two generations, he nevertheless had a true smith's physique: the shoulders and biceps to wield a fourteen-pound hammer, and the rumbling voice with which generations of his ancestors had soothed nervous horses. He was thirty-eight and was still much as he had been at thirty: even his hair remained thick and had kept its tow colour. His wife, however, had fallen victim, some years back, to the strange marshland disease of premature ageing and their children had not thriven well. It remained to be seen how the one surviving son, who resembled his mother in looks, would fare.

But one thing was sure: if he outlived his father, he would one day have a hundred and twenty acres, virtually of his own. He was nineteen now and looking for a wife.

Who would not, however, be Nicola. 'I'm *really* sorry,' Osbert said, since, although he had paused, William did not speak. 'I've always lived in peace with my neighbours. And I know how hard you've tried for your girl's sake . . .'

William looked at him. His blue eyes, set a little close in a face narrower than was typical of the district, was not offended; only miserable. 'I daresay everyone knows for miles,' he said bitterly. 'I overindulge my girl, they say, and maybe they're right. I've tried one family after another, over all the three manors: going round trying to sell her . . . that's what it feels like. I said to her once: do you really want me to go round offering you like goods in a pedlar's pack? Saying to people; look at my daughter, see how pretty she is. Telling them: she can bake, she can milk, she's healthy, . . . and she can gut fish in her sleep,' he finished in despair.

'Will you have some ale?' said Osbert. 'To show there's no hard feelings?' William nodded. Osbert went into the adjoining room and came back with two brimming tankards. Handing one to William, he said, 'I've only seen your girl from a distance, in church, but I know she's a nice-looking lass. And if she's set her heart on marrying a freeman . . . I'd have said yes, William, except that my boy's already set *his* heart elsewhere. Truth to tell, he's got a fancy for that second daughter of Richard Grosney's.'

'What, one of the bailiff's girls?' William took a drink of ale. He looked surprised, as well he might. Everyone who owed rent or customary service to Sir Edward Rushley, loathed Richard Grosney. He was a cousin of Walcher Grosney who held the big farm which had once been called Normansland but was now called Norsland. Rushley bailiffs, as they were called now rather than reeves, nearly always were Grosney connections; it was a tradition. Richard was literate, and used his skills for keeping meticulous records of everything that happened on his lord's estate, so that Sir Edward should lose not one pot of honey or a single fresh-caught eel, not one heriot beast due as payment for the right to inherit, and not one hour's bonded labour.

Added to which, he was Rushley's other constable, which gave him an extra right to poke his nose into other people's business, a right he had no compunction in using. The sound of Richard Grosney's official footstep and the sight of his taut face approaching one's dwelling usually made the occupant want to slide out of the back door or hide under the bed and some people had actually been known to do these things.

He had a house of his own and a wife called Elinor. He treated her quite well but had no reason to do otherwise. He had married her when she was fourteen and trained her carefully to regard him – said Rushley cynically – as God. Asked for an opinion on anything at all, even on whether it was likely to rain tomorrow, Elinor would start her reply with, 'Richard says . . .'

Their trio of meek and soft-voiced daughters, similarly, began every other sentence with, 'Father says . . .'

And your boy wants to marry into *that* family? said William's expression now.

'She's a taking little thing,' said Osbert apologetically. 'Chatters quite

174

merrily when she's out of Grosney's hearing. And, of course, there's the dowry.'

'Quite. That's the point, ain't it?' The bitterness was back in William's voice. 'What I can give Nicola ain't bad, but . . .'

'If my boy had his eye on Nicola, the dowry wouldn't matter so much,' said Osbert. 'But as things are . . . well, if I can get him the girl he wants and she has a good portion to go with her, that's doing right by him. Now isn't it?'

William took a long swig from his ale and sighed. 'I suppose so. When I started all this, I did have hopes. This sort of thing's happening more these days. Girls do make these marriages. But somehow or other . . . her portion's just not enough and we're too far down, that's what it is.' He took another swig and produced a smile, albeit not a very mirthful one. 'The smell of fish puts them off. And she's twenty already and I'm getting tired. Every time I set off on another of these tries at . . . at . . . taking her to market, I feel dead weary before I start. What am I to do?'

Osbert regarded him with sympathy. 'If I offer you a bit of advice, will you mind?'

'No,' said William. He did not know Osbert well, but once or twice, when out fishing early in the morning, they had met and joined forces for an hour or two, and William had taken a liking to him. He did not think that Osbert Smith would wound or offend him intentionally.

'Look,' Osbert said now. 'Your girl's got all these notions in her head, but going along with them may not be the best thing for her. You thought of that? Maybe you're a better judge of what's right for her than she is. You want to look round for the sort of lad *you* think she ought to marry and fix it up. She'll come round, you'll see. What's her mother think about it all?'

'Syb? She thinks what you think. She's said it, too, to Nicola. But Nicola just breaks down and cries.'

'Ah. You'll have to be hard-hearted, maybe, to be kind in the end. What good would it do her, if I forced her down my boy's throat? He wouldn't be happy and he wouldn't make her happy either. You tell her, better a plain man, villein or not, as long as he likes her, than someone with all the world's goods and privileges, that doesn't.'

'Better a dinner of herbs, where love is, than a stalled ox and hatred withal?'

'Aye. Father Matthew talked on that last Sunday, didn't he? Nicola should have listened to him. There's plenty more ale. Fancy another?'

The masculine atmosphere of Osbert Smith's house was very agreeable. His own house, William thought, was too much under female influence. It would be better when Will was grown, perhaps. Meanwhile, Osbert was first-class company.

They settled down to another round of ale.

*　　*　　*

It was well on in the afternoon when William poled home up the Meadbrook. His dwelling was welcoming enough to his eyes as he punted to his little landing place, where he had flattened and paved a few yards of bank and installed a couple of mooring posts. It was a pity Nicola had this ambition to better herself. What was wrong, he'd like to know, with her parents' way of life and her parents' home? All right, if you were gentry, used to a stone house and panelled walls in the dining hall, then William of the Lea's house no doubt looked as if it were made of earth and growing from it, a mere bulge in the ground with a shaggy wig of reed thatch on top. And no doubt gentrified eyes would find the inside small and sooty. But daub was as good a material as stone for keeping you warm and dry and some said it was better, and the reed thatch was rain-proof all right. The vegetable plot which extended along the river bank for a good way on either side kept them in beans and peas, cabbages and onions, parsnips and radishes and there were six apple trees on the sheltered side of the house, and a watercress bed further upstream.

There was a byre too, for the small herd of cows he pastured on the commonland, and the smokehouse where his catch was dried was properly built; anyone could see that this was a place run by a man who knew what he was doing.

He'd improved the place a lot since Sir Edward bestowed it on him at the time when he married Syb. It had belonged previously to a family of Eelfishers, that half-savage clan which had somehow never been assimilated into the pattern of lord and villein which held everyone else as though in an iron web. As more land was drained and the marshes retreated, the Eelfishers had followed them, because marshes were their natural habitat and they seemed to be unhappy anywhere where it was possible to walk about normally instead of on stilts.

Sir Edward Rushley, usually a fierce defender of his rights, never tried to stop them drifting off the manor. He merely observed 'Good riddance' whenever another waterside plot was abandoned, and found better tenants. In this case, William and Sybil.

All right, Sir Edward, damn him, did grab far too many barrels of fish and far too much of his, William's, time on Sir Edward's land, but when was life ever perfect?

Just now, the smoke rising from the roof vent, which was set to one side because one of his improvements had been a hearth delved out of the thick wall, with a flue through the wall above it, and the promise of something tasty cooking on the fire, was good enough for him and he was mighty sorry it wasn't good enough for Nicola, too.

He found Sybil busy, as he had hoped, with the stewpot. Will was sitting cross-legged in a corner, repairing a fishing net. Beside him, giving an amiable hand, was his Uncle Dick.

'Hello,' said William to his elder brother. 'What brings you here? Haven't seen you for a while.' He caught Sybil's eye and gave her a

176

tiny shake of the head. She nodded and devoted herself once more to the cooking.

Neither William nor Dick were young men. William had been forty when Nicola was born, and Dick was six years his senior. When their father, Stephen Carpenter, died, Dick had taken over the carpentry workshop by right, but without regret on William's side, because William frankly preferred to fish and raise vegetables. Dick, who now worked with his grandson, had formed a mutually useful partnership with the Woodcarver family whose house and workshop were only a couple of doors away from his own. Dick and John Carpenter made things: Ed Woodcarver and his son Thomas decorated them.

But when Thomas proposed for Nicola's hand, with his father and Dick Carpenter as intermediaries, and was refused, an unease had fallen between William and his brother. Dick had not called round casually like this for a long time.

'Can't keep it up for ever,' Dick said now. 'Got to be reasonable. The offer's still open, Ed says. Thomas knows what he wants. But I gather from Sybil here that you've been talking to Osbert Smith about his boy.'

'Aye, and I've been turned down flat,' said William shortly. 'Where's Nicola, Syb? I'd have thought she'd be agog for Osbert's answer, not that she'll like it when she hears it.'

'I sent her over to Mistress Sixacre with a few early apples. Meg Sixacre's been ill. And it was a way of getting Nicola out of my road,' said Sybil. 'I didn't think you'd be back with good news, somehow. She won't be here yet. Sit you down; you look tired.' Broad-built Sybil was rarely tired, but she was always considerate when William, who was slighter and beginning to develop a rheumatic knee, flagged as he sometimes did. 'She's putting you through it,' she said crossly.

'She *was*,' said William, with emphasis on the past tense. He looked at his brother. 'But I've had enough of it now.' Something in his voice made Sybil pause once more in her cooking. She glanced at him sharply but did not speak. 'If Thomas truly has a mind to her, still,' William said, 'and his father's agreeable, you can carry a message to them from me, if you will, Dick. Tell them I consent. And that so will Nicola.'

Silently, expressively, Sybil raised her eyebrows almost to the edge of her linen headdress. and pursed her lips.

'I don't like doing it,' William said, when Dick had taken a share of the stew and gone. 'I don't, Syb. But Osbert is right; he only said what you've been saying and what I know at heart is true. We're doing Nicola no favours, carrying on like this. When she comes in, I'll tell her.'

'She'll howl her eyes out,' remarked Will from his corner.

His father turned. 'And no gibes from you, boy. You only make things worse, with your sneering at her.'

'She doesn't like me, so I don't like *her*.'

177

'She won't be here for long for you to like or dislike each other but until she goes, you can behave yourself. Go and fetch the cows in.'

'That's Nicola's job.'

'Do as you're told!' snapped Sybil, and watched with satisfaction, as her son departed unwillingly for the common. 'Mistress Sixacre lives a good way off,' she said as the door banged shut. 'Nicola won't be home for a while. I just wanted to put off the moment when you told her that Osbert had said no, because I was sure he'd say no. I heard a rumour, this very day, about his boy being after one of the Grosney girls.'

'Did you? Well, it's true. I wish we'd known before. Or maybe not. Talking to Osbert cleared my mind. I see,' said William, dryly jesting, 'that you still like Nicola to be charitable and take treats to the sick and elderly.'

'Well, I do, though I grant you it wasn't always a good idea.' Sybil piled used stewbowls and spoons into a net ready to be left in the river overnight to get clean. 'That's how all this trouble started. I meant well, William. I was sorry for poor old Mistress Isabel, out there in that lonely house, and I thought it was good training for Nicola to take butter and apples to her and help out with the hoeing. If I'd known that Isabel was stuffing her up with stupid ideas about marrying above herself . . . I put a stop to it when I found out but by then it was too late. The harm was done.'

'Though Nicola was only ten. She can't have been more; Isabel died just before Will was born and *he's* ten. Amazing, that what Mistress Isabel told her stuck so long,' William said.

'I think Isabel went a bit funny before she died,' said Sybil, 'and what she said sounded impressive. It's an odd thing but people's who're not right in the head can sound no end convincing. Remember that Rohese woman that lived with Isabel and died about six years sooner? *She* was a bit funny, if you like! I used to take the butter and whatnot up there myself then; Nicola was too small. Rohese gave me the creeps. She'd spend hours sitting in front of a scratched old silver mirror, combing her hair – she had yards and yards of it, all grey and dirty – and patting lotions on her pockmarks and talking about the marriage she'd make when she'd cleared her skin. She was clean off her head, but she'd talk in such a reasonable voice and make it sound so real that I'd come away wondering if I was barmy instead of her! I'd have to shake myself to realise that it wasn't so. I think Isabel had an effect like that on Nicola. Perhaps Isabel sounded reasonable and natural to her, and Nicola's never learned enough sense, even now, to work out that she was hearing a lot of foolishness.'

'You may well be right,' William said. 'I daresay Isabel did go a bit strange. First living with Rohese and then being alone up there would be enough to make anyone odd, but maybe Nicola took her seriously. I couldn't make out why Isabel stayed there, after Rohese died. The

Woodcarvers would have given her house-room; they were some sort of cousins to her. Come to that, so am I, though it's pretty distant.'

'She said once that being alone was the only freedom she'd ever known, whatever that may mean,' said Sybil. 'As for being related to you; well, I'm glad we weren't landed with her. I can't work out how you were kin to her anyhow.'

'Nor can I, but it's what the priest said when I was getting married to my first wife and he looked up the kinbook to make sure it was all right. He just mentioned the link in passing. My mother was a Lightfoot, and the Lightfoots and the Northfields – Isabel was born a Northfield – were related. In fact, I checked that relationship again, not long ago, just to make sure there was no impediment to Nicola marrying Thomas Woodcarver.'

'Did you, indeed?' Sybil looked at him thoughtfully.

'Well, it was just after we first heard of the proposal and I thought maybe we'd talk her round. Father Matthew said it was all right, that the link is too far back to matter.'

Sybil cocked her head. 'I can hear Nicola coming. Well, Dick's gone off with your message, so now we'll have to talk her round.'

'No, we shan't,' said William, with the surprising resolution which just occasionally appeared in him. Sybil had seen it only once or twice before but it always impressed her. 'I'll deal with it,' he said. 'And I'll be *telling* her.'

'Not Thomas!' Nicola wailed. 'Someone else, if you like, if it's all no good and you can't find me what I want, but not Thomas Woodcarver!'

'Now what on earth's all this?' In spite of his resolution earlier, William of the Lea now looked exhausted. It had been bad enough, seeing Nicola come in with her face all bright with a hope he would have to destroy, and knowing that she would make a fuss when he told her that he had fixed on Thomas. But he hadn't expected quite this kind of fuss, as if Thomas, in addition to being a mere villein, was also some kind of monster. It was too much. His weariness sparked into anger. 'See here, Nicola. I've had enough. You're making us all into a laughing stock, turning your nose up at good chances and making me go after impossible ones. Remember what Master Dorrard at Redesmarsh said to me? "You've nothing to offer," he said. "If there was a big dowry now, things might be different but as it is, your girl may be the prettiest climbing rose on earth but my son isn't a trellis." And he sent me away without even a cup of ale. I can't face any more of it. It's got to stop.'

'I won't marry Thomas! I don't like him.' Nicola sat rigid on the settle by the wall-hearth of which her father was so proud (no Eelfisher would have taken the trouble to build one). Her parents, sharing the settle on the opposite side, had a shoulder to shoulder air which frightened her.

'But why not?' said Sybil. 'What have you against the boy?'

'It's not fair. Why should Osbert Smith and everyone look down on us as they do?'

'Seems to me that you're doing a bit of looking down on people,' said William. 'You're looking down on Thomas and that's not right. He's the same kind that we are ourselves.'

'It's not just that! I don't *like* him, I tell you.'

'All right, then. Why not? Come along, Nicola.'

'Yes, explain,' said Sybil. 'Can't you see your father's tired out with your tantrums? If you've a reason for not marrying Thomas, let's have it, and quick.'

Nicola clenched her fists, summing up the courage to say what she had to. 'I'm scared of him,' she said and glanced, embarrassed, at the floor.

It had been five years ago. She was fifteen and her brother Will was five and he'd come and jogged her arm when she was making butter. Angry, she'd shaken and slapped him and then her mother rushed in and clouted her for it and she'd run off to sulk.

She'd run out and along the river bank, to where the track from Rushley village crossed on a bridge. It had been a wooden bridge when she was small but had since then been rebuilt in stone. There, leaning idly over the parapet and tossing twigs into the water, was Thomas, the son of Ed Woodcarver.

She knew Thomas slightly. He was the same age as herself and his father Ed worked with her uncle. There was a scandal about Ed's birth; the tale was told sometimes round the fire in winter, when the dark evenings needed enlivening. Ed's mother had been Annet, cousin to old Mistress Isabel, but Annet's husband hadn't sired him.

Back in the days of the first King Edward, one of the Grosneys had married a connection of the Rushley family, a lady called Eglantine. She was the widow of a knight killed in the fighting in Wales and when the lord of the time, Sir Simon Rushley, brought her back to Norfolk, a Welsh girl called Bronwen came with her.

Both she and Bronwen feared for the safety of friends they had left behind, but eventually Sir Simon returned to Wales and at length reappeared with the friends in question, a brother and sister called Myfanwy and Owen. They had survived their perils after all.

Bronwen, later, had married Owen and gone home again, because it was safe by then, and Bronwen missed the mountains so. But before he left Rushley, Owen had put his mark on it. The Welsh, everyone said, were as lax in some ways as the Eelfishers were. Until Bronwen married him (she'd tame him, said public opinion with a chuckle), Owen never saw why he shouldn't bed any girl he fancied and he was very good at persuading them; he was a minstrel by trade and what girl could resist a man who made lovesongs for her? After he and Bronwen had gone, Annet was found to be with child by him and had had to be provided with a husband in some haste.

There was no doubt that Owen was the father of Ed Woodcarver, for even as a boy he looked very much like Owen and if anyone's memory of the Welshman were blurred, there was Myfanwy, who closely resembled her brother, still in Rushley, attending on Lady Eglantine in Bronwen's place, to remind them.

Ed had one feature from his mother: a head of pale red hair. Otherwise, he had Owen's swooping eyebrows and dark eyes and deep voice, and almost certainly from the same source came an imaginative streak which made him, in fact, rather a good craftsman. His stepfather Arthur carved wood as part of his living and taught the work to him. Arthur always behaved in public as though Ed were his son and had inherited his skill from him. But there were stories that, behind closed doors, he ill-used the Welsh cuckoo in his nest.

Myfanwy said so, anyway. She stayed on, unmarried, looking after Eglantine and, later, the children which Eglantine produced – to her own surprise and Herbert's, since she had had no children by her first husband. Myfanwy was said to have caused some of the trouble between Ed and his stepfather, by acknowledging the boy too openly as her kin.

Time had passed. Myfanwy and Annet and Arthur were dead and Ed, now, was fifty-five and his son Thomas was fifteen and the image of Ed at the same age.

He called to Nicola as she came up to the bridge. She was in too much of a temper to want his or anyone's company, but he called again and, dragging her feet, she joined him.

'I've invented a game. See these two twigs here?'

'Yes?' Nicola looked at them without interest.

'One's got this knob halfway along and the other's got two knobs, so we can tell which is which. You take this one. Then we lean over the bridge on the upstream side, see, and drop our twigs together, and then look over the other side to see which comes out first. It's a race.'

It was easier to say 'all right' than to detach herself, so she said it and they dropped their twigs. Then they peered over the downstream parapet. Thomas's twig had been caught in the faster central current and came out first.

'I win!'

'Yes,' said Nicola, bored.

'But I ought to have a prize. Winners of contests always have prizes. I know! I'll award myself this!' said the grandson of Owen, Welsh minstrel, and with that, flung his arms round Nicola and kissed her. He succeeded in doing it thoroughly before she in turn succeeded in flinging him off.

'How dare you?'

'Why? Do you mind?'

'Yes, I do mind. What do you take me for?'

181

'A girl,' said Thomas. 'A very nice-looking girl. Hair like honey, you've got, and eyes the same.' He had a funny turn of phrase at times. William of the Lea had once said he got it from Ed, who had it from his Aunt Myfanwy. 'I've been wanting to kiss you for a long time,' said Thomas. 'Only waiting my chance, I was. Oh, come on. Let's race some more twigs. You might win this time. Then you can kiss me, instead.'

'Kiss *you*?' The rage which had sent Nicola flouncing out of the house, frothed up anew, this time to expend itself on this impertinent, horrible boy. 'You leave me alone! I don't want to mess about with you; why should I? *Welshman*!' said Nicola, simultaneously summing up in one single word the whole of Thomas's scandalous heredity and dismissing him as a descendant of a conquered nation.

A split second later, she was backed against the parapet and half over it, with the stone grinding into her spine and Thomas's furious face above her. The swooping eyebrows made him look alien, almost devilish, and his dark eyes were so angry that they were terrifying. And his knee was in her stomach and his hands were round her throat.

'It isn't,' said Thomas through his teeth, 'that I mind being called a Welshman. I mind being called it *in that tone of voice*! Don't ever say *Welshman* to me in that tone of voice again. Do you hear? *Do you hear?*'

Nicola choked, heaved, tried to kick him, rolled her eyes. He seemed at length to realise that it was pointless to demand an answer from her unless he allowed her to speak, and relaxed his grip. He let her stand upright and Nicola, gasping, clutched protectively at her throat. He had hold of her shoulders now and he was shaking her. '*Do you hear?*'

'Yes yes!'

He released her and she twisted away from him and fled.

She had seen him since only across the church. She had been horrified to hear that he wanted to marry her. 'No!' she had said. '*No!*' And she was still saying it.

She tried, stammering with the strength of her fear, to explain.

It fell flat. 'All this to-do is because he had a fit of boyish temper after you'd been rude to him?' her father said. 'Come off it! You'd do well, Nicola, to make an effort to like a boy who apparently likes you.'

'I can't. Not Thomas. You don't understand,' said Nicola desperately.

She had begun to taste defeat before this, when she had been rejected by one after another of the fathers of promising sons, whom William had approached on her behalf. Some of them, like Master Geoffrey Dorrard at Redesmarsh, had been very scathing about the lack of a dowry.

She could bear defeat, she thought. But not if it came in the form of Thomas Woodcarver.

'The Woodcarvers are a good family. They're fine craftsmen and well respected,' William was saying. 'Do you think we don't want the best for you?'

Sybil looked at the misery in her daughter's face and her own softened. She moved across to sit beside Nicola and put an arm about her. 'There's no need to worry over what Thomas was like as a boy. He's grown up now. But so are you, and you've got to see that you can't have everything you want, just for the asking. You have to settle for what's there. That Isabel Plowman,' said Sybil, as Nicola's unhappy face did not change. 'She did you no good. I wish I'd known sooner what she was saying to you.'

'She was interesting,' said Nicola defensively. 'She used to tell how she'd been to Norwich to the trial of a witch and to London for a coronation . . .'

'I know! I heard her myself once or twice. But she did more than that,' said Sybil. 'She gave you big ideas. I haven't forgotten.'

Nicola said nothing. She was remembering her final errand to Isabel. It was the last time Sybil had sent her. She could recall sitting on the hard dirt floor of the cottage out on the edge of Norsland: arms wrapped around her ten-year-old knees and eyes wide, listening while Isabel, who felt the cold and looked like nothing so much as a bundle of shawls with sharp black eyes and clawlike hands, squatted by the fire-trench and brewed them a tisane, and talked. She could remember with perfect clarity everything Isabel had said.

'The young can be both very wise and very foolish. I was wise enough to know the difference between things that are symbols and things that are real. Our priest, Father Benedict, used to talk about that. "You bow the knee in church to the rood and the statue of the Virgin, but they're not what you're worshipping," he used to tell us. "They're just to put you in mind of Christ and His mother. They're symbols." I understood what he meant; really understood, and some people didn't. Alfred always used to talk about the Virgin's statue as though it was her, herself, somehow.

'But it was seeing Abbess Christiana at that Christmas feast, that started me off thinking properly about what was really a symbol and what wasn't, and I worked out at last that if the medallion was a symbol for the things I wanted like clothes and travel, then those things in turn were symbols. What I really wanted wasn't them but what they stood for; having power and being respected, not having to crawl and be humble and always a bit scared. Having people listen to what you wanted. Rohese could get food served when she wanted to, and the abbess could sweep in late and not pay a forfeit, and have her hand kissed by Sir Henry, and make all the other ladies look trivial.

'Of the two of them, the abbess had the most power, the most respect, and she didn't even have to please a husband. I thought: of the two women I'd rather be like her. And that's where I was foolish. She had more power than I bargained for.

'Not that I did any better when I got away from her,' Isabel had added viciously. 'I've told you all about how I did that. Hanged, she was, and good riddance. But then I went back to the idea of bettering myself through a man and that was no good either. I loved him, too! Didn't help. He let me down. I didn't have anything to fight with, that was the trouble. You've got to have looks or money in this world; best of all, both. I had neither. You're going to have looks, though.' The sharp black eyes had taken Nicola in, scanning her face and hair as though playing a light on them. 'That's one thing you'll have that I didn't. And times are changing. People move about more and not only from place to place. They get free more easily. Girls marry above themselves oftener.' And then, in a sing-song voice as though she were talking as much to herself as to Nicola, 'I got my revenge on the abbess but I never got it on that man. I was kept down for being born into the wrong sort of family; as if that was my fault! You'll have the looks; you marry well, Nicola. Make yourself into a lady with servants of your own and do it for me as well as for yourself. *Get my own back for me!*'

Nicola could remember every word even now. She had at the time tried to repeat to her mother what Isabel had said, and that was why her visits to Isabel had been abruptly stopped. But she had never told her parents that, on that last day, Isabel had given her a keepsake, an old silver medallion with a device on it supposed to be that of some freeborn forebear of hers – and Nicola's too, possibly, since she had once heard her father say that Isabel was a distant relative. She wore the medallion often, but always out of sight, and it had indeed kept her in mind of Isabel.

Years later, when the question of her marriage came up, she had asked her father to find her a freeman but she had carefully not reminded either of her parents that this course of action had been recommended by Mistress Plowman. Now it seemed that they had known all the time.

'I'll do what you say,' she said to them. 'I'll marry who you say. But not Thomas, please not Thomas Woodcarver.'

But it was too late.

'I have to tell you, Nicola, that I've already accepted his proposal,' said William. 'I can't back out, not after refusing him once already. There's no call to back out either; there's nothing wrong with the boy that I can see. What if you did have some childish squabble with him? You've got a timid streak, I know that. If anyone raises their voice to you, you look at them as if they've done something dreadful, though you never minded your little brother being scared of you when he was small. Thomas is all right.'

'He's not. *Not* Thomas,' said Nicola again, weakly defiant. 'I won't. Even if I'm dragged to the church, I won't say *I will*.'

'All right.' William got up and reached his hooded cloak down from its peg. 'If that's your last word. I'll go for a walk along the river. I'll see you presently.' Nicola and her mother gazed at him in astonishment

184

at this sudden capitulation. And then realised that it wasn't capitulation at all. 'It's Thomas or St Peter's Abbey at Redesmarsh,' William said, swinging the cloak round him. 'Girls who won't marry go into the abbey. That'll mean no nice dresses ever again, just gowns of black for the rest of your life. They'll cut off all your hair that you're so proud of, my girl. You get bored in church even once a week; you'll spend hours in church every day, at the abbey. And coming from this background, your work there'll be scrubbing floors and pounding dough and weeding the garden and nothing back for it; no man to love you and no children. Think it over.'

'William!' said Sybil on a note of expostulation, but caught his eye and fell silent.

'The abbey? But I can't . . . I don't want . . .!'

Nicola could not believe that her father was saying these things. He had loved and indulged her all her life and she had believed he always would, even if she threw tantrums sometimes or bullied Will. This was as unbelievable as though the sun had risen in the west.

'I'm tired of hearing what you want and don't want,' said William. 'I've spoilt you and I know it. It's Thomas or the abbey. Take it or leave it. I'm off for my walk now and you can tell me when I get back which it's to be.'

He went out. Nicola fell weeping into her mother's arms. 'I can't go into the abbey, I can't! I can't wear black and have my head shaved and . . . and . . .'

'There, there. Don't take on like that. There's no need to go into the abbey. You'll be all right with Thomas.'

She would have to marry him. The abbey was unthinkable. But she wouldn't be all right with Thomas. He hadn't changed since he was fifteen; she knew it. She'd felt it in him that day on the bridge. That anger in him, that hidden violence; they were part of him and would be for always. They would grow as he grew.

She would spend her whole life in his power.

Chapter Eleven

The Clouded Marriage

Thomas Woodcarver's marriage took place under a cloud, literally. It was October and, a week before the wedding date, a spell of clear weather broke suddenly in wind and rain.

There was no flooding; the drainage channels did their work well and the harbour and sea-wall which had been constructed on the orders of Sir Edward Rushley's energetic grandfather Sir Simon and where a new village called Wendmouth had now grown up, did their work well. But the dark skies and the swish of the rain were hardly festive and, besides that, the Woodcarver workshop was busy. Sir Edward's son was soon to be married too and the Carpenters had made a settle for Sir Edward to present to his future daughter-in-law. It had to be carved now, on back and arms, with the Rushley device of a heron between two spears.

The work itself was straightforward enough. Sir Edward was for ever wanting his device on this or that and they had carved it a thousand times before. Thomas would have welcomed something more challenging. He knew that in his strong brown fingers were skills like seeds waiting to germinate. But they needed to be called forth and sometimes he grew angry because he was not free to leave home and apprentice himself to a master craftsman in Norwich. Here in Rushley, he could not learn what he desired.

But though the work on the settle was familiar, it was also rushed. Sir Edward, as usual, hadn't given them enough time. 'It's got to be finished on your wedding day, as luck would have it,' said Ed.

They did get it finished, but only just in time. In the morning, when Thomas was waking up the fire (Nicola would be doing that henceforth), hooves splashed in the rainswept road outside, booted feet descended squelchily into mud, there was a commanding rap at the door, and there was the bailiff, Richard Grosney, demanding to know if the settle were ready.

Richard Grosney's taut face and tight mouth always made him seem as if he were in a state of suppressed rage. Thomas, who was frequently in such a state himself, but reckoned he had better reason than the free and well-paid Richard Grosney, often wondered why but suspected that Grosney simply enjoyed it.

186

No one but Richard Grosney would have come through such a downpour and broken in on a man's wedding morning on such an errand. Indeed, the bailiff's work was not normally concerned with domestic furniture. Grosney was here, thought Thomas with venom, out of pure nosey-parkering and to enjoy the pleasures of harassment.

But Sir Edward's bailiff must be treated with respect. Politely, they told him that the settle would be sent up by ox-cart within an hour, gave him some ale and said that they hoped to see him at Thomas's marriage feast. Grosney rode off again and Ed said, 'It won't be so bad when you've got a wife here. Doing everything ourselves; it's a lot too much. Beth's been dead two years and it feels like twenty. If it weren't for your sisters and a few good neighbours, you'd have no marriage feast. Well, let's hope the bride don't drown on her way to the church. What weather! Oh, perk up, boy. What's wrong with you, got doubts about yourself? You don't want to worry. You're a proper man. I saw to that.'

Thomas was six years old, no more than that, when the second King Edward was flung off his throne, and he was just turned seven when the King was murdered.

It came about because neither Queen Isabella nor the barons had been able any longer to stand his preference for sleeping with men instead of women, or his habit of listening to his favourites instead of to his Council. The Queen had fled to France and taken a lover and then reappeared, accompanied by both her lover and an army. King Edward the Second was deposed and the year after that he was very horribly dead.

Father Amyas, who had the parish of Rushley in between Benedict and Matthew, and to whom sex – in any form – was merely an alternative word for sin, stood up in church, gave his parishioners the full and lurid details of how the King was killed, warned them that such was the just due of anyone who indulged in unnatural practices, and urged all fathers to be vigilant in checking such tendencies in their sons.

When they came home. Ed Woodcarver beat the seven-year-old Thomas 'as a warning of what to expect if you ever take to unnatural goings-on'.

From Ed's point of view, it was a reasonable thing to do. His stepfather had regularly used his belt and his fists both on Ed and on Ed's mother Annet. Any excuse would serve. If a meal were late or not hot enough, if either of them said anything that could be called answering back or hummed a snatch of song the way that mucky old Welsh minstrel, Ed's natural father, used to do; these were reasons enough.

Ed had grown up taking violence for granted. True, his wife Beth had stood up to him and he stopped hitting her after she'd half-brained him with a poker. But he treated his children as he liked, which was roughly.

The seven-year-old boy hadn't understood very much of the priest's homily and didn't know why his father was beating him, and Ed didn't think to explain. On that day, Thomas for the first time experienced the black rage which ever since had risen up in him on occasion, drowning reason and fear in the longing to strike at whatever had offended him. Unable at the age of seven to attack his father, he had rushed away bellowing and banged his head on a wall until his fury at the injustice had discharged itself. Two years later, when a bigger boy teased him into the same quality of rage, he had banged the bigger boy's head on a wall instead. No one tried to tease him after that.

He had never forgotten or forgiven his father's unprovoked attack, although he did his filial duty because it was to his advantage. He was the only boy in the family. His sisters were married and provided for and Thomas would one day have his father's house and workshop and his partnership with the Carpenters. That Dick Carpenter was Nicola's uncle made the marriage with Nicola very fitting.

He also hoped, and did not pretend to himself about it, that the day of his inheritance would come soon.

The outrageous injustice which had alienated him from his father, had alienated him from religion, too. It had after all stemmed in the first place from Father Amyas. He went to church because one must, but spent most of the time looking at the carving in the roofbeams. He had noticed woodworm in them lately.

Now he said shortly, 'It was never likely that I'd grow up to be anything else,' and knew that his father had understood the oblique reference because Ed replied, equally shortly, but defensively, 'I got Nicola for you.'

'Yes.' Thomas privately thought that Dick Carpenter had had more to do with it since it was to him that William had finally given consent, but he decided not to say so. 'I wish I knew her better,' he said as he prepared for the bridegroom's obligatory wash-down. 'I've seen her about and I've admired her all my life but till we were betrothed I'd hardly ever spoken to her and even now I've only taken her walking a couple of times and she hardly said a word.'

'So? We want a girl who'll work, not chatter. Never given her any cause to dislike you, have you?'

'Course not,' said Thomas.

The incident on the bridge wouldn't shock Ed, who would think it unimportant, but Thomas didn't propose to tell him about it. Thomas knew in his heart that if you wanted a girl to love you, if you wanted to bury your face in her soft, brown-gold hair and see her eyes grow melting and lambent for you and feel her body move with joy beneath you, then you were more likely to achieve your desire if you refrained from trying to strangle her.

*   *   *

188

The wedding feast was over.

Nicola, dressed in a gown of blue fustian (everyone had fustian these days – there was a new fabric called velvet for the rich), had stood beside Thomas Woodcarver at the church door and exchanged vows with him, amid a crowd of onlookers who overflowed the porch and spilt into the church (though not out of it, because of the rain). With hoods over their heads, and Nicola's gown buried under a mantle but still trailing its hem in the mud, they had hurried back at an undignified trot to the Woodcarvers' house, where the big workroom had been swept clear of woodshavings and the marriage feast was spread on what, normally, was the workbench.

There were pasties and fish, bread and fruit and honeycakes; mostly contributed by neighbouring goodwives, and the drink was ale or elderflower wine and Richard Grosney, of course, was there, his mouth as compressed as ever, but *saying*, anyway, that he wished them well, and drinking all the toasts with loud enthusiasm.

Nicola was engaged, consciously, in doing as she was told. Since the day when her hitherto indulgent father told her to choose between Thomas or the abbey, she had been like someone suddenly benighted in a tangled and dangerous forest, knowing that only by being very, very careful could she find her way and avoid falling into a morass or being eaten by wolves. She was helpless in the power of others and she could only keep herself safe from harm by pleasing them.

She had even had to cry in secret. 'Don't you dare show Thomas a miserable face when he comes to supper,' William of the Lea had said, and she had been afraid to defy him. She did not know that her father, too, had shed secret tears in the night, hating himself for the unhappiness he was causing her. But he had given his word and it was for the best. Once married, he told himself, Nicola would surely find that after all, she had a good bargain.

Unaware of this, Nicola had neither smiled at her father nor spoken to him as he brought her to church that morning, and now here she was in the Woodcarver house, with most of Rushley crowding in, full of rejoicing over what was to her a catastrophe. Her sisters-in-law came to kiss her; her elderly Uncle Dick and Aunt Blanche embraced her and their grandson John came up to present a gift of a new iron cauldron. She forced out words of thanks.

During the meal, she had sat next to Thomas, who squeezed her hand and said things like, 'My sister Anne Potter made these pies for us,' and 'Just look at Richard Grosney. I've never seen him drunk before.' She had made suitable replies and compelled herself to smile, while the pit of her stomach seemed to be occupied by a solid lump of lead.

The meal and the toasts had been followed by dancing, with hand-drums being tapped and Osbert Smith, who had come from his outlying home to join the festivities, had produced one of the six-stringed lutes which were sometimes called guitars and began to play it. Nicola watched him with concentration. He looked good-humoured, she thought. She would rather have had him for a father-in-law than Ed. His son, whom she had hoped to marry, was here too. Oddly enough, it was the first time she had really had a good look at him. He struck her as rather quiet and dull, but that would have been preferable to Thomas. With him and Osbert, she would not only have been free; she'd have felt safe.

And now it was coming, the moment she feared. Her mother and her sisters-in-law and Blanche Carpenter were advancing on her, to take her up to the loft where Thomas and his father usually slept.

The room was heated with braziers, and with so many people crammed into it, it had become very hot. Perhaps that was why she was sweating and felt faint. 'Al . . . already?' she said, and Blanche Carpenter laughed and said, 'You want to go on dancing? And you the bride? Might as well go on downing the ale when someone's offering you a taste of Sir Edward's wine.'

'That's right.' Her mother's voice was a little sharp, and held a warning. *Don't misbehave now, please.* 'Come along.'

She stood up obediently and someone cheered. Embarrassed, she let herself be hurried towards the ladder to the loft. Halfway up, she trod on the hem of her dress and stumbled. Her mother pushed her impatiently from behind and she turned to say, 'Just a moment.' In the room below, the guests' faces were upturned to watch her; faces red with ale and perspiring with heat; eyes full of knowing laughter.

She never quite knew why her own gaze at once sought out Osbert Smith, where he sat perched on the edge of the table, only just below the ladder, strumming his guitar.

But it did. And from her place on the steps which were leading her to the bed she must henceforth share with Thomas Woodcarver, Nicola of the Lea looked straight down into the eyes of the man she had once thought might be her father-in-law, and knew, as surely as she knew that the sun rose in the east and nowhere else, that this, and no other, was the man she should have married.

It was a moment of revelation as complete and irrevocable as her kinswoman Isabel's had been when she fell in love, all in one moment, with Herbert Grosney, except for one thing.

Herbert Grosney had not reciprocated. But Osbert's kindly blue eyes responded on the instant. She saw it happen, saw the flame of recognition, the redness that suddenly stained Osbert's weathered face, saw an understanding that penetrated her mind more deeply than any physical union would ever penetrate her body; saw the beginnings of a smile.

Saw him drop his eyes to attend to the fingering of his guitar strings, and was pushed by her mother once again, and freed her skirt, and climbed on once more, through the trapdoor at the top of the ladder, leaving Osbert behind.

*   *   *

Her heart was thudding and her brain whirling but she had little time in which to think it over. No sooner had the women finished putting her to bed and gone down the ladder again, than Thomas came up. Most of the party apparently wanted to come too, but as he scrambled through the trapdoor, he put a foot in someone's face by way of discouragement, and then slammed the trapdoor shut and bolted it, ignoring the disappointed bellowings and poundings from below.

There were no curtains round the bed. It was a plain affair of a frame with a webbing of leather thongs and a straw-stuffed pallet on top. There was one linen sheet and one good squirrel rug plus an old, worn one made of martenskins, and a couple of thick fleeces. Two more fleeces had been put downstairs, where Ed would sleep for a night or two, before coming up to snore on the other side of a screen which he and Thomas still hadn't had time to rig up but on which Thomas had insisted, although his father had snorted about it. 'You think I'm interested in what you young things get up to at night? I *work*, boy. And I *sleep*.'

For tonight, Thomas and Nicola had the loft to themselves. A candle had been placed on a shelf, in a bronze holder, and lit. Thomas came over and sat down on the bed and, by the light of the candle, they looked at each other.

The room was shaking slightly, due to the buffeting of the wind outside and another outburst of thumping from beneath the trapdoor. It seemed necessary to say something, so Nicola cleared her throat and said, 'I hope the bolts are strong.'

'Strong enough. I didn't want everyone pushing in. I thought you mightn't like it.'

'No, I . . . I wouldn't.'

There was a silence. Then Thomas said, 'I've got a feeling you haven't forgotten what happened a few years ago. I think I'd better say, it won't happen again. You'll be treated properly here. You can have anything you want, within reason. Clothes or things for the house. And you won't have to gut fish, like you used to.'

Nicola nodded. She was trapped now, the vows taken, the step irrevocable. She had been pushed out of her own home, even out of her own identity. This unfamiliar loft, its roofbeams slanting up to meet overhead and its walls sloping so steeply inwards that she would probably bang her head whenever she got out of bed, would henceforth be where she slept. At home, they had all slept downstairs, and she was so homesick now for her solitary pallet in the back room that she would have liked just to curl up and sob herself to sleep.

She would also have liked to lie still and think about that strange moment on the ladder, when she looked down into the face of Osbert Smith.

She would have to forget that, as quickly as possible.

Thomas stood up and began removing his clothes. The body which emerged from them was smooth and strong, dusted with reddish hairs on the chest and back. There were a few scars on his forearms, the result of misadventures in the workshop.

'I believe,' he said conversationally, 'that you would sooner have married a freeman. Your father tried to get Osbert Smith's son for you, didn't he? That's the gossip, anyway.'

'Has there been . . . gossip, then? I didn't know.'

'Everyone knows everyone's business in Rushley. And most of them know everyone's business in Oxfen and Redesmarsh too.' He finished stripping, and threw back the rugs. He climbed in beside her. With a tremendous effort, Nicola didn't move away. 'That side all right for you to sleep?' Thomas said, and added, without waiting for an answer, 'You'll be better off with us than with the Smiths. You'd have had to gut fish there, too.'

'Yes. I'm sure that's true. I'm very happy', said Nicola untruthfully.

'I wish I were a freeman, too,' Thomas said. 'I'm sick of that Richard Grosney thinking he can come in here and give orders over every little thing. Work extra days on the lord's land at harvest time and get that carving job done yesterday, or we'll take away your cornpatch. My Welsh grandfather was free. If only he'd married my grandmother, so would I have been.'

'I can see you're proud of your Welsh grandfather,' said Nicola carefully. 'You must tell me about him.'

'I will. But, you know,' said Thomas unexpectedly, 'it wasn't really him I was so angry about when you said *Welshman* to me that day. I was just pretending about that. I was really angry because you didn't want my kisses. Well,' said Thomas, sliding down under the rugs and drawing her towards him, 'you can't avoid them now.'

No, she couldn't. She must yield to him, respond to him, allow him to do things to her and pretend that she enjoyed it.

'Can we put the candle out?' she asked.

'Why? I want to see you.' Thomas had not pulled the rugs fully over them. Now he thrust them right off, exposing them both fully to view. 'You're beautiful, Nicola, did you know that? Look at you, how wonderful you are, all in proportion and just like milk. Don't you want to see me? Come on, put your hand here, like that . . . Nicola, lovely Nicola . . .'

Nicola, that night, tried very hard, because there was no escape and for her own sake she must please Thomas if she could. When he buried his face in her breasts, she stroked the back of his head and that wasn't so bad; there was even a curious, disturbing beginning in her own body of an answer to his caresses.

But when he knelt up and came between her thighs to complete the act, all her muscles stiffened. She had wished to put the candle out because she hadn't wanted to see his face. She knew that when his face was above hers, as it had been that day on the bridge, she would be terrified.

Now the terror turned her rigid. He had to force his way in and it was for Nicola like being impaled upon a spear. Unable to help herself, she screamed.

And there, in the hovering face, was the fury she remembered and dreaded. He was already past the point of no return and he went on, but not kindly now, as when he had started, but roughly, using her, shoving himself home as though he were stabbing an enemy. When he rolled off, she was crying wildly though softly.

'Oh, for the love of God,' said Thomas, exasperated. 'What a fuss. All over something as ordinary as this. Anyone would think I was murdering you!'

'That's what it felt like,' Nicola whimpered.

Thomas turned his back, pulled the rug over his head, and without another word went, or appeared to go, to sleep.

Precisely four weeks after her marriage, Nicola awoke, as usual, with reluctance, opening her eyes to see Thomas by her side, and the curtain, only five feet away, which hid his father, and to look at the sloping beams around her, and realise anew that this was for ever.

She slid, shivering, out of the bed. There was, as usual, work to do. The first job was to go down and through the workshop to the sooty little room where food was cooked and eaten, to make up the fire and prepare some breakfast. After that, she must see to the cows. She dressed, hurrying, and not only because of the work or because the morning was cold. If she could get out of the loft before Thomas or his father woke up, she would avoid the risk that Thomas would want to start the day by making love to her.

This morning, she managed it, arriving unhindered in the little room. It was a one-storey affair which seemed to have been tacked on to the workshop like an afterthought. To Ed and Thomas, the workshop was the centre of their lives and the hearth a mere adjunct. It consisted of an old-fashioned firepit in the middle of the floor, with a louvre in the roof above; no one had troubled about wall-hearths in this house. She knelt to take the clods off the fire and found, depressingly, that it was almost out. Nothing remained but a mass of ash and a dull red glow. She blew on it to encourage it, reached for the woodbasket and then discovered that she had forgotten to refill it last night. Only half a dozen small twigs were left. She fed them to the hearth and saw them catch, and then went out in search of more fuel.

It was a discouraging morning. It wasn't actually raining now but there had been wind and heavy rain yesterday and it was blustery still, with more rain to come. The sky was angry, its eastern half strewn with red clouds, menacingly reflected from the pools in the marshland out towards the sea. Worse, the wind had driven yesterday's downpour into the lean-to shelter where they kept the wood. If she had remembered to bring some in at nightfall, it would have been dry by now. As things were, she would have to get the fire going with damp wood before she could even begin to cook the porridge and fish with which the Woodcarvers customarily started the day.

When she returned with her dubious supply of fuel, she soon found that the fire was not in a mood to be cooperative. It was more difficult to get an unwilling fire to brighten in a firepit than in a wall-hearth, which would draw better, and this was not the first time that Nicola had been convinced that the flickering red beast in the Woodcarvers' pit had a mind of its own which was inimical to hers. Some of the better pieces of wood should have caught after a spluttering few moments while the surface damp was burned off, but all they did was give off clouds of smoke which refused to dissipate through the louvre but were instead blown back and downwards by the wind.

When her husband and father-in-law came down, she was still on her knees, red in the face, coughing and covered with smuts, struggling with a flame which looked, Thomas remarked disagreeably between his own coughs, too feeble to light a candle.

'I thought when we had a woman in the house,' said Ed, coughing as well and waving smoke away from his face, 'that we'd be coming down to hot food every morning but you don't seem to know what you ought and you don't learn fast, either.'

'I'm sorry. I forgot the woodbasket last night.'

'Well, you'd better start remembering, girl,' said Ed. 'Let me know when the meal's ready and get rid of that sodding smoke.' He stalked off to the workshop and Thomas, not looking at her, said, 'I was feeling . . . that way . . . when I woke up but you weren't there. And then I thought: oh well, there's something to be said for a warm room and food as soon as I get down there. But that isn't to be had, either, it seems. Just a cold room full of smoke.'

'I'll have it right in a moment,' said Nicola distractedly, attacking the fire with a poker. 'I'm so sorry. I'm still not used to bringing wood in at night in case it needs to dry. At home we kept it in a corner of the byre, right out of the weather. It didn't need bringing in.'

'This is your home now,' said Thomas coldly, and followed his father through to the workshop.

She forced the hateful fire into some sort of life at last and set the food to cook. Outside, the promised rain began, sharpening the chill of the morning and causing the light to fade. She lit rushdips and then, shivering, slipped through the workshop, where Thomas and Ed, busy at their workbench, took no notice of her, and up to the loft for an extra shawl.

When she came down again, both the fish and the porridge were scorching. She rescued the fish, scraping the blackened scales off, and scooped the porridge out into wooden bowls, leaving, she hoped, all the charred part behind. She poured ale, went to the workshop door and called.

They came in, sat down, and began to eat, silent, as they had been every morning since her marriage. The Woodcarvers, father and son, were never conversational between themselves. It had occurred to her sometimes that, although they seemed to work smoothly together, they did not really like each other. At the beginning, she had tried to talk to Thomas at breakfast but had now given up. She busied herself with her own share of the food. It didn't taste very nice, and she hoped Thomas and Ed would have their minds so much on their work that they wouldn't notice.

Thomas took three mouthfuls of porridge and one of fish, picked up his fish by the tail in one hand and his porridge bowl in the other and hurled them across the room. 'They're bloody burnt! What do you mean by giving us burnt food for breakfast? Can't you even cook? Can't you even do *that*?'

'I'm sorry. I'm sorry.' Frightened, Nicola dropped her spoon clattering into her bowl. 'It was just that the fire wouldn't burn . . . I'm not used to this kind of hearth yet, we had a wall-hearth at home . . . I mean at my father's place, and . . .'

'*This is your home! How many more times*?' Thomas shouted. He sprang to his feet and came round the table at her. 'I don't want to hear about your father's wall-hearth or the way he stores wood! I said you'd be treated properly here but that's if you do your part, and doing your part doesn't mean making out you're bloody well above me! You didn't want to marry me because I wasn't good enough! The whole village was laughing at you, my girl, and at me too for being fool enough to want you! Well, you are married to me now and you can just stop giving yourself airs and try learning to kindle a fire and get a decent meal. By God, I think I'd better teach you!'

Nicola gaped, terrified alike by the tirade and by his face, for there, once more, was the look of fury which she secretly called his devil's face. She scrambled up and backed away. It was no use. One blow sent her stumbling across the room and, as she bumped into the wall, another sent her sprawling.

'Don't, please don't!' She tried to get up. Thomas, ignoring her appeals for him to stop, knocked her off her feet once more.

'Can't you do anything right?' Thomas yelled. She crouched, shielding her head in her arms, shuddering with pain and sobbing out wild apologies and excuses. 'I'm sorry, I'm sorry . . . the fire was so weak, I didn't think it would cook anything fast . . . I was cold; I wanted another shawl. I'm sorry, I'm sorry.' She kept on saying it, over and over, like a prayer.

'Let her up, Thomas,' said Ed's voice indifferently from the table. 'Tell her to cook some more food. I can't eat this.'

Thomas pulled her to her feet. She jerked away from him, trembling. He pulled her back. His face was still devilish. She began to cry, loudly and hopelessly. Thomas shook her. 'Stop that, stop it! Be quiet! Oh for the love of God! I'm sorry too, I'm sorry too. But we're hungry and it's cold; it's a wet, wretched morning . . .' He folded his arms round her and, as though the blows of a moment ago had never happened, pressed her head against his chest and patted her lovingly. Nicola swallowed her sobs, fearing to rouse the demon again.

'All right. All right.' Thomas was almost crooning. 'That's it, now. Now just make some more porridge. Forget about the fish. Just some nice, hot porridge that isn't burnt and we'll forget all this.'

'Oh, give over and let her get on with it,' said Ed from the table. 'I'm hungry.'

'Come on, now.' Thomas put her head back so that he could gaze down into her face. She looked up into his and found him smiling, as though nothing very much had happened, as though her temples and her right cheekbone were not filled with a huge throbbing which soon would show itself in purple bruises. He did not know how terrifying he was or how much he had hurt her.

'Come on now,' said Thomas. 'The world hasn't come to an end.'

Yes it has! she wanted to cry. *Yes, it has! My world has ended because in my world, I had people who loved me, who would never have hurt me as you have! You say you love me but you don't know what love means. I want to go home to my own world. I want to go home!*

But she could never go home again. Her father had given her away, given her to Thomas and this, God help her, was her home now. Thomas had said it, twice.

Tremulously, aloud, she said: 'I . . . I'll do that porridge.'

Later, when they had eaten and she was clearing up the mess which Thomas's rejected breakfast had made on the floor, she suddenly ran for the door, and Thomas, hearing her retch, ran after her. 'Does that mean what I think it means?'

'I . . . I'm not sure. I think it might, yes.'

'Then I'm sorry again for that just now. You should have said. I'll watch my temper. It's just that . . . when I'm angry, it's as if I can't help myself.'

Nicola nodded. 'I'm all right now. I'll just stay here in the open for a moment.' He hesitated, and then went back inside. Nicola watched him go and said inwardly, 'If you can't help yourself, who's going to help me?'

But she knew the answer, of course. Nicola must help Nicola. Not by fighting back; she wasn't brave enough for that. But she could protect herself by being careful, by making no mistakes in her daily tasks and devoting herself only to pleasing these two men, her husband and her father-in-law. And by somehow responding to Thomas's lovemaking in the way he wished, so that he would not again come at her with that angry shout of, 'Can't you do anything properly?'

It was a kind of death.

Chapter Twelve

The Hope of War

The enormous longbows which had been invented by the southern Welsh could send a shaft for more than a hundred and fifty yards and pin a man's leg to his horse's girth on arrival. A longbowman could reload much faster than a crossbowman could, and a second arrow could follow the first almost instantly.

Accuracy didn't always matter. If you were shooting into massed ranks you were bound to hit someone. But there were times when it was desirable to pick off a special target; a crossbow sniper, for instance, or a standard bearer whose disappearance would confuse the enemy. A man who could do that could get himself noticed, win promotion or reward.

Times had changed since the Norman kings forbade peasants to keep bows in their homes. Skill with the bow was encouraged now, even in villeins. Sir Edward Rushley had set up butts just outside Rushley village and ordered all the men to practise at least twice a week, and there was an annual competition, with prizes.

Thomas Woodcarver ignored the competitions and avoided practising whenever he could, claiming that he was too busy, what with the workshop and the holding where he and his father grew corn, and the bonded labour on Sir Edward Rushley's land.

In fact, although he now had a profitable sideline in making bows, he was poor at shooting and self-conscious about it. Today, attending practice because Richard Grosney, in his dual capacity as Sir Edward's bailiff and one of Rushley's constables, had sent word that his slackness had been noticed, he was in a temper because he couldn't hit the target even at eighty yards, let alone a hundred and fifty. Gilbert Pecher, with whom he was supposed to be having a friendly contest, was showing him up. And Richard Grosney had ridden up and was sitting there on his gelding, watching.

'The wind's swinging. You want to allow for it,' Gilbert remarked mildly, observing Thomas's scowl. Gilbert was lanky and good-natured, the youngest son of a man who had been half-brother to old Isabel. Most people liked him, including Thomas, but just now he was annoyed with Gilbert. He didn't need to be told the wind was changing. He could see the weathercock on the church. He took his stance, stared angrily along the field at the brightly coloured concentric rings of the targets, pockmarked from the shafts of better archers. He drew, loosed evenly without any lute-players' plucking, and missed the damned target by at least six feet.

'Your mind's not on it,' said Richard Grosney, who had ridden up so close that his horse was almost breathing down Thomas's neck. 'But it's natural, under the circumstances. You're to be congratulated, I hear. A daughter, was it not?'

'Yes, sir. Your shot, Gilbert.'

'How have you called her? Your wife is all right?'

'Alison, sir. Yes, she is.' Gilbert had got his shaft into the target; not in the centre, but in.

'I'm pleased to hear it. I take it that she was the reason why you didn't present yourself for your half-day yesterday? Well, it's understandable. We'll say no more about it. But time has to be made up, of course. You're expected at the Hall this afternoon. There's work to be done on the stable roof. That's a good bow you're using, by the way. Did you make it?'

'I did, sir,' said Thomas briefly, taking his stance again.

'What wood did you use?'

'I used yew-wood, sir.'

'Why? The Welsh bows were of elm and there's elm available from Sir Edward. He's had some trees felled lately. Where did you get the yew from?' said Grosney.

One of his black rages instantly surged in Thomas. Anyone would think he'd been stealing yew trees from Rushley churchyard at dead of night. He forced himself to speak quietly.

'Yew is more flexible, sir. I bought a consignment in Lynn, last time we carted wheat there. It comes from the continent. It's better than English yew.'

'Sir Edward would prefer you to buy from the wood he has for sale.'

Sir Edward, thought Thomas, could . . . could . . . he seized a shaft from his quiver, fitted it, loosed wildly without taking aim and to his own astonishment hit the target dead centre.

'Excellent,' said Grosney, in tones of faint surprise, and spurred his horse, and cantered away.

'They think they own us!' Thomas turned furiously to Gilbert. 'Practise archery because they say so! If you're ill or your wife's having your baby and you miss a half-day, they say make up the time, and still they expect you to fool about here at the butts! There's a table and a bedstead half-done in the workshop, all for Rushley Hall; Sir bloody Edward's already sent two messages about those; he thinks things ought to be ready the day before he bloody orders them! My father can't finish them all on his own. He doesn't even pay a fair price for the work when it's done! *And* we've our own sowing to do and a fence to repair to keep *his* bloody sheep out of our corn and now it's make bows of *his* wood, so he can sell it to us. Never mind what's the best wood or the cost to us! Him and his kind, they're all the same. *They* think we're just there to use, cows to be milked for work and money . . .'

'I know,' said Gilbert. 'You're a treat to listen to. You've set the whole alehouse laughing, more than once. But it's got nothing to do with real life. Things are as they are and . . .'

'And we just put up with them and anyone who says different is to be laughed at! I tell you, Gilbert, I call you my friend but sometimes you make me angry. You accept things that no one should accept. You . . .'

'It isn't a question of accepting things. It's a matter of what just is. You're always getting into rages about things these days, Thomas, but it's no use trying to change them.'

'It ought to be some use! Why isn't it any use? One day it'll be different!' Thomas threw the words at Gilbert. 'One day men won't be able to own each other, wait and see! It can't go on for ever.'

'I expect it will, though,' said Gilbert Pecher placidly.

It was true that he was always in a bad temper these days but neither Grosney nor Sir Edward were the fundamental cause. He loathed them heartily, but he would have talked about it far less, had he not, so badly, needed to relieve another bitterness. Climbing the ladder to his bedloft later on, to ask after Nicola's wellbeing and that of his daughter, he knew that the wellspring of his anger lay at home.

Nicola's smile when she greeted him, was itself exasperating. He had seen her become happy, on the day and at the moment when Mistress Meg Sixacre, the Rushley midwife, informed them both that as Nicola's pregnancy was now well advanced, they should cease from lovemaking, and should not resume until three months after the child was born.

He had tried so hard, ignoring his father's crude advice. 'Take what you want, boy, when you want it,' Ed had said. 'And never mind her vapours. Just tell her to remember what a wife's for and remind her who's master.'

'As you did with Mother?' Thomas had asked, effectively silencing him.

But Ed knew too much; it was maddening. He was always there, just on the other side of the curtain, and he wasn't always asleep. He had probably heard all of Thomas's attempts at courtship, during those early days of marriage.

'The very first time I noticed you properly, Nicola, I was out on the banks of the Meadbrook and it had just got dark. It was January, with snow on the ground and I wouldn't have been there only I'd run out because my mother and father were quarrelling. You were rowing down the stream. There was a moon. Funny, your hair's such a warm colour, but in that light it was pure silver. You looked magical.'

She lay there, letting him caress her hair, but she did not seem to take pleasure in it, he thought. 'I'm not magical,' she said. 'I'm just me.'

'I think you're magical. Oh Nicola, we could make magic together, you and I. I want to. I was all nervous and blundering on that first night; I always get bad-tempered when I'm nervous. I'm sorry for it now. I want it to be enchantment and revelation for you. Let me make it like that for you. . .'

But when he tried, taking her in his arms, stroking her back and whispering endearments, it was no use. She whispered to him and stroked him in return but he knew that it meant nothing to her, that it was only a task and that he had not aroused her. Once more he had to hold down his anger. And he knew that it was there in his voice, all the same, when, unable to help himself, he demanded: 'Oh, why won't you love me?'

'You keep saying that. But I do love you. I know you were nervous that first time. That's all forgotten now, truly.'

'It isn't, I can tell. There's no one else, you say, and I believe you. So what's wrong with me? You're a woman, you're made for making love, why don't you want to?'

'But I do want to. Only I get tired. There's so much to remember; everything's strange to me yet . . .'

'You *don't* want to. You're making excuses. You don't take fire from me. Your face always looks so *patient* . . .'

'It's the candlelight; it makes people's faces look different from what they are. Blow the candle out!'

'But I like to see you. I want you to see me. Oh Nicola, please, darling Nicola, I know you have to work hard, but you're young, it shouldn't matter so much. Give way to me, melt to me. If I put my hands here and here, surely that's nice . . . oh, damn you, you're pretending, all you ever do is pretend . . .'

'I'm not pretending, Thomas, truly I'm not.'

'You are, and I don't want you to pretend. I want it to be real. Why can't it be real?'

'Oh God, I can't please you!' Her face in the candlelight looked white and exhausted. 'I try so hard but I don't know what you want. Nothing's ever right.'

'Don't whine! I hate it when you whine.'

'I'm not whining. I'm so tired.'

'All right, be tired then. Hide away from me in being tired. No, by God, you shan't hide away. I'm tired too: it's just one job after another, dawn to sunset, carving wood . . . oh, I'm so sick of spears and herons! . . . ploughing our land, ploughing bloody Sir Edward's land, making bows, practising archery, back in the workshop with more carving to do; but that doesn't stop me wanting love and I'm going to have it!'

200

'No . . . no, oh no, Thomas, not like that, not with that look on your face . . . oh, don't, don't . . .'

Again and again she had defeated him, souring the love he wanted to give her, awakening anger in him instead. Driving him back into the likeness of his father Ed, whom he did not want to resemble and could not escape.

He had got used to it in a way. One learned to manage, to live with what could not be helped. But he hadn't learned to like it and he never would.

Nicola had been glad to be pregnant because once it was established, it freed her for a time from Thomas's embraces and was certainly a protection against his temper, for he took care about that. She would be exposed to his temper again eventually, she knew, however hard she might try to please. She wished that she could stay pregnant for ever.

But that, of course, was impossible. Her time came in due course. The birth was free of complications though painful and exhausting. Sybil, who had helped Mistress Sixacre to look after her, visited her often and William of the Lea came too. His wish to be friends again was obvious and almost pathetic and Nicola was too tired to resist. She would never forgive him for forcing her into this marriage; the love she had once had for him was gone for ever. But she had come to understand that he hadn't meant her to be unhappy, hadn't known to what fate he was sending her and it was a relief to receive affection which would not express itself in physical demands to which she could not respond. They were on speaking terms again.

Her sisters-in-law came, and various neighbours, to congratulate her and advise her on caring for the baby and even Ed was quite amiable, telling her she could take it slow after she got up, and holding his grandchild, if awkwardly, to display her to the visitors.

'Though it's a pity she ain't a boy,' he remarked, the day after the child's birth, climbing up to the loft after Thomas when the latter returned from the archery practice complaining that the half-day he'd missed on Sir Edward's land would have to be put in after all. 'We could do with another pair of hands round here for doing men's work. Still, maybe next time.'

'Yes, let us hope so,' said Nicola, rather too brightly. Privately, she was thinking *at least I've still got three months' reprieve, so Mistress Sixacre says.*

Then she saw Thomas watching her and knew that he had read her thoughts. She looked away.

'Time we got back to our work,' Ed said, and Thomas, summoned by a jerk of his father's head, followed him down to the workshop below. They had Sir Edward's table and bedstead to finish and a chest to make for Nell Ketels, at the end of the village. Nell was only a cottar's wife and couldn't afford much but, like any other woman, she needed a private chest for her clothes and her little ornaments, and her old one had fallen to pieces.

They were constructing it themselves, since the Carpenters, although usually insistent on doing basic construction, were glad enough to pass on what they called 'piddling little jobs'. Nell had offered a farthing extra 'if you can put just a bit a of carving on it, to make it pretty'.

But, Thomas thought as he and Ed squatted down on opposite sides of the bedstead and set to work, although there was plenty to do, it was all quite simple, to the point of being dull.

There was a new church at Redesmarsh and once, while over there for the May fair, Thomas had gone in. He had heard that the church had a rood screen there which was worth seeing.

It was. It crossed the church between congregation and altar, oak panelling three feet high and a delicate tracery arch and lattice above, with an arched opening where the aisle passed through. It was all exquisitely carved and painted but Thomas had been riveted most of all by the beam along the top. He had never dreamed of such complex craftsmanship. The beam was decorated with a pattern of oak leaves on twigs, which had been left attached to the parent timber only here and there. The leaves had been gilded, creating an airy, gleaming fascia, which seemed to have nothing to do with the beam behind it.

It was work he couldn't match; to reach that standard you had to study under a master craftsman of the woodworkers guild, and gain knowledge distilled from a thousand dedicated lives. Tricks picked up from a father and grandfather who had carved wood in between pushing ploughs and harvesting other men's corn as well as their own, couldn't compare.

But had he been taught, he could have learned. Sometimes, his fingers itched for fine detail and for three-dimensional marvels like the oak leaves on the Redesmarsh rood screen.

Instead, he must content himself with a pattern like a length of rope run round the edge of Nell Ketels' walnut chest, and a few dog roses, maybe, on the lid. The table and bedstead for the Hall, of course, needed only the Rushley herons and spears which Sir Edward always had put on everything.

He began, automatically, to carve them now. And although he was simultaneously bored and angry, nevertheless, there was something quietening in the task, and the smooth way the curls of wood slid from under the chisel. Here in the workshop, with his tools in his hands, was the potential for peace of mind. Here, if anywhere, was something that could turn his mind away from Nicola so that he could cease to think of her as special, a potential giver of enchanted gifts beyond the power of commonplace woman, and simply regard her as his wife, quite pleasing, with nice brownish-fair hair and eyes to match and little work-roughened hands; that and nothing more.

His father was talking. It was something about the archery practice. 'Folk are saying that we might have to put in more of it; Sir Edward reckons there'll be another war in France before long. Hope he don't take you off to the wars, boy. Don't know if you fancy fighting, but I don't fancy being left here on my own, trying to do everything.'

'I don't fancy fighting,' said Thomas shortly. 'I prefer my work.'

But if only his chisel had something more exciting to do than rope patterns and dog roses, and the damned old Rushley spears and herons. Then, even though he remained a villein, with Sir Edward and Richard Grosney harrying him all the time; even though his Nicola never learned to love him, he could be fulfilled.

'Another war' was the wrong way of putting it. Wars were long-running affairs, although it was true that different kings concentrated on different enemies. Edward the First had fought the Welsh, Edward the Second had fought the Scots – not very successfully – and Edward the Third, having tackled the Scots with a similar lack of success, had turned his attention to the French.

Everyone on the three manors understood why.

Ships' crews, sailing into the Rushley harbour, had lurid tales of being attacked in the English Channel by Norman pirates, and from a variety of sources, including the travelling friars and the pedlars and minstrels whose circuit regularly brought them to Redesmarsh Fair and at other times as well, came stories of the shocking, underhand way in which the King of France had sent men and arms to help the Scots.

Most alarming of all, to a community which bred sheep and sold wool, were the reports by the visiting wool-buyers, who said that in Flanders, where so much of the wool was sold, the count was more friendly to the French than to the English and that there was no knowing what would happen to the market there; unless someone did something soon, the Flemish burgesses might have to buy their wool elsewhere and the Flemish ports might soon be harbouring French raiding vessels.

At the time of Thomas's marriage, Sir Edward had only just returned from Flanders where the King had led an expedition to protect English interests. Sir Edward and his two sons, Roland and Eustace, had volunteered with enthusiasm, in the hope – they made no secret of it – of winning renown and raising the family fortunes. The Rushleys were still not as far up the social scale as they would have liked to be, and everyone knew that Sir Edward had had trouble in finding a match for young Roland because he had aimed too high. Little, in fact, had changed since Sir Henry had failed to marry his ward Eglantine to a de Montalt. The de Montalts were gone, and Castle Rising had for years now housed Queen Isabella, the widow of Edward the Second, whose behaviour had once made Ed so unjustly chastise his son, and who had for a time become so savage and bitter that she had been called a She-

Wolf, until her son, taking the throne, had drawn her teeth and put her in a luxurious but unmistakeable cage.

The Rushleys didn't visit Castle Rising now, or look for advancement there. But war might provide opportunities. The Rushleys had set off amid great excitement, going overland to Norwich to join one of the King's ships, since their own had already been requisitioned. It had been all trumpets and banners; horses with red and blue caparisons; Sir Edward and his sons and two score of hired knights all in new armour, with high-pommelled saddles and long stirrups which made them look as though they were standing astride their horses rather than riding them.

The return, after the signing of a not very satisfactory truce, had been a muted affair, by water all the way to Rushley, in a ship now returned by the King, with Eustace's coffin on board.

No one thought the truce would hold and Sir Edward certainly didn't want it to. He had a personal hatred now of the French. The Rushleys had gained nothing from fighting them, but it was a French spear which had gone through Eustace's stomach and caused him to die after hours of horrible misery. Sir Edward would be only too happy to set out to France again and get his revenge.

Alison was five years old when his chance came.

'The truce, good people, is ended.' Brother Ailred was one of the friars who paid regular visits to the district. He was a Franciscan and he came every May for the Redesmarsh fair but usually stayed on to preach in Rushley and Oxfen too. He generally began his sermons with some general news items as a way of fixing the attention of his audience, although his reputation was now such that this was hardly necessary.

Brother Ailred was in his thirties, a fit and gifted orator who took a wicked delight in being controversial. Audiences gathered at his open-air sermons in the hope of being scandalised and usually came away with wide-stretched eyes, saying, 'Ooh!'

Parish priests eyed him doubtfully, but he had a knack of making himself agreeable to them in private conversation, and Father Matthew found him rather exciting. In bad weather, he allowed Brother Ailred to use Rushley Church as a venue. The weather had been reasonably good during the fair, but now the rain was slanting mercilessly down on field and marsh and the shelter of Rushley Church was welcome.

Ailred had not, however, climbed into the pulpit. His vows were those of total poverty and although he had stretched them to the extent of wearing sandals, a pulpit counted as a luxury. He was tall, and simply standing on a bench gave him the few extra inches which were all he needed to dominate any crowd.

'The truce was ended last year, in truth,' he announced. 'The French have presumed upon it. They are putting forward their own claimant for the succession in Brittany and challenging ours, and they continue to elbow for influence in Flanders and the English lands of Gascony. King Edward has had enough.'

Brittany, Flanders and Gascony were, to most of his hearers, names without accompanying mental pictures, but they had a general idea of what he meant and they liked the feeling of being informed.

'War will come,' Brother Ailred declared. 'It is inevitable, as inevitable as the last battle that must one day come between good and evil here on earth. And while knights and archers and men-at-arms furbish their weapons for war against France, it behoves us all to furbish the weapons of the spirit for the Day of Judgement. If the trumpet sounds tomorrow, how many of you will be ready?'

He was about to slide into his sermon. Thomas Woodcarver, who had thrown a mantle round himself and abandoned his workshop for the sake of the news, would now have liked to slide out of the church but it was impossible. Most of the village had crowded in and he was near the front and firmly wedged. He had to listen.

'I go about the country,' Brother Ailred declared, 'and I grieve at times to see how few people understand what the weapons of the spirit are. I see men and women everywhere setting store by the weapons of the world, and by that I am not speaking of sword and spear. I speak of money and possessions; the quick profit which makes your neighbours envious because with it you can buy what he can't: the pretty gewgaw that a girl hopes will make a young man look at her: houses full of needless comforts, spare rugs and pots and lamps; store-rooms full of meal-sacks and ceiling beams groaning with hams in the curing, while outside, others go homeless and cold and hungry.'

He paused for breath and someone in the crowd said protestingly that they'd only got one ham hanging from their ceiling and they'd need that, with a family to feed, and another voice added, 'And whatever we got, we *worked* for it.'

Brother Ailred swung round to identify the owners of the voices. 'Worked? Yes, indeed, no doubt. No doubt you worked day in and day out. Could you not work less and let some less fortunate neighbour do the remainder and earn the goods you do not need? Not that I can blame you for the way you speak. Your Father Matthew is a good man, a true priest, but I have seen and no doubt you have also seen, other priests growing fat on tithes taken from those who can ill afford them, and abbots with goshawks on their wrists. Such men are no better than heretics. With such examples, you can hardly be blamed for valuing the wrong things. But as Christ, the humble man, once disputed with the learned doctors at Jerusalem, and set an example to the Pharisees, such folk as yourselves can set an example to those above you. Yes, you can! You . . .'

Thomas had lost the thread. Something interesting was happening. Brother Ailred's voice was powerful and it seemed actually to be shaking some of the fabric of the church. Bits of wood appeared to be showering down on him. He glanced up in surprise, feeling them. 'Take care! Brother Friar, take care!' Thomas suddenly shouted.

205

Brother Ailred glanced up again and then jumped for it. Above him, with a cracking sound and a heavy shower of dust, one end of a roof beam gave way. The beam swung down, passing through the space which the friar had occupied only a moment before, and then, as the other end broke off as well, crashed to the floor. There were cries of alarm and a hasty shuffling backwards on the part of the gathering, with anxious eyes upturned to see if any more of the roof were coming down.

Brother Ailred had jumped into their midst, but was unhurt and still on his feet. 'Out of here!' he barked. 'Everyone! But in orderly fashion; don't shake the building!' He shepherded them all out, himself emerging last. As they stood anxiously in the churchyard, in the rain, he added, 'You have woodworm in your church roof. How very appropriate! Take it as a warning! For there is a canker like woodworm in the way Christianity is lived in these modern days, and if the Trump for the Judgement were to sound tomorrow I fear that nine Christians out of ten would find themselves among the goats. If you would save your souls, you must do more than go regularly to Mass and Confession . . .'

Thomas, who didn't go regularly to either, was once more not listening. He was already drifting unobtrusively away. He supposed he ought to have warned Father Matthew about those roofbeams. They'd all have to be replaced now. Oh well, that would be work for the Carpenters. He couldn't see much in it for himself and Ed.

'The arrangement Father Matthew suggests is perfectly acceptable to me,' said Henry Peyton, the master woodworker from Norwich.

On Ed's workbench, examples of his and Thomas's skill had been set out. There were a couple of bows from a consignment Thomas was making for Sir Edward, a wooden bowl with a decorative carving round the rim, partly finished, and what would eventually be a lift-up seat for a settle-cum-chest which they were making for Sybil. Henry Peyton was examining one of the bows. Bowmaking was one thing and carving another but the crafts were of course related. The finish on this bow was all that it should be. He set it down, linked his hands and let the fur-trimmed cuffs of his long, formal gown slide concealingly over them, for all the world as though he were a lord who never had to work with his own hands.

'Some master craftsmen don't allow it,' he said, turning to Ed. 'With them, it's guild workers for the whole job, or they won't take it on. But I don't agree, not in a case like this. I think the local craftsmen should have a chance to put the work of their hands into their own parish church. It keeps them proud of it and reverent. There is so much absurd talk these days. Some of the wandering friars preach dangerous doctrines, likely to undermine respect for the church. I've heard them say things that are not far off heresy.'

'It was a friar brought that beam down,' Thomas remarked. 'I've never heard such a booming voice.'

'It would have collapsed soon in any case. It was worm-riddled through and through,' said Peyton. 'And, as I said, I'm agreeable to Father Matthew's request that you and your father should do a little of the work on the new, ornamental beams, although my journeymen will do the rest. That's the kind of arrangement I commonly make in these cases and my men accept it because if they don't, they're out. Your Father Matthew,' he added, 'won't give me the contract if I don't consent, anyway. You're lucky in your priest.'

Thomas grinned faintly. Father Matthew, arriving in advance of Peyton to warn them of his visit, had said, 'And I hope, Thomas, that once the new roof is on, I shall see you in church oftener. After all, you'll owe me something for this rare opportunity.' He supposed that he might go along now and then, at least for a while, to keep Father Matthew content.

'You understand what's wanted?' Peyton said. 'I brought a plan with me . . . perhaps you'd care to look at it.' He took a roll of vellum from under his arm, untied it and carried it to the light. Ed and Thomas followed him. As Peyton enlarged on his explanation, pointing here and there, Thomas's heart began to thump, in a strong, resolute rhythm.

He had been waiting all his life for this.

The whole church roof was going to be replaced, at Sir Edward's expense, and his portrait was to be carved into one of the beams. But apart from this, all the beams were to be decorated. Herons and spears would figure largely as usual, but there were to be other things, too.

'Leaves,' said Master Peyton. 'You have grasped the point? A garland of leaves along the sides and undersides of each beam: the type of leaf varying from one beam to the next: oak, ash, chestnut, what you will. You will undertake two beams, choosing which leaves you like. My men will carve different ones. The beams I want you to do are these two . . . you follow? At either end of this nave . . .' He pointed to where, at one end of the vellum, was a plan of the whole roof. 'You are free to decide on detail. It will be a great opportunity for you to leave a mark which will last long after you're dead and gone.'

Roofbeams, high over the heads of the congregation, wouldn't be looked at overmuch and Thomas knew it, but one couldn't have everything. He could carve them and within limits, please himself over the design. Oak leaves, with serrated edges, like the ones in Redesmarsh Church! But he'd include acorns, cup and fruit, in tiny detail. And horse chestnuts, with prickly conker cases . . .'

'Reckon you're up to it?' said Ed.

'We're both up to it! When can we begin?' said Thomas.

'In a month,' said Peyton, sounding amused. Thomas gave him a brooding look. So this master craftsman from Norwich thought enthusiasm amusing, unsophisticated, did he? But Peyton had brought him a chance for which he was starving. 'In a month,' he said. 'We'll be ready.'

After Peyton had gone, he said to Ed: 'We ought to practise the design a bit, on some spare pieces of wood.'

'You ought to, you mean. I'll be leaving the job to you,' Ed said. 'I'm not as sure as you that I'm fit for it and you're ravening to get at it. Don't mess it up, that's all.'

'You mean – me do both beams?'

'Yes, you. Who else? Haven't got half a dozen odd sons hiding in the corners of this workshop. Pity you haven't got a few yourself but I suppose there's time yet.'

'These things are as God wills,' said Thomas sententiously.

Nicola, cooking in the room next door, heard the exchange and bit her lip. In the five years since Alison's birth there had been no other successful pregnancies. Thomas, now, seemed able to take her as she was and not ask for what she couldn't give. But somehow or other, as though this very acceptance had put out some essential flame, she had conceived only twice and lost both pregnancies early. Thomas had been disappointed but fair. It wasn't her fault, he said stiffly; no one could prevent these things, and he had stopped his father from grumbling at her.

He tried to be a good husband; she knew that. He had lost his temper and struck her only two or three times since that first occasion and every time he apologised and seemed stricken by his own behaviour. On her side, Nicola strove to avoid provoking him, by keeping the house in a manner above criticism, by doing her best in bed and by smiling at him until her jaws felt stiff with the effort.

But it was like being under siege. That latent anger in him was always there and she could not forget it. She wondered if she would have been better able to bear it if she had never heard Isabel Plowman's life story and never been given that medallion which she still kept hidden in her private chest. The answer, she thought wryly sometimes, was that probably she would indeed have been happier, for the very good reason that she probably wouldn't be married to Thomas. Had she never harassed her father with demands for a freeman, he might have let her turn Thomas down.

Fate, given a chance, might even have . . .

But it was better not to remember how she had turned on the ladder up the bedloft, on her marriage night, and looked into the eyes of Osbert Smith.

In the other room, Ed grunted in reply to Thomas and changed the subject. 'Before you start practising for them beams for the church,' he said, ''the bows still want finishing, so that Sir Edward can go off to war with them. Better get down to it.'

Sir Edward Rushley was in a bad temper.

It was impossible to concentrate on checking his steward's monthly household accounts while his son Roland and some of the stable lads, aided by thick sticks and joyfully barking dogs, were hunting rats just outside in the courtyard, and immediately overhead there was all that thumping and screaming from the chamber where his daughter Ghislaine was locked up.

The rat hunt he could have put up with. The house was always getting overrun with them and every time a heavy stick went *thwack*, it meant the end of another long-tailed little pest. But Ghislaine was another matter. The girl had no sense. It was true that the husband he had found for her was nearly sixty, with gout and a limp which dated from the fit he had had two years ago. But he was rich, with a London house and an Essex manor and such elderly, ailing men rarely lived long. With luck, Ghislaine would be a wealthy widow before she could turn round and then she'd be welcome to disparage herself with a good-looking archer or a sexy groom. No one would interfere. But meanwhile, he expected her to do as she was told. Dear God, he'd even kept her at home instead of sending her off to be brought up by friends or relatives, because he wanted to oversee her upbringing himself. No girl had ever had a better father and this was how she repaid him.

She had said, passionately, that she wouldn't do as she was told, and he had finally been compelled to take steps. Not violent ones: the bridegroom would be here within a month, and bruises sometimes faded slowly. It would be a pity if on her wedding day the bride carried such marks. But there were other methods. She wouldn't, for instance, be the worse for not being quite so plump as usual. 'You'll be locked in the empty guest room over the hall and you'll have one bread and water meal a day until you come to your senses,' he had said that morning. It had taken the combined efforts of himself and his wife Lady Margery, plus Roland, to get Ghislaine into her prison and she was still at the stage of thinking they didn't really mean it and that making an uproar would induce them to change their minds.

Well, it wouldn't, and fortunately Margery – an excellent woman who always agreed with him – and Roland and Roland's hero-worshipping little wife Anne were of the same mind as he was.

He couldn't wait to get away to the war, which had developed far too slowly for his taste. Middle-aged he might be, with a corrugated brow and grey in his wiry hair and red veins on his jutting hawk-nose, but he was still active. His protuberant, hooded eyes had excellent vision and his joints still moved smoothly. He was fit to fight and he'd enjoy it. His temper was slightly soothed, therefore, when his captain of archers came to say that Thomas Woodcarver had brought a consignment of bows. 'Do you wish to examine them personally?'

'Yes.' He flung the steward's wooden tallies into a handsome box with the Rushley device inlaid in ivory on the lid, and locked it. 'Bring them in. And bring Thomas. I want to see him.'

Thomas, informed of this, was surprised and uneasy. He had worked at the hall on the decoration of some new panelling and Sir Edward knew him by name as a result. But usually, when delivering bows or going to the Hall on any other ordinary matter, he expected to see only the steward or the captain of archers. He could think of no reason why Sir Edward might want to speak to him and felt instinctively that it was ominous. The bows were of good workmanship, he knew, and made of Rushley elm. He didn't think they would incur criticism and he couldn't think of anything he had done which might. Also, he was impatient to get away. With the order for bows now completed, he wanted to begin experimenting, on spare pieces of wood, with leaves and acorns and horse-chestnut cases. He came into his lord's presence reluctantly and with caution.

He sensed at once that Sir Edward was irritable, although the irritation didn't seem to be directed towards himself. There was a lot of disturbance going on: shouting and laughing somewhere outside, and upstairs, a woman crying and apparently beating a door with her fists. As directed, he set down his cloth-wrapped bundle on the table and opened it. Then he waited while Sir Edward, who had greeted him with a short nod, took up one bow after another and subjected them to an intense examination by eye and fingertip.

Having finished, he looked up. 'Good. No rough edges or knotholes there. Your work, Thomas, will be carried to France and God willing it will help to win battles, to defend our interests in Flanders and Gascony. Richard Grosney tells me, by the way, that you are now becoming an adequate archer yourself.'

'I'm a poor shot, sir. I still miss the target too often.'

'Anyone might say that, out of modesty.' Sir Edward stopped. Upstairs, Ghislaine was now clearly hysterical. He beckoned sharply to a page who was crossing the hall. 'My wife is in the solar. Go and tell her from me to put a stop to that noise up there. I don't care how. Now, Thomas. I've seen you at the butts myself. Your marksmanship has unquestionably improved with time and, in any case, as you well know, the ability to get the full range out of a bow matters as much as accuracy of aim. You have that ability. That, put with your skill in making the bows in the first place, makes you a valuable man. I have need of as many good men as I can find, to take to France. You may regard yourself as one of my archers from this day on.'

Thomas stared at him, staggered.

In other circumstances, the prospect might have been agreeable. It would have meant getting away from Rushley, seeing other places, going forth to adventure and, perhaps, to opportunity. But . . .

'But what about the church roof, sir?' he blurted.

'The church roof?'

'Yes, sir. I've got to work on the beams, carving them. The job won't start for two or three weeks and it'll take a bit of time, sir. I'll have to do that first, sir.'

'Rubbish. Your father can do it or Peyton's men can carry it out, whatever it is. Oh yes, I think Father Matthew mentioned to me that he'd arranged for you to have a hand in the carving. But you're not essential. Don't concern yourself about that.'

'But, sir,' said Thomas protestingly, 'it's . . . it's . . .'

Like virtually every other villein, he always felt nervous in the presence of anyone from the Hall, most of all Sir Edward. But, unlike most of the others, he resented this. Looking at the angry gleam now showing under Sir Edward's heavy eyelids, he hated not only Sir Edward but himself; his own fear and his certainty of defeat. He heard his voice die away in stammering.

'It's what?' demanded Sir Edward. Overhead, his daughter had become quiet. Lady Margery's voice could be heard, speaking on a note of warning.

'It's . . . I've never had the chance to do any work so important before,' said Thomas, knowing it was useless but saying it just the same. 'I'd like to carry it out before . . .'

'You'd *like* to carry it out? Who the devil cares what you like or don't like? You're my villein, which means that you do as I bid. Go home and tell your family, collect whatever personal gear you want to bring – which includes your boots, a cloak and your own bow – and then come back. Captain Fulbert here will be in charge of you. You'll live in the Hall from now on and train with my men. You're not the only one. Gilbert Pecher – I've seen you shooting with him – I'm taking him to France too and he's already here. That's settled then. Off you go.'

Lady Margery's voice had sunk to a murmur and the rat-hunt seemed to have withdrawn to some remoter region. Thomas hadn't moved. He stood where he was, staring at Sir Edward.

'I said,' remarked Sir Edward, 'off you go.'

He had come up here with his bundle of finished bows, thinking he would just hand them over and be off back to his workshop. He couldn't take in the speed at which his world had changed. He'd been going to carve those beams. He wanted to carve them. His fingers lusted for spiky conker cases and the zig-zag outlines of oak leaves as though all the satisfaction Nicola had not given him, could be found there instead. And yet it would not be a second-best. His need for his work was a thing in its own right. Given that, almost anything else was bearable.

He couldn't be taken from his craft *now* and turned into something alien and irrelevant like an archer. He felt this so strongly that it seemed to him that Sir Edward ought to feel it too, to understand it by instinct.

'Well?' said Sir Edward. 'What are you waiting for?'

'Sir,' said Thomas blankly, 'I . . . I *can't*.'

'Do you realise who you're talking to, man?' Captain Fulbert was scandalised. 'Sir Edward has taken the trouble to speak to you personally on this matter, a courtesy to you because of your good bowmaking. It's a courtesy that seems to have been wasted!'

'Quite,' said his lord. 'Captain Fulbert's reminder is timely, Thomas. I am Sir Edward Rushley. I have given you my orders and that's the end of it. Now go and do as you're bid.'

'Please, no. Sir, I . . .'

He stopped. Sir Edward was leaning back on his seat, arched eyebrows raised and forehead deeply furrowed and the expression in his eyes was intimidating. 'I'm tired of this,' he said. 'Captain Fulbert, just take him off, will you? He's under your control from this moment on. Send someone else to his home for his belongings . . . oh, for the love of God!'

The shouts and snarls of the rathunters had surged close to the hall once more, almost drowning his voice. Sir Edward sprang to his feet in rage. The racket faded again but as it did so, a door slammed overhead and bolts were shot and then, from Ghislaine, there came this time not screams and banging, but a grievous and heartbroken sobbing which plucked at the nerves.

Sir Edward's face darkened to a rich crimson. The sound of new footsteps made him turn with an angry movement. 'Ah. Richard Grosney. Come here, man. You gave me a very good report of this fellow's prowess with a bow; he was improving considerably, you said, which agreed with my own observations. But there was one thing I didn't observe and you apparently didn't either. He's been trained for war but he doesn't want to fight. He says he wants to carve beams instead. What have you to say about that, Grosney?'

'He'd rather carve beams instead of men?' Grosney remained calm in the face of what amounted to a rebuke from his lord, and regarded Thomas with contempt. 'Well, sir, one often comes across this sort of thing with villeins. I daresay he can't help it. He's craven, I expect.'

Thomas's face also darkened. His hands curled into fists and his whole body made a curious, jerky movement as though he were a cat on the verge of making a spring.

'I'm sorry if I misled you, sir,' said Grosney. 'I don't like being made a fool of, Woodcarver.'

Sir Edward stared at Thomas and then beckoned to Grosney. He whispered into Grosney's ear and Richard Grosney smiled. They both turned to gaze at Thomas, who stood still, a coldness seizing on his bowels. The trouble with overlords was that they were not only powerful, but incalculable. They might use their power for anything.

'So,' said Sir Edward. 'You don't want to be an archer. You prefer – or perhaps you'd feel safer – carving wood?'

'Safety doesn't come into it, sir. I'm not scared of the French; it isn't that at all. It's . . .'

'Not concerned about your safety?' Sir Edward cut him short. 'That's just as well. For you're not safe, Thomas. No man who defies me is safe.'

'I'm not defying you, sir. But this . . .' It was no use and he could see it was no use. 'I'll get my things,' he said, and knew that the very civility in his voice was an insult. 'And come to France.'

'Too late, Thomas.' The pathetic whimpering in the room above was still continuing. Sir Edward glanced upwards and his mouth hardened. He looked as though, in Thomas, he had found an outlet for pent-up fury. 'I no longer want you. I'm grieved to waste a good man, but archers and bowyers can be hired and so can craftsmen. You will be none of these things henceforth,' said Sir Edward. 'Instead, you shall be a warning to others and a reminder of their duty to those above them. Grosney, as my bailiff, and constable of Rushley, you will act as witness. Captain Fulbert, these are my orders . . .'

Nicola was washing her hair and taking a bath; and preparing to perform the same service for Alison.

She had first begun washing her hair and body regularly at the age of ten, when she realised that they were part of the good looks which Isabel Plowman had pointed out to her. She kept it up even during the winter, at least when the weather was not too bitter. Her mother had prophesied lung-rot and marsh ague but neither had overtaken Nicola as yet, and the beauty of her hair and skin were her reward.

Now, despite the heavy burden of work on her married life, she still persisted, growing the herbs to sweeten the water and saving a little buttermilk for her face. There was self-respect in her efforts; a feeling that life had not quite defeated her. She kept the dwelling well-swept too. And she wished Alison to appreciate cleanliness as well.

Alison had Thomas's rare combination of dark eyes and light red hair and might one day have striking looks. If so, Nicola meant her to make the best possible use of them. The good marriage she hadn't been able to make herself might yet be achieved by her daughter. Five-year-old Alison might grumble and wail, but once every two weeks or so, Nicola filled a small tub with hot water and relentlessly scrubbed them both with a soap of wood-ash and animal fat. She had finished her own toilette, put on an old gown and an apron, tied her damp hair up in a scarf and was just dunking her reluctant offspring when from the adjoining workshop, Ed's voice cried out in horror and she heard blundering footsteps. Thomas's voice, with a queer, hoarse note in it, was gasping something in reply to his father.

She picked Alison out of the water, wrapped her quickly in the thick woollen cloth she used as a towel and sat her on a stool. 'Stay there,' she said, and hastened through to the workshop. Ed was leaning on his workbench as though he were about to faint. And Thomas, who had set out earlier with a consignment of bows on a pack donkey, was slumped, ashen-faced, on a bench by the wall. His clothing was splashed with water and his hair was soaking wet. His left hand cradled his right, which was buried in a great ball of bloodstained cloth. He turned as Nicola came in and looked at her with eyes in which there were not only tears but a disbelieving horror. She ran to his side.

'What's happened? Thomas, what's happened?'

'It was him up at the hall. Sir Edward,' said Ed. 'They sent him back alone. All the way, alone, on foot. They kept the bloody donkey.'

'But what did they do to you, Thomas? And why? Weren't the bows all right? Oh, what has *happened*?' Nicola knelt beside him, trying to touch the ball of bandages. Thomas held it away from her.

'The bows were all right. He wanted me to go to France as an archer. Didn't want to go. Because of the beams; the beams for the church. Wanted to do those.' His voice was jerky and faint. 'So he said . . . he said . . .'

'Yes, Thomas, what did he say? Oh Thomas. What did they do? Tell me!'

'He said I shouldn't be either an archer or a carver of wood,' Thomas mumbled. The tears brimmed and began to stream down his face. 'He told his men . . . they chopped off the two first fingers of my right hand. That's what they did. On a chopping block . . . in the kitchen. Used hot iron to stop the . . . the blood . . . I fainted. They threw water over me. Richard Grosney was there. He laughed. Oh, God, it hurts so much, I didn't think anything could hurt so much. I've lost my fingers, Nicola, I've lost the fingers I hold a chisel with. I'll never be able to carve wood again.' His weeping now was rage as much as pain. 'That's what they've done to me. That's what that bastard that calls himself Sir Edward wanted. Sod him. Sod him. I hope he fries in hell for all eternity. I'd like to be there with a pitchfork. I'd like to hear him scream, and laugh at him. There's nothing I can do to get back at him, *nothing I can do . . .* !'

With her arms tightly wrapped round his shoulders, Nicola said, 'Father-in-law, go to the well and get some cold water. Then send for my mother. She makes good medicines. She may have something for the pain.'

'You go. I'll see to Thomas. Women go to the well, not men.'

'No. I want Nicola,' said Thomas thickly.

'Then I'll stay. And I can't be in two places at once!' Nicola snapped to her father-in-law. 'So will you please *go to the well*!'

Ed blinked at her and then did as he was told. Thomas muttered, 'Good . . . good girl. On my side, that's right,' and attempted a grin, which twisted into a dreadful grimace. Nicola set about coaxing him to let her undo the wrappings. She saw Alison peering fearfully through the doorway and called to her to fetch some of the elderberry wine which Nicola had made the year before. 'You know how to draw it. Get it in a jug.'

By the time Alison came back, clutching the jug with both hands, Ed had brought the water and rushed off again to find Sybil, and Nicola had the bandages off. What was beneath was very ugly and Thomas, leaning against the wall, moaned wretchedly because even the act of removing the wrappings was so agonising. He cried out when Nicola plunged his hand into the cold water but the Rushley well was very deep and the water very cold and it numbed the pain somewhat. Thomas grew quieter. She lifted his hand out and dipped it into the wine jug. Wine was cleansing; everybody knew that. Father Matthew told the story, sometimes, of the Good Samaritan who had looked after the man attacked by footpads, and poured oil and wine into his wounds.

It was some time before Ed returned, but when he did. Sybil was with him, armed with a cordial. 'This may help. It's brewed from some kind of foreign poppy seed; my mother got the recipe years ago from old Isabel. I'll help you get him up to his bed. Come along now, Thomas . . .'

'It's wicked, that's what it is, wicked!' When Thomas, who had become very faint, had been steered on to his pallet and was sleeping heavily under the combined influence of the poppy cordial and a strong dose of the elderberry wine, which Sybil reckoned was as beneficial inside as out, they returned to the living room and Ed spoke his mind. 'Just because my boy didn't want to do what Sir Edward said . . . to do a thing like this to him! We're no better than slaves, that's what it is. We've no rights, no nothing. He'll never be able to hold a chisel again. He's right there. He's no good with his left hand.'

'He's got his other fingers left,' said Sybil. 'And his thumb. If he survives this, maybe he can train himself to use them.'

Ed had collapsed on to a stool. 'All the trouble I took to bring him up right and teach him his work and now this. Whatever he does, he'll never be as good as he was.'

'We'll see,' said Sybil kindly. 'Nicola, I think we could all do with some of that elderberry wine. Your father-in-law certainly could.'

'I'll fetch it,' Nicola said, making for the door to the little stone storeroom.

Once there, she paused to lean against the wall and wipe eyes which were suddenly brimming. She had never thought she could feel so sorry for Thomas. She had never been nearer to loving him than today, when he had such need of her and when, for once, the help he needed was something that she had the power to give.

She caught sight of Alison, once more peering from the doorway. She had never noticed before how often her daughter peered round doors, watching the adults and listening to them. She straightened herself quickly, blinking her eyes clear. All this must be very frightening for the child. She must be wondering what was afoot.

'Your father has been hurt but he will be all right. He's asleep now,' she said. 'Fetch some of those earthenware goblets and come and sit with us. I'll find you some milk to drink.'

Chapter Thirteen
Death and Opportunity

Healing took place gradually. Thomas, raging and cursing, swore he was finished as a craftsman but Sybil had been at least partly right. The skill once housed in the first two fingers of his right hand began to be transferred to the last two, though the process was slow. Efforts to work with his left instead, however, were quite useless, as his father had prophesied. The co-ordination was simply not there. Again and again, he was driven back to his maimed right hand with its two surviving fingers and its thumb.

He fought them as though they were enemies. Many times, he threw his tools down in angry despair at his clumsiness and many times too he was forced to drop them because the unaccustomed fingers had gone rigid with cramp. A measure of success came at last; enough to get by with, Thomas said with a delicate curl of the lip. But the fine edge, the ability to carve and tiny detail with unerring precision, was gone, lost before it was fully developed. It was still latent in his eye and brain but the fingers he had left would never respond with quite the smoothness of the fingers he had lost.

With those fingers had gone his chance at the roofbeams, and now, even if such a chance came again, he could not do it justice. Ed had done the beams instead, but Thomas would have done the work better, and knew it.

The edginess between father and son, of which Nicola had been aware from the first, although she did not know the cause, mellowed for a while after the catastrophe, because of Ed's clearly genuine distress on his son's behalf. But this did not endure. Thomas, in a fit of bitterness at his mutilation, let out his opinion of Ed's oak and chestnut leaves. Ed retorted that there was no need to point out his limitations; he knew them already. He wasn't a fool. The only fool in the house was Thomas, who'd still be in one piece if he'd had the sense to do as he was bid. 'You'd be in France, maybe, but you'd have your fingers with you!'

After which the household sank back into its accustomed uneasy state, and Nicola sank with it, her moment of supremacy gone. Thomas sometimes took his frustration out on her, finding fault where no fault was, shouting that perfectly good food was overdone or underdone or not hot enough, that clothes she had made for him didn't fit properly

216

although she knew that they did, or that Alison, who had done nothing worse than run indoors calling loudly or letting the door slam behind her, had no manners. He struck them both on frequent occasions. Ed regarded such behaviour as normal and never commented but to begin with, Thomas would say afterwards that he was sorry. But when it had happened three times in four days Nicola, tired out with fear and the strain of trying not to give offence, only turned away her head. It was after dark and they were in bed, and Thomas, enraged because his apology had been rejected seized her and took her as though he were attacking her.

When he had done, he rolled off, leaving her bruised and rigid, and lying on his back beside her, he told her of his childhood and Ed's treatment of him and how he had hated Ed. She knew why he was telling her. It was another attempt at justifying himself, oblique this time. It was frightening, she thought, how much hatred Thomas carried within him. But then, Thomas had always been frightening. That was nothing new. She said nothing in answer to his story, because the only thing she wanted to say, just then, was that she wished Sir Edward had amputated more than the two fingers on Thomas's right hand, and that she dared not say.

Thomas, receiving no response, gave up, and thereafter ceased to apologise for his violence, although it became less frequent, as though he were trying to restrain himself.

Sir Edward had left for France. News came of a great victory at a place called Crécy, where English archers had destroyed a much larger French army, by breaking up its cavalry charges and reducing it to confusion. 'I suppose *he* was there,' Thomas remarked. 'Pity I didn't go, after all. In all the uproar, I might have managed to swing round and put a shaft into him instead of into the French.'

Crécy was followed by further news, of Calais being besieged and taken. And then, so report said, the King was bringing his army home. But Sir Edward and his son Roland did not return at once, although some of the men they had taken with them from the three manors did and reported that Sir Edward had served valiantly and been given some land in the north of England as a reward, and had gone to inspect it.

These men told marvellous stories of sieges and battles and stormy voyages, of danger and bravery and stratagem, of peculiar food and strange diseases. But not all came back whole and there were some who never came back at all. Gilbert Pecher was safe, and rejoined his father on their holding as though he had never been away. But the Oxfen miller would never see his son again and Osbert Smith's boy came back on crutches, with one leg cut off below the knee, because his shin had been smashed by a terrible new weapon called a cannon ball.

For a long time, no one talked of anything but the war. Until, in the autumn of the following year, Lady Ghislaine, Sir Edward's married daughter, arrived with her elderly husband, hotfoot from their Essex home, with a horrifying story of a pestilence which had completely wiped out a household only four miles away from them. Hard on their heels, came the friar, Brother Ailred, to demand audience with Lady Margery, who was running the estate in Sir Edward's absence.

The pestilence, he said, was of a new kind and represented a most alarming menace. For the safety of the three manors, no ships which had touched London or any south-coast port should be allowed to unload either people or goods at the harbour, nor should travellers from the south be given hospitality.

'I warned Redesmarsh Abbey on the way here, since their guest-house is so widely used by travellers. The sickness is widespread in London and already moving northwards.'

'We already know of it. My daughter and son-in-law have told us,' Lady Margery informed him. She was a small woman, fashionably pale, with light-blue eyes and a small, narrow nose and eyebrows plucked almost out of existence. She sat quietly, very upright, with white, slender hands folded on her lap, by the fire in the handsome wall-hearth which her husband's innovative forebear Sir Simon had installed in the hall to match the one in the solar. The fine panelling around it, however, was Sir Edward's idea, and the Rushley device carved into it here and there had been put there by Ed and Thomas. Hearth and panelling made the hall look both comfortable and dignified.

Lady Margery prized dignity. The news of the pestilence was alarming but she refused to give way to it. 'I doubt if we can turn ships away,' she said. 'We are expecting consignments soon, of goods ordered by various people in the locality. They're arriving on one of my husband's ships, returned to him after the French campaign. Refusing to accept them would be somewhat drastic. After all,' said Lady Margery valiantly, as became the wife of Sir Edward Rushley, hero of Crécy, 'epidemics are commonplace. Marsh ague, smallpox, scarlet fever . . .'

'This is different,' said Brother Ailred. 'People recover from those other illnesses as often as not. Very few survive this and it's an evil way to die.' His naturally resonant voice had been trained for effective preaching and or overwhelming hecklers. Now he used it deliberately to transmit dread. 'There's a raging fever and swelling – neck, armpit, groin. When they're dying, people turn bluish, as though they were a mass of bruises.'

'You've seen cases?'

'I've had the disease. I travelled to Italy two years ago and I caught it there. I was one of the fortunate few who lived. As I said, there are not many. I urge you, my lady, most sincerely, to follow my advice and keep ships and people from the south from entering your domains.'

'That's how it started at Whitmead.' Ghislaine came through the door from the solar. Uninvited, she came to the hearth, the train of her very elegant blue overgrown whispering across the rushes. 'With visitors from the south,' she said.

'Whitmead?' queried Lady Margery sharply. 'Was that the place near you where the disease broke out just before you left?'

'Which drove us out,' said Ghislaine. 'It's a holding not far from our Essex house, Brother Ailred. It's part of a neighbouring manor, but quite big in its own right and isolated too. There was a celebration there; a marriage or something of the kind.' The tone in which Ghislaine said the word *marriage* made her opinion of that institution quite clear. 'They had guests from London. After the guests had gone home, the whole household fell ill. Somebody who called there found them . . . well, they were all dead. We knew there was disease in London. In fact, that's why we were in Essex; we'd left London to get away from it. As soon as we realised that this was the same, my husband said we should leave again for somewhere healthier.'

She finished her account in an expressionless voice which actually concealed turbulent depths of feeling. Ghislaine, starved and terrified into saying *I will*, would never forgive her husband for being lame and gouty and sixty, and his terror at the prospect of catching what was now being called the plague had disgusted her. A man who was often so painfully ill should in her opinion positively welcome the chance of release from life. She was the one who was entitled to be afraid, but he was the one who had shouted at the servants to get baggage and horses ready at once, and banged his stick on the ground with rage over some minor delay, exploding that they must, *must* get away before the pestilence caught up with them and not caring that the kitchen scullions could hear him. He had in fact made an exhibition of himself.

Ghislaine had made an exhibition of herself once, and had suffered imprisonment and privation as a result and had been defeated in the end, after all. She would never make that mistake again. Ghislaine too had learned the value of dignity and, as she sat down at Lady Margery's side, she looked very like her mother.

As the wife, however reluctant, of a man with a London house and a manor in Essex, she had also learned to take decisions.

'I think, Mother, that we should accept the good friar's advice and protect the three manors.'

'I would remind you,' said Lady Margery, 'that I am in charge here in your father's absence, and should I be incapacitated, your brother Roland's wife Lady Anne will take my place. You have no power to make decisions.'

'Neither has Anne,' said Ghislaine shortly. 'Anne can just about decide between gold thread and silver thread for her embroidery. I say that we should turn all ships and people away.'

'Where,' asked Brother Ailred mildly, 'is Sir Edward at present? Is there any means of getting in touch with him?'

'He is still in the north. He has been taking over new property there and there was a great deal to do. The steward who was acting as caretaker had proved dishonest,' said Lady Margery. 'He hoped to return for Christmas but I believe he is now snowed in.'

'Mother, we *must* do as Brother Ailred suggests!'

Lady Margery's face was cold. The friar and Ghislaine were right; she knew it. She had a brief and shocking mental vision of a ship sailing into Wendmouth harbour, with sails of black and a skeleton for steersman. But Ghislaine should have kept quiet and left the choice to her. She hesitated.

Brother Ailred came to her rescue. 'Obviously, it can't be done unless people understand why but there I can help you. I will go round the three manors, explaining and preaching. I shall preach on the theme that none of us knows the day or the hour when our souls may be required of us.' He stopped and let out a sigh. 'I know this disease. I very much fear that whatever care we take, God will be swinging his scythe here as elsewhere, before long.'

'Why?' said Lady Margery. Her shoulders had sagged. She was going to agree to isolating the three manors; her consent, or defeat, were there in the lines of her body. 'Why do these things happen? Why does God allow it?'

'Perhaps to remind us what sinners we are,' said the friar.

'I think,' said Ghislaine in a practical voice, 'that we had better start by informing Richard Grosney and sending him to warn Gerald Harbourmaster at Wendmouth.'

'I'm not turning out to see Sir Edward Swift-With-The-Chopper come home,' Thomas said. 'I've digging to do in the vegetable patch, now the frost's broken at last. I want you to give me a hand, Nicola.'

'You'd best not call Sir Edward names where other folk can overhear you,' his father warned him. 'Might get repeated.'

, 'No one's likely to overhear me with the church bell making that racket,' said Thomas sourly. 'I can hardly hear you, even. I notice,' said Thomas sourly, 'that no one talks about turning *his* ship away. Suppose he brings this disease in with him?'

'He's come from York, not London or Norwich,' said Ed. 'Richard Grosney's made a point of telling us that.'

'I'm glad to hear it.' Thomas lifted a spade from its wall-hook. 'So it's in Norwich now, it seems. It's creeping closer.'

'Perhaps it will pass us by,' Nicola offered hopefully.

'We'll be in trouble if it doesn't,' Thomas said. 'We've heard what happened near where Lady Ghislaine used to live in Essex. What was its name? Whitmead, that's it. A whole family, gone inside of a week.'

Nicola said anxiously, 'The church bell means that the ship's coming up the river. Master Grosney said we'd all got to be there to see Sir Edward and Sir Roland come ashore. They're coming to the Rushley Hall landing stage so it isn't far. We ought to go, really, Thomas.'

'You just want an outing,' said Thomas with a snort.

'No.' Nicola spoke hurriedly. 'I don't want to see them, not after what Sir Edward did to you. But it's Master Grosney's orders. We could just stand at the back, just so as not to give any offence.'

Her menfolk made growling noises, but these indicated unwilling agreement. For villeins, not giving offence was important. Once, Thomas had not known how important. But he knew now.

After eight years of marriage Nicola had not still produced any more living children, although she had had another miscarriage and one stillborn son. She had wept over the son and Ed had complained loudly, but Thomas had scarcely been moved. 'What sort of life would a son have, anyway?' he had demanded savagely. 'He'd be just Sir Edward's creature, same as us.'

Nicola had got over it, slowly. Alison at least was thriving; she wasn't completely childless. Life had other compensations, too. Thomas rarely lost his temper with her now and she had friends among the other women in Rushley. She gossiped with them round the well and took an occasional cup of ale in their houses, exchanging tips about weaving or brewing. There was a good deal of unsolicited advice about improving her fertility, but she had grown used to that.

These days, her worst enemy was the tedium. Every day seemed exactly like the one before, and the years stretched ahead with no prospect of change except that of growing older. Although she had so hurriedly denied that she wanted an outing, it was true that she enjoyed anything that amounted to a break in the monotony. It was a clear day; cold and windy as March weather so often was, but the sun was out. The banners would be bright for Sir Edward's homecoming. She was pleased when Thomas said, 'Oh very well, then. Come on.'

It was a special excitement because, since Brother Ailred's visit, no ship at all had been allowed to moor in Wendmouth Harbour, still less to sail upriver to Rushley landing stage. And people had missed the ships. Sails in the distance meant new faces, information from outside and, of course, commodities. The crowd which gathered on the stretch of grass between the landing stage and the encircling wall of Rushley Hall, had been told by Richard Grosney that they had to be there, but most would have come along anyway, and the cheers which greeted Sir Edward's ship as she came in, under oars and with sails furled, but with pennants bravely flying and a gilded figurehead catching the sun, were largely spontaneous.

The oars were stowed as she came alongside. Sailors leaned over the side with fending poles to keep her from bumping the jetty until she had settled into place; mooring ropes were thrown and made fast to bollards and presently the gangplank was lowered and Sir Edward and his son Sir Roland marched down it. They had come in armour as befitted men who were returning victorious from war. The Rushley heron between two spears was embroidered in gold thread on their red

221

surcoats, *or* upon *gules*, and their armour was polished. They wore their long swords and carried their helmets. They bore no shields. Mail grew thicker and more comprehensive every year and Sir Edward had provided the latest armour for himself and his son before they set out. He had had new swords made as well, and they were massive weapons which needed two hands. Shields were superfluous.

Behind the knights came their attendant squires, new to Rushley, hair neatly bobbed, sleeves dagged in the new zig-zag manner, looking about them with interest as they came ashore for the first time at their employers' principal home.

The ladies came out of the gate and down across the grass to greet their returning menfolk. Lady Margery, Lady Anne and Lady Ghislaine were beautifully dressed for the occasion in their most formal clothes, although the effect was somewhat spoiled by the thick mantles which the cold wind had obliged them to put on.

Only when the mantles chanced to blow back were the interested audience, especially the female part of it, regaled by a glimpse of the tight-sleeved, thin wool underdresses, and the graceful sleeveless overgowns cut away under the arm, with long trains that trailed across the grass and the Rushley device woven, silver on green, into the front of the dresses worn by Lady Margery and her daughter-in-law. Lady Ghislaine's gown bore her husband's device of martlets and roses, in gold thread on blue.

The greetings were as formal as the clothes. Hands clasped elbows, polite kisses were exchanged. The more passionate embraces would come later and more privately, despite the whistles and whoops of encouragement from the livelier members of the crowd.

At the edge of the gathering, Thomas found that Gilbert Pecher was beside him and said viciously, 'Anyone would think it was the Second Coming.'

'Well, Crécy was quite an affair,' said Gilbert cheerfully. 'I was there, remember. Sir Edward and Sir Roland are good leaders on the battlefield. They know their business. They knew how to instruct their captains of archers and they were always near us, keeping our spirits up. We were outnumbered at Crécy – God's Teeth, we were outnumbered! I remember standing there, bow drawn, seeing a line of cavalry charging towards us. It was like seeing death coming for you. Then we heard the order to shoot . . . and by God, that cavalry charge broke up. It just . . . just dissolved. And then Sir Edward and young Roland were in there, leading a squadron of knights on horseback, chasing the enemy, laying about them like boys killing rats! You were a fool to refuse to join us. We were well rewarded.'

'Were you?' said Thomas, in an unpleasant voice. Nicola recognised the signs of bad temper and her pleasure in the outing faded. She wished they were better placed. She could hardly see the ladies' dresses from here. Her view consisted mainly of the ship's figurehead, the muddy river purling by at her feet and a section of Ed's right shoulder. 'They took it for granted you'd risk your life for them,' Thomas said to Gilbert. 'But it didn't occur to them afterwards to repay you by giving you your life back, did it? Going to war for them like that, you should have been given your freedom afterwards. Well, were you?'

'Are you still on about that? Oh, well, I suppose it's natural.' Gilbert glanced at Thomas's right hand. 'But I reckon it's best not to spend your life hankering for things that can't happen.'

'You should have been a friar and gone about preaching,' said Thomas, still in a disagreeable voice.

Nicola tried nervously to think of something to say to distract him, caught sight of something floating in the water, and said quickly, 'What's that in the river? Look, coming downstream.'

'Where? Looks like a dead sheep.' Gilbert also craned his neck. Then he stiffened. 'It's not a sheep. I can see an arm.'

'It's a body!' said Thomas.

Other people had seen it now. A cry had gone up. A sailor from the ship appeared with one of the fending poles and reached into the river with it, trying to pull the sodden thing to land. Ed, who was tall, snatched a stave from an elderly neighbour who had been leaning on it, and joined the effort. The river current, which at this point swirled in close to the bank, assisted them. The thing bumped against the landing stage and hands reached to drag it out.

Then Ed, with a horrified cry threw the stave away from him into the water and sprang back. 'Stop! Don't touch it! Leave it be!'

'But I recognise him!' said Gilbert. 'It's one of the Eelfishers – it's Stig, that lived by himself out by Duckwater Ditch. He must have had some sort of accident. He's all bruised.'

'Wait. Stand back, everyone!' Sir Edward had come striding down to the bank. He stared at the body bobbing at the water's edge. Those standing close him saw him whiten. 'Those are not bruises,' he said. 'I've seen marks like that before, overseas. If he had an accident, he had it because he was ill. Fell in, maybe, trying to fetch water to drink. Those marks are the sign of plague.'

The ship had sailed again by the next morning. But not with Sir Edward or his son aboard it. The word round the well, when Nicola went to fetch water, was that the Lady Ghislaine's husband had been carried aboard on a litter, moaning with the pain of the gout which would not let him walk, but absolutely determined to flee ahead of the advancing plague.

The Lady Ghislaine had gone with him, of course, but no one else. Mistress Ketels' niece worked at the Hall, cleaning and serving food, and she had actually been there when Sir Edward called the rest of the household together and announced that he had never run away from an enemy in his life and didn't propose to start now: he was staying where he was.

Three days after that, there was a rumour at the well, that somebody at Redesmarsh was sick with the strange new disease. Nicola, having drawn her bucket of water for the day's needs, went home again in a pensive mood, wondering what, if anything, could be done to hold the foe at bay. Would it be useful to clean and sweeten the house and the family's clothes? Were there any herbs which could be hung up to make the air wholesome, or any prayers or charms that might be recited? Father Matthew had said a special service might be held on Sunday to intercede for protection. They must all attend that.

Meanwhile, ordinary life must go on. She had the dinner to get. She carried the bucket into the house, setting it down with a slight clatter in its accustomed corner. The sound brought Thomas hurrying through from the workshop. 'Nicola. Come here, quickly.'

'What is it?' Nicola followed him back through the workshop door. Ed was leaning on his table, nervously feeling his armpits. She looked in alarm at his grey, drawn face.

'I'm ill,' he said. 'I can't eat and I'm hot and . . . and I've got lumps under my arms. I feel like death.' His eyes widened in fright. 'Like death,' he repeated.

Thomas had never been a doting father. He paid Alison little attention as a rule, apparently regarding her as an extension of her mother, expecting her to help as far as she was able with the work of house and holding. He never played with her and complained angrily if she made a noise while playing by herself. But the first thing he said now was, 'Where is Alison? We've got to protect her.'

'She's milking.' The Woodcarvers had always kept a cow or two, and Nicola's modest dowry had included a heifer. They had five milking cows now, and Alison looked after them. Nicola thought quickly. 'Help your father to his bed, Thomas. I'll see after Alison.'

Hastily, she collected rugs, linen, a spare dress, and a basket of food: some cured bacon, cheese, honey, ale. She carried everything to the byre, which was at the back of the house but not built on to it. Beyond it was the path that led away from the village to the marsh pastures. Alison was sitting on a stool, her head against the flank of a cow, rhythmically working. She looked up when Nicola called her name, startled by her mother's tone.

'I think your grandfather has plague,' Nicola said. 'No, it's all right, don't be frightened. I haven't got it. But until I know it's safe, you're not to come back to the house, or enter anyone else's house. We don't know where's safe and where isn't and, anyway, the chances are people won't let you into their homes if they think yours has the sickness in it. So you'd better stay here. You'll be warm enough; there's plenty of straw and you can sleep in that spare stall at the end there. I've got rugs and clothes and some food for you. There's ale as well, and you can always drink milk. Don't go to the well, even. Stay right away from everyone. You can go out into the open. You'd better turn the packhorse out to grass. Take the cows out, and if you plant the onions, that'd help. I'm going to have my hands full. I'll come and shout news to you each day and leave you more food. I'll make bread somehow today. I'll bring some to you.'

'But what if you and Father . . .!' Alison's small face was frightened. She had heard all about the plague. Her parents didn't know, but she had sometimes dreamed about it.

'Quite. But that,' said Nicola, 'is in the hands of God. Be a good girl and do as I say. We'll try not to die, I promise.'

Nicola woke from a shallow doze. Thomas was calling for water. Half-asleep, she rolled off the pallet, fumbled in the gloom for a dipper and fetched him a drink from the bucket she kept always filled.

She tried to give Ed a drink too, but he was barely conscious and, when she propped him up and tried to pour it into his mouth, half of it dribbled down the sides. He couldn't swallow properly.

Having done her best, she staggered back to her pallet and sat on it, to go wearily through the check which she made automatically whenever she awoke. Had she any sign of fever? Was she too hot, or too cold? Could she face the thought of food? Was her throat sore? Did her bones or head ache? Had she any swellings? Under the arm? In the neck? In the groin?

Once again, miraculously, she had not. But she had no strength either. She sat with her head in her hands, trying to regain it. Outside, the birds were singing their dawn chorus as though nothing in the world were wrong, and a flight of geese were honking across the sky. The light that found its way through the louvre was flushing now with what she knew would be one of the pink and gold marsh dawns barred with cloud and smelling of the fresh rain and the sea.

The loft room smelt – no, reeked – of other things. She must fetch fresh straw and burn that on which her patients lay. Except for her own pallet and its cover, all their slender supplies of bedding had been burned days ago. She had settled Ed and Thomas on straw on the floor, with rugs on top of them. She had to roll them aside to get them off the old straw and on to the new when she changed the bedding. She had not had more than an hour or two of uneasy sleep at a time since Thomas sickened, a week ago now, two days after his father.

She must get up and go on. She must fetch more water and eat something and take food to Alison. For Alison had not sickened either. She was still in the byre, miserable, frightened, but safe. Nicola did not know why either of them had so far escaped; whether it was to do with her insistence on cleanliness or simply due to inborn good health. But so far, healthy they remained.

She forced herself to move, to begin seeing to things. When she

225

fetched the water, her sister-in-law Anne Potter was at the well, and they exchanged rapid, grim-faced news.

'Ed's worse. Thomas is the same.'

'Both my sisters are down and Nell Ketels died last night. And it's up at the Hall now, did you know? And Richard Grosney's on the mend but his wife's gone and so have his daughters.'

'Aye, that's right,' Blanche Carpenter joined them. 'Even that Grosney girl that married the Smith boy, One-Leg, down on the marsh, she's dead as well, and One-Leg with her.'

'What about One-Leg's father?' said Nicola sharply. 'Osbert Smith?'

'All right, far as I know. Saw him yesterday with his spade. He's always got a spade over his shoulder nowadays. Father Matthew'll be the next to go; he won't last, they say.'

The first time Nicola had gone to the well, the day Ed fell ill, she had chosen a time when not many others would be there and had shouted a warning when she saw someone approaching. 'Don't come near! There's plague in our house!'

Now there was no need for such precautions. There was not one single house in Rushley, or Oxfen or Redesmarsh either, that the contagion had not touched.

All the priests on all the three manors were dead or dying. There was no one now to perform burial services and although Osbert Smith, muscularly powerful and apparently immune to the disease, had taken on the task of gravedigging, stating that as a constable of Rushley he had a responsibility for its management, he could no longer keep up with burying the dead separately. With whatever helpers he could find, he had dug a row of pits on the commonland out towards Lower Rushley and each day, filled one with the night's harvest of the dead, and threw earth in on top.

When she went back with the water, Thomas was calling weakly for it once more, and Ed was conscious but in a hopeless and horrible fashion. Though the abscesses in his armpits made it agony to move his arms, he had nevertheless shifted one outside his rugs and was staring at it with dazed and red-rimmed eyes.

'Nicola, come here, look at my arm. It's going black, isn't it? It's the black death come on me.'

'Have some water. Richard Grosney's getting better, I hear. Just like him, isn't it? Hardly anyone would miss him, so he recovers. But it shows people *can* recover. You will, too.'

'Don't be stupid,' muttered Ed. He moved, jerkily, against her hands as she once more tried to help him drink. 'Pain,' he said. 'Whole body . . . full of pain. Frightened. They're putting us in pits, aren't they? Heard someone talking in the road outside, yesterday. Don't want to be buried in a pit. Bury me decent. Promise me. In a proper grave of my own and say some words for me. Say a Paternoster or something.'

'I'll try.'

'Please, I don't want to go in a pit.' The reddened eyes were spilling tears. Hot fingers closed on her wrist. 'Promise!'

'I promise,' said Nicola in the most reassuring voice she could manage.

'Water!' Thomas called again. 'Thirsty.' She laid Ed gently back and went to her husband. As she held the dipper to Thomas's lips, she heard a shuddering moan behind her. When she turned Ed's mouth had flopped open and his eyes were fixed.

One did the next thing, the task immediately in front. One's body obeyed as though in a dream. She had learned that already. She had long since forgotten what squeamishness was like. Caring for people with plague had soon seen to that. She gave Thomas some more water and a few spoonfuls of broth with a little bread broken into it. She found time now and then to make bread, because it was essential. Then she turned once more to Ed.

He was dead. She arranged him as best she could, crossing his hands on his chest and closing his eyes. Presently, he was cooling. So she must deal with the task of getting him down from the bedloft. She wrapped his rug over him, hiding his face, found a piece of rope and, with difficulty, wound it round him, creating at last what amounted to a ghastly parcel. Then she set about dragging him to the ladder which led down into the workshop.

But she couldn't possibly carry him down it. She squatted beside him, considering. Bumps and broken bones wouldn't matter to him now. She must just tumble him through the trapdoor.

The body bounced down the ladder to land with an ugly thump. Nicola descended after it. Some squeamishness still remained, she found. Foulness was oozing from the bundle and, at the sight and the stench of it, she wanted badly to cry or retch. A lot of use that would be. She choked back her disgust, dragged Ed – only he wasn't Ed now, someone she'd spoken to just a short while ago, but a thing which would never speak or move again – to the door and went back for a spade.

She hadn't liked Ed but he had depended upon her in his illness and he had begged her for a promise. She had made that promise and she ought to keep it. If she could.

The proper place to bury people was in the churchyard but she couldn't drag him that far alone. She went to fetch the packhorse from the common where it had been turned loose for the time being. It was unwilling to be caught. They had acquired it to replace the donkey sequestered by Sir Edward, and the donkey, thought Nicola, had been much less temperamental. She haltered it and led it to the house eventually, and tied it to the door while she lugged Ed out. But it took violent exception to the corpse, squealing and plunging and she gave up the attempt before even trying to solve the problem of lifting the body across the animal's back. She pulled Ed back inside the house. The only thing she could think of to do was to bury him in their own vegetable patch. It would be a grave, at least, Ed's own, and she would say the prayer he wanted. God would understand. She couldn't ask anyone else to help. No one had time to spare and they'd only say that Ed wasn't entitled to special treatment.

Alison was milking the cows out in the pasture and needn't see. The ground in the vegetable patch was reasonably soft but the hole would have to be deep. Half an hour later, she seemed to be getting nowhere and her strength was giving out. She rested, with the spade wedged upright in the soil and her forehead on its handle. And behind her, Osbert Smith's rumbling voice suddenly said, 'What the devil do you think you're doing? Is that a grave? Nicola, what are you doing?'

He had never spoken to her directly before, but he did so now as though they had known each other well for years. When she raised her head and answered him, it was in the same manner. 'It's my father-in-law. Ed Woodcarver. He died today.'

'Whoever it is, you can't go digging graves among your cabbages and onions. I'll see to him. I'm on my rounds. The ox-cart's in the road.'

'He begged not to go into the pit and I promised him.'

'He'll have to.' Osbert spoke seriously, though very kindly. 'God will know where to find him on Resurrection Day, you know that. He'll be quite safe, with all the others. Put that spade down; you'll kill yourself with exhaustion. I saw you from the road and wondered what you were about. How's Thomas? Is he still alive?'

Once, one could not have talked of the possible death of one's closest relatives in such a casual way. Now it was a commonplace. Bereavement now was the common lot.

'Yes. He's up in the bedloft.'

'All right. Now, leave this to me.'

It was a relief to realise that Osbert didn't intend to be gainsaid, a blessing to be able to give in. All the same . . . 'Let me help,' said Nicola doggedly. You just couldn't live in the same house as someone for nearly nine years and not acquire feelings of duty towards them. She must go as far as she could towards keeping her word. She took Osbert to where Ed lay and said: 'He wanted a Paternoster recited for him. I'll say it when he's on the cart. Can I do that?'

'Course you can.' Osbert stooped and deftly heaved up the rug-wrapped bundle. 'That'll be nice, very proper. But don't come near the cart. Just stay where you are. I'll put him aboard.'

The ox-cart was already laden with half a dozen bodies, although they were concealed by sacks and old clothes which Osbert had thrown over them. He carried his burden to the cart and laid Ed on top. One of Ed's ankles slipped free of the rug and dangled over the side of the cart. Nicola, who had followed Osbert after all, went forward automatically, to lift it back.

'No!' said Osbert sharply. 'Don't! Let me do it; I'm used to it . . . get back, Nicola . . . Mistress Woodcarver . . . I don't want you to . . .'

It was too late. Nicola, trying to push Ed's ankle back out of sight, made the shrouded shapes below him shift and settle and the sack that hid two of them slipped aside. She found herself looking straight down on two dead faces.

'Nicola!' Osbert snatched her away. 'I didn't want you to see, or to know, it's better you shouldn't . . . you shouldn't have come near: I said, leave it all to me . . .'

'Oh dear God, sweet Mary, it's my mother! It's my father! I've had no time to go out to the Lea but it's away from other houses and I'd hoped . . . one of the women said last week that she'd seen my father in his boat . . . oh no, you can't throw them into a pit, Osb . . . Master Smith . . . you can't . . .!'

'I must. There's no choice. My poor wench, there's no choice . . .'

'No, no!' What felt like a pent-up lifetime of tears flooded out. 'Help me finish that grave! Please, please help me. They and Ed can share it. But don't take them to the pit!' She broke away from him and tried to climb on to the cart to drag her parents' bodies clear. Osbert pulled her down again.

'Hush now, hush. Your brother Will gave permission. He had it too but he's getting well. He was there and he helped me bring them out. I didn't just take them.'

'Will! Oh trust Will! God damn his soul; I always hated him! You can't take them, I say! You can't . . .'

She was not only crying now, she was shrieking. She hammered at Osbert, trying to make him let her go. He did not. Instead, he wrapped his massive arms round her and held her like that until the hysteria passed.

When it did, and she stood still, hiccuping, she found herself where she had longed to be for nearly nine long years, ever since her wedding day, when she had looked down from the ladder on her way to Thomas's bed, and met Osbert's eyes. She was in Osbert's embrace, held firm and warm and utterly secure. She wanted to stay there for ever.

Above her, Osbert's deep voice said, 'I must take them, Nicola. You know that.'

She released a long, trembling breath. 'Yes, I know. Let me go; I . . . I'm better now.'

'What about that Paternoster? You can say it for them all and I reckon that'll make you feel easier. I'll say it with you, if you like.'

They knelt side by side on the ground next to the cart, and spoke the old familiar words. Nicola was weeping again before they were finished, but in a gentler, healthier way. When the prayer was finished, Osbert helped her to stand. 'Grief's natural and good. Your tears'll do you no harm,' he said. 'Now, let me take you back inside.'

With an arm round her because she was unsteady on her feet, he led her back to the dwelling, pushing past the horse, which was now standing across the entrance, and guided her in. The door led straight into the living room and he steered her to a settle. 'You'll be all right. If you've got any ale or elderberry wine, you'd best have some. Tell me where to find it. I'll get it for you.'

She told him where the elderberry wine was and he fetched it and handed her a beaker. 'Here. This will help. What's that horse doing tethered to the door, by the way?'

'I'd thought first of taking Ed to the churchyard. But the horse was too frightened. I'll put him out to graze again presently.'

'Sure? Or shall I do it?'

'No. No, it's all right.' His eyes, watching her as she drank, were kind and concerned and seemed to be searching out the very depths of her. She wanted to say yes, please see to the horse, let me give my whole life, my whole self, into your hands. She must not. 'I'll take the horse back presently. Thank you for . . . for everything.'

'Very well. I must be on my way. Take care of yourself, my girl.'

He smiled at her, patted her shoulder, and went, quite rightly, about the business which waited outside on the cart behind the patient oxen. And that was that. She had stood in Osbert Smith's arms but she could not stay there. The quality of his touch and the expression in his eyes had told her that he had not forgotten that extraordinary, silent exchange nearly nine years ago, any more than she had. But he had said nothing and nor had she and, while Thomas lived, they never would. Osbert was gone, and she was made more lonely and more bereft by his going even than by the sight of her dead parents. For he was alive. And out of reach for ever.

But there were things to do. Always, these days, regardless of exhaustion and distress, there were things to do. Once more, as when she woke that morning, she forced herself to move. She took the horse back to the common and then, returning, climbed up to the bedloft to attend to Thomas. His accusing eyes met her as soon as she appeared. 'You left me alone so long,' he whispered.

'I'm sorry.' Nicola fetched water for him and helped him to drink. Like Ed, he could hardly bear to move his arms because of the huge, painful lumps beneath them. 'I . . . Thomas, your father's dead.' She didn't know if he had realised it or not.

He nodded, however. 'I heard. He wanted you to bury him. Silly old fool. You didn't, did you?'

'I tried, but Osbert came along and wouldn't let me. Thomas, I'm so sorry.'

'What for? That he's gone or that he had to go in the pit? Either way, don't be. Old bastard,' muttered Thomas. 'You never saw, yourself, what he was like when I was small.' There was a silence. Nicola looked helplessly at her husband, not knowing what to do or say and much too tired to think. 'I ought to be glad he's gone,' said Thomas defiantly, and tried to raise a hand to brush his eyes. He dropped the

230

hand at once with a moan which suddenly became a gasp. 'Nicola . . .!'

'What is it?'

'Turn back the rug and look in my right armpit. I think . . .'

She obeyed. 'Has it . . .?' said Thomas weakly.

'Yes.'

The horrible bubo had burst. Yellow pus was running from it. 'I think the one in my right groin's broken, too,' he said huskily. 'Is it good or bad?'

She knew the answer. All the details of the disease, and the significance of every symptom, were known to her now.

'It means,' she said, 'that you're probably going to live.'

Their cornfield had been safely sown before the plague struck but the spring gales had damaged the fence which divided it from the commonland, and it was some time before they could attend to it. Thomas's physical weakness limited him to the vegetable patch at first and this, in any case, needed attention, having been attacked by rabbits. These had escaped, Thomas surmised irritably, from Rushley Hall or Redesmarsh Abbey, where they were bred for the pot. Neither Thomas nor Nicola felt much grief for Ed but 'the old bugger would have been an extra pair of hands, I grant you,' Thomas said once. When they did at last visit the cornfield, somebody's sheep were wandering in the young crop.

They were shooing them out and Thomas was saying that he must mend the fence and thank God he was just about well enough to tackle it now, when Richard Grosney came riding past, not on his usual horse, but on one of Sir Edward's sturdy riding cobs. His own grey horse was on a leading rein and laden with a pack, and a woman, bundled in a mantle against the dull, chilly April weather, was seated on the cob's pillion. The sheep, streaming across the track, obliged the riders to halt.

'I see you're on your feet again!' Grosney called to Thomas.

Thomas scowled and caught Nicola's eye. They were both thinking the same thing. Richard Grosney was no doubt about to tell them that normal day-work on Sir Edward's land must now be resumed and that his corn came before theirs. In mutual resentment, they chivvied the woolly river of sheep out of his way.

'I can walk,' Thomas said coldly. 'But if I work too much yet awhile I could still drop dead. Some have.'

But Grosney did not raise the matter of Sir Edward's fields. His face was still taut: the skin stretched too tightly over his sharp cheekbones, the muscles of his jaw too bunched. But the haunted expression in his eyes was new. 'Sorry to hear you lost your father, Thomas, and Osbert told me both your parents went, Mistress. My family's all gone as well and Osbert's sickened now. Just after he got the last of the bodies out of the manorhouse. They're all dead, did you know?'

The words came out jerkily, as though of their own accord, and because he couldn't stop them. He had been shocked to the point where he would confide in anyone, however far beneath him, just to ease the horror. 'Every man jack and woman jill in the place except for Nan here,' he said. 'She'd had it and got up and looked after the last of them and . . .'

'I was Lady Margery's tirewoman,' said the woman on the pillion in a high voice. She slackened the fold of mantle which had been half across her face and was seen to be middle-aged, with a face which should have been soft and a little crumpled with the years and blue eyes which should still have been bright with interest in small everyday things. The face was now blanched and frozen and the eyes, like Richard Grosney's, were focused on some appalling private vision. 'When Master Grosney and Master Smith came, I was shut in a room with my lady's body and Sir Edward's, with the dogs baying outside. No one had fed them in days. The house was full of death and what it was like in there after dark . . .'

She broke off, shuddering. 'We're going north,' said Grosney. 'We're making for Sir Edward's new lands in Yorkshire. My lady Ghislaine should be there. I'm taking Nan to her and taking the news of what's happened here. Someone's got to.' The sheep were off the track now. He nodded to Thomas and Nicola, shook his reins, jerked on the packhorse's halter, and set off once more. Thomas and Nicola watched him go in amazement.

'He's running away,' said Thomas. 'He's just running to get away from here and leave all the horrors behind. Well!' He went on gazing after Grosney and Nan, oblivious of the fact that some of the sheep had now drifted back towards the corn. 'Well!' he said again.

'What's the matter? Thomas, why are you standing there like that? You look as if you'd been struck rigid.'

He turned to her. 'Nicola!' His face was very thin from the illness, but his eyes, all of a sudden, were alight. '*Nicola!*'

'What is it?'

'If they're all dead at the Hall and Grosney's going north, then . . .'

'Then what?'

'I did a deal of thinking while I was lying there waiting to get my strength back,' he said slowly. 'Only, I never thought Grosney would take his eyes off the manor and somehow I never thought the Hall'd be left empty. I always felt that Sir Edward would be there for ever, like God. But now! Do you realise? We can walk out of Rushley and no questions asked. *This is our chance*''

'Thomas, you're mad!' As though corn, sheep, fences and his own physical weakness had never existed, Thomas had set off homeward at a pace so fast that Nicola couldn't keep up without intermittently breaking into a run. 'Thomas, we can't just take to the roads! What about the workshop – the cornfield – everything your father left you? What about . . .?'

'What about making a new start? What about making ourselves free?' They arrived at their dwelling and Thomas crashed through the door. Alison, no longer obliged to hide in the byre, was scouring pots. 'Leave that!' said Thomas. 'Put your things together, girl, ready for the packhorse. We leave this house tomorrow. For good!'

Alison stared at him, speechless and bewildered. Her father was already striding here and there about the room, apparently bent on tearing it to pieces, snatching up this and that, flinging back the settle lid, sweeping objects off a shelf. 'But if we go away, what about the cows?' she protested.

'We'll drive them on to the common tonight. Someone'll see to them. They won't be the only ones abandoned.'

'But we can't,' said Nicola desperately, 'just *go*.'

'I *told* you,' said Thomas with furious impatience, 'this is our chance. When Grosney comes back – if he comes back – we'll be far away and he'll likely think I had a relapse and died and that you two caught it and died too. Osbert Smith's sick; the burying business'll all be just a muddle. And it won't matter what he thinks anyhow. He won't know where we've gone.'

'But where *are* we going?' It was being borne in upon Nicola that he actually meant it. She was terrified. Rushley was the only home she knew. Besides, Osbert Smith had caught the pestilence. He was lying sick, perhaps untended. She wanted to rush to his side, to take care of him, to nurse him until he was strong again or if not, then to be with him while he died.

She dared not say so. Rushley was full of the sick and the dying; why should she want to pick out Osbert for special attention? Oh Osbert, are you suffering badly? Or is it already over? Please God, have mercy on Osbert; make him well or end it swiftly. And let him know, somehow, that I am thinking of him . . .

'Get your clothes packed up! Come on, Nicola, don't stand there making objections. What is there to keep us here? You never liked your brother, and I've lost all my sisters and their families now. Do as I say!' Thomas's sudden temper flared. 'Get up to the loft and bring down your things!'

Nicola found herself clambering up the ladder and doing as she was bid. Coming down again with an armful of clothing, she saw Thomas shoving his woodworking tools into a bag. He observed the wild, questioning expression on her face and said, 'When Friar Ailred was going round the manors warning us about the plague coming, he mentioned a place in Essex called Whitmead. Remember? Lady Ghislaine told him about it. Sounded like a freeman's holding, from what he said, and it sounded lonely. We'll make for there. He said it was left deserted, and that the whole family were there for a marriage just before the plague broke out. Likely enough, there are no relatives. We might be able to take it over.'

233

'Take it over? Just walk in? But . . . someone else is sure to be there by now!'

'Really? We've seen what the plague can do, haven't we? We need a definite place to make for, Nicola, that's right enough. We might find somewhere else along the way – likely there's plenty of places left empty. But if anyone asks us who we are and where we're going, we're kinsfolk of the Whitmead people, on our way there to move in. If you're asked that sort of question, it's as well to have an answer, or folk might be suspicious and think we're running away from our manor.'

'We are!'

'Yes, we are and we're going to get away with it. We're going to be free, don't you understand?' Thomas suddenly grinned, a fierce grin, full of imagination and aggression in equal proportions, which came straight from his Celtic ancestry. 'We're going to take over a place on freeman's terms. *Only* on freeman's terms. If we find ourselves at this place Whitmead . . .'

'We don't even know where it is!'

'It's in Essex. That's due south, far side of Suffolk.' Thomas had never been beyond Norwich, but he had talked to men who had. 'We can find it if we want. But wherever we stop, Whitmead or anywhere else, we won't settle if it's on villein's terms. I won't stand for those, ever again. There'll be no work on the lord's land, no paying fines when Alison marries, no crawling about politely asking the bailiff if we can go to Norwich or whatever. Dear God, I can hardly believe it! Sir Edward's dead! He's down in hell now where he should have been long ago and he'll never do to any other man what he did to me! And I'll let no man have that kind of power over me again! Or over you! That's what you've always wanted, isn't it? You didn't want to marry me because I was a villein. You wanted a freeman. Well, you're going to have one. So what are you whining about?'

'I'm not whining! But . . .'

'But, but, but!'

'Wherever we go, there'll be someone who'll want rent, who'll want to know all about us.'

'Of course there'll be *rent*, but it'll just be money or produce. I *said* we won't settle anywhere where it isn't. From now on we're freeborn people on our way to claim an inheritance. Maybe Whitmead, maybe not. But we'll find somewhere, right enough, somewhere without heirs, and then we'll claim that we're the heirs. What's wrong with you? You managed very well when my father and I were ill; why can't you be some help now?'

The answer was that she felt as though she were running frantically at the stirrup of a madman on a bolting horse. 'I can't!' she said, and sat down with a thud on a stool. She dropped the pile of clothes she was carrying in a heap on the floor. '*No*, Thomas. I'm saying no. We mustn't do this. We'll be caught and questioned and . . .'

234

Thomas threw aside his bag of tools and clamped his hands on her upper arms. Even the hand with two fingers missing had an amazingly powerful grip. He pulled her to her feet. 'You'll do as I say, do you hear? If you don't, I swear I'll kill you!' His hands shifted and closed round her neck. 'We're going away from this place and out of this life where a man can be mutilated for a whim, and I'm taking my wife and child with me, and *that is final*. You're to be on my side! God knows it's in your interest too but, even if it wasn't, it wouldn't make any difference. You and Alison only stay behind if you're dead. Do you understand?'

Once more, it was like being back on the bridge when they were both fifteen. Once again the face above her, with its swooping eyebrows and furious dark eyes was the face not of Thomas Woodcarver, but of a diabolical stranger infused with a paralysing hatred and anger. Her teeth began to chatter. Thomas's hands tightened. '*Do you understand?*'

Nicola, unable to speak, managed a nod. Thomas let go.

'Good. Then stop gaping at me and get on with the packing! Thank God we've got a packhorse. Alison, go and catch it and put it in the byre, ready for tomorrow. We'll have to try and get riding animals,' he added thoughtfully, calming down. 'It'll look better. As though we're what we say we are.'

He had terrified Nicola, but not, she found, hurt her throat too much after all. Now, in the spirit of one who humours a madman, she said, 'We turned our horse out when your father fell ill. Others must have done the same . . .' Her voice trailed away again. Horse-stealing was a hanging matter.

Thomas was unconcerned. 'Good. Yes. By God, we'll try Sir Edward's home pasture. He still owes me for that donkey.' That fierce grin appeared again. 'In fact, we might do better than just rob his pasture . . .'

'You mean . . . loot the manorhouse!' Nicola's protest was timid but she made it just the same, watching Thomas fearfully. 'But . . . that woman Nan said no one had fed the dogs. They're hounds, Thomas! Great big mastiffs!'

'We've a barrel of cured meat left, haven't we? We'll keep them quiet,' Thomas said, 'with that.'

Alison was as frightened as her mother but Thomas was like a river in flood. Obstacles seemed to disappear as soon as he reached them. All their goods were packed and piled ready on the floor before they lay down that night to sleep and when a neighbour tapped at the door, Thomas made them keep still and remain quiet and wouldn't let them open it. 'No one's to see that we're getting ready to go.' Even the bread and meat with which they would break their fast in the morning were put ready. Next day, he roused them when the first faint light was stealing over the marshes. 'Come on, quickly. There aren't many people left alive to see but we don't want *anyone* watching us. Eat but hurry.

Then help me carry this stuff to the byre. We've got to load the horse.'

'You haven't changed your mind in the night?' Nicola had not slept. She had lain open-eyed, listening to Thomas's snores and praying that sanity would have prevailed when he woke. But his lunacy appeared to be of a highly enduring nature. 'Of course I haven't changed my mind!' he snapped. He went to the door and glanced out. 'There's a sea-fog drifting up. All the better.'

When at length they set out, they were a quiet little procession, invisible from any of the Rushley houses because of the mist. Thomas led the way with some roughly made rope halters in his hand and Nicola followed with a pail of oats. Alison came last, leading the packhorse. Alison, young enough to be adaptable, seemed now to have accepted this incredible adventure but Nicola could not believe that they were really about to leave Rushley for ever. She was either, she thought, on her pallet and dreaming, or else she had caught the plague after all, and this was delirium. But if so, she must have a high fever, and it was odd that she still felt so cold and astonishing that the wet grass now soaking the hem of her long skirt could feel so real.

Thomas's plans were clear-cut. He led them to an elm copse near the home meadow and stopped. 'Tie the horse here and then follow me.'

It was so easy that it was absurd. Sir Edward's horses were used to being handled and were not at all averse to answering Thomas's persuasive calls, or to munching the oats he and Nicola offered them in the pail. He picked out a pony and two sturdy cobs like the one Richard Grosney had taken and haltered them. Then he led the party back to the elms. The packhorse whinnied in pleasure at the approach of other horses and Thomas swore, but no one was within earshot but themselves. The misty world remained quiet except that, somewhere in the distance, dogs were howling.

'We've no saddles,' said Alison. 'Or bridles.'

'I'm going to get some,' said Thomas, heaving down the barrel of meat which had been balanced unsteadily on top of the packhorse's load. 'Wait here, both of you. I won't be long.'

To Nicola and Alison, waiting under the elms, it seemed an eternity before he came back. Wisps of mist drifted among the trees. They were not yet in leaf and Nicola could look between the trunks towards the distant gatehouse of the hall, although the fog kept her from seeing so far.

What if someone were there, after all? What if Thomas did not come back? She'd give him . . . well, till she was sure something had gone amiss. Then she'd loose the manor horses and take Alison home. They'd unpack and make everything look as usual. She must protect Alison. What if they were seen getting the packhorse back? What if . . .?

Thomas materialised out of the mist. He was dragging a small handcart. On it was a cloth-covered heap which looked as though it included another barrel, and saddles were piled on top. Bridles were hung over his arm and beside him trotted two large dogs. 'I've fed them,' he said. 'Fed all the dogs; I found some meat barrels in there. In fact, I've got one here, to feed these two on the road. I thought we'd be more impressive with a couple of dogs of our own. How we look, that'll make a difference to whether folk believe what we say. These saddles are about right for size. Here, give me a hand.'

Halfway through the business of saddling, he paused suddenly and said, 'The gate was barred outside; I suppose Grosney did that, to keep the dogs from the sheep and cattle. He didn't care about the dogs, poor brutes. I threw some meat over the wall and then pulled away the beam he'd left jammed across the gate, and walked in. The dogs were too busy with the food to care about me. It was eerie in there, Nicola. Awful. No one's been in since the bodies were carried away. There were beds left with rugs half dragged on to the floor, and such a stench . . . and the place is big. You can fill a dwelling like ours with yourself, so to speak, but that place is all arched doorways with shadows on the other side . . . I wonder that woman Nan didn't go mad when she found herself in there at night with a lot of dead bodies. Even in daylight . . .'

Nicola blinked at him. She had never heard him talk in that hushed tone before. He shook himself, did up the girth he was holding, and then went to the handcart and pulled off the cloth.

'I didn't just bring dogmeat away with me. There were chests of clothes and things all over the place. I've got us all some more clothes, better ones, and a cornelian necklace for you. And I found this.'

He turned to her with a box in his hands. It was shaped like a miniature hooped chest and had the arms of Rushley inlaid on the lid in ivory. It had once had a lock, although this was now broken. The splintering round the keyhole was fresh; Thomas had evidently done the breaking. He opened the lid.

Inside, the chest was compartmented. One side was empty but on the other were a number of small leather bags with drawstrings at the neck. Thomas undid one to show her. 'Silver.' His eyes were sparkling with satisfaction. 'I threw out the tallies. We don't need reminders of how much he was going to grab from us on Lady Day. But there's enough money here to pay us back for some of what that grasping bastard snatched over the years, and to pay me for my chopped-off fingers, too.'

Nicola said nothing. It would be no use. She was trembling and would have liked to faint. This was worse than horse-stealing.

Thomas seemed unconcerned. He loaded the stolen goods on the packhorse, picked up his round-eyed and silent daughter and put her on the pony, and said to Nicola, 'Well, mount. You can manage the horse, can't you?'

She could manage. They all occasionally rode the packhorse, and if none of them rode very elegantly, still the back of a horse was more or less familiar. They set off.

They went warily, since the mist had now begun to clear. Thomas avoided the village, taking them on a circuitous route which used paths through the marshes and kept trees and dykes between them and habitations.

But they met no one. There were few enough people now to meet, in any case. They went unmolested and unnoticed.

Except for the lack of human figures, the places that Nicola had known all her life looked just as always.

Somewhere behind her, Osbert Smith lay on his sickbed and their abandoned cows lowed, and her brother Will must be up and about by now. Somewhere in the village was the neighbour who had tapped on the door yesterday and received no answer.

Now, at this inappropriate moment, she had discovered that she was after all quite different from old Isabel Plowman whose image she had tried to be. She did not want to travel, to see London or Norwich or anywhere else. She wanted to stay in Rushley, in the place she knew.

In all probability, she was leaving it behind for ever.

Chapter Fourteen
Defending the Future

Denis Astleigh of Quensted Manor was once more modelling castles in clay.

It was something to do, since he hardly ever felt well enough these days for active things like the falconry he had once liked so much, or for riding round his lands. He had been very proud of those lands once. Because of the efforts of himself and his forebears, through loyal service to the Earl of Essex and through well-chosen marriages, he was lord of many wide and fertile acres. As a boy, he had dreamed of distinguishing himself in battle and being knighted. He had never, in fact, had the physique for fighting, and there had been a time when he minded about this. It had mattered. But not now.

Nothing mattered very much now. Even the wide acres were little more than a worry. He sat at a table in his walnut-panelled hall, patiently shaping the crenellations of a keep. The sun, slanting in through the green-tinged glass of the tall, narrow windows, cast streaks of light, also greenish as though filtered through water, across the knotted veins and liver spots of his hands.

He couldn't understand why he was still alive and he wished he were not.

Of all people on earth, why should he, Denis Astleigh, have escaped the plague? He had had creaky health from childhood. His entire life had been a succession of sneezes and catarrh, bad throats and aching sinuses and grating coughs. He had been three times diagnosed as having the lung-rot, with only months to live, but somehow he had never reached the point of coughing up blood and his symptoms always subsided. Never strong, never feeling entirely well, he had nevertheless tottered on and on, and when the plague came he had stayed in the condition which with him passed as normal, while his dear wife Constance, whose vitality he had always envied, was carried to her tomb, and most of the family and household with her.

His hands faltered on the clay as the misery of it all swept over him again. In accordance with custom, he and Constance had sent their children away to be reared by others and he had not been close to any of them, but he'd known they were there. He had attended their marriages and his first grandson had been named Denis after him.

They were all gone. Every one of them: sons, daughters, their spouses, his grandchildren. Gone too were the young people, the children of friends whom he and Constance had brought up in return, and grown fond of, almost as if these too were their own.

And here he was, left to wander about the hall and the chambers of a house so empty that it seemed to echo, with only one maidservant and two menservants – all of whom he had personally nursed through the plague – to help him. They were grateful to him, which was actually a nuisance in a complicated way. When the epidemic was at its worst, he had got into the habit of sweeping the floors and the courtyard, and cooking meals and grooming horses, but now, his surviving servants wouldn't let him help them any more. They said it wasn't fitting. But he would rather have swept the courtyard than be left unoccupied except for his clay castles.

'You ought to get out, round your lands. See what's going on,' Theo had said, more than once. Theo had been his butler and was now steward, chief cook and valet as well. At times, he behaved in addition like a schoolmaster. He was for ever advising his master for his own good.

But Denis didn't want to go out. He didn't wish to ride past fields going wild because those who had once tilled them were dead, and what use was it to order thatch to be mended when all the thatchers were dead too and the dwellings concerned had no occupants anyway? He'd sell his horses if he could find a buyer offering a fair price. But the market for them had collapsed and it was unthinkable to sell for less than seven shillings an animal that had cost him forty.

'Your dinner, sir,' said the maidservant, Peg, and added disapprovingly, 'You at your castle-building again?' Peg was nearly as bad as Theo. She helped in the kitchen, did the sweeping and mending and washing, spun wool when she could find time. She also backed Theo up in urging their master to get out and about. Denis, pushing his clay fortress aside to make room for the food, glanced at her face and sighed.

'World ain't quite come to an end,' said Peg bracingly. 'There's a good few people left. Things'll get right again.'

'Will they? I doubt it,' Denis said.

The other manservant, Joseph, saw to the horses, did repairs, acted as gatekeeper and lent a hand to his colleagues as necessary. He turned from where he was setting platters for the servants' meal at a second table and said, 'Peg's right. The place'll fill up again. There's those new people at Whitmead; look at them. They only came a year last spring but they've taken a harvest. They've got their little girl herding the sheep and they're shearing now for the second time.'

'Yes. I know. But they're only one family . . .' Denis Astleigh let his voice trail away and began to eat.

All the same, Joseph was right. Whitmead paid its rent at Michaelmas, not the more usual Lady Day, in the form of wool and silver. Last year, they'd paid two thirds of the normal rent but this year, in all likelihood, he would receive the full amount. The new Whitmead tenants ought to represent encouragement, a sign of improving times.

But they didn't, because the newcomers at Whitmead, hardworking though they were, somehow vaguely worried him. He sighed, finished the meal which he was compelled to eat in solitary state, and began once more to shape the battlements of his miniature keep. But he raised his head, roused to interest at last, at the sound of hooves in the courtyard. No one had called at Quensted now for a very long time.

He must not, of course, go out to meet whoever it was. His domestic tyrants wouldn't allow it. Joseph must take the new arrival's horse and Theo must bring the visitor to his master, who must wait patiently for these formalities to be concluded.

Theo brought the visitor in. He was a stranger, not young, but spare and brisk, and well-dressed, though in what Astleigh considered the deplorable latest style, with a long liripipe attached to his cap, and a tunic and hose parti-coloured in blue and sanguine, with much elaborate dagging. To Astleigh, the result suggested that the tailor had run out of his client's first choice of colour, and then had to rescue the garments from the teeth of a savage dog. Astleigh preferred the simpler clothes of his youth, and certainly these fantastic fashions did not suit men with taut faces like this, in which the lips were pressed so tightly together that when their owner parted them to speak, one wondered if he found it an effort.

The stranger cut straight across Theo's attempt to introduce him. 'Good day. You are Master Astleigh, I take it.' The brusqueness was businesslike and not, Denis thought, intentionally rude. 'I am here on behalf of the Lady Ghislaine, relict of the lord of Herneham manor, six miles from here . . .'

'Herneham? Oh yes, of course.' Theo was courteously placing cushions on a settle and Denis, rising, motioned his visitor to it and sat down beside him. 'Theo, we'll have some wine. The Lady Ghislaine is widowed, then? Was it the plague? I am glad to hear that she at least, still lives.

'Both she and her husband caught it,' said the stranger. 'They fled all the way to Yorkshire but it followed them. He died, but his lady survived and has inherited Herneham, and her father's lands in Yorkshire and Norfolk. Her parents died too, you understand. She's in Norfolk now.'

'I hope her father's estates are in better fettle than Herneham is,' said Astleigh. 'I haven't been over there myself but my maidservant has a cousin there who is still alive. He told her that they took only half the harvest in last year.'

'Quite right,' said the stranger in his brusque way. 'I've just come from there.' He accepted a goblet of wine put in front of him by Peg,

241

and added, 'Herneham's in complete disorder. So are my lady's lands in Norfolk and Yorkshire. We are trying to set things straight again. I'm here, sir, because the Herneham land marches with yours and I can't find anyone at all who can tell me where the boundary line is across the common land in between. I want to make an accurate report to Lady Ghislaine. Her husband, it seems, never gave her much information about his properties. It occurred to me that you would probably know the answer.'

'There isn't a boundary line as such. Roughly, my people use the half of the common nearest here and the Herneham folk put their animals on the commonland nearest Herneham. We've always been on good terms; it hasn't caused any trouble.'

'Indeed? It seems a little haphazard,' said the stranger.

His voice was disapproving and Astleigh bristled. 'May I know your name, sir? You haven't given it to me and you gave my servant no opportunity to announce it. You are the Lady Ghislaine's . . . representative? She was not able, I take it, to come herself. You are her bailiff? Steward?'

He received a strong impression of controlled anger in the other man and the reply came out in a voice whose very evenness reinforced that impression.

'The lady of Herneham cannot travel just now. She is with child and it would not be safe. I beg your pardon; I should of course have told you my name at once. I am Richard Grosney and I am the Lady Ghislaine's new husband.'

'My Order, good people, is that of the Franciscans and my principal vow was that of poverty. And since the Franciscans as yet have no house established in your land, I and all my brethren who go about among you and preach to you, are truly men who, like Christ himself, have no place to lay our heads. Believe me, when I preach to you of the virtue of poverty, I know what poverty is!' declared the Grey Friar, standing on his upturned box in the middle of the main street in Chelmsford.

'You have a perfectly good and very well-financed College of Theology in Oxford!' The grey Franciscan friars and the black-clad Dominican friars usually got on well but the Dominican friar standing close to the box was plainly disposed to be aggressive. Among the thin smattering of bystanders were some who knew that this was because the Dominican had arrived late at his usual midsummer market pitch and found the Franciscan already in possession. There were a few sly grins. 'Any of you would be welcomed there at any time!' bellowed the Dominican. 'None of you understand the concept of poverty at all!'

'I am aware that we have a college at Oxford University!' boomed the Grey Friar. 'I studied there. But it is a place of learning and not a shelter for those who are tired of cold winds and short rations. It is also a long way from Essex! And so I repeat, good people, that when I say you are blessed because you have so little, I understand what I am recommending to you. I am part of the church but wealthy abbots and fat friars please me no more than they please you . . .'

The Dominican himself was rotund. He turned crimson. 'What you are preaching is near to heresy! You undermine respect for the authority of the church and if that is once destroyed, then all respect for authority is destroyed! At the end of that road is anarchy, where there is no law . . .'

'We could do with a bit less law!' someone shouted. 'They're trying to make a law now that the lords can't pay us fair! They make us do three men's work each, these days, but they can't pay us three men's wages, oh no!'

'Move,' muttered Thomas in Nicola's ear. 'Sideways. Slowly. Don't attract attention.' He nudged her along and they eased themselves out of the little crowd. No one took any notice. Everyone's attention was taken up by the two wrangling friars.

'And why *should* abbots be wealthy? You friars are supposed to be poor, *all* of you!' A new heckler joined in, addressing the Dominican. 'But you still expect us to listen to you, so why do abbots have to be wealthy to keep their authority?'

'Most abbots ain't fit to have any authority!' A large man joined in the dispute with an angry roar. 'I'm a miller at Herneham and our mill competes with the abbey mill up the river. The abbot sent men to smash our mill up last autumn! If I ever catch Father Abbot Gregory in a lonely place I'll break his bloody neck and I reckon if our lord were at home, so would he and just for once I'd agree with him!'

'It's not possessions which are sinful, but the being in thrall to them,' retorted the Dominican. He had swung round to face the bystanders. 'If you cleanse your hearts of desire for material goods . . .'

'Go and preach to Abbot Gregory!'

'Our brother the miller is right! An abbot who has had a rival's mill destroyed is unfit to hold office. So would any lord be who acted in such a fashion!' The Grey Friar made a bid to reclaim his audience. His black-clad challenger was outraged.

'Heresy and treason! My friends, do not listen to this Franciscan. He will imperil your souls and put your bodies in jeopardy too unless you take care. If you set yourselves against natural authority you will incur the wrath of the law . . .'

'Quickly,' said Thomas, as he and Nicola retreated. 'Let's collect our cart from the inn and go.'

'But what's the matter? What's wrong?'

'What's *wrong*? Don't you know who that Grey Friar is?'

'No. Who is he?'

'It's Brother Ailred that used to come to Rushley! Lucky we weren't too close or he might have recognised my face.'

'Ailred!' Nicola was horrified. 'Oh, no! What a mercy you recognised him in time.'

'We've sold all we brought,' Thomas said thankfully, as he steered them quickly into an alley. 'We won't lose anything by making for home at once.'

'Let's get home quickly,' Nicola agreed, still shaken.

She repeated Thomas's word *home*, referring to Whitmead, with determination. It still didn't come naturally. But Whitmead *was* home now, and one day she might even come to believe it.

It had taken a week to travel between Rushley and Whitmead but it had been the transition from one world to another and in her memory it did not seem like a week, but more like a lifetime.

For the first three days Thomas had made them press on as fast as they could. They rested at night, and found food too, in deserted dwellings but he would not approach any occupied house or pause on their journey. 'We must get well away from our home country. We want to be where we shall be complete strangers,' Thomas insisted.

Later, as they made their way south through unfamiliar country and past villages where there were few hearths smoking and scarcely anyone about in the fields, they came across several places which Nicola thought might do, because surely they could take them over unchallenged, but Thomas always shook his head.

'No, not here. Look at the sort of place it is. It's a villein dwelling if ever I saw one.' Or, 'No, there are still quite a few people round here, and they'll want to know every single thing about us, and what we don't tell them they'll find out somehow. We need somewhere a bit isolated. If I can find out where this place Whitmead is . . .'

Whitmead. Whitmead. His mind seemed to be fixed on the name Whitmead, although there could be no certainty that it was unclaimed, and although he knew only that it was in Essex and that to get to Essex, you travelled south. After the third day he judged it safe to make inquiries here and there but it proved to be not as safe as he thought. The first village they approached boldly instead of slipping past it through the fields, greeted them with a barrier of carts across the track, and two men on guard with bows. With shafts pointed at Thomas's heart, they shouted across the intervening space that no strangers were being admitted in case they brought in the plague. 'We've not had a case here and we don't want one, neither!'

Thomas shouted back that they didn't want to come in, but was this Essex yet, and could they tell him where to find a place called Whitmead?

'You're in the middle of Suffolk and we ain't never heard of any Whitmead! You can pass the village on a track down there!' shouted the one who was acting as spokesman, lowering his bow in order to point. The other man's bow remained steadily drawn.

'Good day and good health!' Thomas shouted back, sardonically. He jerked his head at his family. 'Come on. This place is no use.'

They met with a similar reception at two more villages before they reached Essex. Others were more hospitable, although it was clear enough that this was because the pestilence had overtaken them before they had had time to barricade themselves in. No one seemed to find their inquiries suspicious; the good, sturdy cobs, the big dogs trotting alongside, and the good quality clothes, filched from the manorhouse, which Thomas had insisted they should all wear, saw to that. But no one had heard of Whitmead although someone did eventually explain details of the landmarks which indicated the Essex border.

They crossed into Essex and continued south. The land, which had been flat but fairly open for most of their route, now became more heavily wooded and for two days they travelled through deep forest. The were following a good track, but one nightfall overtook them before they could find shelter and they had to camp as best they could under the trees.

Nicola had seen only small woods before this. She was used to wide skies and open marshlands. The forest, even though it was still leafless and so afforded glimpses of the sky, alarmed her. The trunks loomed in the dimness and there were unexplained rustles in the undergrowth. She spent a long and wakeful night lying, rolled in rugs, between the roots of a huge oak, remembering that she must not let Alison sense her fear, but taking more comfort from the protective presence of the dogs, with which she had made friends, than from Thomas.

The next day, Thomas was suddenly overtaken by the weakness of his recent illness. Excitement and purpose had buoyed him up till then but now he turned faint and they had to rest and then proceed slowly, with Nicola leading Thomas's mount while Alison had charge of the packhorse. Fortunately, since Nicola was far from being a skilled rider, the cobs Thomas had chosen were steady in temperament.

Fortunately too, they found, within a couple of hours, a hamlet which although still populated, was not barricaded, The plague, weirdly capricious in its choice of victims, had apparently struck, but taken only a few souls and then departed. Here, they found not one, but three people who had heard of Whitmead and were able, after some putting together of heads, to give them directions. 'It's a few miles past a place called Quensted. Summat to do with it − same landlord most likely. But Quensted's bigger. You keep asking for Quensted, and keep on this track and you'll get there.'

By the evening of the day after that, they had arrived.

And Thomas had been right. They had considered other places, but he had had Whitmead in mind from the start, like a talisman, sure that it would be empty and unclaimed, as though he had some secret, esoteric source of knowledge.

And empty and unclaimed it was, its gate standing open as if to welcome them. It was not unnaturally in a neglected state, but it was far better than any of the other prospects they had rejected along the way. All the other farmsteads they had seen had been in a much worse condition than this.

Whitmead was lonely, as Thomas had thought, up on the side of a low hill, a cruck-framed building with daub-faced timber walls, a dry, flagstoned cellar store-room, a hall and kitchen at ground level and four slope-ceilinged rooms above.

It had an encircling palisade with a shallow ditch, although there was no gatehouse, just a stout gate which could be barred at night. There were stables and byres at the back, inside the palisade, and outside it, the place had three fields of its own, two respectively growing wheat and beans, while one was fallow meadow. There were two villeins left, both men, living beside the meadow in round, thatched dwellings. The younger was silent and sombre-eyed, as so many were who had watched their families die. The other was old with few teeth, but although his empty gums made him hard to understand, he was obligingly talkative when Thomas began to ask questions.

So Thomas was his old master's cousin? No, no, no one else was coming to take over, that he knew of. They'd all been here for that wedding just afore the plague broke out and likely it got the lot of them. Surely, yes, he could tell Thomas all about Whitmead. Yes, it was a freeman's holding and the rent was in wool and silver coin. As well as its three home fields, it also had shares in the open fields of its landlord. Rushley had not used the system by which vast fields were divided into strips held by various people, but Thomas had heard of it and nodded when it was mentioned. 'Master Astleigh, Denis Astleigh of Quensted, he's your landlord,' the old man said. Drawing lots for strips, he added helpfully, was a practice which had been discontinued ten years ago. 'People have their strips all together now and the same all the time. John Bulmer, your cousin that'd be; he had thirty acres of Astleigh land, this nearest end. And sheep out on the common pasture.'

Thomas gave Nicola a glance which meant: Praise be for this garrulous old idiot because now I know who my landlord is and whose cousin I'm supposed to be. In lofty and casual tones, he said, 'We must call on Master Astleigh tomorrow.'

'Ah, best do that. Rent's due come Michaelmas. Yours to him, that is. Ours to you is corn and cheese on Lady Day and a bit of day work all the year,' said the old man with a gummy grin.

And unbelievably, when they presented themselves at Quensted Manor, Denis Astleigh showed no disposition to do anything but accept them. So they were cousins of John Bulmer? He'd tried hard enough to find heirs to the tenancy, but he only knew who the nearer relatives were and when he tried to send word to them, he couldn't find a single one left alive.

Thomas, who had gambled on his strong if inexplicable instinct that

Whitmead was still untenanted, had come ready to gamble anew, on his ability to make imaginary details of a distant cousinship sound convincing, and was not after all obliged to provide any details at all.

It was enough that they were distant connections, too remote to be asked to the disastrous wedding, who had heard by roundabout means that Whitmead needed an heir. They'd come, and Astleigh was thankful to see them. Whitmead, he said, would fall into ruin if someone didn't take it over. 'My own shepherd's kept an eye on the sheep – it's not a big flock, only four hundred – but I've no one to till the fields.'

Nicola restrained a gasp. Four hundred sheep as well as thirty extra acres on top of the Whitmead fields! They'd only had ten acres all told before, and a couple of cows.

But Thomas had shaken off his attack of weakness and merely said, 'Certainly,' and when Nicola, on the way home, said anxiously, '*Can* we do it?' he replied that he felt well enough now to confront a dragon; a flock of sheep and a few extra acres would be easy.

That night, they retired to bed at Whitmead, as its official tenants, and they rested in comfort.

On entering Whitmead, which presented no difficulties because not only was the gate open, but the door of the house was unlocked too, they had had to clear up a high degree of mess. They had spent the first night on the floor, rolled in rugs, in the way they had grown used to during the last week.

But next day, after returning from Quensted, Nicola had co-opted Alison, found brooms and buckets and cleaned the floors. Then they had taken down the dusty curtains round the big bed in the main upper chamber, and thrown out the old pallets, all of them rotting and unpleasantly stained, which had been in use on that and various smaller beds about the house.

In a chest, they had found fresh curtains, and some fleeces in good condition which could be used in place of pallets. Nicola had set up a truckle bed for Alison in another room, and installed herself and Thomas in the big curtained bed, thinking that this was luxury.

Yet, on her first night in that new luxury, she was wakeful, listening to the faint creaks of this strange house as a brisk wind blew from the east, and to the occasional click of claws in the hall below, where the dogs were. The former tenants' dogs were gone; sold, Thomas suspected, by the two villeins for what they would fetch. He had said he didn't propose to pursue the matter. The cows and sheep were there, and there were three Whitmead horses in the meadow as well as those they had brought from Rushley; it was good enough.

Too good, thought Nicola, considering that they weren't entitled to any of it.

In the darkness, Thomas said, 'Are you awake?'

'Yes.'

'There's going to be a lot of work. You and Alison'll have to help in the fields.'

'Could Alison learn to look after the sheep? She was good with the cows at home.'

'This is home now. Yes, Alison could take the sheep on, though she couldn't do the shearing and she'll need help at lambing time.'

'We must just do our best,' said Nicola. She added, 'You'll miss your woodworking.'

'I've missed that,' said Thomas with bitterness, 'since I lost my fingers. Not that it matters any longer. I've taken my pay for that and now I'm going to be a freeman farmer, what they call a yeoman. A farmer's a farmer and a craftsman's a craftsman. Can't be both. I'll make some furniture for this house, if I get time. The stuff here's a bit plain. I'll make you a new settle and a chest. Nicola . . .'

'Yes?'

He turned on to his side and slid his arms round her. She returned the embrace, preparing to yield. But then, unexpectedly, he eased himself away again, rolling on to his back.

Once again, he said, 'Nicola . . .' and once again, he broke off.

'Yes? What is it?'

'I . . . I want to say I'm sorry. I've frightened you badly, haven't I? Dragging you here from Rushley as I have. You must have been terrified. You've always been afraid of me. I've tried to show you that you needn't be and then I force you to follow me into the unknown and threaten to kill you if you refuse. I'm sorry. A devil gets into me at times, that's all I can say. But I *want* to be kind to you, I *want* you to trust me.'

'I know. But . . . suppose some real Bulmers still turn up?'

'They won't. Astleigh would have found them if there were any. They'd be here already. And if they do . . .'

'We'll be arrested!'

'No, we'll raise our eyebrows and ask for details of their relationship and, if necessary, gracefully withdraw. I'll see we're safe, Nicola. I said, *trust* me.'

'I do,' said Nicola, thinking that she had little choice, after all.

'Do you? Do you?' He had sensed the doubt in her. He turned to her once more, and gathered her into his arms a second time. 'This is our bed now, but no bed is rightly ours until we've laid claim ceremonially,' he said.

He took his time, coaxing and persuasive, and she did her best to respond. At last, apparently contented, he slept, still holding her. She pressed close, glad of his warmth, a little reassured by his kindness. Able to hope that perhaps, in time to come, she might after all find in Thomas some of the safety and protectiveness she longed for, which she had never hitherto dared rely on him to give.

Which she would have had, assuredly, from Osbert Smith.

She woke next morning, once more afraid that their luck wouldn't hold, that some real Bulmers would appear to challenge them but no such thing occurred. They set about putting Whitmead in order. When it was midsummer and time to shear, they braced themselves to tackle the task alongside their villeins but, as if by magic, a small gang of itinerant shearers arrived. 'Sorry there're so few of us but we'll see to you as usual. New, aren't you? Plague get John?'

'I'm afraid so,' said Thomas gravely.

Inch by inch, Nicola's fears subsided. At times, as she swept the unaccustomed expanses of floor in the big rooms of Whitmead, and kindled fires in a wall-hearth just like the one in the hall of Rushley manorhouse and admired the new furniture which Thomas, keeping his word, made for her, although lack of time made it a slow business, she could hardly believe in her good fortune.

It was true that the work was hard, with the land and stock to be tended as well as the house, but she was free, well-fed, and was treated by Denis Astleigh and his people, on the rare occasions when they met, with a respect she would never have received at Rushley.

She was not even troubled, here, by homesickness for marshlands. They had marshlands of their own. They had come right through the forest and were, she understood, not far from the estuary of the great River Thames. The common pasture below the slight hill on which their home stood, which formed a flat green triangle, six miles across at one point, between Whitmead, Quensted and the big manor of Herneham, was reclaimed from bog but threaded, like the Rushley pastures, with drainage ditches. The land was very fertile; close at hand was a place where in summer the daisies grew so thickly that they were responsible for Whitmead's name which had once, the villeins said, been Whitemead.

In addition, away to the south-west lay the wide green expanse of Fobbing Marshes, with pools and streams and clumps of reed. Their nearest neighbour in that direction was the village of Fobbing, five miles off. Another village called Corringham lay beyond it and then the estuary. It was a landscape very much like that of Rushley and what had there been at Rushley to hold her? Even her parents were gone.

It should be easy to think of Whitmead as home. So why was she still finding it difficult when the second midsummer shearing came round?

On the day when they went to Chelmsford to sell their wool, and almost came face to face with Brother Ailred, she found herself wondering about this. The near-encounter had alarmed her; it seemed that she had been right after all and they were not as safe at Whitmead as Thomas thought. Why, Brother Ailred might come to Quensted next! Perhaps that was it.

And yet, she thought as they rode home through the summer

afternoon, perched behind the oxen, somehow that was not the reason, or at least not all of it.

Home, after all, meant more than a particular place. It meant people, too. She had had time, before they left Norfolk, to accept the fact that her parents were dead, but Osbert Smith had fallen victim to the plague just before they fled and she did not know what had happened to him.

Thomas had been considerate since they came to Whitmead, and she ought to be content. What was Osbert to her? They had exchanged glances on her wedding day; he had been kind on the day of Ed's death. She had believed that something deep and unspoken lay between them but she had grown older in spirit since she left Rushley. Now she asked herself: had he ever said anything to prove it? Was it real? Perhaps it was all her imagination.

Whether Osbert were in his grave, or well again and walking about the fields of Rushley, should not matter to her.

But it did.

'Everywhere is in disorder, I know,' Denis Astleigh remarked, agreeing with his guest. 'Much needs to be done. But sometimes there seems no point. It means going on, doesn't it? Leaving people . . . leaving the dead . . . behind.'

Richard Grosney regarded his host across the wine and growled inwardly. A guest must be polite, of course, but Astleigh's watery eyes and air of despondency were exasperating. Grosney himself had been bereaved by the plague and he had mourned his lost family, as any man would, but he had done it privately and set about replacing the loss as quickly as possible. When a child died, you buried it and sired another as fast as you could; when a wife died, you buried her and got married again.

As for 'going on and leaving the dead behind', well, naturally. What else?

'You have to do what's in front of you,' he said, putting it carefully. 'When Lady Ghislaine and I returned to Norfolk, to her father's house in Rushley, we found signs of looting, and somebody had stolen horses and let the dogs out. They'd been preying on the sheep. We had to straighten the house in order to live in it, and round up the dogs. Nearly wild, they were, the ones that hadn't had a shaft put through them. I'd like to know who'd been in there, I must say. Couldn't find any traces of stolen goods in any Rushley house. But as I say, you just have to do what's there in front of you. You're alive and you have to go on living.'

'I suppose so,' said Astleigh sadly. 'Well, I have tried. Funny; some things arranged themselves regardless of me. Take that place Whitmead, where the plague first broke out – Lady Ghislaine will have told you about that, I daresay. . .?'

'Yes. That will be the place four miles from Herneham.'

'That's right. Well, I searched hard enough to find an heir for the tenancy. Bulmer, that was the family that had it. John Bulmer had a brother London way and a first cousin on the other side of Chelmsford and some distant cousins in the fulling trade at Thaxted. I sent after each set in turn. Those are the letting terms, you see. It's a freeman's let, £3 a year, half of it in wool and half in cash, and it passes from heir to heir. But the whole lot turned out to be dead. It took months, finding out. One man I sent to inquire, never came back because he got the plague and died on the road, and so I had to send to trace him as well as the Bulmers he was after . . . and then I had so many other things to think about . . .'

My wife. My beloved Constance. But I kept you out of the plague pit, my love. When we first understood the danger, when the first case of plague appeared in Quensted village, I ordered coffins and had the tomb vault under Quensted church unlocked. You were reverently buried, you and the four young people we were bringing up for our friends. No plague pits for any of you. Oh God, why am I left here to mourn and remember without one single grandchild to lead my eyes towards the future? My coffin's upstairs, waiting in one of those empty rooms. Why can't I be in it?

He checked his thoughts before they found their way into words. Judging from the telltale lines round his eyes and mouth, Grosney was better at anger than compassion.

'I gave up trying to find heirs for Whitmead, in the end,' he said, attempting briskness. 'But then some remote Bulmer cousins found me instead. They said they'd heard by some roundabout means or other all about Whitmead, and come along, reckoning they were probably the only Bulmers left. I'm not altogether happy about them, to tell you the truth,' said Astleigh gloomily, 'but they're taking care of the place and paying their rent, so I'm not complaining.'

'How do you mean, not happy about them? You think they're not Bulmers? Just strangers who saw an empty property and grabbed it?'

'More or less.' Earlier, he had called for more wine, and now picked up the flagon to pour fresh goblets for them both. 'Though they seem well-conducted and respectable,' he said. 'They weren't just ragged strays, by any means. They arrived with good horses, decent belongings, a couple of dogs. They'd been upper servants on some manor or other in Norfolk, I think they said. Well-paid but not with land. They've got Norfolk accents.'

'So why do you feel doubtful about them?'

'They said so little about themselves.' Astleigh, even now, was interested in detail. His clay castles were mostly models of castles he had seen. He hadn't had the spirit to question Thomas much, but he had sensed an unnatural lack in the details Thomas had vouchsafed. Most people, trying to establish their identity under such vague circumstances, would have been much more anxious to thrust information under his nose.

'They came here and talked to me,' he said, 'but they never told me the name of the manor where they used to live or the name of the lord there. They said the plague got nearly everyone, so it was no use sending there for confirmation of their story.'

'How very convenient! Yet you've allowed them to stay?'

'I said, they're looking after the place. And very well, too, even though there's only the man and his wife and a young daughter, and a couple of villeins that were left on the holding. Until these people came along, there were only the villeins, Sim and Robert, and they're the sort that need someone telling them what to do all the time. I was at my wits' end. I could see all the fields going back to forest and the sheep and cows turning wild. I'm glad to have someone in Whitmead who's willing to do an honest job. They knew John Bulmer's name, anyway, though they call themselves just Whitmead. My man Joseph went over there not long ago to drop in and pass the time of day – he does that of his own accord sometimes, just to keep an eye on things for me, he says – and when he came back, he said that the man's made some fine new furniture for the house. Made it and carved it. He's a skilled woodworker, apparently, for all he's lost the first two fingers on his right hand.'

'Really?' said Grosney. 'How unusual.'

Denis Astleigh had had a good deal of wine by now. He did, just in passing, wonder why the Whitmead tenant's skill at furniture-making and his missing fingers had caused that expression of intense alertness to cross his guest's face, but he could not be bothered to inquire. Presently, Grosney took his leave, saying that he had business back at Herneham, and rode off into the sunny afternoon. Astleigh went to his chamber and went to sleep, and Grosney's momentary air of sharpness, and his own brief curiosity, were already forgotten. He never remembered either of them again.

'Well, here we are, safely back, in spite of Brother Ailred,' said Thomas, as he drove the ox-cart through the gate of Whitmead. 'Seems a long way from Chelmsford, doesn't it? If we do as well with our wool next year, Nicola, I might begin replacing these oxen with heavy horses. They eat more but they go faster and they can keep going longer. Right, get down. Let's see if Marge can give us some food.'

Denis Astleigh, remarking that the population of Whitmead consisted of only a man, a woman, a young girl and two villeins, was slightly behind the times. Just before shearing, the younger villein, Sim, had found himself a wife, a widow from Quensted. Marge was a few years older than he was, but she was already expecting and she had proved herself to be very handy in kitchen and dairy.

Alison too would not in future be on her own with the sheep. The

252

Quensted shepherd and his three sons had all survived the plague and the youngest son, Wat, who was now fourteen, wanted shepherding work. Henceforth, he was to help Alison with her four hundred charges. Until now, she had had only the two dogs from Rushley to assist her, although she had done well in training them. One of these days, perhaps, Alison might resume a more normal way of life for a young woman. Thomas and Nicola had told her to take charge of the sheep, but neither of them felt entirely happy when she went off to her work, morning after morning, whistling like a boy, with the two big dogs gambolling round her. But Sim was needed for heavy toil on the land and old Robert wasn't fit to be out with the sheep in all weathers. Wat would be a blessing. All they needed now, Thomas had said, was another pair of hands to help Sim. He'd let the fact be known as widely as possibly, but there were difficulties . . .

Marge came hurrying from the house to meet them. 'There's someone to see you, sir, looking for work. I seed you coming from a distance, so I said to this fellow to wait, and I give him some ale . . .'

'Splendid,' said Thomas. 'Pour me some as well and tell him I'm coming.' He took a bag from the corner of the cart. 'Put the oxen away. Nicola. I'll just lock this silver in our money chest upstairs, and then I'll see our caller. We might be in luck this time.'

'I can't agree to pay you fourteen shillings a year. For one thing I can't afford it, for another thing it would be outrageous even if I could, and for a third thing it's against the law,' said Thomas with irritation, to the applicant who had presented himself for employment. 'And I'm getting tired of saying so. You're the fourth, wanting the law broken to please him. Ten shillings is the most I can pay and you know it.'

'That's it, then.' The man was a short, tough, good-humoured individual who sat calmly consuming Thomas's ale and showing no desire to haggle. 'I'm only asking for the rates everyone wants these days and as for the law . . . when people want work done badly enough, they'll pay for it, no matter what the law says. I'll be on my way, then. Sorry about it. Nice place, this.'

'It's insufferable!' Thomas fumed to Nicola, calling her in as soon as the man had gone, which he did with a blithe step and the air of one who can afford to pick and choose employers, leaving the outer door open behind him. 'It's ridiculous! Do you know what he was asking? *Fourteen shillings*! Has Marge got any food ready, by the way?'

'Yes, I'm just heating it. I've sent her home. She's got to get Sim his late meal. Thomas, we do need another man. Maybe we ought to pay what others are paying.'

'And what if some busybody reports us to the sheriff's men? It happens. Men talk too much in alehouses and some people get rewarded for having big flapping ears. We don't want anyone here making inquiries and you know it. They might want to know exactly who we are and where we come from. Do you want to be dragged back to Rushley?'

'No, of course not.'

'Well, then. I did ask around in Chelmsford. I might go to Thaxted or Brentford sometime too, and see if I can hear of anyone suitable. Nearly everyone there is in the wool trade in some way or other; I might be lucky.'

In little over a year, Thomas had acquired an impressive knowledge of the geography of Essex. He knew which were the wool towns, had gone across Fobbing Marsh to visit Fobbing, and when one of the oxen died, had bought a replacement at a fair in a village called Brentwood, to the north-west. They sold their own surplus stock and produce, however, at Chelmsford, the town to the north-east. It was a bigger centre and selling was easier.

'Be careful if you do,' said Nicola. 'Seeing Brother Ailred in Chelmsford like that gave me a fright. I wouldn't have expected us to meet anyone we know, so far from . . . so far from Rushley.' She almost said *from home*, but stopped herself.

Thomas wasn't listening. 'I wish I could find someone to come for less than ten shillings a year. We're not doing badly, considering, but we got almost nothing for the spare saddle horse we sold last year and there are things we need. I said I want to buy draught horses, and even everyday things seem to eat money. We get through enough candles in this house to light the King's palace.'

'But Thomas, what about the silver we took from Rushley?'

'*That!*' said Thomas. 'Let me show you!' He sped up to their chamber and returned with the money chest which he had taken from Rushley Hall. He banged it down on the table, unlocked it and threw back the lid. 'Look at this. These bags here, they're what we brought back today. And these are what we've saved from working Whitmead so far. There's just enough there for one good draught horse, if prices stay low. But we won't be able to save so fast in future, because *this* little bag is all that's left of the Rushley money, after paying the rent and getting the corn milled at Quensted, and buying in salt and the food we can't grow ourselves, and those everlasting candles. We've also had to pay the shearers twice, buy an ox, pay the taxes . . . dear saints, the taxes . . .!'

'It's harder than you expected, being a freeman with property, isn't it?' said the voice of Richard Grosney. 'I daresay you'll be quite relieved to lay the burden down, won't you, Thomas Woodcarver?'

They spun round, Thomas slamming the lid of the money chest down as he did so. Grosney stood in the middle of their hall, regarding them with grim amusement.

'Most people,' said Thomas with fury, 'announce themselves before they walk into other men's houses. Most people shout or knock or blow a horn.'

'The door was open. Besides, I didn't want to announce myself. You might have run away.'

'How did you find us?'

'Oh . . . chance information, which I found intriguing. When I got back to Rushley and began setting it in order, you'd disappeared and no one seemed to know what had happened to you. No one could say for sure that you'd died, and when I went to your dwelling, half of your goods had gone too. So when I was in this district, and chanced to hear of a man called Thomas, of mysterious but possibly Norfolk origin, who hadn't been here long and who carved wood rather well but had the first two fingers of his right hand missing, I came along out of curiosity, as you might say. I reckoned you could well have got to Whitmead. Friar Ailred talked about the place enough.'

Nicola, speechless, was leaning on the table for support. A moment ago they had been safe within these walls, believing that danger lay only outside, for instance in towns like Chelmsford, where they might encounter Friar Ailred. And now, here in this very hall, Richard Grosney had appeared, like a . . . like a demon.

He was better dressed than she remembered. He had been accustomed to wear simple, dust-coloured clothes. He looked very strange in his new sky-blue and sanguine, with all that dagging on sleeves and cape. The cape was attached to a hood which had the longest liripipe she'd ever seen, trailing in front of his left shoulder like a girl's plait.

But there was nothing girlish about Grosney himself. His gold-buckled belt had a dagger stuck into it at a businesslike angle and from the midst of his fantastic ensemble, the taut face and cold eyes which Nicola and Thomas had always disliked and feared, regarded them unchanged.

'A polite host,' said Grosney, 'Asks guests to be seated.' He stepped round Nicola and deposited himself in a settle. 'Such a host,' he added, 'also offers refreshment.'

With a half-formed idea of placating the enemy, Nicola said faintly: 'There is food . . . and ale, of course . . . have you got men with you? Would they like . . .?'

'None of them eat a mouthful of my food or drink a cup of my ale!' snapped Thomas.

'My men are at Herneham,' said Grosney coolly. 'That needs as much setting to rights as Rushley and they've work to do. I'd ridden over to Quensted to see Denis Astleigh — I may as well tell you that it was Astleigh who told me about you. Craftsmen with missing fingers aren't that rare; accidents do happen with chisels. But Astleigh described your family and it fitted so well. I started off back to Herneham and then changed course and came here instead. Some sort of instinct made me sure it was you. And I was right.'

'Yes.' said Thomas pugnaciously. 'So what next? Do you want to be bought off? Astleigh may not be too pleased to lose his tenants. What did he say when you told him?'

'I haven't, yet. I was still thinking it over when I took leave of him. He thinks there's something odd about you but he doesn't know what and he can't be bothered to find out. But he won't want you here once I tell him who you are. Buy me off? That would set a bad precedent and I hardly think you could afford it. This place seems prosperous but, after all, it's Astleigh's, isn't it? Not yours. I hadn't got as far as putting a price on your liberty, I must say.' Grosney smiled in his tight-mouthed way, enjoying their discomfiture. He opened his mouth to say something more. And then stopped short.

Moving to the settle had placed him close to the table. On it, was the money chest. Grosney was looking at it. 'So it was you,' he said slowly to Thomas, 'who looted Rushley Hall.'

'What are you talking about?'

'The Rushley device is staring me in the face, from that chest-lid. Well, that changes things, I fear. Theft, Thomas my friend, is a hanging matter. You can't buy your way out of this. You have been foolish, haven't you?'

'I took what I was owed,' said Thomas. 'For my fingers and for a lifetime of toil for which I was never rightly paid. Who are you, Grosney, to set yourself up in judgement? You're not the sheriff's man. You're not even Sir Edward's man any longer. Sir Edward is dead. You're not my overlord.'

'As it happens,' said Grosney, 'Your overlord is precisely what I am. Sir Edward's heiress, may I remind you, is his daughter Lady Ghislaine. When I went north to find her and tell her of her parents' death, I found that the plague had widowed her. She's a woman of possessions now and in need of a man to help her run and defend them. I am that man. We were married in York.'

'You? *You?*' Thomas's voice contained amazement, fury and disgust, in equal parts.

'Yes, me,' said Grosney. 'I am in Sir Edward Rushley's shoes, now. I am your owner, Thomas, and the owner of the chest on the table there and all the silver which you've by now spent out of it.'

'Poor Lady Ghislaine!' said Thomas, in tones of the utmost commiseration. 'The poor, poor soul.'

Nicola, still leaning on the table, found her voice. 'Oh, why didn't you die of the plague? Go away, Master Grosney, go away and leave us in peace! What harm did we ever do you? Go away!'

Grosney raised his eyebrows. 'Go away? You can hardly expect me to do that, Mistress Nicola. One doesn't just ride off and leave a thieving runaway in possession of his stolen goods.'

'But,' said Thomas in a queer tight voice, 'I am going to remain in possession. You've made a mistake, Grosney.'

Nicola, looking at Thomas's face, almost stopped breathing. But Grosney seemed amused. 'You believe I can't deal with you because I'm here alone? Really? You're Timid Thomas, aren't you, that didn't want to go to war? Now listen to me, my friend. You have a wife and daughter. I am not accusing them of the theft, or even of running away. No doubt you compelled them to do as you said. Come with me now, as my prisoner, without resistance, and I will swear an oath, before a priest, that your family will be cared for. They must return to Rushley, of course, and you'll swing, but a suitable new marriage will be found for your wife; she and your girl will have good prospects within the station of life which is properly theirs . . .'

'Don't be afraid, Nicola,' Thomas said quietly. 'None of this is going to happen.'

'Isn't it?' Grosney, still oblivious to warnings which to Nicola were as obtrusively visible as Grosney's own garments, continued to talk. 'That is one choice, Thomas. But if you defy me and force me to go back for my men, or try to run off while I'm fetching them, then I will catch you just the same, and I will make what is left of your life into a foretaste of hell, and when you're dangling from a gibbet, your wife will marry the lowest and most worthless cottar I can find and your daughter likewise, in due time. So you see, you have a very easy decision to make.'

Nicola glanced at Thomas's face once more, pushed off from the table and edged back to the wall.

'Yes. Very easy,' said Thomas. This time there was something in his voice which did penetrate Grosney's self-satisfaction. He stiffened and Nicola saw the beginnings of fear flicker in his eyes. 'Be careful, Thomas,' he said. 'I am your overlord.'

'You're Richard Grosney, same as you always were. And you're here alone.'

'I told Master Astleigh I intended to call here. Thomas, I warn you . . .'

Grosney had risen. His hand was on his dagger hilt.

'I don't think you told Master Astleigh anything of the sort. You told me you were still thinking it over when you left him. I don't believe anyone knows you're here,' Thomas said. He moved, not towards Grosney but to the other side of the table, and faced his adversary across it. 'You're quite fool enough to do a daft thing like that. You never did have any respect for other people, Grosney, and I'm only Timid Thomas, aren't I? And you didn't know then that I was Thomas the Thief as well. You didn't know then that I was gallows meat. But even if you told the sheriff himself you were coming here, what have I to lose? I'll chance it!'

Then he grasped the table with both hands, and flung it over, to send Grosney staggering.

To Nicola, what followed seemed both fast and slow. There was time to watch every detail, and yet when it was over, it had apparently taken no time at all.

The overturned table hurled the money chest to the floor. The lid came off and the contents fell out. Bags burst open and the coins scattered. Grosney's hand slipped off his dagger-hilt as he stumbled back and Thomas, leaping over the fallen table, made to seize his enemy's throat.

Grosney grappled with him. They tripped on the chest lid, crashed to the floor together and rolled, fighting, amid the rushes and the strewn silver. Grosney's hand found his dagger again and drew it. Thomas, cursing, seized Grosney's wrist and twisted savagely. The dagger fell to the floor and Thomas, clawing and groping, got hold of it. Grosney snarled and fought to get it back. Thomas was undermost. He was still cursing, in gasps. Then he struck upwards, into his adversary's body. Grosney emitted a gurgling scream, arched, kicked feebly, made queer animal noises, and sagged. Thomas threw him off, dragging the bloodied dagger out of him. He knelt over Grosney and used the dagger again, twice, grunting with the effort of driving it in and tugging it loose.

He came to his feet, breath rasping. When he could speak again, he said, 'I brought us here to make us free. He wasn't going to take it away from us.' He looked at Nicola, who was pressed against the wall with her knuckles in her mouth and her eyes enormous. 'He held me in contempt,' said Thomas. 'He knew better before he died.'

'Y . . . y . . . you've killed him!'

'What else was there to do? He'd have had me hanged.'

'He . . . you . . . suppose s . . . s . . . someone comes looking for him?'

'We haven't seen him.'

'But if Master Astleigh *does* know he was coming here . . .'

'I reckon he doesn't, but what of it, anyway? We haven't seen him, understand? He never got here.'

'But he's *there*!' Nicola pointed at Grosney's body, grotesque in its fashionable dagging and parti-colours.

'Well, we've got to get rid of him. Then we're safe enough.'

'We should never have come here! Lady Ghislaine's still alive; she owns Herneham. It's only across the common! What if she sees us and recognises us?'

'When did Sir Edward ever let his precious daughter go near his villeins? I never came face to face with her in my life; did you? She won't know us, Nicola. Anyhow, Whitmead isn't part of Herneham. Why should she ever come here?' He prodded Grosney with his foot. 'We'll have to bury him.'

'Bury him?' Nicola recoiled. 'I c . . . couldn't touch him!'

'Why not? You would have buried my father! You dragged him from his bed by his heels and tumbled him down the ladder! I saw you do it. You can help with this, too!'

'But there's no time! Alis . . . Alison must be on her way home by now!'

'Sweet Christ! Yes, she must.' Thomas looked round as though expecting to see Alison come through the door. She was not there. But for a moment, passing an exhausted hand across his forehead, he seemed irresolute.

Nicola made an enormous effort. Her bowels wanted to loosen and her knees wanted to give way but she mustn't let them. Thomas was dangerous; she'd always known it, since the day he half-throttled her on that bridge at Rushley. He had to be placated. She must be on his side, as he would put it, and that, just now, meant being practical, thinking what to do. 'All right, all right, I'll h . . . help. We'll have to hide his body now and bury him during the night. But we must get him out of sight quickly. Behind the barrels in the store-room, won't that do?'

'You always prove yourself in times of trouble,' Thomas said with grim amusement. 'I've noticed it before. You're right. Come on. Let's get him down there.'

And somehow or other, there she was in the kitchen, hastily propping open the door to the steps which led down to the store-room, hurrying back to find that Thomas had put the table on its legs again and was already dragging Grosney towards the kitchen by his feet. Fortunately, there didn't seem to be all that much blood. Redistributed rushes would hide what there was. Between them, she and Thomas got Grosney down the store-room steps and dumped him in a concealed corner.

'We can bury him here,' Thomas said, scanning the room in the faint light from the door above. 'Move the barrels, dig up the flagstones beneath them, put him there and then put back the stones and the barrels. That'd be best. We'll have to come down quietly, when Alison's asleep.'

'She'll be here any minute . . . Thomas, his horse! Where's his horse?'

They ran, up the steps, through the hall and out into the yard. The horse was standing patiently, its reins secured to a ring which some earlier tenant, perhaps John Bulmer, had fixed in the doorpost, no doubt for this purpose.

'I don't think Marge would have seen him ride in,' Nicola said shakily, going to unloose the reins. 'She'd gone by then. She takes the little path that doubles back round the palisade so she wouldn't have met him. What . . . what's the matter?'

'The horse! I don't want to have to kill and bury his horse as well!' said Thomas furiously. 'It's too big and I don't want to kill it, anyhow. No horse ever threatened to hang me.'

'But why should we kill it? Can't we hide it in the stable? For the time being? And then . . . oh, turn it loose on the pastures or something? We can take its tack off and bury that. There are a lot of horses running on the common; some of them aren't even claimed. Their owners died in the plague and . . .'

'Nicola, *look at it!*'

Nicola looked and saw. Richard Grosney's new-found passion for cutting a dash had evidently extended itself beyond clothing to his

259

mount. This was no common bay or brown or even grey nag which could be lost in a crowd on the pastures. It was, in fact, a spectacular animal, whose description would be unmistakeable. Nicola had never seen such colouring before. Grosney's gelding was chestnut in front, but with white hairs beginning to intermix at the shoulders and increasing towards the rear, so that its coat shaded through roan along its body until its hind legs and its hindquarters near the tail were virtually white, save for a sprinkling of golden-brown hairs. Its saddle and bridle were just as striking, all crimson and blue with silver studs and scalloped reins. But they could be made to vanish more easily than the horse.

'Oh, God,' said Thomas. 'I'll get the animal into the stable for the moment and push that tack under some straw. You clear up the hall. Alison's late. Just as well, but I hope nothing's wrong with her. Hurry, now!'

In the hay-barn adjoining the stable, Alison lay crouched and shivering, her arms round the dogs for comfort.

As far back as she could remember, she had had the habit of watching the adults, whenever possible, without letting them know it. She had always been aware of secrecies among them, of things below the surface which she did not understand. She had always known, for instance, that her mother was afraid of her father though she did not know why. To observe unseen, to peer round doors or listen on the other side of thin walls, was a means by which, one day, she might penetrate these grown-up mysteries.

And so, seeing a strange horse just inside the gate when she returned home, she had gentled the dogs, told them to sit so that they would not go gambolling into the house and announce her presence by barking, and then moved on quiet feet to the open hall door, and looked in.

To see the hall in a shambles, with the table overturned and the money chest in wreckage on the floor, and her father fighting a man in the midst of it all. To see her father stab him. And to catch sight, for a moment, of the other man's face, and know that he was dead, and to recognise Richard Grosney, the hated bailiff from Rushley.

She had been back with the dogs, looping her fingers into their collars, dragging them quickly past the house and into the shelter of the barn, so swiftly that she could hardly remember doing it. And now she lay there with them, in a corner behind a stack of haybales, her heart banging against the board floor beneath her, afraid to go into her own home and trying to understand, to make sense, of the awful, inconceivable scene she had witnessed in the hall.

She heard the horse being led inside, heard hay and water being fetched and a violent rustling of straw a little further off, in the end stall. Then she heard her mother's voice.

'The hall's tidy now. There's still no sign of Alison. Thomas how *are* we to get rid the horse?'

'The other side of Fobbing Marsh, that's the answer, Nicola. There's not that much coming and going between here and Fobbing. We'll have to take him Fobbing way and turn him loose on the common there. Likely enough he'll be found in the end but there's no link between a horse running wild at Fobbing, and us here. You'll have to do it tonight.'

'Me?' Her mother's voice was shrill with alarm.

'Well, I can't leave you alone in the store-room with Grosney's dead body, digging up flagstones by candlelight. You do all right in a crisis mostly, but I reckon that'd make you panic. You'll take the grey cob and lead this fellow on a halter. Then ride back. There ought to be a half-moon; you'll see your way all right. There and back will only take a couple of hours, even by night. By the time you get back, I'll have the worst of the job in the store-room done. Now don't argue, Nicola. The whole thing's got to be over and done with before Marge arrives in the morning. When Alison comes back, we'll have to make sure she doesn't come into the stable. She ought to be here by now. I'd like to know where she's got to . . .'

His voice faded. Her parents were leaving the stable.

Habits of concealment and pretence saw her through when, presently, she nerved herself to bring the dogs out of the hay-barn, and go into the house and pretend that she was returning a little late because a sheep had strayed. Her parents did not question her. They seemed a little distracted although the hall now looked ordinary enough. She succeeded in eating some food, in talking about the sheep, and, presently, in retiring to her bed.

Once there, she lay tense in the dark, listening for movements in her parents' room next door and wishing to be out on the sheep pasture again with Wat, the son of the Quensted shepherd. Wat was serene and cheerful and open of face and temperament. There was nothing about Wat to suggest hidden dangers or frightening secrets. Wat was all that was calm and sane.

After a time, she heard the movements she was waiting for with so much dread. A little later, she heard the snort of a horse and the thump of a restless hoof in the yard outside and, peering from her window, she saw her mother, riding with bunched skirts astride one of the Rushley cobs, lead the strange horse away. Very timidly then, with trembling hands, she opened her door and peered into her parents' room. Moonlight slanting through a window showed her the drawn-back bedcurtains and the empty bed within. On tiptoe, she stole across the room and down the staircase on the far side, down to the moonlit hall and into the kitchen.

She saw at once that the door to the store-room steps was open, for it was faintly outlined in candlelight, from below. She crept halfway down the steps and heard the sound of her father breathing heavily. A few more steps brought her a glimpse of him, back bent as he heaved up the edge of a flagstone with a crowbar. Close to him, was a heap of what looked like colourful saddlery, and there was something else, too, lying on the floor, half in and half out of the shadow of a barrel.

She did not wait to see any more. Silent as a shadow herself, with a palm pressed over her shaking mouth, Alison fled for the security of her bed and lay there, shivering. Hours later, she heard a horse come back into the yard, and a long time after that, when dawn was already breaking, she heard her parents return into their room.

In the morning, she broke her fast with her parents in the hall as usual. They were very silent and looked exhausted but otherwise, everything seemed as usual.

Two days later, she found an opportunity of visiting the store-room. She was afraid of it but the need to know was greater than her fear. There was little to see but she thought some of the barrels, of ale and salted meat, had been shifted and when she peered closely between two of the barrels, she saw fresh earth along the edge of a flagstone.

She had nightmares, regularly, for a long time afterwards. It was always, in essentials, the same dream. She was in the store-room, fetching flour or counting cheeses, when the flagstones cracked apart and Grosney rose up, gigantic and leering, and reached out to clutch her. She would wake in terror, aware of Grosney's buried body as though he were a monstrous seed which had been planted in the ground below the house.

Only out in the pastures, where Wat was as normal and as refreshing as daylight and spring water, could she find ease.

In Rushley, the Lady Ghislaine waited for Richard Grosney to return but the two men who had accompanied him from Norfolk came back, eventually, without him.

He had vanished, they said. Simply vanished, man and horse, after paying a visit to a neighbour called Denis Astleigh. No, no one suspected Astleigh of harming him. Astleigh's servants had all seen him ride away and take the track for Herneham.

After which, his fate was lost in mystery.

They had asked at every habitation for miles, they said, in Quensted's village and on its outlying farm at Whitmead, and they'd been as far as Chelmsford, hoping to learn news. But no one had seen him and they knew of no one with any grudge. After all, he was a stranger there.

But the track to Herneham was lonely, partly running across commonland and partly through a tongue of the thick Essex forest. Grosney had been alone and there was always the chance that he had met with robbers. He could have been murdered and buried in the deep forest, and his horse stolen. It was their belief, anyway, that he was dead.

At the end of their narrative, Lady Ghislaine showed the proper signs of distress, and withdrew to her chamber, to grieve alone, she said to Nan, who was her one female attendant.

Once alone, she knelt, rather awkwardly because of the advanced state of her pregnancy, in front of her prie-dieu and besought God, most earnestly, not to let Richard Grosney reappear.

Marriage to her elderly and unattractive first husband had been enough to turn her against marriage for ever. After that, she could think of men only as invaders. But she hadn't been able to withstand Grosney. 'You will inherit considerable possessions, my lady. Yorkshire, Norfolk, Essex – and I believe your husband left you a house in London, did he not? You will need someone to help you administer it all and to defend it. You will need an heir. Why not marry me? After all, you know me and I know your Rushley lands well, and I'm accustomed to administration. I can be a great help to you, and I'm still a fit man and not so very old. I'll be a better lover, my dear Lady Ghislaine – or may I call you Ghislaine? – than your first husband was. You will not know it, but when you were a young girl still at home, I admired you greatly. My dear, we have both suffered great bereavement. Could we not comfort one another?'

He had taken a few weeks to put all that to her, but reduced to its elements, that was what it came to, and she hadn't been strong-minded enough, not after just recovering from the plague herself, to hold him off. If she didn't marry him, she supposed that the Earl of Norfolk would push her into marrying somebody else. It was true that she was acquainted with Grosney and that he knew Rushley well. It was easier to give in. She had regretted her weakness bitterly since.

For one thing, although less repulsive than her first husband, he wasn't at all a better lover, for he was rough and hasty, taking his own satisfaction and indifferent to hers. And worse than that was watching him lord it over the manors that were hers, *hers*, not his, not the property of Richard Grosney, arrogant ex-bailiff. He spent her money on fine clothes and a splendid horse for himself and, when she protested, made it plain that to him she was property, just as much as the horse.

If he had been murdered by outlaws, good. She was grateful to them. If his body were never found, better still, since no one then could compel her into another marriage. 'But how can I? My husband may be living yet,' she would say.

She did not want ever to get into bed with a man again and, while Richard Grosney remained lost, she wouldn't have to.

Her son was born a month later. She even had an heir now. She regretted that his father was Richard Grosney but at least he seemed healthy. She had a bad moment a few weeks after that when word came that the Herneham steward, visiting relatives in Fobbing, to the south, had seen a horse that looked uncommonly like Richard's, grazing on the marsh pastures near the village.

But nothing came of it. The steward had spoken to the Fobbing constables, inquiring who owned the horse, but it seemed to be one of the ownerless strays which were now such a common sight.

If this had been Richard's horse, then perhaps, for reasons of his own, he had abandoned it there and gone away, perhaps to the Thames to take ship to the continent. It was hard to imagine what his reasons could have been, unless he had committed some crime or other and feared discovery.

In Ghislaine's eyes, Richard Grosney *was* a crime, walking on two feet. She only hoped that wherever those feet were now, they would continue to walk away from her and not turn back.

The possibility that he was alive after all worried her for a long time but gradually the fear faded. On her son's behalf, she ruled Rushley and the three manors, and the Yorkshire lands, and Herneham in Essex, and the house in London, as undisputed mistress, and enjoyed it.

In the thick darkness of the curtained bed, Thomas completed what he knew was nearer to an attack than an act of love, rolled away from his wife's compliant body and said bitterly, 'Why do you put up with that? Why don't you complain?'

'Complain?' He couldn't see Nicola's face but he could hear the wary note in her voice.

'Yes, complain! Fight, push me away, bite me, sulk!'

'Is . . . is that what you want?'

'No, it isn't what I want.'

'But you said . . .'

'I want you not to be so afraid of me. Oh God, the day that man Grosney came here, I stabbed him to the heart and cut my own throat at the same time, didn't I? I did it for you and Alison as well as for me but you've looked at me with terror in your eyes ever since. Just as you did on that bridge when we were children, and on our marriage night and the day I said we were leaving Rushley. And this time it won't fade, will it?'

Nicola said nothing. He knew that she did not know what to say, that she was thinking of answers and rejecting them in fear.

'Six bloody months he's been buried under that floor but you'll never forget he's there, if we live here six centuries.'

'Thomas, you know I'll do anything you want.'

'Yes. I do know that. Funnily enough, I do know that.'

'Well — just say what you want.'

He'd said *push me away, bite me, sulk*. He was just a little too proud to say *cuddle me, love me; it's a dangerous world and I'm afraid of those bones under the store-room floor as well; I need shelter too.*

'It's all right. I'll settle for things as they are. Forget all this. Good night,' said Thomas.

PART IV
John Watson:
The Taking of the Prey
1375–81

Here, then, for an end of this ancient picture, is the day of our first kill.

Chapter Fifteen

The Acknowledgement

'I could do with another strong young fellow about this place,' said Thomas, coming in out of a muddy March afternoon and sitting down by the fire to drag off his boots. 'Well, Wat Shepherd's dead now so I won't have him crowing. I'd better bring John here. He's the only heir I've got and he's not going to inherit after me without doing some work for it. I'll ride over to Quensted tomorrow. What are you staring at me like that for, Nicola? I haven't said anything so odd that I know of. And where's my supper? I'm cold to the marrow with that wind.'

'You're going to fetch *John* here?' said Nicola faintly, half-rising in order to go to the kitchen, but stopping halfway. 'But . . .'

'I said; he's the only heir I've got,' said Thomas, banging caked mud off the boots. And avoiding his wife's astounded eyes.

Nicola would never, all her life, forget the day that Alison announced that she not only wished to marry Wat Shepherd, but had betrothed herself to him in the presence of his father.

'A betrothal stands in law,' she had said, facing them gallantly, having nerved herself to speak one midday after dinner. 'I know you won't like it but you can't stop me now.'

There was a silence, long and heavy. Nicola could feel the astonishment radiating from Thomas and turning into anger as iron in the forge turned from cool and dark to red-hot. She was aware too of her own disappointment. She had had such hopes for Alison, taken such trouble to teach her how to care for her hair and skin, instructed her in the lore of being well-dressed. When they first came to Whitmead, they had had to send the girl out to look after the sheep, but she had hoped it would do no harm. And now this had come of it.

In a tone of the deadliest calm Nicola had ever heard, Thomas said, 'No, I can't stop you. Not if you're betrothed as you say. But I can forget you. You want to go to Wat Shepherd, a common villein with nowhere to live but a dirty hut and no land beyond half an acre of beans and cabbage. I daresay his father was delighted to be your witness. You're a catch for a boy like Wat. I've no doubt they're rubbing their hands, thinking of your portion. You won't have one. Leave my house.'

Now, this moment. Go to Wat's parents and marry him as soon as you like. As far as your mother and I are concerned, you no longer exist.'

Alison stared at him, suddenly turning white. Then she mumbled, 'All right. I'll take my things and go. Mother . . . I . . . I'm sorry . . .'

Thomas cut the apology short. 'You didn't understand me. I said go now. *Now*. Just as you are. Go on!'

And then, when Alison began to protest that it was winter and cold, that she must at least take a cloak, he caught hold of her and, although she fought and cried, dragged her out of the house and across what had been the yard but was now paved and called the courtyard, and thrust her through the gate, which he then slammed shut.

Nicola had not dared to intervene. When Thomas came back, he found her sitting at the table where he had left her. Marge was there too, and both of them were stricken silent.

'She's gone,' said Thomas. 'I looked through a crack in the gate and she's stumbling away. Serve her right.' He glared at Nicola. 'And you won't go chasing after her do you hear? You're never to speak to her again. If she comes whining back here, throw her out. And you, Marge, you don't take messages between 'em. Do you hear?'

His fury filled the room. All they could do was nod. But a few weeks later, when Thomas and Nicola were alone, he said gruffly, 'I hear Alison's married. I suppose you'll be yearning to steal off there sometimes when my back's turned but too scared of me to do it. Well, go. I won't stop you. But I don't want to know about it and it's no good her asking for anything from me; she won't get it. Dear God, when I think what we risked to get our freedom and this place so that she could grow up to make a fine marriage . . . She won't be happy. Mark my words: they're just after her portion. Probably hoped to get this place in the end. Well, Wat can say goodbye to that.'

Nicola did not think Wat had been after Whitmead. He reminded her strongly of Osbert Smith. He was a kind boy, she thought, and it was likely enough that he really cared for Alison. She was sure that Alison loved Wat.

Well, she had permission now, of a sort, to see her daughter sometimes although she might be wise not to do so too often. She said, 'Thank you.'

'I need a son,' said Thomas. 'Women your age still have children sometimes. Why can't you give me a son?'

But there had been no son. Nicola sometimes thought that all her fertility had finally died on the day that Thomas murdered Richard Grosney.

But Alison, in the beehive-shaped hut at the nearer end of Quensted village, four and a half miles off across the pastures, had provided them with a grandson. Thomas had merely grunted when told of his birth and Nicola had been under the impression that her husband didn't even know that Alison's little boy was called John.

*   *   *

268

Alison was used to Wat's hut by now but adapting to her married home had been a nightmare. She had only done it by remembering, over and over again, how much she loved Wat, and by calling her pride to her aid. Alison had a great deal of pride, which she realised she probably inherited from her father. If she was hungry, or short of fuel, or the babies fell ill because the hut was cold and damp, well, she had chosen to live here.

But all the same, she had been glad of her mother's occasional clandestine visits and often grateful for the extra food or clothing which Nicola smuggled to her. But it had been hurtful, too, to see the pity in her mother's eyes.

She had never asked for help, but once or twice Nicola had let out that, in spite of Thomas's prohibition, she had attempted to coax him into letting go of the feud. 'I don't like to see you thin and tired and grubby, and after I brought you up to be so clean, too,' she would say, looking at her daughter's home in gentle despair.

'It's all right, Mother. I'd sooner you took care of yourself. You know what Father's like when he's in a temper. I don't want you being hit for my sake. I wanted to marry Wat and he's good to me,' Alison would say stiffly.

'He doesn't hit me much now. He just pretends not to hear what he doesn't want to hear,' Nicola told her. Once she added with a sigh, 'If only Wat could get on a bit. Villeins can, sometimes, but he doesn't seem to have any push.'

'There's no time, Mother. The sheep keep him so busy. We're always shearing or lambing or tarring them to keep the parasites off, and Master Astleigh won't pay a halfpenny a year over the set rate, so we can't save to buy our own flock. He's as bad as Lady Ghislaine is, over at Herneham. Wat says they're all alike, the people with land and power. They just wring all they can get out of people who can't stop them. But there's no way out, unless somebody helps.'

She hadn't meant to say that. It had slipped out and she heard the resentment in her voice. But even then she added proudly, 'Only Wat wouldn't accept help. He just lets you give me the odd gift because a mother can give a present to her daughter; that's all right. I've no regrets. I couldn't have a kinder husband than Wat and no one's perfect.'

If there was an implied criticism in that last phrase, an admission that Alison too considered that Wat could have achieved more if he'd pushed harder, Nicola was wise enough not to comment.

Most of the time, Alison, loyal and determined, had put on a great show for Nicola, serving meagre food as if it were a banquet and talking affectionately of Wat and their son John, who for a long time was the only child to survive the life in the dark, cramped hut.

And now Wat was gone, after taking a chill while shifting sheep in a rainstorm and dying of congested lungs, just as his father had done, only a few years ago, and here she was, with John aged fifteen, trying to take Wat's place, and with the latest baby, miraculously still alive so far, whimpering in the cradle. Thin as a hazel wand herself, she was somehow or other making enough milk to keep the infant Walter breathing. She wondered how long she could keep it up.

The door opened, to admit a stream of chill air, as John returned for his midday meal. He was taller already than either of his parents and had to duck his head. His light red hair was beaded with drizzle and his clothes were damp, and in his arms he was carrying a dead lamb.

'Can you skin this for me while I eat? Usual thing. I want to put the skin on an orphan lamb and persuade this one's mother to suckle it but it's got to be done quickly. Poor little mite's bedded down on straw in the stable and we got some milk into it by letting it suck a soaked cloth, but it needs a foster-mother; it's a weakly little thing. You're so handy at this job.'

'Done it often enough in my time,' Alison said. 'Get those wet things off and put them to dry while you eat.' She had learned from long experience never to be lax about this. The row of sad little mounds in Quensted churchyard bore testimony to the effects of ignoring damp clothing. She shooed him into the dark, curtained-off compartment at the back of the hut, where they slept. 'Take the blanket from my chest! I'll have the skin ready by the time you've had your meal.'

She had already set about the work when he reappeared, blanket-swathed and carrying his wet tunic and hose. He set them by the hearth to steam, and helped himself to his ryebread and stew.

He ate hungrily, too hungrily. That tall frame of his needed better food than it was getting, Alison thought worriedly. Lack of good food did not help to keep a body strong against the weather. She looked at him sometimes, when she thought he wouldn't notice, thinking how much her son he was, far more so than any of the others had been, or than the infant Walter was likely to be. John had her hair and her dark eyes and he was growing handsome. But he wouldn't fill out, not properly, on their dismal rations.

The meat from the skinned lamb would be tender, but the lamb belonged to Master William Astleigh of Quensted and its meat was for him, not for the shepherds who tended his flock in the wet. His predecessor and distant cousin Denis Astleigh had been generous about these things sometimes, but William was not. The death of any animal had to be reported to his bailiff, who was always on the prowl to make sure that no one cheated.

The light in the hut was bad. It was exasperating; open the door to let in light, and you let in the cold as well. Keep the door shut and you needed rushlights at noon, which was costly. 'I'll have to take this outside,' Alison said. 'It's that fiddly.' She fetched a blanket wrap for

270

herself, pulling it over her head, and took her task into the daylight. She was back in a moment, still clutching the half-skinned lamb, her eyes wide.

'I don't believe it! Your grandfather's on his way here! He's not two hundred yards off. I know the way he sits a horse and I'd know that black mare with the star anywhere!'

'He can't be coming *here*,' said John with his mouth full.

'The only place in Quensted village that he ever calls at is the smithy and I've just seen him ride straight past it,' said Alison. 'He's coming from the manorhouse direction but if he was just making for home, he'd take the short cut like everyone else, for sure . . . and that's his horse outside!' Alison thrust her gory task into a corner, threw her blanket over it and went to the door. 'Father!'

'Can I come in?' said Thomas Whitmead.

He made his request in a brusque voice and, once inside, looked round at as much of the dim interior as he could see, disparagement written all over his face. John put down his food and rose politely to his feet, beginning a greeting, but Thomas said shortly, 'Never mind that. Get on with your meal. It's as well you're home. I thought you might be, at this time of day. Haven't you anything to offer me, Alison? Not even a drop of ale?'

'Of course.' The ale was produced. Thomas accepted it and sat down on the stool Alison pushed towards him. A silence fell.

'Well, Father,' Alison said candidly at last. 'I never thought to see you here, I must say.'

'I'm not here to forgive you, either,' said Thomas, with equal candour. 'Though I've an offer to make that may please you. The fact is, Alison, you got yourself into this mess you're living in, and you can get yourself out of it, if you can. But' – he glanced towards John – 'the boy couldn't choose his father and I recognise that I'm a fair man, I hope. I've been to see William Astleigh this morning.'

He stopped as though expecting them to comment. They stared at him in bewilderment.

Thomas sighed, apparently at their slow wits. 'You, boy – John, that's your name, I think – your father was a villein of Quensted and so are you. That right?'

John said civilly, 'Yes, sir.'

'But in the natural course of events,' said Thomas, 'when I die, the tenancy of Whitmead would come to you. Not because I want it to but because it just would.'

'Though what Master William Astleigh would think of that,' Alison remarked, 'the dear Lord alone knows. He's the landlord and we're still his villeins.'

'He'd take your value out in death duties,' said Thomas. 'I asked him this morning. And I said that if you were willing for what I'm offering, I'd buy you out of villeinage now instead. Then you could inherit when the time came, and pay only the ordinary duties.'

'And what,' said Alison quietly, 'are you offering, Father?'

'A chance for John to learn his trade,' said Thomas. 'A chance to know Whitmead inside out before he has to run it. If I buy you out, John, you'll be free to come and work for me instead of for William Astleigh and that's the offer. To work for me, I mean. Not to live with me; I'll have no son of Wat Shepherd living under my roof while I'm alive myself. But you can come every day and help me at Whitmead. I'm offering no favours!' Thomas's eyes flashed as angrily as though someone had suggested that he was. 'You'll work like all the rest and be treated like all the rest. You'll be paid what you are now and you'll work for every farthing. You'll be in my debt, remember, and I'll get my money's worth out of you. But I'll see that you learn and by the time you've earned Whitmead, you'll understand it. That's all.'

Silence fell again. Then John said slowly, 'I'm to work for you instead of Master Astleigh, and it won't be much different, except that when you die, inheriting won't be so expensive.'

'That's a good enough summing up,' said Thomas. 'I'm glad your wits aren't slow. I wondered about that, seeing the stock you're bred from.'

Alison stood up, with a quick, angry movement. 'You'll decide for yourself, John. It's between you and your grandfather. Meanwhile, there's an orphan lamb out in the pen, needing a mother and I've a task to do for it.' She removed the half-skinned carcase from under the blanket and took it outside.

John, his face thoughtful, chased the last of his stew round the bowl with a piece of bread. Thomas watched him. 'Well?' he said.

When John walked through the gate of Whitmead to begin his first day's work there, it was the first time in his life that he had ever been through that gate.

He had passed Whitmead often enough, of course, and his mother had told him about it. He had known, ever since he could remember, that his grandfather and grandmother lived there. But it had been a place he must never expect to enter. Alison had made that clear.

Beyond the gate was an expanse of paving and then the house, which took him aback because, compared to the beehive hut which was all the home he had known, it seemed so big. It was in fact much smaller than Quensted Hall which he had seen often and indeed, entered, for Christmas feasts or to accompany his father to pay the Lady Day dues of ewe's milk cheese. But Whitmead belonged to a member of his own family, and might one day be his, and that was an idea to take one's breath away.

Slowly, looking about him, he crossed the courtyard. To the right of it, alongside the house, was a patch of bare earth where hens clucked and pecked and there were barns beyond. The door of the house was open, and there was smoke emerging from its single chimney. Though he had risen before dawn and set out briskly, fearing to be late, the place was awake and active. Thomas came out of the door as he approached it and regarded him unsmilingly, a strongly-made man in his fifties, with fierce dark eyebrows, fading hair which had once been the same colour as John's own, and working clothes with a minimum of dagging. 'So you're here. All right. Come inside.'

He obeyed, and found himself in a flagstoned hall full of astonishing furniture. Even Quensted had nothing so decorative as these stout settles of oak and walnut, with what were obviously lift-up seats over storage compartments – he could see the corner of some bright fabric showing under the edge of one of them – and backs lavishly adorned with carved leaves and fruits and flowers, and arms and feet ending in carved paws like those of monster cats and hounds.

'Carving is my amusement,' said Thomas. 'I manage, even with two fingers short.' John nodded. He knew from his mother that his grandfather's right hand had been maimed in some kind of accident and, when Thomas came to their home, he had seen the injury for himself, in the hand that held the ale tankard. 'It's amazing, what you can do when you have to,' Thomas said. 'Now then. We'll run through what your duties'll be to start with . . .'

The list was alarming. There were other men on Whitmead, apparently, an elderly one called Sim and his two sons, but Thomas made it sound as though John would be responsible for everything, personally and single-handed, from grooming the horses to getting in the corn. He listened politely and nervously, reminding himself that someone must have been doing all this work before he came and that his grandfather was probably trying to scare him intentionally.

It was at the end of the lecture, when he was about to make his way out and begin his first day's labour for Whitmead, when at the kitchen door, at the far end of the hall, his grandmother appeared, neat and rounded, in a maroon gown and clean white headdress. Behind Thomas's back, she gave him a smile, and it was a smile of welcome.

In the succeeding days, he was often very grateful to his grandmother, Nicola. He knew her, of course. She came, just now and then, to see his mother, usually bringing a gift of food, and she had always taken an interest in him and had a kind word. Now, she was a secret source of encouragement in a life which proved astonishingly hard.

It wasn't that he was unaccustomed to hard work. But, as one of the Quensted shepherds, he had worked either alone or with his father or his father's colleagues and the operative word was *with*. He had been expected to know what he was doing and had then been allowed to get on with it and if he needed help, he just asked for it and no one thought any the worse of him. Michael Shore, the bailiff, was often about, making sure that no one made off with a dead lamb or more ewe's milk than their entitlement, but Master Shore wasn't a shepherd himself and at least didn't tell them how to do their jobs.

Thomas, on the other hand, hardly ever left his men alone. Whatever you were doing, whether it was ditching or ploughing or sowing or seeing to the horses which Whitmead now used for draught instead of oxen, Thomas was likely to appear behind you and tell you you were doing it all wrong. He would then demonstrate how to do it right, but in a rough, angry way which made it plain that he thought you were a fool. Sometimes he lost his temper and would then administer backhanders freely, his face dark with a fury quite out of proportion to the offence. It was almost as though, John thought, his grandfather used other people as substitutes for some hated enemy who was forever out of his reach.

At Quensted, at times when the sheep didn't need too much attention, the shepherds had to help with other tasks and John knew himself to be fairly competent at most of the things he was asked to do. He resented the continual criticism and the physical bullying, but he would remind himself that one day, one day, Whitmead was going to be his, and he would bite his tongue and say nothing. After all, he wouldn't have dared say anything at Quensted, and there he would have had no reward in view.

At midday, he ate in the kitchen at Whitmead and the food was certainly better than at home. But he could never take any good things back with him for his mother; Thomas had a watchful eye on everything that went on and made it clear, when he caught John trying to slip a cut of meat into a napkin, that no charity was to leave this house for the beehive hut. The clarification took the form not of one clout, but two.

But later that day, when John was in the courtyard picking out the feet of one of the stolid horses, Nicola came out to scatter grain for the hens and passed close to him. Into his hands she slipped a small, cloth-wrapped package. 'Just a little chicken pasty for your mother. Put it inside your shirt,' she said, low-voiced.

Since then, she had often covertly passed him edible gifts to take home and once, when Thomas had really lost his temper with his grandson over some task he considered skimped, and actually set about him with a broomhandle and a string of insults concerning John's base origins, Nicola waited until Thomas had gone off to plague the young Simson brothers, and called John in to bathe the places where the broomhandle had broken the skin.

'It's all right,' he said awkwardly. 'It's nothing much.'

'Yes, it is. I can see by the way you move that it hurts you to walk, and there's blood seeping through. Bathe it in these herbs, though, and it shouldn't fester.'

'I can put up with him hitting me,' said John suddenly. 'But he had no right to say those things about my father. He didn't know my father! At least Dad was good-natured. Why is Grandfather always so *angry*?'

'He was brought up hard,' said Nicola, 'And there've been hard things in his life since. He's as he is and it's best not to provoke him. I heard you shout back, defending your dad. That was right in a way, but if it happens again, just let it go.'

'Keep him sweet? You've had to do a lot of that,' said John thoughtfully.

'Don't worry about me,' said Nicola. She added, 'You're gentle, yourself. I've seen that, watching you with the horses. Don't ever change, John. Your grandfather can teach you a lot but don't let him teach you to be angry.'

She left him alone to bathe his abrasions but came back presently to remove the basin of water. 'I'll get rid of that. You get off to your work before he comes back.'

'Grandmother, is there any little thing I can do for you in return?'

'I can't think of anything,' said Nicola.

'Please. Let me know if you do.'

'Very well,' said his grandmother, laughing at him. But she did find a small task for him, and brought it to him the next day when he was mucking out the byre. 'If you want to do something for me, can you get this old silver medallion clean? I've tried and tried but I can't shift the tarnish. It's just an old thing but I'm fond of it.'

He took the medallion home and did his best. It was tarnished nearly black but he managed, after several evenings' work, to remove most of the dark deposit, exposing a pleasing if somewhat meaningless pattern made of curved lines arching like a bridge over wavy ones. He also worked hard to clean the silver chain on which the medallion was strung. When he returned it to his grandmother, she looked at it admiringly, and thanked him.

It was June and warm, and haymaking had begun. He worked in the hayfield all day, stripped to the waist, and was still carrying his jerkin over his arm when he came back to the house that evening to say goodnight to her as he usually did before going home. Nicola came out to meet him with the medallion dangling from her hand and to his surprise, put the chain over his head. She admired the effect of the shining silver disc against his sun-browned young skin and said, 'That looks well. You keep it. I said I was fond of it but . . . it reminds me of things, too, things I'd as soon leave behind.'

'But isn't it valuable? Where did you get it from?'

'Oh, an old woman – some sort of distant relative – gave it to me when I was a child. It was just a fancy of hers; she was fond of me because I used to take apples and butter and things to her. My mother used to send me. No, you take it; you can look after it. It'll just be neglected and get tarnished again if I keep it.'

'But . . . will my grandfather mind you giving it to me?'

'He doesn't even know it exists. I told you; I never wear it. It's just been lying in my chest, all these years.'

'All right. Thank you,' said John a little shyly.

He was touched by the gift, in a way that wouldn't go easily into words. It formed a new link between himself and his grandmother and seemed to bind him closer to Whitmead. He wore the medallion often and showed it proudly to Alison who said, 'My mother's always been kind. She'd have done more for us if she could. God alone knows what sort of life she's had with my father all these years.'

In the autumn, Thomas won the first word of praise he had ever had from his alarming grandfather and the first privilege.

'You've put your back into it, boy; I can't deny that. Want to go to Chelmsford with the Simson boys when they take the corn there to sell?'

Chapter Sixteen

The Hawk Rouses

The first time he helped to take the surplus grain to sell in Chelmsford, it was fun. Wilbert and Phil Simson, the two young Whitmead villeins, had been making the trip each autumn for years and knew exactly how to go about things. In their company, John tramped the roads beside the laden cart, climbing up every now and then for a ride on the load or on the back of one of the big plodding horses. They stayed at Chelmsford overnight, sleeping under the cart and sharing packed food, an ale flask and a singsong before they settled down to sleep.

It was not a particularly profitable expedition; for the first time, John learned that people like his grandfather, who held places such as Whitmead and appeared always to have enough to eat, still had their worries. Corn prices were depressed and the Simsons shook their heads about it. Thomas Whitmead would probably put the blame on them, they said, but they'd done their best and, of course, he had the upkeep of the place on his hands.

But profitable or not, it was an adventure and he looked forward to repeating it the following year.

But the following year, when it came, was different.

It had a different atmosphere from the start, for times were hard at home and, although Alison never said so, he knew that they were poorer than the year before. They both needed clothes and hadn't had them, and the food in the beehive hut was getting worse. He set off with the Simsons in a depressed state of mind, thinking, at first, that the trip would be a relief.

They arrived in the evening and took the corn to the market next day, and after that they joined a crowd streaming towards the main square, where there was supposed to be something worth seeing. And with that, John's exciting trip to town turned into a nightmare.

As his grandmother had said, he was a gentle boy and at Quensted, although life had often been hard in one sense, it had been sheltered in another. There had been things he hadn't known about, except by hearsay, and his father Wat Shepherd had always said of those tales, 'Awful to think about, that sort of thing. How anyone can take pleasure in watching, or even go out of their way to be there, I just can't think.' If a lambing ewe died, Wat would grieve afterwards as much because

277

of her suffering as because he had lost a valuable animal. He was a far kinder man than Thomas was, or, apparently, than most of the current population of Chelmsford.

John sat now in an almost empty alehouse, wishing he had never gone to Whitmead because then he would never have set foot in this hateful town, trying to swallow the ale without letting his stomach heave, trying not to think about the unbearable scene from which he had just, blindly, fled.

He hadn't been quite the only one to run away. He'd seen maybe two others forcing their way out of the crowd, and a couple of women hastening their children from the scene. But most people had just stood watching and some even shouted exultantly, or laughed. Some women, far from removing their children, had held them up for a better view, and a man close beside him . . . had come erect and rubbed himself and danced with pleasure while he spurted his seed through his hose on to the ground.

John Watson, sitting deliberately with his back to the street which was also empty because nearly everyone in the whole of bloody Chelmsford was apparently at that diabolical scene in the square, wished he could destroy his own memory at will.

'Found you!' said Wilbert Simson triumphantly, ducking in at the low door, his brother behind him. 'Been searching all over, we have. You can come out now. It's finished.'

'You stayed to watch,' said John accusingly.

'She was a witch and she'd made someone's cattle sicken and made her neighbour's child die. That's what happens to witches nowadays. They burn.' Phil sat down and made impatient gestures at the girl who served the ale.

'Cattle are always getting ill and children are always dying. Some of them even die after their mother's had an argument with the woman next door. Doesn't mean the woman next door did anything to the child. She was old and she was terrified and she was alone and . . .'

'It was interesting,' said Wilbert thoughtfully. He and Phil were both well into their twenties, but both had young, freckled faces with very round eyes. Just now, their eyes were even rounder than usual. They were not stupid but they had no imagination. 'It took so long, longer than I'd have thought. I didn't think it would smell like that, neither . . .'

'Look, lad,' said Phil, rising quickly, 'you can't throw up in here. Wilbert . . .!'

Between them, they hoisted John to his feet and steered him out into the street, which was empty no longer since the show in the square was over and people were now coming away from it. A drift of smoke followed them, blurring the cool, grey, late September sky and carrying a stench strong enough to make itself known even above the smell of horse droppings and rubbish which infested every town.

'What's wrong with him?' someone shouted, as Wilbert held John's head and John threw his last meal and the ale he had tried to drink into the gutter. 'Couldn't stand the sight back there? He wants to be careful. No good showing sympathy to the likes of her.'

'Piss off!' John yelled, and threw up again.

The passer-by laughed. He was festively dressed in red and yellow with plenty of dagging on sleeves and cape, but the materials were cheap and the dagging crude and some of it was accidental, the result of simple raggedness. He was also very thin. 'Pity you're wasting good food like that! There's some would have been glad of it! That witch woman ate well for years, on account of frightening her neighbours into giving her things to eat!'

He went on his way, still snorting with savage laughter and John, straightening himself gingerly, said, 'I'll kill the next person who mentions food to me. Or witchcraft.'

The relationship between the Simsons and John Watson was odd, because while they were villeins and he was now the master's heir, he was villein-born as they were, and they were his seniors in age and knowledge. On the Chelmsford trips, they considered themselves to be in charge of him. 'We'd better get you back to the cart,' said Wilbert, now. 'Got the corn money safe, have you?'

'You shouldn't have gone off alone like that,' Phil said. 'You could have been robbed.'

'There isn't that much to steal,' said John, accepting the change of subject thankfully. 'Prices are even worse than last year. My granddad won't be pleased,' he added gloomily.

'No, he won't,' Wilbert agreed. 'Though Whitmead's well off compared to some places. We won't go hungry. But my dad says nothing's been the same since the plague come, and it keeps breaking out again and setting things back. Bound to be hard to sell things when there's fewer people to buy and they've hardly any money because pay's so low. And this year, there was that damned poll tax.'

'It's daft,' John said as they set out to where they had left the cart, 'making laws saying that men can't be paid more for the work they do. Even William Astleigh thinks that. Corn and wool would fetch more then. My mother's heard him say so.'

Phil laughed. 'Your mother's got a gift for hearing things. *My* mother says if ever she wants to know what's happening anywhere in Whitmead or Quensted or Herneham, she asks Alison Shepherd.'

Wilbert said, 'What're all those people doing round our cart?'

As the Simsons had told John the previous year, they didn't get to Chelmsford often and, after finishing at the corn market, they never wanted to set off home at once. But before going for what they called a look-around, it was their custom to take the cart back to a patch of commonland on the outskirts of the town, where horses and oxen could graze, hobbled, on a stretch of good grass beside a small wood, and carts be left under the eyes of some urchins who earned a halfpenny from every client and were reasonably reliable.

279

They had done this before getting caught up in the people surging to the square. Now they discovered that, urchins notwithstanding, their cart was the centre of a large and interested crowd. John stopped short in alarm, automatically connecting rapt crowds with horrible sights. But Wilbert exclaimed, 'Someone's standing on it, making a speech,' and urged them forward.

'It's a friar!' said Phil. 'He's gone and picked our cart to preach from.'

John, as they caught up to the friar's audience and stopped once more, said 'It's Friar Ailred! But I haven't seen him for four years at least – he used to come to Quensted sometimes but then he stopped coming. I thought he was dead!'

'He don't look very dead,' said Phil, standing on tiptoe for a better view. 'Looks a bit old, but no worse.'

'Want to listen?' said Wilbert.

'We can't do much else,' John said. 'Can't turf a friar off his platform, even when it's our cart.'

Brother Ailred was just beginning his oration. He seemed very much as he had four years ago, except that his tall figure was a little skinnier than it had been then, so that his grey robe hung more loosely. But he had all his old charisma. '. . . my friends!' he was saying, in a voice which was still resonant despite his age. 'My brothers and sisters! It is with great joy that I find myself among you once again! I see that I am welcome! Have you missed me?'

'Yes!' cried a chorus of voices. A couple of dissenting shouts of 'No!' were heard on the edge of the crowd, from a couple of well-dressed burghers, and a group of men wearing the sheriff's badge on their plain and soldierly clothing, but their neighbours drowned them with shouts of, 'Garn!' and '*You* wouldn't!' and some jostling accompanied by histrionic exclamations of apology. 'Sorry, good sirs. Didn't see you just behind me . . . careful where you're putting your big feet, Dickon, lad, you stepped right on the gentleman's toe.'

Brother Ailred waved his arms for silence and obtained it, more or less. 'My friends, my good friends. This day in Chelmsford, we have witnessed a most grievous spectacle. We have seen a woman lose her life for the sin of destroying the lives and livelihoods of others through witchcraft!'

'Oh no,' muttered John. He looked round for a way of escape but the crowd had already closed in behind him.

A moment later, however, he realised with relief that Brother Ailred was not embarking on a defence of the horror in the square. 'It is not for me,' shouted the friar, 'to comment on the rights or wrongs of that execution. I never heard the evidence. But I know this. That it is easy, very easy, for men and women to be condemned for merely saying things that those above them do not want to hear!

'My friends, as a friar of the order of St Francis, I have at times kept pet beasts and birds. I once had a tame crow which would imitate the sounds other birds and animals made and could even croak a few words of human speech. But it didn't understand what it said. I fear that some of you mouth words at times which you do not understand! Witchcraft is heresy; I have heard those words said in the town this day. But how many of you know what heresy really is?

'A moment since, I asked if you had missed me. For I have been absent from you and all the other people up and down the land, who were accustomed to hear me preach, for four years. And do you know why?'

'No!' replied his audience obligingly.

'I was recalled to the headquarters of my order in Assisi and I too was accused of heresy. The laws of the continent are harsher than those of England. A man here may be imprisoned for heresy, but not burned, not yet. But in Italy, I was lucky to escape the flames.

'And why? What was it that I said or did that put me in such danger? Well, I hadn't ill-wished anyone's cattle or children. I hadn't ill-wished anyone or any creature. But I had criticised certain people, yes. Those who wear velvet and silk and sleeve tippets that trail to their very feet, and ride on fine horses while others go hungry, and still call themselves representatives of Christ, to be looked up to and obeyed; those men I had criticised, and publicly.'

At the back of the crowd, the burghers, who were both wearing much-dagged velvet cloaks and long tippets from the elbow, discreetly began to drift away. The sheriff's men also moved off, but more purposefully, glancing over their shoulders and consulting together as they went.

'I escaped,' cried Brother Ailred, 'because no one could gainsay me when I repeated that Christ was born in a stable and brought up by a carpenter and throughout His ministry was a man with neither home nor income nor position. But it was a narrow escape, very narrow. There were those who argued against me, with passion.

'However, here I am again though I was not allowed to set up my pitch in the town itself, I fear. But I take heart, for in these days, I have a new supporter. I am not the only man to have these ideas, and not the only man to preach them. In London at this moment is a great and educated doctor called John Wyclif. He is a scholar of the great University of Oxford and he has the protection of a mighty lord, son of our late and lamented King Edward the Third, uncle to our young King Richard the Second: John of Gaunt, no less . . .'

This produced a restless stir. Everyone knew the name of John of Gaunt; he was one of those controversial personalities who, despite the remoteness of royal status and enormous wealth, got themselves discussed round the hearthfire of even the meanest hut. John of Gaunt lived in sin with Katherine Swynford, the woman originally hired to instruct his lawful children. He had had a whole new family by Katherine. He had been embroiled in complicated quarrels with various ecclesiastics; he had backed up a newly appointed and very unpopular Marshal of England, Harry Percy.

The post of Marshal was purely military but Percy had tried to extend its authority in a hitherto unheard of fashion. The outraged Londoners considered that he should confine himself to controlling the army, and let civilian citizens be, and both John of Gaunt and Harry Percy had had to escape from a mob and flee south of the Thames to save their lives.

As if all this were not enough, since the Black Prince, the eldest son of Edward the Third, had died before his father, leaving his own young son as the heir, rumour had accused Gaunt of scheming to thrust his youthful nephew aside in order to become the heir himself.

The scheme had failed, if there had been such a scheme. King Edward was dead now and the ten-year-old Richard had been crowned on the 16th of July, only two and a half months ago. The citizens of London, too, had made their peace with both John of Gaunt and Harry Percy. But the shocked excitement engendered by so many scandalous rumours still lingered. If this John Wyclif were a pet of John of Gaunt, something was probably wrong with him.

Brother Ailred perfectly understood the murmur and grinned. 'Rumour does not always speak the truth, my friends, or at least not all of it. Great sinner though my lord of Gaunt may be, his nephew *has* become our new king, has he not? And in supporting the scholar Wyclif, Gaunt has again proved that in some ways his heart is in the right place. Few sinners, my friends, lack *any* redeeming features. Let me tell you what Wyclif has been preaching!

'He has been standing in pulpits in London and declaring what I have always declared: that all authority within the Church should be founded upon grace and goodness and that if priest or abbot, bishop or archbishop, abuse his property, cling to it greedily and add to it by snatching bread from the mouths of the hungry, then he should be deprived of his office and that the secular authorities have the right to take it from him. A worldly prelate, my friends, is a heretic. That is the true meaning of heresy; claiming to represent Christ while behaving like a worldly lord; claiming to be a shepherd and behaving like a wolf . . .!'

'You're a Lollard!' somebody shouted. Brother Ailred waved a hand in reply and let out a roar of laughter.

'Aye, you're right! That's what I am! That's what a Lollard is, my good friends! How many of you know the word? That is what they're calling us, those who believe in what Wyclif preaches and are teaching it to others in turn! It's a rude slang name: it comes from a Low Countries word that means a mumbler of prayers and from our own word lolling, which means lazing about! But I and those like me do not mumble – am I mumbling?'

'No!' shouted a chorus. One lone voice expressed the opinion that Brother Ailred, though certainly not mumbling, was bellowing a lot of dangerous and irreligious nonsense, that would end by wrecking society, but was shouted down.

'No, my friends! I do not mumble, neither do I laze! There is no time for idleness in this world! We have work to do, to put right the evils of our times . . .!'

282

'Break it up! Back to your homes! Come on, out of the way!' Shouts and scuffling broke out at the back of the crowd. The sheriff's men had come back with reinforcements. They were laying about them with staves and the flat of their swords and barking orders for the crowd to disperse. 'Get down off that cart, Friar! Get about your business if you don't want to be taken in for causing a disturbance and preaching bad doctrine!'

'This is my business!' shouted Brother Ailred superbly. Someone jumped up on to the cart and pulled at his elbow, speaking urgently into his ear. He was dragged down to safety.

John Watson and the Simsons began to push their way out of the gathering, avoiding the sheriff's men. 'Leave the cart awhile,' Wilbert muttered. 'Come on, in among the trees. We'll come out later, when it's all quiet again. Don't want anyone thinking we lent the cart or they'll think we're mixed up with the friar somehow.'

'He's right, though. Pity, while he was at it, he didn't say a few things about sheriffs and lords who snatch bread out people's mouths,' Phil said as they plunged into the shelter of the hazel brake which edged one side of the grass patch. 'They're as bad as any prelates and I don't see that not being in the Church is any excuse. The people they grab everything from feel hungry, just the same. William Astleigh's no saint and the folk at Herneham hardly know what a square meal is. At Herneham, the labourers don't even get a midday meal, except at harvest time.'

'There's no point in saying it,' said Wilbert. 'No point in all that preachifying either, if you ask me. Nothing's going to change.'

On their return to Whitmead, John left the Simsons to see to the cart and the horses, and went straight into the house to find his grandfather, carrying the corn money with him and wishing there were more of it. Thomas in shirtsleeves, since no one could do such work in a tunic with elbow tippets, even the small ones he preferred, was squatting on his heels in the middle of his hall, chisel in hand, carving a new stool. At the sight of his grandson, he put the chisel aside. 'So you're back. I thought I heard the cart come in. How did we do?'

John handed over the leather bag. Thomas tipped out the contents and counted them. 'You're not much good at haggling yet, are you? Prices seem to be worse than last year.'

'Yes . . . well, Grandfather, that's true. People can't afford to pay much. There was the poll tax . . .'

He stopped. He did not want to discuss the poll tax with Thomas. They had had one dispute on the subject already.

'Whole world's gone mad, these days,' Thomas grumbled. 'Good wheat not worth the effort of growing it, and still men come wanting wages more than the law allows. Unbelievable.'

To John's relief, he seemed only mildly annoyed, but his grandson still watched him with some disquiet. With Thomas, one could never be sure. He could become angry so quickly. John usually hesitated to question him, but after a moment, because of something inexplicably harried in Thomas's expression, he did so. 'Has something happened, Grandfather? Something else? I mean . . . I know this has been a difficult year for you.'

Thomas, frowning, was counting the corn money for the second time. 'Aye, it has. It's a great pity you couldn't do better than this because we needed a worthwhile profit on that corn. Something's happened, right enough. French pirates, that's what's happened. The news came two days back. They captured a ship called the *Guinevere* in the English Channel. She sailed in the spring and she was almost home. They didn't murder all the crew as it happened; three surrendered at swordpoint and they dumped them in a dinghy without any oars and set them adrift. By God's grace, they were picked up by another ship. They told the news. The Frenchmen stole the *Guinevere* and all her cargo. She had a fortune on board, in spices and silk and foreign silver. And I,' said Thomas, 'had shares in that voyage. I invested three hundred pounds in the *Guinevere*, so let that be a lesson to you. Never gamble on merchant ships unless the seas are clear.'

John stared at him. Thomas smiled grimly. 'Yes. Three hundred pounds. And I've lost every single last penny of it.'

'But . . .!' John was speechless. Three hundred pounds was a fortune.

'It's appalling,' Thomas said. 'Time was, we used to beat the French at war, but Crécy's a long way behind us now. Let's hope the new reign means a new wind blowing. We've been thrown out of Brittany and Gascony and you can't sail from Dover to Calais in safety now. That poll tax at the start of the year – no one liked it, boy; it was a nuisance to us all – was supposed to be to raise money for giving the French a lesson in manners but we've yet to see any results. I never went to Crécy,' said Thomas reminiscently. 'Didn't want to at the time but since then I've regretted it. I'd like to think I once put a shaft into a Frenchman. You'd better be getting home. I daresay your mother'll be waiting. Your baby brother's thriving, for a wonder, in that hovel that was all your father could ever provide for you.' And as he spoke of John's father, a sneer came automatically into his voice.

'Three hundred pounds,' said John jerkily. Words were rising up in him which he must not utter, let alone shout into his grandfather's face, but he wanted to shout them. A black rage, hitherto quite outside his experience, had seized hold of him and he wanted, indeed, to do much more than bellow insults at Thomas. He would have liked to strike or strangle him. His hands were trying to curl into fists. 'Don't let him teach you to be angry,' his grandmother had said. A vain hope. But he had discovered by now that it would be possible for Thomas, if he wished, to change his mind and will Whitmead to someone else. By inheriting it one day, John would have a chance, and probably it would be his only

284

chance, of improving life either for himself or for his mother. He must not give in to his rage.

It would be advisable, he thought, for him to do as Thomas said and go home at once.

Normally, he would have stayed to see his grandmother, who was probably in the kitchen, but this time he couldn't face her, although she would certainly have given him a bite to eat and perhaps slipped him something to take home. Thomas hadn't even asked if he were hungry after his journey. At Whitmead, John had a seat at the table for the noon meal and that was all. Not that he'd have accepted anything offered by Thomas now! If he stayed here for another moment, his fury would burst him apart. He bade his grandfather a curt farewell and departed, on foot as usual, making for home so lost in angry thought that he was nearly ridden down by a party of horsemen. At the last moment he became aware of hoofbeats behind him, and sprang aside. The party consisted of a woman in the midst of an armed escort. One of the escort yelled 'Stupid peasant!' at him as they passed and a contemptuous foot shot out and caught him on the shoulder, knocking him down.

The foot did not, however, belong to one of the mailed escort. It belonged to the woman. He knew who she was. Scrambling to his feet, John Watson stood by the roadside and scowled after the departing riders. Lady Ghislaine of Herneham, that's who she was, riding astride like a man, haughty nose in the air, though in fact she wasn't lady of the manor in her own right, since she had a grown son, although he rarely came to Essex.

John had never seen her close to before; for some reason his grandfather thought she was a person to keep away from and had brought his mother up to think the same. But he'd seen her from a distance and he recognised the red and silver livery of her men. It was her all right.

She did not come to Herneham much more frequently than her son. According to Thomas, they had greater lands in Norfolk and in Yorkshire. But she occasionally descended on the Essex manor to go through its accounts and reduce its steward and bailiff to a state of quivering nerves. Both of them were in fact reasonable men continually forced to act out of character by extracting excessive rents from luckless tenants and harrying villeins to perform customary services. They had large families living in houses owned by Lady Ghislaine and were as much at her mercy as anyone else. Thomas had been heard to say that he felt quite sorry for them.

John stood at the wayside, watching the riders vanish into the distance, rubbing his shoulder, and seething. That woman had never been hungry, never had to worry about where the cloth was coming from to make new clothes when her son grew out of the ones he was wearing. She had buried one husband, it was said, and then married a second one who had disappeared. Perhaps he had run away, thought John savagely. Perhaps that chilly profile had chilled him a little too much. Perhaps she had kicked him, too.

He strode on, more angry than ever. He was home in another ten minutes. And his home, when he came in sight of it, had never looked so squalid.

Having lived in it all his life, he had never really noticed it until he began going to Whitmead, and could observe the contrast, and even then, it hadn't actually hurt. Home was home and Whitmead was Whitmead, that was all.

But back in his grandfather's hall just now, listening while Thomas talked about the unimaginable sum of three hundred pounds, he had seen his home in his mind's eye and understood with absolute clarity not only what that contrast meant, but how unnecessary it was.

His mother was looking out for him, his small brother Walter perched on her hip. Despite Nicola's secretive gifts, Alison was still much too thin, and she had not bothered to put a headdress over her hair, which was plaited and bound up, but straggled out of its fastenings. 'You're back,' she said flatly. 'You've delivered the money to your grandfather? Did he . . . did he give you anything for your trouble this time?'

'No. I'm sorry.'

'Your grandmother didn't by any chance . . .?'

He shook his head. 'I didn't see her as it happens . . . what is it, Mother?' He put his arm round her and steered her into the hut. 'What's wrong?'

'Maybe you should have kept some of the money back,' said his mother. 'He owes you, seeing the amount of work you do. You've earned that freedom he bought you twice over by now.' Once back indoors, she gestured towards the firepit. 'There's a pottage cooking in the pot, and there's bread and some ewe's milk cheese, but that's all, and you must be hungry.' She sank down on a stool, holding Walter in her arms. 'We're that short, that's all. I'm worried we'll run out of flour. I just can't afford to get any more ground at Master Astleigh's mill, and you know what trouble I'll be in if I cheat the mill and grind my own and Master Shore catches me at it. He did once before and he let me get away with it that time – he's not so bad at heart – but he said himself, it'll be more than he dare do, to look the other way twice. He could lose his place and he's got his own family to think of . . . There isn't a halfpenny in the house. Ever since that poll tax . . . there's a rumour,' said Alison harshly, 'that there may be another, one of these days. And if there is, I just don't know what we'll do. I heard the rumour today. I've been keeping it from you, how short we were but I can't keep it back any more. If there's another tax, I just don't know how we'll pay! I can't manage even now.'

'Hush, Mother. It hasn't happened yet and perhaps it won't. Now don't worry about food. I'll make time to do some fishing; I'm allowed to do that and we can salt some down and . . .'

'If only your grandfather had helped us with the poll tax!' Alison's

286

voice was bitter. Walter woke and cried and she soothed him. She looked haggardly up at John. 'I begged your grandmother to try and get him to help; I never told you, but I did. And he wouldn't. She came over to see me next day and said he just shut his mouth like a trap and walked away from her and never even answered. Fourpence for each of us! It's more than a month's worth of that miserable pittance he gives you!'

'And I never told *you*,' said John, 'that when it was announced, I asked him myself for help and he said no, he hadn't any spare money. I believed him, *then*.'

'He's got spare money all right,' said Alison, not taking in the significance of that emphatic *then*. 'I know that one day you'll have Whitmead but that's no help now. We'd have that much more flour in the crock and a couple of decent mutton hams hanging up, if he'd just put his hand in his money-chest that once. I tell you, there are times when I'd like to *kill* your granddad. I'll never forget him sitting there and making it clear that all you'd get from him till he died would be villein's pay . . . If it wasn't that Whitmead ought to be yours by right and I want you to have it . . . well, that's why I left it to you to decide. I couldn't stand in your way, but I say again, I'd have liked to kill him, that day, and I'd like to now.'

'I know. So would I,' said John. 'He's complaining because a ship's been lost that he put money into.'

'Money?' said Alison. 'A ship? He's been hazarding money on the seas while we're . . .?'

Mother and son looked at each other in mutual anger, out of the selfsame dark eyes. 'Three hundred pounds he ventured on it,' John said. 'He told me. The poll tax was before the ship sailed, from what he said. He still had all the money then, that he invested in it. He could have paid the tax for both of us and never noticed it and he wouldn't spare us *one* bloody fourpence!'

'But you have to go back,' Alison said, over the pottage. 'You must, John. Go back tomorrow as though nothing's happened and well, just *pretend* nothing's happened. It's our only hope. You never know; he may treat you better as you get older, give you more money or something.' She shook her head. 'It's not pretty, waiting for him to die. But that's what we are doing, I suppose. Well, stick to him and it'll all be worthwhile in the end. John, we're depending on you, me and Walter. My father's never said he means to do anything for Walter. I reckon he thinks that if you get Whitmead one day, then you can look after your brother and me. So you've got to get Whitmead; it's up to you. Just forget about the poll tax and so on. We'll manage, and very likely you're right; there won't be another.'

John was still angry but his innate good humour was reasserting itself. 'Oh, all right. I'll turn up tomorrow as usual and I'll keep the old skinflint happy instead of throwing him in the trough. Times may improve,' he said.

                    *   *   *

But they did not, and within two years, the rumoured second poll tax
came. Less was asked from poorer households this time, however, and
John and Alison, grimly determined never to seek a favour from Thomas
again, paid it somehow.

But at the end of 1380, there came a third.

Since the day when Thomas had said, grudgingly, that she might visit
Alison sometimes, Nicola had never quite given up hope that one day
he would soften a little further still. More than once, though it had taken
all her courage, she had nerved herself to make cautious appeals on
Alison's behalf. All had met with angry rejection but still, she tried once
again.

'They *can't* pay a whole shilling each. And there is an instruction that
the rich should help the poor. Compared to them, we're rich, and we're
Alison's parents!'

'I don't call myself rich,' said Thomas, 'and Alison's no daughter of
mine. Don't you know that yet?'

'But there's John . . .'

'I've bought his freedom. What more does he want?'

As ever, his aggression frightened her off. She fell silent. John and
Alison themselves did not ask. They were not alone in their anxiety, and
there were other ways out.

Master Elias Westbrook, Tax Commissioner in the employ of Simon
Sudbury, Archbishop of Canterbury and Chancellor of the Exchequer,
hitched his cloak hood more firmly over his ears to protect them from
the biting wind, decided that February was of all months the coldest and
filthiest for travelling, and gave the lazy nag he was riding a resentful kick.

He'd bought Whitenose in haste when his elderly piebald Jester died
in the midst of a journey, and Whitenose was a mistake. He was young
and sturdy but possessed of an obstinate mind of his own and he didn't
like hurrying. Herluin, the senior man-at-arms of the four who were
accompanying Elias, said that Whitenose's mealy-coloured muzzle
probably meant that his sire was one of the semi-wild ponies which
roamed the moors in the west of England. 'The stallions often get at saddle
mares turned out to graze. Those ponies are more obstinate than mules.'

At the moment, Elias could have done without Whitenose's
waywardness. He was in haste. Wrathful haste, at that.

His father, a freeman farmer with a few acres of land and an elder son
to inherit it, had done what he could for his younger boy. He'd sent Elias
to school and it had been the schoolmaster who, when Elias was fourteen,
had by some means or other coaxed or wangled a lowly position for him
in the employ of the See of Canterbury.

He wasn't in orders and had no desire to take them but there were still
career openings there for an able and willing layman and Elias had set
out to exploit them. He had a good knowledge of Latin and he wrote

an elegant hand and he could use an abacus rather well. In fact, he had the uncommon ability to visualise one in his head and thus work out the answer to arithmetical problems without resorting to physical aids.

Elias, put to serve in the See's accounting office, had sharpened quills, set out parchments, replenished sandboxes, taken dictation on letters to do with financial matters, and when figures were quoted in the letters and totals were required, he had shown signs of being able to provide the answer faster without an abacus than his superiors could with one.

This had annoyed some of them but attracted the attention of others. He obtained first one promotion and then another. He saved his salary, bought land and let it, bought a house which he did not let and installed a wife there, carefully chosen for her good health and good dowry. He had a family growing up satisfactorily in Hertfordshire. When his master Simon Sudbury became Chancellor as well as Archbishop, Elias had found himself in the Exchequer, had become a Revenue Collector for the Herneham and Quensted district of Essex, and then received this commission to go personally and collect overdue taxes in that area. If he did well, he had the prospect of at least one more promotion before he retired. He had done it all by working hard, never, never being complacent and never, never letting anyone get the better of him.

Which was why he was furious now. There were, at present, a number of people trying very hard to get the better of him and he wasn't going to stand for it.

Of course, it wasn't surprising. There had been any amount of grumbling even over that first poll tax back in 1377, though it was a mystery to him why these stupid peasants couldn't see that everyone's standard of living would drop if the French were allowed to go on attacking English vessels at sea, terrorising merchants and shutting off trade with Gascony, and that a successful renewal of the war was going to cost money.

The second tax, in 1379, hadn't been much more popular although no one could say that the government hadn't tried to be fair and graduate it so that wealthy men paid more. When the plans for this latest tax were announced; one shilling a head on everyone over the age of fifteen, with no relief for the poor except for a vague, pious hope that the rich would help them, well, anyone but a fool would have known that there'd be trouble. He'd realised it at once.

Even so, he hadn't foreseen the extent of it. Because, all right, there'd been government mismanagement and military disasters but once a situation was there, it was there. It was hard on people but when a government had to borrow five thousand pounds from the city and sell off some of young King Richard's crown jewels, it was obvious that a tax of some sort was bound to be levied. One would expect at least a few people to have the sense to realise it. Instead of which . . .

The first time round, in 1377, they had set about the business of collecting the tax by taking a census. The same census, updated, had been employed in 1379. The population seemed to have shrunk rather surprisingly, considering that there had been no dramatic outbreaks of the plague for nearly ten years, but still, people did die, and there were plenty of things for them to die of.

But when, three months ago, he and his fellow revenue collectors began trying to call in the third poll tax on the basis of those earlier records, one third of the population had apparently vanished since the original census.

Which was why he was riding round Essex in February, to deal with what seemed evasion on a grand scale, hoping to win preferment through his efforts but beginning to fear that unless he were very determined, he'd be more likely to end up facing a reprimand.

He had started by holding a sitting in the hall of Herneham manor and summoning witnesses from all over the district which he had to cover, which included the neighbouring Quensted estate and a number of separate holdings scattered round about.

His principal witnesses had been William Astleigh from Quensted, the chief officials of Herneham – since Lady Ghislaine and her son Sir Stephen were both absent then – and various other freemen, or yeomen as they were now commonly called, who had standing in the locality; the substantial and responsible group who acted as constables or jurors.

And what had happened?

Granted, William Astleigh had been outwardly co-operative, handing over the rolls on which he kept details of rents and services owed and by whom, which gave quite a good picture of the Quensted population.

But the Herneham officials, Laurence Dubois the steward and James Att Brigg the bailiff, had been shifty and evasive beyond belief and said that they couldn't produce the manor rent-rolls because somehow or other, these had been mislaid. Manor rent-rolls were *never* mislaid; it simply didn't happen. But that was their story, and they refused to budge from it.

And even Astleigh's records hadn't been straightforward, because Astleigh's own bailiff, a man called Michael Shore, had challenged them, saying that they were out of date, that this or that person had died or gone away. And Astleigh had just said oh, well, no one's been through the rolls in detail for well over a year now. And then, a number of the yeoman witnesses had spoken up in support of Michael Shore.

The yeoman witnesses were infuriating. It wasn't that they were ignorant. Many had been to the wars; others had been on pilgrimage to Rome and some had been to school, even to school in London! But all of a sudden, these worthy individuals who a year ago had been keen-eyed and articulate, with accents only moderately local, had developed dialects which verged on the incomprehensible and such gormless expressions that you automatically looked for the straw sticking out of the sides of their mouths.

One in particular, Thomas Whitmead, who, although unlettered, had seemed last year to be prompt and law-abiding, a man who understood the need for taxation, was behaving like the stupidest villein and didn't seem to know how many people worked on Whitmead.

In a vague, argumentative fashion, with much calling on one another for corroboration, these maddening folk had given Elias to understand that scores of young men had gone off to join the army ('Well, it's these here wars, like. All the lads want to do their bit.'); that young women had been wooed and wedded by swains from far distant parishes in such numbers that the abduction of the Sabine women by the Romans now looked by comparison like an unambitious project; that mortal diseases had raged through the district; that lethal carelessness with scythes and bad-tempered bulls had reached epidemic proportions. And that William Astleigh, being a busy man and accustomed to delegate, just didn't know the half of what was going on. And when that was said, Astleigh didn't contradict it.

But if you looked for the graves of these hordes of dead, you couldn't find them, and on the rare occasions when anyone named the distant parish to which some young bride had gone, a cross-check with the said parish revealed no trace of her. A colleague of Elias, one John Bampton, who was currently chasing unpaid taxes in the neighbouring district of Brentwood, reported a precisely similar state of affairs. He had the villages of Fobbing and Corringham within his area, together with a third village to the south-west, called Stanford-le-Hope, and never, he said indignantly, when encountering Elias by chance on the boundary between their two districts, in his whole life, had he come across such sly intransigence, such a lack of respect for authority or position.

It was possible, Elias thought, that Bampton had created some of his own difficulties. His commission was an interruption in his normal life as the steward of some great lord or other and he set too much store by show. The hard-up villagers had probably taken offence at the sight of his fine horse and his magnificent clothes, and the number of armed men who rode with him were more like a small army than a normal mounted escort.

But even he, Elias, who had tried to avoid such conflict by adopting quiet manners and dress, couldn't claim to be doing much better. He knew well enough what he was dealing with. The instruction that the rich should help the poor had missed its mark. Rich men didn't like parting with taxes any more than their peasantry did and, as a result, the landlords and their tenants were virtually conspiring to tell lies which would keep down the amount they must pay between them.

Well, he'd settled Herneham, because Lady Ghislaine had been a welcome breath of honesty and virtue. Her son Sir Stephen was actually Herneham's lord, but when Elias sent after him, the messenger, trying their Norfolk estate first, found that Sir Stephen was away in Yorkshire but that his mother was willing to come on his behalf and come she had, swooping on Herneham the very next day. She had produced the missing rolls, threatened her steward and her bailiff with dismissal and eviction if they ever misbehaved in such a way again, and fined them then and there 'as an example and a warning'.

But the highly proper attitude of Lady Ghislaine only served to highlight the improper attitudes of practically everyone else. Elias was now doubly convinced that the information he had been given about Quensted mainly consisted of lies.

He wasn't standing for it, and the only thing to do, he had decided, was to carry out checks in person. He must accompany his men and see for himself; never mind the time it took and never mind the weather. He caught sight of Quensted village at last, kicked Whitenose again and decided that it was time to give up trying to be quiet and not provoke people, too.

Dusk was coming on. At this hour, most folk would be indoors. Well, well, what a surprise! Girls who had married and gone to Suffolk or Kent; boys who had run off to be soldiers, folk of all ages and both sexes who were said to be in their graves: he'd catch them all scraping their boots and having their suppers. Hah!

Michael Shore, the Quensted bailiff, was the half-brother of Laurence Dubois, the steward at Herneham. Shore was a hard man who regarded his master's interests as his own, at the expense of the peasants if need be. But just now, William Astleigh's interests and those of his peasantry were unusually close together. Astleigh had said as much. 'If I have to help out all these villeins of mine, I'll go bankrupt. If not this time then next time and there'll *be* a next time, that's certain. And more villeins by then, no doubt. They breed like mice. Do something about it, Shore!'

He had complied and, therefore, when Laurence arrived from Herneham, riding headlong across country to say that Elias was on his way to Quensted to conduct a personal survey, Michael Shore took action. From house to house through the village, the word was spread. 'If you're supposed not to be here any more, hide quickly.'

John Watson – he preferred the name Watson to being called Whitmead – did not hear the news until Elias was already in sight, and had no time to escape to the misty marsh pastures or the nearby woods. When the jingle of bridles was heard outside, he was lying in the rear room under his mother's pallet. His own had been hurriedly stuffed into a lidded barrel.

According to the solemn oath of Michael Shore and the two other Quensted shepherds, he, John Watson, was dead. Under the pallet, he tried to lie as motionless as though it were true.

The horsemen he could now hear dismounting were not necessarily coming to this house. Likely, they'd pick out a few dwellings at random and they might miss his. No. Footsteps were coming in at the door. He froze, trying to reduce even his breathing to a minimum.

In the bigger room at the front, his mother, Alison, was cooking the usual evening stew. He heard men's voices speaking to her, in a hectoring manner. Her voice, which was clearer than theirs and closer to the doorway between, came plainly to him.

'My son died two years back, that is, if it's John you're wanting. He's the only one that ever got to be older than fifteen. Walter's not six yet. Oh, what are you *doing* here? I've only got Walter, now, I tell you!' Alison sounded convincingly distressed and exasperated.

Fear could sound much the same.

A man's voice, on a loud note of command, said, 'Search the place!'

To be forced to be passive while in danger was difficult. One's body thrummed with the desire to run or fight. A wrinkle in the edge of the pallet gave him a worm's eye view of a booted foot, six inches away. There were thumps and rustlings. Then triumphant exclamations. They had opened the chest which held the family clothes and discovered a young man's garments there. His mother, who had followed them in, was saying, 'I couldn't stand to throw them away. He was my son. Haven't any of you got sons?'

'You're lying, woman. There's nearly fresh mud on this cotehardie.' The man's voice was immediately above him. 'Look, green grass blades caught in it. Someone wore this yesterday.'

'I lend things sometimes! Nearly everyone in this village is short of clothes!'

'You're lying, I say! The fellow's hiding! Where is he?'

'In his grave!'

'And where's the grave? We've looked in the churchyard.'

'He died away from home, in Chelmsford; he . . . let go! Let go . . .!' Alison's voice broke off in a shriek. There was the sound of a blow.

'*Where is your son?* We'll have the truth out of you sooner or later; you may as well tell it now!'

There came the sound of another blow and his mother cried out again. John threw the pallet off, leapt up and flung himself on the mail-clad man who had hold of Alison. Two more, who had been ransacking the chest, instantly turned and caught his arms.

'Leave my mother alone!' shouted John.

'Ah,' said the plainly dressed man who was standing to one side, dispassionately watching, 'There you are. Right under our noses, too. You are John Watson, I take it?'

'Who are *you?*'

'Elias Westbrook, Tax Commissioner. You're in trouble, my friend. All right, Herluin; bring him along.'

Alison cried, 'No!' and tried to break free but she was hustled aside as he was manhandled through the outer room and into the road.

Outside, standing in an interested semicircle round the door, were Michael Shore, Laurence Dubois, and about a score of the other inhabitants of Quensted, including his two fellow shepherds, both

293

carrying their crooks, the blacksmith with an immense hammer and various other men, grasping staves.

'What's all this?' demanded Elias.

The horses were tethered on the other side of the track, in a clump of trees. Michael and his companions were in the way. The faces of Elias and his men became wary.

'Nothing to worry about,' said Michael. John blinked at him. Before Christmas, the bailiff had come round the village telling people that as far as the tax returns were concerned, they were welcome to have left the area or died, but he had made it clear, somehow, that this was because William Astleigh wanted it so. He was still Astleigh's henchman. But now, although his hard face, with its straight brows and mouth and cold grey eyes, looked the same as ever, Michael had suddenly become a man of Quensted, as his father had been. 'We just want everything to be peaceful and good-natured,' he said evenly. 'And we don't want any of our folk dragged away like criminals.'

'This man *is* a criminal. He has tried to evade the poll tax,' said Elias.

'We can't pay it! We haven't enough to buy food!' Alison, had run out after them. She was in tears and her face was bruised. Blood oozed from a graze on her cheekbone.

Elias, ignoring her, spoke sharply to his men. 'Take him to the horses and tie his wrists to someone's stirrup.'

'I think not,' said Michael. The semicircle closed in. The two men-at-arms who had hold of John stiffened and the others reached for their swords, but shepherds' crooks instantly darted out, hooked themselves round the mailed forearms and jerked. The swords flew up and were torn from their owners' grasp.

Then John was thrown roughly aside as his captors abandoned him in favour of reaching for their own weapons. Another crook lunged, a stave cracked against flesh and bone; there was a sudden, brief scuffle and a lot of swearing and then the four men-at-arms and Elias were in a disarmed huddle, while the blacksmith stood in front of them casually swinging his hammer to and fro, and there were four swords in the hands of the villagers. One of the men-at-arms was cradling a damaged hand.

John had been helped up by Alison. He put his arm round her. 'I'm all right,' he said. 'Better than you are. Your poor face.'

'You're outnumbered,' said Michael to Elias. 'You'd better leave. All right, let them pass to their horses. Stand back!'

'This,' said Elias, 'is an outrage. You realise that this won't be the end of it? I may have to leave now, but I shall be back, and with reinforcements.'

'We'll worry about that when it happens,' said Michael. 'Maybe we'll have reinforcements too.'

'The men of Herneham are in the same mood; you'd better be warned, Master Commissioner,' said Laurence. 'And we've been hearing news from other places.'

'That's right,' said the blacksmith. 'My brother-in-law in Fobbing says they're not too pleased with the commissioner that's been harassing them there, either.'

Elias' small, somewhat expressionless features were stained red with anger but there was no help for it. He snapped 'Come!' and strode forward, followed by his men. Someone put out a foot and he stumbled over it, almost falling, whereupon a stave cracked against his rear.

'That's right!' Suddenly John let out a shout. His mother's injured face had made him angry, as he had been in his grandfather's hall when he heard about that three hundred pounds. For the first time it occurred to him that he, who in the presence of his grandfather, and indeed of anyone with authority, always felt like a mouse before a hawk, might have hawk-like characteristics of his own. 'Give them something to remember!' he yelled.

He let go of Alison and ran forward and suddenly, Elias and his escort were sprinting headlong for their horses, with all the villagers shouting at their heels. John snatched a stave from someone, caught up with Elias just as he was untying the knot in his frightened mount's reins, and gave him another hefty crack.

Elias squealed and scrambled into the saddle and tried to kick his horse into an speedy departure but the animal, apparently blaming its rider for all the disturbance, laid back its ears and bucked. Elias fell forward, stomach arched over the high pommel and hands clutching at the wiry mane in front of him. He cursed the horse at the top of his voice.

The men-at-arms, quicker at emergency mounting than their master, were already up and fleeing. Elias shouted imprecations at them, too.

He got his steed going at last and departed in pursuit of his men; in very slow pursuit, clinging frantically on because the horse was still much more inclined to bounce up and down than to go in a straight line. Elias stayed in the saddle probably because he dared not topple out of it. John, running alongside, kept up for some distance and landed several more wallops on Elias's person before the horse finally broke into a canter and outpaced him.

He had been infuriated, shouting insults as he ran and walloped. But suddenly, as he fell back, he found himself laughing. The commissioner, trying to make his mount stop bucking, clutching at its mane, shouting curses at it and his escort, and yelping whenever the stave landed on him, heading, one hoped, for the career setback of a lifetime, was a very funny spectacle.

That was how it began. John Watson remembered that afterwards. With laughter and absurdity; with farce.

Chapter Seventeen
The Hawk Flies

The next event at Quensted took place nine weeks later, when the blacksmith's brother-in-law arrived from Fobbing, accompanied by half a dozen of his fellow-villagers and also, unexpectedly, by an elderly Franciscan friar, no other than Brother Ailred.

They announced that the tax commissioner covering their area, John Bampton, had been chased away and that a Chief Justice called Robert Belknap had come in his stead 'and set up shop in Brentwood'. He had then proceeded to inquire into everyone's behaviour and had threatened to try, imprison and fine to starvation point virtually every adult soul in Brentwood, Fobbing, Corringham and Stanford-le-Hope.

'Except that we've seen him off too,' said the smith's brother-in-law, with a roar of laughter. He was a tanner, hands and arms stained dark brown from oak-gall tannin, in startling contrast to his round red face, which explained his nickname, which was Redbrown. His baptismal name was John but he preferred not to be known as that. There were thousands of men called John, he said, but only one Redbrown.

'We were all thinking,' he told the impromptu meeting which had assembled on the green in the middle of Quensted, 'that we'd have to run for it or hide ourselves in the woods like outlaws till he'd gone, but then we had a better idea. We all packed the court out, blocked the doorways and when I give the signal, we rose up, grabbed Sir Robert and his pack of clerks, pushed a bible under his nose and told him he'd better swear on it to go away and never take on such an inquiry again, and that if he wouldn't swear, we'd slit his gullet for him.

'Funniest sight I ever saw,' said one of the other Fobbing men happily. 'All the clerks with big round eyes like pennies and Sir Robert opening and shutting his mouth like a fish in a stagnant pond. The armed escort were outside; they didn't know a thing. We made it clear we'd finish off anyone who as much as squeaked for help.'

'Did he swear?' cried a chorus of voices, led by Michael Shore. Most of Quensted, male and female, was in the gathering, and someone from the Fobbing party had, on the recommendation of Redbrown, who knew the district, peeled off to Herneham and reappeared with Laurence Dubois, James Att Brigg and four of the villeins, all young unmarried men whose chances of being able to afford marriage were getting slimmer every year and who resented it.

'Oh aye, he swore all right,' said Redbrown. 'Swore the oath and then a good few curses along with it. He's off to London again with his tail between his legs but there's no time to lose. It'll be more armed men next time, Gaunt's lads and Sudbury's men if we're not careful. That's what the friar here says; ain't that right, Friar Ailred? He came over the river from Kent, got to us just after we'd got rid of Belknap.'

'That is so!' Friar Ailred was now very skinny indeed and his height had diminished. He had a fragile, withered-leaf look and although his companions had all come marching on foot, they had perched him on a jennet. 'He can't walk so far, 'tisn't reasonable, at his age,' one of them had explained.

But his spirit gleamed through his frailty like a sword in a transparent sheath. 'The men of Kent are up and they have a leader who is calling on men from other counties to join him in a march on London to demand that the King hears our complaint against Simon Sudbury and his lawyers. Sudbury has oppressed the people and tried to silence priests like myself. A good man, a travelling priest called John Ball, is in Simon Sudbury's jail for doing no more than say that the likes of you have as much right to eat as Sudbury has.'

'That's right! It's got to stop,' the blacksmith said. 'Lawyers in dusty rooms, dreaming up taxes fit to break men's backs; poor folk harried and made into criminals just because they're too poor to pay; commissioners and justices swaggering about the land, prating of the law and behaving like bullies . . .'

'Great lords like Gaunt, spending other folks' money and then saying, oh dear, we can't afford the war on what we've got, quick, let's have a few more taxes!' That was one of the Quensted shepherds.

'Gaunt's not so bad,' said Friar Ailred. 'At least he protected the thinker Wyclif . . .'

'We don't need a Wyclif to tell us we're being treated unjustly. We don't need a Wyclif to tell us that men like this Belknap ought to be ashamed of themselves!' Michael Shore spoke vigorously. 'And John of Gaunt has an income of more than sixty thousand pounds a year. I've heard William Astleigh say so. A man like Gaunt can't even imagine what a shilling means to the likes of us.'

'Well, never mind that now. Just now, we've all got to move as quick as we can,' said the friar energetically. 'Fobbing, Corringham and Stanford-le-Hope are already on the march to Gravesend where they'll cross to Kent. Men are coming from Brentwood; people who have kinsfolk over the county border in Hertfordshire have sent word to them . . .'

'Anyone here got kinfolk at a distance? Chelmsford? Over in Suffolk? If so, send for them. Have you understood, all of you? This is serious.' Redbrown's sentences came out like punches from a fist. 'It's rise or

297

go under. It's march and demand justice or be dragged off by the justices. It's fight or die in a prison or a ditch! *Do you understand?* There aren't any other choices!'

'And before you set out,' added another of the Fobbing men, 'get rid of the records these ten-times-damned lawyers have been using to snatch our money. They look at the rent-rolls to see how many folk there are in a village or on a manor! March on the manorhouses and burn the rolls! Do that first!'

'Oh, here now,' someone demurred. 'William Astleigh's all right in his way. He didn't let us down with the commissioner.'

'Only did it to please himself!' shouted someone else. 'He didn't want anyone asking him to pay up for us! And if it had come to the point he'd have said no, anyhow!'

John Watson had met the Fobbing men while on his daily journey to Whitmead. He was not sure if he should turn back with them; his grandfather would surely not approve. Then he remembered his mother's bruised face. Now he was here beside her.

'That's right!' he shouted. 'He'd have made us find the money and we all know it!'

'Yes! It's true!' Alison was holding Walter's hand. Now she picked him up and held him over her head. 'Look at my little boy! He's skin and bone as it is!'

'But Astleigh stood by us in his way.' Michael Shore was still partly Astleigh's man. It didn't extend beyond his own employer, however. 'But Herneham's rent-rolls ought to burn! The lady of Herneham didn't stand by anyone! Laurence'll tell you! Let's make a start with Herneham!'

John Watson never afterwards had a clear memory of how it came about. Redbrown and Brother Ailred and their companions seemed to sweep in like a great wave and bear them all away on a crest of excitement.

He had only a dim recollection of hurrying his mother and Walter home, thrusting a knife through his belt and snatching some money out of the coffer where they saved coins for the taxes, putting some clothes and small belongings in a bundle, asking Alison for some bread and bacon, wrapping them in cloth and putting them into the bundle too.

He remembered kissing his mother, who, though she had taken a vociferous part in the meeting, was now frightened and tearful. She understood the plans that were afoot and was horrified by them.

'March on Herneham! Go to London and hand the King a petition! You can't do things like that! They're dangerous!'

He said he'd be back soon, that nearly all the men in Quensted were joining in and he couldn't be left behind. The idea of attacking a manorhouse and calling on the King actually seemed fairly incredible to him too, but that was what Brother Ailred said they were going to do, and he was an educated man and full of years; he must know what was what.

'You mustn't go! You'll never come back!' Alison cried as John went out of the door. But he joined the other men back on the green and when they set off, with Brother Ailred leading the way on his jennet, flanked by Michael Shore, and Laurence Dubois and James Att Brigg, it didn't feel dangerous at all.

It was exhilarating, swinging along in the May sunshine with his friends. Others joined them as they went, coming in from outlying farmsteads. Phil and Wilbert Simson, who had not been scooped up when the Fobbing men passed Whitmead but had somehow learned what was happening, suddenly appeared, armed with scythes. No, they hadn't asked Thomas Whitmead's consent. 'Catch him giving it! Oh aye, he tried to get us off the poll tax, but only in case someone dunned *him* for it,' they said, their view of Thomas clearly much the same as John's opinion of Astleigh. 'He'd have said: you stop here and behave yourselves and work! So we didn't ask him.'

And that, of course, was the source of the exhilaration. No one had asked permission to be here. They were breaking rules, flexing muscles in their minds. It made you want to sing.

Then somebody started a song and the rest took it up. It gave a rhythm to the march. It was glorious.

Before they reached the manorhouse itself, they came upon the fence of the Herneham sheep-run.

This unpopular innovation was only three years old and had been erected on Lady Ghislaine's orders. It took a huge bite out of the commonland and encircled a piece of excellent grazing which the Herneham sheep now had all to themselves. There was no need for a discussion. It was a plain wooden fence, with a gate where the track to the house passed through. They opened the gate wide and attacked the fence on either side with whatever weapons they had.

Everyone had brought something and some were well supplied. Several had bows and shafts and a few, who had been to war in France, had swords and good daggers. But even those who had none of these things still had knives and choppers, hammers, scythes, sickles, billhooks, crooks and staves.

The fence was down for fifty yards on either side of the gate and alarmed sheep were already escaping on to the common before the leaders cried, 'Enough!' and marshalled them all forward again. They marched on, past a beech spinney, to the house. It was encircled by a wall and, unusually for the middle of the day, the gate was shut fast. Someone, clearly, had seen them coming. They hammered on it and kicked it and then Brother Ailred shouted and they gathered round his jennet. He told them what to do.

John found himself back at the beech spinney, helping to cut down a tree. As soon as it crashed, men were swarming all over it, lopping its branches. With so many at the task, it seemed to be done at magical speed. They strode back to the gatehouse equipped with a battering ram.

They were greeted by a volley of arrows. Those with bows at once shot back, hoping to discourage the enemy while the battering ram got to work but the first blood was drawn at the gate of Herneham. At one moment, Wilbert Simson was heaving at the ram and shouting 'Hah!' with the others every time it struck the gate; the next, he had let go, and with a look of amazement on his face, was plucking at the shaft sticking out of his chest.

Then he made a choking noise and blood came out of his mouth and he collapsed. There was a roar of fury. More shafts were loosed in retaliation, and the gatehouse arrow slits were pelted with stones. The ram was carried backwards for a new and harder run at the gate. Its double leaves groaned and buckled and burst apart. They poured into the courtyard. The mood of exhilaration was gone. Now, they were angry.

Michael Shore had once accompanied William Astleigh to war. 'Those arrows – there's no more than six archers in there! I can tell!' he shouted. A dozen men instantly pounded into the gatehouse, which had archways on the inner side, but no doors. They emerged, dragging what proved to be only five archers. Their bows and shafts had been confiscated. Michael looked at Laurence Dubois, who after all was Herneham's steward. Laurence hesitated.

Then James Att Brigg, the bailiff, barked. 'It's join us or you die, here and now!' and after that there was no more to be said. With five frightened conscripts in their midst, they surged across the courtyard, through another archway, across a width of greensward and up the steps to the door of the hall.

John was up with the leaders. He was trying not to think about Wilbert; after all, this was war; this was what it was like. Phil, beside him, wasn't crying or wanting to stay beside Wilbert's body; Phil, on the contrary, was bellowing war-cries and flourishing a scythe.

The hall door was not barred. Whoever was inside must have decided that it was more dignified to let the uninvited guests enter than to wait for them to break in. They jostled and shoved their way, unopposed, into a hall of very gracious proportions, bigger than the Quensted one which John saw on manor court days and sometimes at Christmas, and much, much bigger than his grandfather's hall at Whitmead.

The door was halfway along one side of it. At the left-hand end was another door through which some alarmed kitchen-hands were peering. At the right-hand end was a hearth in which a small fire burned and, beside the hearth, turned so as to face towards the invaders, was a settle, On this, with an arm along the back of it, her knees crossed under a skirt of blue and tawny, and one foot ominously swinging, was the Lady Ghislaine.

Two scared-looking girls stood behind the settle, and four men-at-arms, with their hands on their swordhilts were grouped close by, ready to defend the ladies.

'Laurence,' said Michael, halting in the middle of the hall but speaking loudly enough to be heard all over it, 'you know where the rent-rolls are. Fetch them.'

'They're upstairs.' Laurence pointed to an archway close to Ghislaine. A spiral stair could be seen beyond it. 'They're kept in a bedchamber.'

The Lady Ghislaine said, also in a voice pitched to carry, 'May I know the reason for this outrageous intrusion?'

Someone snapped that she'd just heard it. But Brother Ailred raised a hand for silence and stepped forward. 'We are here to destroy the rent-rolls which have been for too long used as a means of oppressing your tenants and assisting those who burden them with intolerable taxes, contrary alike to the laws of justice and Christianity. Is that answer enough?'

'No, it is not!' Lady Ghislaine's chilly gaze had now identified familiar faces in the crowd in front of her. 'Laurence Dubois! James Att Brig! My steward; my bailiff! How dare you come into my hall in this fashion?'

Laurence seemed unable to answer but James Att Brigg said resolutely, 'We dare because right is on our side, as the good friar here says. And we want those rent-rolls.'

Lady Ghislaine gave him and Laurence a look of blistering scorn and said something to the four guards. They drew their swords and moved into position in front of the arch.

Behind the leaders, more of the crowd had entered the hall. They were roaming round it, talking noisily, whistling at Lady Ghislaine's girls, fingering tapestries and panelling. Some were talking persuasively to the kitchen-hands. Michael, Laurence, James and Brother Ailred conferred rapidly and then Ailred shouted for silence again and Michael called three names and an order. Three men with bent bows stepped out of the throng and positioned themselves with shafts pointing at the guards.

'You are not wearing mail. We can shoot you before you get near any of us with those swords,' Michael said. 'Throw the swords this way.'

'Keep your swords in your hands!' Lady Ghislaine, furious, stood up. 'They will not shoot! They are villeins. and they wouldn't dare. They won't put ropes round their own necks, never fear. Guard that door!'

'Laurence,' said Michael Shore. 'James.' They came to his side and the three of them walked steadily towards the guards, taking a path which would not interfere with the flight of the archers' arrows.

'Throw down those swords!' called Ailred. 'Or . . .'

'*Deal with them*!' Lady Ghislaine's harsh voice broke in.

None of the guards moved. The swords were wavering in their hands. Brother Ailred snapped another order and an arrow whistled through the air to bounce off the top of the arch behind them.

'That was not a miss,' said James. 'It was meant to land there. The next one will land in somebody's guts.'

The men-at-arms, as Michael had said, were not wearing mail. They had only padded jackets. One of them said 'My lady, fighting is one thing but suicide's another,' and then muttered something to the others. It was evidently an order. The four swords were flung across the floor and eager hands picked them up. The guards moved back and Michael, with his brother and James behind him, vanished up the stairs. Lady Ghislaine shouted 'Cravens!' at the guards but could not interfere, for she had been surrounded.

'No harm will come to you,' said Brother Ailred, standing in front of her. 'Or you.' He glanced at the horrified girls who were still standing being the settle. 'But we have come to carry out a certain task and we intend to do so.'

'You! A friar, a man of God!'

'Of the Christian God, my lady. Is it in accordance with the teachings of Christ that poor men should have their last farthings snatched from them by lords who wouldn't notice the loss of ten thousand farthings?'

There was a short and simmering pause. Lady Ghislaine's gaze darted this way and that, as if seeking supporters. There were none to be seen. The crowd was everywhere in the hall now. Someone asked one of the girls for a kiss and was pushed off with a sob of disgust.

'Here, come on now, pretty; Hal Piggott of Fobbing might smell a bit but he's a nice fellow when you get to know him.'

'Leave her be!' Redbrown strode forward, frowning, and pulled Piggott away. 'We've no quarrel with the wenches.'

'I ain't quarrelling with her. I asked for a kiss, that's all!'

'You're frightening her. Redbrown's quite right; let her be!' ordered Ailred. The scruffy individual called Hal Piggott withdrew, muttering.

John was close to Lady Ghislaine. It was interesting. So this was what she looked like when one had a chance to see her properly. He never had before. He'd only been close to her once in his life hitherto, and you couldn't take in much about someone who had just kicked you flat while cantering past on a horse.

She was middle-aged, of course; she must be nearly fifty. But she'd be handsome still if only the expression on her face and in her blue eyes were not so hard. Her skin was well-kept despite the lines between her brow and round her mouth, her eyebrows were meticulously plucked and he was near enough to know that she smelt of rosewater. When young, she must have been beautiful.

'We've got them! Here!' Michael, Laurence and James bounded down the stairs, waving the parchment rent-rolls over their heads. A delighted roar went up. 'Out of our way!' shouted Michael. 'Let's put some fuel on that poor little fire.'

'Laurence Dubois! James Att Brigg! Have you lost your senses? What are you doing? Give me those scrolls!'

302

The Lady Ghislaine, elbowing and pushing, skirts swishing, broke out of the crowd encircling her and caught at Michael Shore's arm as he was about to hurl the first parchment roll on to the fire. He shook her off and John, leaping after her, snatched her away.

'No, my lady. Stop.'

The rolls were going into the flames and renewed yells and cheers broke out as they caught. Flame and smoke and bits of blackened parchment went whirling up the chimney. Lady Ghislaine let out a shriek of rage, twisted in John's grip and tried to rake his face with her nails.

It was partly the memory of that kick and partly the deplorable example of Hal Piggott, and perhaps the smell of the rosewater had something to do with it too. At any rate, before he could stop himself, John had grinned, and put his arms round the infuriated Ghislaine and kissed her with enthusiasm, while others whooped encouragement, and in the hearth the rent-rolls merrily burned on.

'When Adam delved and Eve span, who was then the gentleman?' thundered the tall priest, ending the inflammatory sermon he had just preached from a vantage-point on one of the wagons the insurgents had brought from Kent to Blackheath. A roar of applause went up as he finished. John Watson threw back his head and shouted, 'Death to Simon Sudbury!'

And when they'd found Simon Sudbury, Archbishop of Canterbury and Chancellor of the Exchequer, and put his head on the end of a pike, they'd have tall, lean, egalitarian John Ball for archbishop instead.

From where he stood, wedged between Ailred and Michael Shore in the midst of the crowd, thousands strong, gathered on the heath in the scorching sun, John Watson regarded his namesake John Ball as proudly as though he had invented him. When they had freed Ball from the Canterbury dungeon where Sudbury had imprisoned him for preaching on the theme of equality and the unchristian nature of lordship, and carried him out on the shoulders of four men, John had been one of the four.

The John Watson who had said farewell to his mother and set out from Quensted had been a hot-headed boy full of grievance and a fierce excitement in which laughter and fighting were nearly the same thing. And somewhere inside him, too, had been an impressionable boy, who could still be intimidated by a grandfather's frown.

Today, at Blackheath, just south-east of the place at Greenwich where the Thames looped southwards, and only five miles south-east of London Bridge, he felt himself to be a man and a seasoned campaigner.

The cheers, which had been subsiding, were renewed as their leader, the Kentishman Wat Tyler, climbed up on to the wagon beside John Ball. He threw up his hands for silence and silence immediately fell. Tyler was that kind of man. His second-in-command, Jack Straw, was twice his size and much more striking to look at, with his beak of a nose and his wild ginger hair. But when Tyler and Straw appeared side by side, all eyes went to Tyler at once although outwardly he was much less remarkable. He was a stockily built man in his thirties with a very ordinary Kentish face; blue-grey eyes in sockets which were long rather than round, and cheekbones slanting on a line which led straight to the point where the shapely, slightly pointed ears were attached and was then repeated in the slant of the upper earlobe. Hundreds of Kentish folk had features like that. And yet . . .

It wasn't only Jack Straw who shrank in contrast to him. When the marchers from Quensted and Herneham had met Tyler and his men outside Canterbury, their leaders, Brother Ailred and Michael Shore, Laurence Dubois and Redbrown and James Att Brigg, suddenly dwindled. From then on, they were just fellow-marchers or, at most, lieutenants transmitting Tyler's orders.

He took his name from his trade, John had learned. Before the rising began he had made earthenware floor tiles for a living. But he had been to France and learned the arts of war there. He had commanded soldiers. He knew how to run a campaign, how to organise men into groups under leaders through whom he could issue commands, how to galvanise his followers into marching seventy miles, from Canterbury to London, in two days, how to estimate what supplies would be needed and arrange their purchase or requisition (even when they emptied their foe Simon Sudbury's stores in Canterbury, Tyler insisted that this was requisition and not looting, of which he disapproved), and how to insist that wagonloads be brought along on the march.

Yet many men had been to war. Michael Shore had. Many men had the same knowledge and experience as Wat Tyler. The extra thing that he possessed could not be learned. It must have been born in him.

He was now addressing them, explaining tomorrow's plans. They were to march on London. They had a petition for King Richard. He listed its points. The marchers had acquired new objectives since the march began and the petition was now astonishing in its scope. Now, it demanded not only an end to poll taxes but an end to villeinage too, and the execution of those the marchers considered their enemies.

'We have sent a request for King Richard to meet us face to face. Unfortunately, he has not yet appeared.' Tyler flashed a grin at them. 'Perhaps he finds our numbers alarming. He is only a lad of fourteen after all.'

But they dared not wait, said Tyler. Their numbers were too many; the supplies wouldn't last. Tomorrow they would enter London and themselves set about righting their numerous wrongs. There were official records there, concerning the poll tax, which would be best destroyed, and Sudbury was there, and his treasurer Sir Robert Hales, and a whole pack of corrupt lawyers whom they would deal with as traitors if they caught them.

John of Gaunt, the Duke of Lancaster, was unluckily not in London.

Somehow, John of Gaunt had become a target too. 'He has wickedly oppressed the Londoners and is the greatest of the lords behind the miseries that afflict us. He has a palace in London; burn it if you will. But as in Canterbury, my friends, there is to be no looting, no insult offered to decent men and women. We are honest men with a grievance, not common thieves. God have mercy on any man I catch out in dishonesty!'

It was to be another Canterbury, John thought joyfully. The onslaught on Canterbury had been so thrilling that on the hard march to London he'd surmounted aching legs and an empty belly by reliving it.

With Wat Tyler at their head, they had marched right into the cathedral in the middle of Mass in search of Simon Sudbury. 'But he's in London!' gasped the priest, who had been about to elevate the Host when the cathedral door was flung open.

'Then we shall follow him there,' said Tyler grimly. 'Sudbury is a traitor, and we mean to have his head.'

Then he had divided them into squads and sent them to the soldiers' quarters and the stores, to requisition food and utensils and tents, and to open up the Archbishop's prison.

Sudbury had left few of his soldiers behind; too few to challenge such numbers. Some, in any case, sympathised. It was a soldier, not under duress but of his own free will, who showed them where the prison was.

There, in a dank underground cell, they had found John Ball. As they carried him out, they had passed a group of scared-looking monks, and Redbrown had called to them that they need not bother to elect another Archbishop when Sudbury was dead; John Ball was elected already.

The townsfolk, on the whole, were on their side. There was very little resistance in Canterbury, but a good deal of rejoicing instead: bonfires and dancing, and women running from their houses to set up tables in the street and put food upon them. It had been *wonderful*.

There had, of course, been a few patches of opposition and some fighting in the streets as well as feasting, and a number of people named as Sudbury's aides and therefore the enemies of the rising had been seized and executed. John Watson had missed all that. The new John that he had become was much tougher than the boy who had thrown up in the street in Chelmsford, and he regretted missing it. But he had already understood that in a major campaign any one man saw only a small part of it, and now he would have a second chance to be in the forefront of the action.

Brother Ailred said suddenly, 'Thank God Gaunt *isn't* in London.' John turned to him in astonishment and Michael Shore said, 'Well, Gaunt might thank God, but why should we? He's one of the enemy! We want him!'

'You don't understand,' said the friar. He had ridden his jennet all the way from Essex, but the journey had wearied him. He was more frail than ever and his spirit was no longer shining. In the space of a few days, his eyes had become watery and his hands had developed a constant tremor. 'It's going to go wrong,' he said.

'What is? What do you mean?' demanded Michael.

'This whole thing. It's too big, we're asking too much.' The friar sounded desperately unhappy. 'For thirty, forty years, I've preached that it's wrong for a few to take all and leave so little for the rest and I saw no sin in it when the rest rose up and decided to take what was theirs. I still see sin in it. But it isn't going to work. The King isn't going to meet us and that's where we'll fail. He's above all the other lords, you see. If he sees our cause is right, he can order the others to heed us, to stop oppressing us, to give men their freedom. He can make it *law*. But without him . . . we'll take the city, oh yes,' said the friar. 'But then the great men will come and take *us*. Wait and see.'

'Oh, do be quiet,' said Michael impatiently, and added, with a snort of exasperated laughter: 'Jeremiah!'

They had been lucky with the weather. Tyler and Straw had seen to it that tents and oxhides which could be fastened together to make shelters of a sort, had been stacked in the wagons but there were nothing like enough to accommodate the host which had camped on Blackheath. Mercifully, in the warm June night it didn't matter. John Watson spent the night, as indeed he had spent several since he left home, lying out of doors with a cloak wrapped round him and his bundle under his head, watching the stars wheel across the sky, until he fell asleep.

The next day, Thursday, the 13th of June, dawned bright. The skies were clear and there was a dazzling patina on the Thames as they marched beside it towards London Bridge. Their numbers were swelling every moment. There were many poor dwellings here on the south bank and everyone who lived in this tangle of noisome lanes was a potential supporter.

True, not all the houses were poor; a few were of respectable size and there were inns and some strongholds of power. That morning, some of the marchers had already broken open a prison and let the inmates out, and others, who had bypassed the prison and gone on ahead to Archbishop Sudbury's palace at Lambeth had just come marching back, singing and shouting, to announce that they had forced an entrance and made a bonfire of all the parchments they could find 'and that means the Exchequer records!' some knowledgeable wight declared.

John Watson was marching behind Michael Shore and James Att Brigg and beside Phil Simson. 'That's London Bridge, ain't it?' Phil said suddenly. 'It's a bridge, anyhow, and we're making for it. I'm glad to see this day!'

Since they left Herneham, where his brother was killed, Phil Simson had spoken very little. But there was a grim sense of purpose about him. John had lost sight of him in Canterbury but when they fell into each other's company again on the road to London, Phil's clothes had been bloodstained and not, it seemed, with his own blood, for he was patently not hurt. 'The King's scared silly,' Phil added now, with satisfaction.

This was true. King Richard had been sighted that morning, leaving the Tower by barge, going eastward towards Greenwich and the rebel camp as if to meet them after all. But the barge had turned back and it looked as though the King, or at least his advisers, had been alarmed by the sight of so huge a gathering.

Redbrown, who was marching behind John, remarked warningly, 'If the King's in a panic, the bridge may be held. Likely, we'll have to fight our way across. Better be ready.'

But there was no obstruction at London Bridge. They marched boldly across, the timbers shaking under their tread. The people in the houses on the bridge were leaning out of their overhanging upper windows and shouting encouragement. Folk issued from every doorway, eager to join in, men and women alike. On the far side, a huge crowd of Londoners were waiting to welcome the arrivals with further yells and cheers.

It was a colossal, pulsating mass of people and events and sheer feeling. He had hardly been alive before, John thought in amazement. Going to Whitmead, plodding behind a plough, sowing and scything, getting up each dawn to meet another day of familiar tasks and familiar faces, with Chelmsford as an annual excitement, he had never been stretched or fulfilled. It was a small-scale life with no power in it, no means of influencing anything or anyone.

Now, he was joined to a body, a unity, which had already influenced the greatest in the land into a state of fear. And although each individual in it was just one part, like a finger or toe, through each individual surged the power, the unbelievable power, of the whole.

Ahead of them, was an outbreak of new noise. For a moment, unable to see beyond those immediately in front, he thought it was an attack but then the word came back. 'The Londoners know their way round! They'll guide us! *John of Gaunt's palace . . .!*'

They marched on behind their new guides. London was incredible; there was so much of it and it was so full and everyone in it seemed to be shouting at once. Crowds poured down sidestreets to join in and there was a smell of smoke in the air. Phil Simson was still beside him although he had lost sight of all other familiar faces. The way broadened into a wide thoroughfare and the crowd, spreading out, broke into a run. They raced downhill. As they reached the foot of the slope, a squad of armed men burst out on them.

There was a scrimmage. But at the end of it, all the assailants were dead, left to lie in the road, while the whooping mob raced on, and the pike Phil carried was stained red at its tip and so was the blade of the dagger John had requisitioned in Canterbury. They held pike and dagger in the air like trophies as they ran.

It's going to go wrong, Brother Ailred had said, and this morning he had not set out with them. He was quite mistaken. Nothing and no one could stand against them now.

The attack had separated this part of the crowd from those who were making for John of Gaunt's palace. But it didn't matter. There were plenty of targets. He and Phil shortly found themselves in what seemed to be the wine cellar of a big house. Someone said it belonged to a bishop – 'not Sudbury, some other bishop, but what's the difference, they're all the same, the fat, grasping sods!' – and with that proceeded to broach a barrel, using a battered steel helmet as a cup.

Amid riotous confusion, John helped to hoist barrels up into the daylight of the kitchen above and search out bowls or goblets to drink from. The kitchen servants were nowhere to be seen. Some time later, his palate tingling from the first good wine he had ever tasted, the world spinning round his head and a feeling in his guts as though he were so happy and fierce and powerful all at once, that in a moment he might burst or grow wings and fly, he bounded back into the street with his companions. The whirling sky was stained with smoke and somewhere close at hand, a building was ablaze. The street was full of a shoving, noisy horde, all heading in the same direction and the hubbub was like a solid wall of sound.

Phil hit him in the ribs with an elbow. 'This way! Come on! They've found Gaunt's palace! They're sacking it!'

Once, even if sent on legitimate business, he would have been afraid to pass through a gateway so imposing but now he shouldered in regardless. There was a courtyard, enormous, a quarter acre at least. Then another gateway and some noble stone steps and then they were in a great hall which had magnificent proportions and up to a short time ago, magnificent furnishings.

Now, however, a busy mob of Londoners and countrymen were tearing down the hangings, hurling the silver plate on to the floor and stamping on it, ripping up the stuffed, embroidered cushions. Gaunt could back up all the scholars, such as Wyclif, that he liked. But he'd also backed up Harry Percy and his bullies, and prevalent opinion said he'd backed Sudbury and his poll tax and the swaggering justices who'd tried to enforce it, and now he was going to pay.

In the midst of it all was Wat Tyler, hands on hips, bawling instructions. 'Everything that'll burn, on a pile in the middle! Everything that won't goes in the river! The river gate's that way! No looting, do you hear? *No looting!*'

From somewhere or other, Redbrown and the Quensted blacksmith had materialised. They led the way up a flight of spiral steps to the floor above. Excitedly, they stormed through a series of fine bedchambers, tearing coverlets and curtains from the beds, throwing open jewel boxes and coffers, dragging splendid clothes out of chests. John of Gaunt, it seemed, maintained a full wardrobe in all his houses and thus kept his luggage under control when he moved. Some of the clothes made John and his companions gasp. Fashions were growing steadily more extreme but such long-toed shoes and serpentine liripipes, such extravagant sleeves and elaborate dagging, they had never seen.

Shouts from below and the smell of smoke brought them rushing down again with their prizes, to find a fire already burning merrily in the middle of the hall. They flung the combustibles on to it and then ran out with the things that would not burn, on to the river landing stage. Boxes and coffers, shining streams of gems and coins, went splashing into the water. They ran back into the smoke-filled hall, and found barrels being rolled across it, and Tyler, now standing on the only table not so far chopped to pieces, shouting new instructions.

'We've found gunpowder! Clear out! Everybody out! We're going to set the place alight and blow it to oblivion! Open up those barrels!'

Not long after, John, breathless and with the unaccustomed wine churning in his stomach, was outside in the road, hemmed in by the crowd, watching smoke and flame pour from the palace and the gatehouse. Everyone was coughing and soot-smeared and the waves of heat were enough, John thought, trying to edge back, to singe his eyebrows even at this distance. A violent explosion inside the gatehouse lit up its windows with a white flare and flames shot out of the roof. It collapsed, revealing, beyond it, the fire-filled shell of the house itself. There was another explosion and the shell too fell inwards. Cheers broke out and shoulders were thumped by delighted fists.

Then John heard someone screaming.

The screams were coming towards him, from behind. He was thrust aside and a crowd of men came through, making towards the fire. In their midst was Redbrown, struggling and shrieking and behind them, chivvying them onwards like a sheepdog, was Wat Tyler.

As he came, he shouted explanations. 'We're not thieves; we're here in the name of truth and justice! This man was found counting stolen silver! I said no looting! A looter's rubbish same as Gaunt's tapestries! He can go where the tapestries went!'

Once he had fled from a scene not unlike this at Chelmsford. Now, hemmed in by a crowd far greater, he was not allowed to flee. And in some ways, after all, he had not changed, or toughened, in the least.

'What's wrong with him? Too much wine?'

'The man who was . . . was . . . caught stealing was a friend of his,' said Phil. He was holding John's head while John, one hand supported on a wall, went through a dreary repetition of the scene in Chelmsford. At the sound of Tyler's voice, he tried to control the spasms and stand up straight. 'It's all right, Phil. I'm all right.' For some reason, Phil's face was frightened.

He looked at Tyler. Wat Tyler's personality was such that most people never noticed what he was wearing, but he was in fact dressed in a curious mixture of old chainmail and dashingly dagged everyday clothes in green and mulberry. All of it was now filthy.

Tyler regarded him with a degree of contempt. 'You're sorry for him?'

'Yes!'

'He was a thief.'

'It didn't warrant . . . *that!*'

'It did. It betrayed our whole cause and all we stand for. Were you a friend of his too?' Tyler inquired of Phil.

'Yes, sir.' Phil sounded very scared indeed.

'I hope you're more honest than he was. Well, look after your sick pal here. What he wants is a nice girl to stop him having nightmares tonight. But make sure she's willing. I won't allow rape, either, except of bishops' doxies.'

He strode away. John leant on the wall again. 'Oh God, oh God! I'll never forget, never . . . oh, what's that noise, what's happening now?'

'It's trumpets,' said Phil. 'Listen!'

'*Oyez! Oyez!*'

'Someone's announcing something.' John raised his head and swallowed. 'Well, let them.'

'No! We must find out what it is. Besides, you need something else to think about. Come on!'

John was reluctant, but Phil dragged him relentlessly towards the sound. Its source proved to be a man in alderman's robes, flanked by two heralds with trumpets, standing at a crossroads and reading in a stentorian voice from a parchment scroll.

Brother Ailred had certainly been mistaken.

King Richard had not failed them after all. King Richard the Second had ordered that all men between the ages of fifteen and sixty should on pain of life and limb be in the fields of Mile End, east of the city, on the morrow, Friday at seven of the clock, to meet him.

310

Chapter Eighteen

Stooping to the Prey

Someone was hitting him steadily over the head with a hammer and his mouth was full of sand. John Watson opened unwilling eyes and instantly closed them again. The assault of the light was too much. He snuggled his nose against the warm, sweet body at his side and tried to return to oblivion.

A vaguely familiar voice above him said, 'John! Wake up! We've got to get to this Mile End place.'

He opened his eyes for the second time and as the world flooded in, with the sunlight through the open casement and the noises and smells from the narrow street outside, he understood where he was. He was lying on a lumpy pallet in a crowded upper room in the brothel to which Phil had brought him last night, and all around him, on various other pallets and piles of straw and in various states of semi-consciousness, were the inmates and the night's final batch of clients.

His head throbbed and his thirst was unbearable and with wakefulness had come a surge of memories he didn't want. But beneath it all was something different, the delighted gratitude of a body which had never loved a girl before and had been hungry without knowing it, and was now fed.

He would rather remember the details of last night than of yesterday, but these remained blurred, and clearly he wasn't going to be allowed time to think about them. A couple of girls, only half-clad, both with wild hair and faces in which experience had overwritten youthfulness like ugly charcoal scribbles on sheets of smooth vellum, stumbled past, almost falling over his feet, and Phil was standing impatiently over him.

'Come *on*, John, look lively! I said, what about meeting the King? Bet you're thirsty, ain't you? All that bad wine we had here last night and then the exercise you've had since.' Phil's face and clothing were still smeared with the soot of John of Gaunt's burning palace and he looked almost villainous. 'Here's some ale, have a drink.'

'Ugh!' said John.

'Go on!' Phil thrust a beaker at him. You need something and I don't recommend the water. There's some in a pail over there but I think someone's pissed in it.'

John gulped the ale and felt slightly better. 'All right, just let me get myself up.'

'Well, hurry up. We ought to be moving.'

Phil moved away. And John turned to look at his companion of the night. Now that he had had a clear view of some of the others, he had to brace himself to face her.

She was half-covered by a thin and grimy coverlet, and she was watching him, propped on one elbow. She had brown hair and wide brown eyes and a triangular face and what she most resembled was a heartsease flower or a kitten. She smiled at him. 'You'll be off, then. Sounds very grand; going to Mile End to see the King!'

'I can't remember much about last night. I can scarcely even remember arriving here. Did . . . I suppose we . . .?'

The kitten-eyes sparkled. '*I* can remember. We had a nice time.'

He was suddenly aware of his nakedness and hers. And now he began to remember the night: the warmth and excitement, the caresses of small, knowledgeable hands; his own uncertain fumblings, which had changed suddenly into certainty and vigour as some male instinct in him awoke and took control. And the exultant moment when his whole body became charged with molten gold. 'Yes,' he said. 'We did!'

She was enchanting, magical. He didn't want to go to Mile End; he wanted to put his arms round her and repeat the nice time in a state of full consciousness. The contrast between her and the two girls who had just stumbled past his feet was startling. 'What's your name?' he asked.

'Joanna. What's yours?'

'John. John Watson. Joanna, what are you doing here, how did you come to be . . .?'

'Oh, that.' The sparkle died out and the little face looked older at once. The first scribbles of untimely experience were there, after all, although they were only just beginning. 'You don't want to know about that.'

'Yes, I do.'

Joanna looked doubtful. 'Madam tells us never to bother clients with chatter about ourselves.'

'This client wants you to chatter about yourself.' He drank some more of the ale and found that he was gradually feeling less ill. The recollections of the night were good, but those of yesterday he most decidedly wished to keep at bay. Joanna's voice, which was soft and a little husky, was helping.

'All right.' Joanna sat up, hugging her coverlet-draped knees. 'But there ain't much to it. I was born two streets from here. My dad works at what he can. Unloads ships or lugs sand and stones about when anything's being built or whatever. There was nine after me, and by the time the last one got born – well, three or so died pretty small but we was still bursting out of our rooms. Two rooms we had, neither as big as this. And we was hungry and getting hungrier and our clothes was nearly falling off us. We never had no shoes.' She pushed the coverlet

312

aside and waggled a small foot at him, displaying the horny sole. 'Well, I was old enough by then so my mam sold me.'

'She *what?*'

'I don't blame her,' said Joanna defensively. 'She'd got the rest to feed and Madam paid her pretty well. We get clothes and shoes here and enough to eat and if a client slips us an extra present we generally keep it. Well, Madam'd have it off us if she knew, but we don't tell her and she don't inquire too much. I'm saving. Might open my own house one day. So there you are. Story of my life.'

'I'd like you to have an extra present today.' John put the beaker down on the floor. He was distressed, and all the more so because this child – she couldn't be much more than that – with the innocent face, seemed to think her history commonplace. She had no animus either against her parents or against the Madam who had bought her like a pound of meat. Such things did not go on in Quensted. 'I *must* give you something extra,' he said, and then stopped.

'What's wrong?'

'I've hardly any money! I can't even pay your Madam for . . .'

Joanna laughed. 'She don't let you in for nothing, not Madam. You paid when you come in, don't you remember? Leastways, that friend of yours that was here just now did.'

Phil was on the other side of the room, sitting on the edge of a pallet and doing up his shoe-thongs. He caught John's eye, observed that John was still stripped and made a get-a-move-on gesture. John found his clothes, which had been half-pushed under the pallet. He dressed rapidly, said 'Wait,' to Joanna, and went across to Phil.

'Did you pay for us to come in? My girl says you did.'

'Yes. Why?' said Phil in a curiously wary voice.

'What's the matter? Look, I've only got a few farthings left of what I brought from home. I just wondered, could you lend me something? I want to give my girl a present.'

'Good, was she? Tyler was right; that's what you needed. But as for money . . .' Phil shook his head. 'I've only a farthing or two left myself.'

'Well, I'll just have to . . . all I've got's a silver medallion in my bundle. It was a present from my grandmother and I don't want to give it away but I'll have to. It really is silver, so she can sell it. I can't think how you came to have enough to get us in here. You can't have set out with much and we've bought food and that on the way. Phil! You didn't . . . I mean . . . you . . . you didn't do what Redbrown . . .?'

'No, I didn't,' said Phil, and suddenly stopped looking villainous and went scarlet from the chin to the hairline of his essentially uncomplicated and bucolic face.

'Dear God, you did! Well, I won't tell anyone; don't be a fool! After yesterday? Look, I'll pay you back if only you can lend me one penny!'

Phil hesitated. 'Well, there really isn't much left. Not after getting us

313

into this place and buying Madam's wine as well. But to save your keepsake . . . all right, here you are.'

Phil, after all, had not only farthings left, but quite a number of pennies. John went back to Joanna and handed her three silver pence, no doubt the legal property of John of Gaunt. 'Take this and add it to your savings.'

'Coo!' said Joanna, spreading the coins out on her palm and staring at them. 'That's a lot!'

'I wish it were much more. You oughtn't to be in a place like this.'

'Silly. There's worse places. But thank you kindly,' said Joanna, and gave him such a smile that if Phil hadn't come up behind him and pulled at his elbow, he would have stayed, and taken out his threepence worth in love.

'What was all that about her savings?' Phil asked as they made their way down the rickety wooden staircase.

'She's putting money aside. She wants to be a Madam too. I suppose it's the only future she can hope for; girls like that don't marry, do they?'

'Most of them don't live long,' said Phil.

'How do you know so much about it?'

'There's a place Wilbert and me used to go to in Chelmsford sometimes. We never took you. Your grandfather told us once that we weren't to. We learned this and that. Mostly they die young. They get diseased in the end or else a client beats them up once too often. Come back in five years' time and your girl'll either be dead or unrecognisable.'

'Is that true?' It was unbearable to think of the little kitten-face bruised by a fist or sunken with disease; of the life going out of the soft brown eyes.

'Course it's true.' Phil wasn't interested. 'Come on. Seven o'clock, we've got to be there by and it's a mile outside the city, somebody told me.'

'Mile End? How do we know which way to go?'

'Just follow the crowd, I suppose,' said Phil, as they emerged into the street. It was full of people, all walking fast and in the same direction. 'Can't see us getting lost, among all these. Can you?'

In the Mile End fields, where the oxen which had been grazing there wandered uneasily about on the edge of the crowd, they came across Brother Ailred. He tried to smile at them, but despite the King's promise to come, he still seemed tired and unhappy. 'We haven't won yet. Don't think it,' he said.

Wat Tyler, a tireless organiser as ever, had somehow marshalled the great crowd into a rough semicircle facing towards the distant walls of the city. Neither Phil nor John really wanted to be near him but they were foiled by the fact that, for some reason, Tyler seemed to expect Ailred to be at hand. They were only yards from Tyler when the shout went up that the King was approaching. They looked towards the city and saw a small knot of horsemen riding out from it.

Leading them was someone on a white horse. The sunlight was flashing from the steel spears and helms of the knights in the troop behind him, but it flashed more brilliantly still from a circlet on the leader's brow. Presently, they saw that this was of gold, and that his clothes were red and purple and that the surcingle and reins of the white horse were of scalloped crimson leather. 'That's the King!' said someone breathlessly. And then in shocked tones, 'Christ, he's just a boy!'

They had known that beforehand, of course. Everyone knew that King Richard the Second was only fourteen. But knowing it was one thing and actually seeing this slight, fair-haired lad, whose adult height and breadth were still well in the future and whose young face had never known a razor, was something different. John stared at him in wonder and a man just behind him said in a London accent, 'He's brave, coming out to face us like this. We was besieging him in his Tower only yesterday. Was you there?'

'No. We were at Gaunt's palace.'

'Ah. I heard about that. Must have been fun. At least you got in. We didn't get into the Tower. Sudbury's there,' said the Londoner hungrily.

The riders were nearly up to where Tyler waited. Tyler knelt. There was a hesitant moment and then everyone who was close enough to meet the King's eyes, knelt too. The horsemen reined in. The young King Richard the Second, for what was probably the first time in his life, surveyed at close quarters the untitled, unhonoured folk who were the bulk of his subjects and the foundation of his power.

He must be nervous, thought John, studying the King from where he was kneeling, and secretly marvelling because he had never expected, ever, to be close enough to the King of England to see the colour of the royal eyelashes, which were dark gold.

Richard had ridden out here with only this small escort, presumably so as not to alarm or antagonise those he had come to meet, but what, wondered John, do we look like to him? They were all of them dirty from yesterday's rioting and mostly unshaven, and their faces were those of people whose lives had been so different from Richard's that he couldn't begin to understand them, nor they him.

But his expression as he examined them showed only a mild curiosity. He waited for someone to speak first. Tyler, in his best carrying voice, said 'Welcome, King Richard. We wish no other king but you.'

Close behind the King was a stout chestnut horse carrying a weighty man who wore a mayor's chain. 'That's the Mayor of London, William Walworth,' whispered the Londoner behind John. 'I've seen him before.'

William Walworth's heavy face was scowling. 'You're gracious, fellow,' he said, addressing Tyler. 'But maybe the King would wish to have better subjects than yourself. What's your name?'

'I am Wat Tyler of Kent, your grace.' Tyler, still on one knee, had his eyes not on Walworth but on the King and it was to Richard that he made answer. 'I am the spokesman of these commons here assembled and I beseech your grace to hear our petition.'

King Richard raised a gloved hand and Walworth, about to speak again, fell silent. None of the knights or the other gentlemen who made up the escort had tried to speak at all.

The King was looking down at Wat Tyler and John could see that he, like anyone else – or perhaps more so, because royal estate or not, he was so very young – felt the force of Tyler's personality. But in a voice which had great dignity although it was still in process of breaking, he said, 'We will hear you,' and strategically left Tyler on his knees while the petition was made.

Using what sounded like carefully rehearsed words, Wat Tyler began to recite the wrongs of his followers. He repeated all the things he had said the day before, when he explained the contents of the petition to his followers at Blackheath. His followers listened mainly in silence, except that there was a growl of agreement when he spoke of the harshness of the poll taxes and, when he reached the iniquity of villeinage and demanded to know by what right wealthy men claimed to own the bodies of the poor, there was an actual shout of approval.

He went into more detail than he had at Blackheath. 'There is more than one kind of freedom. Men should be free too to bargain for wages. We ask that the Statute of Labourers, which denies that right, should be repealed. Why should our wages be held down to what they were before the plague first came?' This was greeted by more than a mere shout; it was more like a concerted yell. There was, it seemed, more resentment of low wages than of villeinage.

Throughout Tyler's speech, the King did not stir, and once sharply signed to his companions to remain quiet. Tyler, reaching the final stages, began on the subject of Chancellor Simon Sudbury and the Treasurer, Sir Robert Hales, and the Earl of Lancaster, John of Gaunt. 'They are all traitors; to the King's grace and the honest lords of this land as well as to the commons, and as traitors should be brought to justice . . .'

John, who had been listening intently, here lost the thread, as Phil Simson suddenly tugged at his arm. John glanced round. With a small movement of his head, Phil indicated that he should look towards the north-west.

In that direction, north of the city walls, a column of smoke was rising.

In a whisper that was little more than a mouthing, Phil said, 'Jack Straw's not here and that goes for a good few more. I saw some of the others from Quensted earlier, but they've all gone now.'

Very quietly, Brother Ailred said, 'Hales' manor is over in that direction. I should think that's where they are.'

Tyler had almost finished. 'It is our request to the King's grace that all these traitors be sought out and arrested, and given into our hands!' He paused, expectantly.

Still without speaking, the young King studied him.

316

Walworth edged his horse forward as though to say something but Richard shook his head slightly and Walworth stopped. The King cleared his throat and said warily, 'You may, of course, work your will on any traitors who can be proved so by law.'

A spontaneous cheer went up and those who had been near enough to hear the words began calling them to those behind. Walworth stood in his stirrups, made a trumpet of his hands and roared, 'Quiet!' Tyler beckoned to Brother Ailred, who rose and stepped forward, pulling a parchment scroll from under his robe. The crowd took to shushing each other as he knelt once more, beside the King's horse, and offered the parchment to its rider.

'This is our petition,' said Tyler. 'All written out in a fair hand and witnessed by myself and others, all good men of standing. Please to take it, your grace.'

The King accepted it, in gingerly fashion. As he did so, John observed that many besides the friar had now risen from their knees and had gathered closely round the principals. Mainly, he thought, they had just wanted to hear Tyler more clearly. But the royal escort were becoming uneasy. They were glancing about them and whispering to each other. The King, after looking doubtfully at the scroll as though it might be an adder in disguise, handed it to one of his knights, who took it, but leaned forward and spoke in his sovereign's ear. Richard looked over his shoulder.

The crowd had completely encircled his small party and, good-natured though it seemed, there was a restlessness in it; a latent menace. It was like a huge animal which was stirring and stretching its limbs.

Richard had gone rather white. He spoke in a low voice to Walworth, was answered, and nodded. He turned to Tyler.

'Your complaints and your requests seem to us reasonable.' His voice was nervous, pitched a little high. 'We will grant what you wish. All men shall be free. And you may go through this realm of ours and seize whatever men you believe are traitors, and bring them to us. We will see justice done.'

Tyler stood up and began to say something, words of thanks of some kind. But they went unheard. What the King had said was being flung through the mob and the great composite animal was on the move. Someone shouted, 'The Tower! Sudbury's in the Tower!' and the mighty concourse of men and a sprinkling of women began to flow across the field towards the city. John found himself pushed to his feet and thrust onward, past the king and the escort. Phil was on one side of him and Brother Ailred on the other. The shouting all round was now made up of just a few words, repeated over and over from a myriad throats. 'Sudbury! The Tower! *Sudbury! The Tower!*'

The Tower of London was a place of which everyone had heard. It was the mighty fortress at the heart of London; built first by William the

Conqueror, huge and impregnable. The idea of taking it was staggering. Yet it gave one a sense of power just to shout the words *we'll take the Tower!*

And when so many people were bawling them at once, it even seemed possible. What, after all, could withstand an onslaught by so many, armed with such determination?

All the same, as he half strode, half ran, along in the midst of the mob, together with Phil and Brother Ailred, John couldn't see how they were to do it. He had gathered by now that a great many people had tried to get into the Tower yesterday, and failed. Their efforts had induced King Richard to come out on one of the turrets and promise the meeting at Mile End, but they'd come nowhere near breaking in. When the mass of grey masonry loomed up ahead, he saw himself and his companions as over-ambitious ants.

Ailred seemed to agree with him. 'We're fools,' John heard him mutter. 'Just fools. I never thought it would come to this.'

But somewhere in this hurrying horde, were people who seemed to know what they were doing. They were guiding the rest, taking short cuts through smelly alleyways, skirting the north of the fortress, away from the river which was its southern defence. They bore left, circling the walls, and, as they neared the south-west corner, a great gateway loomed ahead. John waited for the crowd in front to slow down and pile up against it and was bracing himself already to be pushed by the eager thrusters behind, and then realised that it wasn't going to happen.

Since yesterday, something vital had changed. The army of servants who looked after the Tower, who cooked and washed and swept for the King and his court, and the soldiers and the prisoners and for each other, were Londoners with friends and relatives among the loudly rebelling city folks outside and they had had time to make contact with their own. Put to the test, their loyalties had veered towards their fellow citizens.

Besides, the King had gone out to meet the rebels, calling them his people, and the rebels themselves had insisted that they were true to the King. So how could it be treachery to let them in?

Somebody had opened the gate.

Amid shouts of triumph, they poured through. Brother Ailred was keeping up somehow, although he was on foot now, like every one else. But he was very pale, and very breathless when he said, as a weird, ferocious roaring broke out somewhere close by, 'It's all right. It's only the lions in the menagerie.'

John had never seen a lion but knew that they were big, fierce animals which ate men, and their roars were frightening. He hoped that the guards wouldn't think of letting the lions out to disperse the mob. But the few guards who were to be seen, showed no sign of doing anything so provocative. They stood back at the sides of the gate-arch and let the intruders pass. They looked, in fact, as though they wished they were invisible. Phil pulled the beard of one of them and said, 'Come on, then!

Join us!' The guard smiled weakly and neither accepted the invitation nor objected to it.

They poured on through the gatehouse and then through another arch and emerged into a wide space of grass and paving encircled by walls and towers and there was the keep in front of them, square and colossal, built of pale stone, with arched Norman windows on three levels and a square, capped turret at each corner.

Someone had jumped up on the steps to the door of a tower, and was shouting. 'They're still here! Sudbury's still here! The bugger tried to get away by river but there were folk in boats waiting for him!'

'Find him! Find him!' A chant broke out. The mob, which had paused and swirled to listen to the man on the steps, swept on again.

It was a hunt, but they needed a sight of the quarry and as yet they lacked it. There was some aimless rushing about, up and down steps, in and out of towers, where there were living quarters which showed signs of having been hastily vacated, and along the walls which linked the towers.

John was running along a stretch of wall when Tyler appeared on the paved ground before the keep, springing apparently from nowhere. He must have been with them all the time, although John hadn't seen him since they left Mile End. He was shouting a summons and pointing at the keep.

Together with Phil and what seemed like several thousand others, John fought his way into the nearest tower, down the stairs and out. The keep was in front of them. They tore across to it and up the steps to the main door. This too was open. A moment later, John Watson, born a villein, was inside England's greatest fortress and most private royal residence.

The place was immense, full of vast rounded stone pillars and high vaulted ceilings, and after the sunshine outside, it struck cold. They milled round a gigantic hall, gasping at the splendour of the tapestries. But this was not Gaunt's palace; no one suggested yanking these tapestries down and burning them. Someone found a flight of steps and shouted to them to follow.

The steps wound tightly upwards. There was a door off at one point but a voice ahead shouted, 'Up here!' and they all continued to climb, emerging at last on to a gallery, running round another hall, presumably above the first. On the far side, someone was shouting robustly, 'Go on then, Jem, I dare you!' and somebody else was bawling, in a strong London accent, 'Come on darling, don't be shy! Strewth! Ain't she pretty, then?' There was a faint shriek, and then a country voice cried, 'Shame on you, trying to kiss a princess! Kneel to the lady; she's King Richard's mam!'

John leant over the balustrade and, through a door opening on to the gallery across the hall, glimpsed some ladies, in beautiful dresses and jewelled crispines, clinging together in a frightened huddle while their grimy and uninvited guests swirled round them, partly friendly, partly inquisitive, and full of a merriment which had an undertone of danger.

Then, from his right, where the gallery turned round the short side of the hall, a score of voices roared simultaneously, '*Sudbury!*' Phil said, 'Come on!' and forgetting the embarrassed pity which had suddenly attacked him, he plunged with his friend into the press of humanity now thrusting its way along the gallery, and burst through a door on to another gallery, with round arches looking out across a chapel, and down on to the floor of it, twenty feet below.

It was a serene place, built of pale, thick stone: austere and yet beautiful, the gallery arches small enough to be homely, the colour of the stone kind to the eye. There was an altar and in front of it, kneeling, as splendidly robed as the ladies had been and looking over their shoulders in a fear even greater were four men. A group of monks peered nervously round one of the pillars supporting the gallery opposite. The yell of triumph from the hunters went up and up and echoed from the roof.

There was a frantic scramble, to be first to find the way down into the chapel, first to lay hands on the quarry. John Watson shoved and shouted, all but lost his footing as he tore down a flight of spiral steps, was jerked up as Phil caught hold of his belt, and burst into the chapel, and found himself on the outskirts of the screeching pack as it laid hold of its victims. He heard names being bandied: '*Sudbury, Hales. We've got them!*' Terrified voices were raised in denial, and another, angry as well as terrified, was saying that it was the Archbishop of Canterbury. 'Take your hands off me! Show some respect!'

Somewhere close by, Wat Tyler's voice rang out. 'Not here! This is the chapel of St John the Evangelist; it's consecrated ground! We can't shed blood here! Take them out to Tower Hill!'

There was clearly no question of taking them to the King, although that was what Richard had told them to do. John and Phil followed the struggling knot as the prisoners were hauled shouting towards the door, their feet scrabbling on the flagstones and their gold-embroidered robes flapping. People hurled epithets at them and someone spat. Someone else aimed a kick at an expensively clad rear. The monks who had been cowering under the gallery trailed along behind, making distraught noises and largely unregarded except for a few encouraging slaps on the back and jolly exhortations not to look so down in the mouth. 'It ain't you we're after.'

They came out into the open air and down the outside steps to ground level. Brother Ailred, of whom they had lost sight some time ago, was sitting on the bottom step but rose hastily to get out of the way. Phil caught his arm and pulled him with them. 'We've got them. We've got them! Sudbury and Hales and two more besides!'

'So I see.' The friar's face was bloodless. 'I couldn't manage the steps; too steep. Where are we going now?'

'Tower Hill!'

'Oh no,' said Ailred despairingly. 'Oh *no*!' .

320

Presently, they were surging back through the gatehouse and past the roars of the upset lions, out into the streets where they found a huge throng gathered. They stopped in a wider space of trodden ground. John had lost his sense of direction and had no idea where they were but this, presumably, was Tower Hill. The walls of the Tower were not far away, and there were houses nearby, too, every upper window crammed with inquisitive faces. He and Phil and Ailred were near the front of a crowd which had formed itself into a rough square. The dishevelled prisoners were being held at one side. Wat Tyler was in the middle, making another speech.

He was naming the prisoners. One was Simon Sudbury the Archbishop and Chancellor and another was Robert Hales the Treasurer; the names of the others meant little to John although it was clear from the growls all round him that they had meaning for some and were therefore probably the henchmen of the other two. Tyler then began to repeat the words of the petition they had presented to the King that morning although it now seemed to John more like a hundred years ago. He had had nothing to eat yet that day and he was beginning to feel light-headed. Tyler was making the details of the petition into an indictment, and saying that the prisoners had been found guilty on all counts. He was pronouncing sentence of beheading.

'This is an unlawful tribunal! The King will have *your* heads for this!' Sudbury bellowed. He was a big, florid, chesty-voiced man, very powerful. He was in the hands of four men and they could barely hold him.

'The king,' said Tyler, 'has given us permission to seek out traitors. A traitor, to his realm and his people, is what you are.'

'Did he give you permission to make yourselves into a court instead of convening one? Did he give you permission to be judge, jury and executioner? Where's your evidence? We're no traitors! You're the traitor!'

Someone had produced a block of wood and it was being carried into the middle of the space. 'You can't do this!' Robert Hales was thin and sharp and his voice was shrill with horror.

'You were at your prayers when we found you. I take it you've all heard Mass today?' said Tyler. 'So you won't need shriving. Still, we ought to have a priest. Things must be properly done. We're executioners, not murderers. Weren't there some monks? Where are they?'

'But,' said a brown-habited monk, when he was propelled forward, 'we're none of us in orders.'

'Well, isn't there anyone here who is? Ah, Brother Ailred! You are, I know.'

Ailred's pallor was now ghastly but he stepped forth. He began some sort of protest but Tyler cut him short. 'You'd better say a prayer for their souls. But get on with it!'

Ailred, facing the prisoners, began to intone. The massed crowd fell

321

quiet. The silence was more terrible than the earlier screeches and insults had been. And inside John Watson, something unexpected was happening.

He had been appalled, yesterday, when Redbrown was murdered but Redbrown had died in a horrifying way and he was, in any case, someone John knew, someone on their own side. John's feelings then had not made him question the rightness of their cause or the desirability of hunting down Sudbury and his fellow oppressors and destroying them. But he was questioning these things now.

It had begun, perhaps, when he looked across the well of the hall and saw the frightened royal ladies. Back in Herneham, he had kissed the Lady Ghislaine himself and thought it hugely comical. In the Tower that morning, he had looked at that crudely jocular mob whose rumbustious compliments could so very easily have slid over the edge of violence and rape and seen himself as Ghislaine must have seen him; as not only rough and dirty but evil.

Now, the change had gone one step further. He looked at Simon Sudbury and saw, not a monstrous Chancellor but a big man whose once-splendid robes were now torn and grubby and whose red face was wet with the sweat of fear and whose jowls were trembling.

Ailred finished his prayer. Sudbury's four captors were dragging him forward. He dug in his feet and cried out hoarsely. They got him to the block and someone kicked him behind the knees to make him kneel and someone else inquired loudly, 'Who's going to be the headsman, then?'

Everyone looked at Tyler but Tyler shook his head. 'The honour goes to plain men such as you!' He looked round. His eyes scanned the front row of the crowd intently, apparently taking them in one face at a time. His eyes locked with John's and stopped. He raised a finger and pointed. 'You'll do.'

'Oh no,' said John. 'No! He can't mean me!'

'Go on!' growled Phil, and pushed him forward. 'You can't say no to Tyler!'

The push was a decisive one. Against his will, he was out in the open, face to face with Tyler and the object of envious expressions on a number of the surrounding faces.

'Ah.' Tyler looked him up and down. There was an unmistakeable gleam of recognition in his eyes. But he gave no public sign of this, as he inquired, loudly, 'What's your name, fellow, and where are you from?'

'John . . . John Watson. From . . . from Quensted.' He preferred not to mention Whitmead. His grandfather would object to that.

'And where is Quensted?'

'Ess . . . Essex. But I can't . . . I'm . . .' He sought for inspiration and found it. 'I'm not worthy! Scores of folk here must have suffered more than me! I'll gladly hand over to anyone with a better right!'

'No, no, you'll do! Someone else's turn in a minute!' shouted an encouraging voice from the onlookers.

'But I've never . . . I'll make a mess of it!'

'Not squeamish, are you?' said Tyler in a loud voice, and then, in an undertone, 'You're the fellow who turned sick after the looter's execution yesterday. I knew you straightaway. That's why I picked you, to give you a chance to get your self-respect back.' The blue-grey eyes were implacable. 'Are you going to refuse to do it? What do you think will happen to you if you try that?'

He didn't need Tyler to tell him. If he refused, the mob now robustly encouraging him, would turn on him. He would be the next to be called traitor, the next to be beheaded.

It wasn't even a question of him or Sudbury. Sudbury was a dead man anyway. But he, John, could stay alive if he chose.

Someone was offering him an axe. It was almost as tall as he was himself, with a polished haft and a patterned handgrip and a curved, savage blade gleaming blue at the edge from recent sharpening. Such a weapon had never been seen in a peasant's hut, not even that of a woodsman. He asked bemusedly where it had come from and several voices informed him that they had robbed the Tower armoury.

The axe was pushed into his hands. It was extremely heavy but not too heavy for him to raise; he was used to hard manual work. He turned towards the block.

Simon Sudbury was sprawled there, defenceless. Two men were holding his feet and his wrists had been roped. Those holding the ropes were standing well back and their sardonic grins told John, unnervingly, that they hadn't much confidence in his expertise, either.

Tyler's voice rang out. 'John Watson of Quensted in Essex: do your office!'

He couldn't see Sudbury's face, only the back of his head. But the man's whole body was shuddering and he was gabbling something that sounded like a Paternoster. One of the other prisoners was sobbing.

He must not prolong this, for Sudbury's sake as well as his own.

He was not only strong; he had a sound link between hand and eye. It was the same link that had made Thomas a craftsman; John had inherited it from him. He planted his feet apart, swung the axe up, felt the balance of it, and let its own weight carry it down, through bone and flesh, to the waiting block below.

And knew as he did so that he had crossed some final and terrible boundary, that the John Watson who had left Essex was gone for ever. He longed to turn back time and be once more the old John Watson, entitled to be sickened by ugly deeds because he was innocent of them, setting out from Quensted for his day's work at Whitmead or going to Chelmsford with the corn-cart, but he could no longer imagine it. He could not imagine ever ploughing the fields of Whitmead, or scything the corn or taking it to Chelmsford in all his life again.

Chapter Nineteen

A Matter of Survival

'I don't know what you're still so miserable about,' Alison said. She was scouring a pot as though it were a personal enemy. 'Your grandfather's willing to take you back. William Astleigh and Lady Ghislaine have taken all your friends back, as well. Even Laurence Dubois and Michael Shore and James Att Brigg. Their wages are down and their customary labour's up, but what else could they expect? They've had generous treatment and so have you. So stir yourself and get on your way to Whitmead. If you go on sending word that you're not well and can't come yet, your granddad might change his mind.'

'Astleigh and Lady Ghislaine aren't being generous,' said John tiredly. 'Nearly every man for miles came along with us to London. Refuse to give them back their jobs and there'd be no one to do the work.'

'There still isn't, where you're concerned! What's the matter with you? Can't you do anything at all except sit about staring into space? Even your little brother's more use than you, these days.' Small Walter was squatting in the open doorway, in the sunshine, peeling onions. Alison paused in the midst of her wrath to cast a benign glance at him before glaring once more at John.

'There's things I can't forget.'

'The others don't seem to be having much trouble.'

'They didn't see everything. I sort of lost touch with most of the others for a while. Only Phil saw Redbrown die and he didn't have to do what I did outside the Tower. He was the only one at the Tower at all. All the rest – the shepherds and the blacksmith and Michael Shore and Laurence and James – they all went off with Jack Straw, that I told you about, Tyler's second-in-command. They were attacking some manor or other to the north of London . . .'

'Oh, yes. Jack Straw.' Alison, as usual, was well-informed. News of the doings in London and the names of the principals, had travelled as if blown on the wind, and she had missed nothing. 'Been arrested, so I hear.'

'I daresay. I didn't really know him. I'm not talking about him.' To his mother's exasperation, John continued to sit on a bench with his hands hanging between his knees, unoccupied and wretched. 'I was saying, only Phil was at the Tower with me and he didn't have to kill Simon Sudbury. Oh, dear God. Why did Tyler have to pick on me like that?'

'I shouldn't talk too loudly about that if I were you. You'd better just forget it.'

'I can't forget it. And I'll never forget what happened the next day, either.'

'Neither will I, if you keep on and on repeating it.' Alison banged the cleaned pot down on its shelf, seized another and began furiously to scour that too.

'The King met us all again the next day,' said John, unheeding. 'Just outside the city. I think they call the place Smithfield. Tyler was there, on a horse. He wanted to look dignified, I think . . . he wanted everything in writing, all the promises the King made to us at Mile End. The King kept on saying, yes, yes, but it was all too easy and Tyler knew it was too easy, and all the lords round the King were glaring and scowling and looking at us the way cats look at pigeons. Tyler shouted at them that he could see they meant to overturn any charters the King signed, that they'd push us back into the mud if they could and there was a quarrel and then someone pulled Tyler out of his saddle and stabbed him and . . . it was just uproar,' said John. 'I was with Phil and Brother Ailred. I didn't know what to do. I hated Tyler but he was our leader and he'd been speaking for us. The King called to everyone to follow him and started leading us all away and we went; it was as if we'd taken him for a leader instead. Then Ailred collapsed. He'd been looking ill the day before and suddenly he just fell down. Phil and me were still there, trying to revive him and everyone else seemed to have gone after the King, when Michael suddenly came up. I hadn't seen him for two days. He said Ailred was dead . . . and that we'd better all get away quick and make for home, that everything had gone wrong, just as Brother Ailred had said it would. And now I can't forget and it was all for nothing, because the King's backed out of everything he said at Mile End and Smithfield. "Villeins you are and villeins you'll stay." That's what he's saying about us, isn't he?'

'You won't stay a villein. You're as good as bought out already. Provided you get up and go to your work at Whitmead.'

'I admired him so much, that day at Mile End,' said John, as though he had not heard. 'The King, I mean. He's only fourteen and he . . . he led us, took control. But now . . . oh well, that's just it, I suppose. He's so young that his great men can work on him. All we did has gone for nothing. And I can't forget Redbrown and I can't forget Sudbury and I wish I could die!'

'There've been a good many times in my life that I wished I could die,' said Alison tartly. 'The dear Lord knows I loved your father and he was the best of men, but there were times I felt it badly that I was born in freedom and my children weren't. Walter's bright; Father Henry at the church says he ought to be taught his letters but it's not so easy to get a villein's son into school unless you buy him in. I went to Whitmead, let me tell you, and asked my father to help. I walked right in on him before anyone could stop me and for a wonder I actually got my piece said! And he turned me down flat, the old . . . But that's by the way. What I'm saying is that you can't die for the asking so you might as well settle for living, the way I did a time or two when I looked at this hut and couldn't stand the thought that life'd never be different and hated myself for wanting it to be. So now get up and . . . well, well! Phil Simson. What brings you here? Come to fetch John?'

'I've not come to fetch him. Just to warn him.' Phil stepped in quickly through the open door and then drew it shut behind him. 'John! You're in danger!'

John looked up in alarm. 'What sort of danger?'

'Arrest,' said Phil sharply. 'By the grace of God, Redbrown's widow heard the proclamation when the King's men gave it out at Fobbing. They're moving northwards, picking up the men they want on the way. You're one of the ones they want.'

'What are you talking about?' demanded Alison.

'They're being moderate after a fashion, I suppose,' said Phil. 'They're only after just a few names; most of us can sink back out of sight and welcome as long as we're prepared to bow our heads and stay there. But John here is on their list because he swung the axe that killed Sudbury. They say they have witnesses, John – the monks who were with Sudbury when he was taken; I think it's them. They heard Tyler shout out your name. Remember? John Watson of Quensted, he called you, right out loud, in front of everyone.'

'He did what?' Alison was furious. 'He was your leader and he pointed a finger at you like that!'

'I told you I didn't like him. But I think he thought he was honouring me, in a sort of way.'

'I daresay! As Abraham honoured Isaac when he almost went and sacrificed him,' said Alison wrathfully. 'I always hated that story. A pretty sort of father Abraham was; I'd have told God to do without!'

Neither John nor Phil paid any attention to this interesting comment on the Old Testament.

'They're taking their time; they've other places to go to,' Phil said. 'So Redbrown's widow sent her eldest boy off to Whitmead straightaway. He didn't know where to find you but he knew me . . .'

'She's sister to our blacksmith,' said John. 'He had to tell her that Redbrown wasn't coming home. But he hated having to do it so much that Phil and me and Michael Shore all went with him, to help both of them if we could.' That's how she knows us. He had risen and opened the door, to stare out at the sheep pastures. Nothing moved on them except sheep. 'We didn't tell her what happened to him. We made up a tarradiddle about him being killed with a spear by a guard at Gaunt's palace, and dying quickly.'

'I said I'd see you were told,' said Phil, unheeding. 'I sent Redbrown's lad home to his mother and came straight on here. I don't know how soon

326

they'll come, John. But they're going to Herneham next, from what the lad said. You've time, just, to get away.'

'But where? How?' said John wildly. 'They'll comb the district, won't they? I need a horse and some money and I haven't got either!'

'I'd give you mine if I had any left.' Phil found it hard to meet John's eye. 'But I really did spend nearly all of it in that place . . . you know, where we spent the night before we went to Mile End.' In Alison's presence, Phil wasn't going to say more. 'But with money or without it, you've got to be away from here, John, as fast as possible! You must!'

Alison, listening, had gone very white, but she was in command of herself. 'There's one person who could oblige with money,' she said in a hard voice. 'And a horse. One person who owes us all that and more.' She threw the pot she was still holding into a corner. 'I'll just hand Walter to a neighbour to keep an eye on and then we'll go. We'd better hurry if we don't want to meet them on the way. John, put your clothes into a pack while I'm seeing to that and be quick about it. If they're making for Herneham first then we shouldn't run into them, but we shouldn't waste time.'

'Where . . .?' began Phil, puzzled.

'She means my grandfather,' said John. 'But, Mother, you know what he's like. He'll only say no again. If he doesn't turn me in, that is!'

'He won't turn you in and he won't say no,' said Alison. 'He's let us all but starve in the past and he sent me away empty-handed when I asked him to do something for Walter's education. But this time, *this time*, he'll say yes. This time he'll help us, I promise. He'd better!'

Thomas Whitmead was out in the sunshine in front of his house, finishing a wheelbarrow. He'd had the wheel and axle made by the wheelwright in Quensted, who had better tools for the purpose, but he'd constructed the rest himself, and now he proposed to turn it into the most decorative and remarkable wheelbarrow ever seen in Essex, or anywhere else for that matter.

He had already finished the garland of carved roses on the rim. The sides of the barrow were now to be covered with a tangle of leaves and fruits. In the oakleaf taking shape under his freehand chisel every detail was as clear and true as he could make it.

He worked in something near to content. Time brought a measure of acceptance, after all. At least, at Rushley long ago, he had been robbed only of two fingers, not of his whole hand, and he had made Rushley pay. Whitmead and his own freedom were that payment; there were worse bargains.

Not that regret would ever quite leave him. His grandson John, in his ignorance, might admire the carved furniture of Whitmead, but Thomas knew where it was faulty, where lines were not as even in their depth or as smoothly curved or unerringly straight as they ought to be; where he had made a design bigger than it rightly should be, because it was easier.

327

He knew, too, that technically, he had been left behind. The whole art of woodcarving had advanced since he was young. There was a new church in Quensted with a rood screen whose beams and panels and slender wooden arches bore such a tracery of tiny, entwined roses, stem and bloom, bud and thorn and rosehip, that the remembered rood screen of Redesmarsh seemed crude by comparison. Seeing it, had made him ache for what might have been.

Because Whitmead was what he had taken in exchange for his craft, he had summoned John to his side. Whitmead was too precious to pass at his death to any but his own flesh and blood. He wasn't going to forgive Alison, though. All through the years since her marriage, he had said to himself: let her lie on the bed she had made and let John see for himself the difference between bond and free. If John ever had a daughter, Thomas hoped he would have more sense than to let her ruin herself.

He'd been relieved when John came home from London, and quite unable to understand why his grandson, heir to this excellent tenancy, had gone away with the rebels as though he saw himself as a downtrodden peasant like them. A nice moment he'd chosen, too. Thomas had been left with hardly any hands to do the shearing and the haymaking; the fact was that without villeins, one couldn't keep the place in order. He'd never realised that until he found himself on the other side of the fence. John would have to realise it too, one of these days.

It was to be hoped that he'd learn now, and not behave in that insane way again. Without John, Whitmead's only heir would be his little brother Walter. So many of Alison's children had died young that Thomas had rather expected Walter to do the same and until John ran off, he had never even considered Walter as a possible replacement.

Even then, he hadn't been willing so to do. Alison had dared, while John was away, to come here – where he had forbidden her ever to come again – to beg for money for Walter's schooling. She'd actually had the nerve to say: 'Walter could be all you've got left.' He'd let her speak instead of having her thrown out at once, because Nicola had said: 'Oh, no, Thomas, please . . .' But she'd gone away with nothing just the same. 'We won't bury John before he's dead,' he'd said. He'd thought, but didn't add, that if John never came home, Walter would come to Whitmead, not go to school. Schools were run by priests and he didn't like priests. But he didn't want to have to train Walter. He'd worked hard on John and the boy had learned well. Walter would mean a new start and he was too young; he might well be only a lad still when Thomas died.

Why, he asked himself for the ten thousandth time, hadn't Alison made a proper marriage and provided him with grandsons who could have been reared from birth to Whitmead ways?

Thinking of Alison, with her obstinacy and impertinence, suddenly spoiled the good mood in which he had begun the morning's work. He began to mutter to himself, as he sometimes did these days when irritated. When the dogs, descendants of the ones he had brought from Rushley, leapt up from snoozing in the sun and rushed to the gate barking and he looked round to see Alison in person, together with John and the villein Phil Simson – who should have been at his work – coming in at the gate, one of his old surges of anger instantly rose up in him. He stood with chisel poised, and glared at them.

Alison spoke first, without preamble, and the moment she was near enough to be heard. 'Father, you've never helped us since the day I was wedded but you've got to help us now. The King's men are searching for John to arrest him. He needs a horse and money so that he can get away and there's no one can provide them except you.'

Thomas laid the chisel down inside the barrow. 'What's all this?'

They tried to explain, all at once and in a babble. He shook his head impatiently at them. 'One at a time. Not you, Alison. You've no business coming through that gate; I told you that when you walked in here last time. Seems that this concerns you, John, so you'd better be the one to tell it.'

John explained, rapidly. 'There's no time to lose,' he said at the end. They'd come all the way from Quensted on foot, walking and running, scanning the horizon for horsemen. He'd been ready to dive into the ditch at the least sight or sound of danger. He looked imploringly at his grandfather.

Thomas, with ominous slowness, said, 'Let me get this straight. When you were in London, you got mixed up with this man Tyler who was the leader there. That much, I supposed already. But I didn't know you let him hand you the axe that took the Archbishop of Canterbury's head off!'

'I had no choice! They'd have had *my* head off if I'd said no. You don't know what it was like! I didn't want to do it; I couldn't help it. And now . . .'

'And now the law's on your heels. Not surprising, is it?' Thomas picked up his chisel once more and addressed himself anew to the oak leaf.

There was a horrified silence. In the course of it, Nicola came out of the house. 'Alison! I was sure I heard your voice. What brings you here?' Nicola looked anxiously from one face to another, and down at her husband, whose head was bent determinedly over his work. 'What's happened?'

Alison told her, shortly and bitterly. 'My father,' she ended, 'won't help. Can you persuade him?'

'No, she can't,' said Thomas, still chiselling. 'Don't try, Nicola. You're wasting your breath.' It would have to be Walter, he thought savagely. John was no use now as an heir for Whitmead. Hanged men inherited nothing and neither did outlaws. It would have to be Walter after all, however much training he needed and however many years he took to grow up. God's wounds! Was any man ever so beset by his own family? The chisel slipped and he swore out loud.

'This is for *John*,' said Alison into his ear as though he were deaf. 'Dear God, it's only a matter of a horse and some silver, nothing else. Father, please!'

329

'You shouldn't have gone to London,' said Thomas to his grandson. 'And if you insisted on going to London, you shouldn't have done what you did. I've been trying to get you ready to be master at Whitmead but it seems you still don't think like its master. You're still a villein in your heart. Only a villein would be fool enough to throw Whitmead away, which is what you've done. Well, isn't it? You've got to run for your life now and even if you get away, what use will Whitmead be to you? You'll never be able to come back here and enjoy it in peace. You'll have to leave that to your brother. You'd better go if you're going.'

'But I can't . . . just take to the forest. I need to get away properly. I need to ride and I'll have to buy food and a passage on a ship and . . .'

'Thomas,' Nicola said pleadingly. 'Thomas, his life's in danger. You can't just say no, you can't!'

'Yes, I can. I'm not wasting what I've wrung from this place, in years of toil, on a fool so crazy that he's capable of throwing *Whitmead* away. Nicola, go back indoors. And the rest of you, go away; especially you, Alison. When will you ever learn that you're not welcome here?'

Nicola let out a sob and Thomas snapped, 'And don't sniffle at me, woman. I've said my last word. Now will you all clear out and leave me to work in peace?'

'John,' said Alison, 'and Phil. Go over and stand by the gate. I've something to say that's private, though not from you, Mother. You'd better stay, Mother. Go on, you two.'

Slowly, John and Phil withdrew to the gate. Alison looked grimly at Thomas, whose head was once more bent over his work and said, 'Father. I think you had better attend to me.'

'I've nothing to say to you.'

'Well, I've something to say to you. You're going to help John, do you hear? Because if you don't, I can't help feeling that, even now, Lady Ghislaine – who is still at Herneham, and her son, Sir Stephen, who is its proper lord and who's supposed to be due there from Yorkshire any day now – might be quite interested to learn what's under the floor of the store-room in this house.'

Phil and John, watching though out of earshot, were startled to see Nicola's hand fly to her mouth, while Thomas sprang to his feet and made a threatening step towards Alison. She did not move, but folded her arms and looked him in the face.

Thomas stared at her. The woman in front of him, with her tired face and her thin body, and the cheap brown overgown stained from the cooking pot and the vegetable patch, gazed back at him out of his own hard black eyes.

'What are you talking about?' he said coldly.

'Richard Grosney.'

'But you knew nothing about that! How did you find out? When?' Nicola was panic-stricken.

Alison glanced at her mother. 'I'm sorry, Mother. I wouldn't have done

330

this to you for the world but if it's you or John I have to choose John. He's my child.' Her eyes locked once more with her father's. 'I saw you kill him; I had just come home and I was peering round the door . . .'

'Oh, you always had that habit as a child!' Nicola moaned. She was much better dressed than her daughter and although she was over sixty now, with hands which showed the years of work, she was better fed. But at the moment, sturdy flesh and good blue gown and clean white headdress went so badly with their frightened owner that they hardly seemed to be hers at all.

'I was scared, so I hid in the hay-barn,' said Alison. 'I heard what you said when you brought his horse inside. And in the night I crept down the stairs and I saw what you did in the store-room.'

'All this time and you've never as much as whispered?' gasped Nicola.

'It's all right, she won't go to Lady Ghislaine,' said Thomas with scorn. His black temper was on the verge of bursting forth but he held it down because this was a dangerous moment and danger was better dealt with coldly. 'How would you explain it, my girl, that you've known all these years and never spoken?'

'I was only a child,' said Alison. 'I'll say I didn't understand till later, from overhearing this and that, and then, well, it was my parents, after all. Not that it matters. If John's taken, I shan't care what happens to me and if he's taken because you wouldn't help, *I'll go to Ghislaine*. I mean it! She won't care why. It's her husband you killed, and Sir Stephen's father. And it's no good making your hands into claws like that as if you'd like to get them round my throat. Phil and John are watching. Touch me and they'll come to the rescue.'

With rage pounding in his head and in his chest, Thomas demanded, 'You'd betray your own father? And your mother?' Onlookers or no onlookers, it was all he could do not to spring at her.

Nicola said tremulously, 'Thomas . . . Alison . . .' She caught Alison's eye in frightened appeal. Alison remained implacable.

'Yes. I would. Help John, or else.'

'Nicola,' said Thomas. 'Fetch my money-chest from under our bed. John!' John and Phil came back, running. 'Saddle the black mare!'

'No. Saddle the bay gelding. The mare's getting old,' said Alison. 'I know what's in your stable,' she added to her father. 'John's told me.'

Thomas almost choked on his fury. 'After all I've done! Yes, go on, John, go on, take the bay. I recognised the boy, didn't I?' he said viciously to Alison. 'He's Wat's brat but I recognised him. And as for you!' He scowled at Phil. 'I've been a good master to you as far as I know; why are you wasting your time rushing to Quensted with warnings for this . . . this . . .? Get about your work!'

He made a gesture which was very like an abortive blow and Phil, though with a faint air of one who has achieved what he set out to do, removed himself.

John saddled the horse and led it out, and Nicola brought the chest.

331

Thomas balanced it on the edge of the wheelbarrow and opened it. 'You can take two of these bags. There's a pound in each of them, in silver pennies.'

Alison reached in, felt a bag of slightly different proportions and snatched it out. 'What's in this?' She undid the drawstring. 'Gold nobles! I've never seen any close before . . . John, take this as well.'

'No, not my gold nobles! They're worth six and eightpence each . . . there's nine pounds worth in that bag . . .!'

'Good,' said Alison coolly. 'Take it, John!'

'Grandfather, I'm sorry. I wouldn't do this if I didn't have to. I'm so grateful to you for helping me. I don't know what my mother said to you but, believe me, I'll always be thankful to you and I'll remember you in my prayers for the rest of my life and . . .!'

'Get out!' shouted Thomas. 'Take my horse and the damned money; take them and go, go, out of my sight; I hope I never set eyes on you again. And you!' He turned on Alison, fist raised. 'And you go too, before I kill you!'

'Thomas!' wailed Nicola. John had one foot in the stirrup already. She reached him as he swung astride and he stretched down and took one of her work-reddened, wrinkled hands in his own brown young fingers. 'Come back one day if you can,' Nicola pleaded. 'But be safe. Put that first. Only, don't forget us!'

'I won't forget. I've still got that old silver pendant you gave me, do you recall? I've got it on me, under my shirt. I've always kept it carefully. It'll remind me of you and Whitmead. Grandmother, I must leave. I've got to dodge the King's men and make for the coast.'

'God go with you, grandson.'

Then he was riding away. Alison ran by his stirrup as he went towards the gate, crying her last farewells, and then stopped in the gateway, clamping a hand over her mouth, to watch him go.

'Oh, what will happen to him?' Nicola whispered.

'You might spare a thought for me.' Thomas was so angry that it was actually painful. His head was pounding more and more and there was an ache in his chest as though a boulder had been rammed behind his breastbone. 'How do you think I feel? Robbed by my own daughter – *your* daughter! She'd have thrown me to the hangman, wouldn't she? Oh God, I always knew those bones under the store-room floor were just waiting their chance. I risked my neck to make a life for us and I toiled and saved, year after year, and now that boy's taken all that gold and my best horse . . . I never thought to see all I've done wasted on a boy so stupid but what else could one expect of Wat Shepherd's brat . . .?'

He broke off. The pain in his head and chest was growing, swelling. He couldn't breathe. He was aware of Nicola's concerned face with the wide, honey-coloured eyes, looming in front of him, felt his knees buckle as the pain became huge, bigger than he was, filling the world, felt his mouth open in a vain, desperate gulping for air . . .

PART V

Piers Whitmead:
The Fledgeling
1399

I thought it was right that I should now be happy to continue as one of a long line. The unconscious of the race was a medium in which one's own unconscious microscopically swam, and not only in that of the living race but of all the races which had gone before.

Chapter Twenty

Out of the Past

Except for a few new dwellings here and there, Rushley looked just the same although she had been twenty-nine when she left it and now she was approaching eighty and she had changed beyond recognition, from a sturdy young woman with honey-coloured hair to an aged crone whose thin hair, where it escaped from her headdress, was completely white and whose body was shrunken and wrinkled. Her hands, however, though speckled with brown and meshed with knotted veins, were still capable and her eyes were still good. She had a silver mirror at home and knew that in her lined face, her eyes were a surprise; like topazes displayed on a piece of worn cloth.

She had kept her health well. It wouldn't last much longer; she knew, with an instinctive certainty which seemed to be lodged in her very bones, that this summer of 1399 would be the last of her life and that her last Christmas was gone by already. When the weather turned cold again, her strength would fail.

But meanwhile, she was still able to pack a bundle and sit in a cart and although Alison had said bewilderedly that she couldn't see why her mother wanted to go to Rushley and that Uncle Will must be dead long since, Nicola had with determination set out.

She had wanted to make the journey for years; in fact, since not long after Thomas's death the day John went away. But she was too wary. As time went on, Lady Ghislaine and her son Sir Stephen, who was also Richard Grosney's son, came to Herneham less and less often and, even when there, would hardly have been interested to learn that the widow at Whitmead – which belonged to Quensted and not to Herneham anyhow – had gone on a journey to visit a shrine or some kinfolk or whatever. But still Nicola waited, afraid lest even the faintest whisper of a link between Whitmead and Rushley, should reach them. Afraid that even now, she and Alison might somehow be dragged back to servitude or ruined by the payment to stay out of it.

Though she was not afraid for Walter. Once mistress of Whitmead, she had paid for Walter's schooling herself. (She and Alison never admitted to each other that Thomas's death was a relief, but it was true.) King Richard hadn't been too hard on the common folk in the end. At least he had quashed the attempt to bring in a law that villeins should

335

not be allowed to send their sons to school. Walter had proved so able that Nicola had decided that it was worthwhile to pay the fine which freed him from Quensted. She had seen a hard season or two as a result, but Walter was now a monk and he had taken priestly orders. No one could ever drag him back to villeinage.

He would, of course, leave no progeny to inherit Whitmead's tenancy, either. The Church might claim it after she and Alison were gone, or else it would revert to Quensted and pass to strangers. She was sorry, but not to Thomas's passionate extent, and Alison only minded because of John.

'I often wonder where he is and if he's still alive,' she said sometimes, when sitting with her mother in the hall at Whitmead, where they now lived together. 'The wars in France have stopped since King Richard's been on the throne, so he can't have gone there as a soldier. But never a word has come back.' Once, just before Nicola set out for Rushley, Alison had said, 'I think John must be dead. It's eighteen years since he went away. If he were living, we'd have heard,' and Nicola had said gently, 'I fear you may be right.'

It was the news that Lady Ghislaine and Sir Stephen had both died, within weeks of each other, that decided Nicola to make her journey. Ghislaine's grandson, young Sir Stephen, was surely no threat; he could not possibly have heard of Nicola and Thomas who fled from Rushley half a century ago. Now, at last, it should be safe.

Alison, who had aged more quickly than her mother and was very lame with rheumatism, wasn't equal to the travelling, but Phil Simson was more than willing to escort his mistress. It would be a journey to see a new place and, since returning from London eighteen years ago, he'd never got further than Chelmsford. 'I'll take good care of your mother,' he said to Alison.

'I've no intention of dying on the road,' said Nicola with slight indignation.

And so here she was, among the flat, familiar fields of her childhood, with the cloud shadows racing across them in front of the east wind and the roofs of Rushley Hall and the house at Norsland visible in the distance, and the calls of the familiar marsh birds and the wheeling gulls in her ears. She considered what to do first and found that although, when she told Alison that she meant to seek news of her brother Will, this had been only a pretext, somehow the call of blood was real. She had detested Will, that jug-eared intruder into her life; yet now that she was here, it seemed necessary to make her lie into truth. Perhaps she should make straight for the Lea. But it might well be occupied by strangers. 'We should go first to the priest's house,' she said to Phil.

This turned out to be one of the recently built houses, and was much bigger than Father Matthew's unpretentious cottage had been, with a stout gable defying the east wind and an impressive door of weathered oak. The priest himself was clearly a recent innovation, too, and Nicola sighed inwardly. This man was too young, she thought, and did not speak with a local accent. He would know nothing of Rushley fifty years ago.

But here she proved to be mistaken. Over wine and cold chicken and good wheaten bread, young Father Edmund told them that he had worked side by side with his predecessor for three years, 'until only two years or so ago, when he went to his rest,' and that the predecessor in question, whose name had been Father Randolph, had been appointed to Rushley after Matthew's death in the first onslaught of the plague. 'More than forty-eight years, he'd been here and he knew every grave in the churchyard; at least every grave that was dug since he arrived. He made sure that I knew them, too. So, if you want to know what happened to relatives of yours in Rushley during his time here, I can very likely help you.'

'I must have married and left the manor just before his day,' said Nicola, dexterously skimming the edge of the truth. 'I went far away, off down south and more or less lost touch with my family. I . . . er . . . I heard my parents died in the plague but I had a brother, living at a place called the Lea. William, his name was. I've wondered ever since, what happened to him.'

'Will of the Lea?' The young priest nodded at once. 'Oh yes. He's been gone since well before my time and his wife too but I know where he's buried. His wife's alongside, and one of their children. There's no family left hereabouts, though. They had five, all told. But when Sir Stephen – the father of the present Sir Stephen, that is – followed the Black Prince to war in France, Will's two elder boys went with him and they didn't come back. There was a third boy but he was a wantwit, poor fellow, and he died before he was twenty – he's the one in the graveyard. The other two were girls, but they both married right off the manor, and went to Lynn, or somewhere. Villeinage started lapsing after the plague and it's gradually grown easier for people to leave. Men have turned their work service into money rents and somehow, after a few years more, they didn't count as villeins any longer. Very few round here still do, as a matter of fact.'

He glanced at the table and noticed that his guests had finished their refreshments. 'We can look at the graves now, if you like.'

In the churchyard he pointed out a mound. 'Your brother lies there, Mistress Whitmead. Would you like me to say a prayer?'

Nicola nodded. She and Phil stood with bent heads while Father Edmund sought a blessing for the soul of Will, whom Nicola had so much resented, and she was surprised to realise how completely the resentment was gone.

But when the *amen* was said, she put Will immediately out of her mind. He was not the real purpose of this pilgrimage.

337

'There was someone else. He was . . . a friend of my family.' That was near enough to the truth. 'His name was Osbert Smith.'

'Osbert Smith? Oh yes. I can tell you about him, if it's the same man, that is.' Suddenly, Father Edmund laughed. 'He was the first problem that my predecessor Father Randolph had to deal with when he arrived in Rushley. He told me the story many a time. It isn't often one's parishioners come to blows in the church, right in front of their priest.'

'Come to blows? Osbert Smith?' said Nicola.

'The wind is cold for you.' Edmund led them back to the church porch, where there were benches to sit on. 'Osbert Smith didn't do the fighting,' he said. 'But he was the cause of the quarrel. He was one of the Rushley constables at the time of the plague and he had a holding down on the marsh . . . was that the man?'

'Yes. Yes, that would be him,' Nicola agreed.

'He died in the plague,' said the priest. 'Just as it was ending, and things were getting organised again – such as Father Randolph arriving to take over the church here. In fact, this man Osbert died the day before Randolph arrived, and the uproar was over his funeral. It appears that, until he fell ill himself, he'd been in charge of burying the plague victims. He lifted a lot of worry off people's hands, and someone had to do it, but he put the bodies in communal graves. Randolph said that happened everywhere; it was usually the best that could be managed. Some of the relations were grateful but not all. Randolph said Osbert sounded like a decent man doing his best, but some people were affronted by the pit burials and a few seemed to feel he'd been tainted by handling the plague dead at all. One faction wanted him shovelled into the communal pit and another faction wanted him given a handsome tomb and, when they met Randolph in the church to discuss it, they fought.'

'What happened?' asked Nicola.

Edmund smiled. 'I gather that he called them to order! Penances all round, for unbecoming behaviour in the church. He wouldn't hear of the pit being used any more – he was trying to get back to normal funerals – and he thought Osbert did deserve a little respect. He had him put under the floor of the church. His name was cut into the slab that lies on top, but it's pretty well worn away now.'

'I'd like to say a Paternoster for him, if you'll show me the place,' said Nicola.

A few minutes later, she stood with Father Edmund and Phil Simson inside the church, looking at a piece of engraved stone in the floor. She could not have read the lettering even if it hadn't already been worn so faint. But she knew that it spelt the name of Osbert Smith and that under her feet lay the bones, all that remained on earth, of the man she had once loved.

For all she knew, he had never really loved her in return. Perhaps she had built her secret dream out of straw and cobwebs simply because she needed the dream so much. One meeting of eyes, before she went to her legal bridegroom. A little kindness at a time of anguish. That was all it amounted to.

And, therefore, it was ridiculous, nonsensical, to feel so much grief. He had been gone for fifty years, had been quiet under his slab, very likely, even before she reached Whitmead.

And she was – she reminded herself again – *in her eightieth year*! She was on the edge of eternity herself. It was utterly absurd to stand here and be swept and shaken by love and longing as though she were a girl of seventeen. Utterly ridiculous to be agonised by the desire for what might have been. Time could not be turned back or lives rewritten and if they could, what of those who would thereby be wiped out of existence? What of Alison and Walter? Or John? Whatever had befallen John, he had once lived and been a part of things. Had he not existed, who would have wielded the axe that killed Simon Sudbury instead?

No, it was foolish either to grieve or to yearn and, of course, she wasn't really doing either. It was just that the church was out of the sun and cool and old eyes watered easily. She put her palms together and bowed her head and said the Paternoster. And, although she had prayed beside the mound that covered her own brother, this was the prayer which she had journeyed so far to make and with this, her mission was complete.

Jolting along in the cart as it came back through Quensted, feeling the heat now, Nicola knew that she was glad to be nearly at Whitmead again.

Whitmead, where she had often been afraid and unhappy, and beneath which lay Richard Grosney, for whom no one had ever said a Paternoster, had nevertheless, somehow, become home. And she was very very tired. She had been riding in the pony-cart nearly all day and she ached with exhaustion. When the cart rolled at last into the courtyard of Whitmead, she sighed with relief. Poultry scattered from the pony's feet and the dogs dashed out, barking, to greet her. Shouting at them to be quiet, Phil climbed out and helped her down. As he set her on her feet, Alison came hobbling out to greet her.

'I heard the dogs . . . oh, Mother, I'm so glad you're home. You're all right, are you? Not ill from so much travelling? We've visitors and I just don't know what to do with them.'

'What do you mean, you don't know what to do with them?' Nicola demanded. She was not ill, but she wanted to sit down and be quiet. Visitors were a disturbance. 'You give them refreshments and ask them their business, what else?' she said crossly. 'What *is* their business? Didn't they say?'

'I know, but it's you they want to see. They've been here since the day before yesterday and I don't know whether . . . oh, Mother, do come inside. Phil, go and rub the pony down. I've really not known what to do . . .'

Nicola, grumbling, went indoors with Alison. Sitting in the hall, quietly stitching something, was a woman. She rose as they came in. Taking her in, Nicola observed that she wore quietly coloured clothes which had never been expensive and were now old, but which had been carefully mended. The woman herself was on the borderline between young and middle-aged; somewhere in her thirties at a guess. Her triangular face was thin and beginning to be lined, and her waist was thick. But she had once been very pretty, and her brown eyes still were.

She curtsied respectfully to the new arrivals, putting aside her work.

'This is my mother, Mistress Nicola Whitmead,' said Alison. 'Mother, this is Joanna . . . she says her name is Joanna Whitmead. She says . . . Mother, she says she is John's widow.'

'You're *who*?' Nicola said to the stranger. She sank on to the nearest settle. 'How . . .? When . . .?'

'He met her in London when he went there with the rebels,' said Alison anxiously. 'So she tells me. Then when he left here, he went back to find her.'

'That's right. We met when he come to London first, with the rebels that broke into the Tower. He took no end of a risk, coming to find me when he was on the run,' said Joanna. She had a surprising voice, pleasantly husky but with a markedly rough accent. 'But he said he'd fallen for me, couldn't get me off his mind. We found a priest to marry us though John was afraid to give his right name. John Whitemeadow, he called himself. I've got a writing from the priest that says we were married.' She pulled at a cord round her neck and brought out a pouch. From it, she produced a small parchment scroll. 'I can't read but I've kept it safe. This is it.'

'We can't read, either,' remarked Nicola.

'I took it to the priest at Quensted,' Alison said. 'He says that what's written on the parchment is as this woman claims. He says it's a record of a marriage between Joanna Porter and John Whitemeadow, at a London church on August tenth, thirteen eighty-one.' Her voice sounded blank.

'He thought someone who knew Essex might have known Whitmead and Quensted were close together. It was John Watson of Quensted the King's men were after, he told me.' Joanna addressed Nicola anxiously, as if sensing a lack of response in her.

'Well, that much is true,' said Nicola. 'Go on – Joanna. Where did you and John go after this marriage?'

'We made for the coast and got passages for Flanders. When we got there, John worked as best he could, unloading ships, carrying luggage and so forth. It was hand to mouth for three or four years. But he knew something about running an estate and looking after animals and eventually he found work assisting a gentleman's . . . bailiff, it would be called here, John said. He might have found that kind of work sooner only he didn't understand the Flemish tongue. Neither did I, and we couldn't get anywhere much until we'd learnt. Once he had the language, he did well,' said Joanna with a touch of pride. 'I was taken into service too, with the lady of the household. I knew how to sew and dress hair, you see. The household travelled about and we went with it. We was . . . were . . . happy. But John was always scared to send word home. He said the law had a long arm and might reach him yet, or if not him, it might reach you, if anyone thought you knew where he was. And then last year, he began to have pains in his stomach and he got worse, and died.'

Nicola said, 'Did you and John have any children?'

For answer, Joanna looked towards the kitchen door. Nicola turned and saw a boy standing there. He eyed them gravely and then came slowly forward. He was about ten years old, well-knit, with his mother's triangular features and pansy-brown eyes, but with light red hair, the colour of a fox's coat. Nicola's eyes fastened on it thoughtfully.

'His hair . . .' said Alison, and stopped.

'I've twin daughters too,' said Joanna. 'Seventeen years old, they are now. They're married, in Flanders. There were others – many!' Something exultant flashed in the brown eyes. Nicola and Alison did not understand it and wouldn't have understood even if Joanna had explained, since it was to do with vinegar-soaked sponges and a way of life beyond their experience. Isabel of Northfield would have comprehended some of it, perhaps.

'Rearing children's never easy,' Joanna was saying. 'And the plague kept coming back. So in the end I only had the three: the twins and Piers here. He's a good healthy boy.'

Just what a place like Whitmead needed, of course. Phil had charge of the men at the moment but he was growing older and Whitmead needed an up-and-coming young master. Joanna had realised it. She was offering Piers as though he were coinage.

But sound coinage, Nicola thought. True enough, hair that colour was not exclusive to one family and chance resemblances could be exploited. Even parchments could be forged. All one needed was a dishonest scribe. And she couldn't take to Joanna, who hadn't said enough about how she and John first met. Something was wrong there. Yet Piers was a wholesome boy if ever she saw one, whoever his father was.

She and Alison exchanged glances but did not speak and Joanna's anxiety became evident again. Nicola's doubts especially showed in her face and even in the way she sat, and Joanna was aware of them. But she ploughed on. 'John told me, if anything happened to him, I was to come to England and bring Piers here. He made me promise. He said he should have inherited the tenancy of Whitmead. He told me carefully how to find it. He said he could never claim his inheritance, but that Piers had the right. If John had lived, he'd have sent Piers over when he was a little older. He said that although he'd been accused of a crime, he was never tried so he was never found guilty and hadn't lost his right to anything he might inherit.' She scanned the faces of both the Whitmead women. 'I'm telling the truth. Straight, I am. I was John Watson of Quensted's wife and here's his son.'

The boy interrupted, though in a mannerly fashion. 'Excuse me. But there is something else.'

'Something else?' Joanna looked at him in surprise.

Piers nodded. 'Don't you remember, Mother? After my father died, you gave me some of his things in memory of him.' His accent was better than Joanna's, though slightly tinged with what was probably a Flemish intonation, but in the timbre of his voice was something hauntingly familiar. 'There was one special thing that he'd once said was a gift from his grandmother.' He looked at Nicola. 'Madam, are you his grandmother? If so, you might recognise it.'

'Show me!' Nicola commanded.

Piers too, it seemed, kept a treasure hung round his neck. His was on a chain. He drew it off and handed it to Nicola.

'That!' said Alison. 'I remember that! John wore it sometimes. He *is* John's son! Well, look at his hair!'

'I remember it, too,' Joanna said. 'Yes, I gave that to Piers. And I keep telling you he's John's son. Why won't you believe me?'

Nicola looked at the boy's keepsake. It rested in her hand, heavy not only because it was of solid metal, but with the weight of years and associations. She was a child of ten again, in old Isabel's dwelling, hugging her knees as she listened to one of Isabel's tales. Incredible: it must be nearly a century and a half since old Isabel had been born in Rushley. Memory moved on. Nicola was Thomas's unwilling bride again, mourning vanished dreams of betterment and harbouring a secret memory of the expression in the eyes of a man called Osbert. And then was once more the grandmother who had hoped to see her daughter's son mature and marry here at Whitmead.

It was a silver medallion, badly worn, but burnished. It was strung on a silver chain. It bore a stylised device of wavy lines, with curved lines arching over them, as a bridge might arch across a river, or long lives span years of change.